TILL ALL THE

Mary found Colin's horse te... ...
of the crag, quietly grazing. ...
saw them, but he continued mooning. She could already hear the roar of the waterfall, as she dismounted and tied Pendragon to another tree, a discreet distance from Prince. She climbed to the top of the crag and felt her way along the path until the cascade came into view.

She stood still, looking down into the ravine and she caught her breath. It was indeed a beautiful sight, the sunlight making the water droplets sparkle like diamonds, forming a brilliant rainbow. But it was not that which made her gasp. There, standing poised on a rock, looking into the deep pool, was Colin, and he was stark naked ...

TILL THE SEAS RUN DRY

TILL ALL THE SEAS RUN DRY

Susan Webb

Till All The Seas Run Dry
First published 1998

Typeset and published by John Owen Smith
12 Hillside Close, Headley Down, Hampshire GU35 8BL
Tel/Fax: 01428 712892
E-mail: wordsmith@headley1.demon.co.uk

© Susan Webb 1998

The right of Susan Webb to be identified as the author of this work has been asserted by her in accordance with the Copyright, Designs and Patents Act 1988.

All rights reserved. No part of this publication may be reproduced by any means, electronic or mechanical, including photocopy or any information storage and retrieval system without permission in writing from the publisher.

ISBN 1-873855-28-1

Cover printed by Pier House Ltd, Bourne Mill, Farnham, Surrey

Text printed and bound by Antony Rowe Ltd, Bumper's Farm, Chippenham, Wiltshire

Prologue

The door was now quite covered by ivy, difficult to find unless you knew exactly where to look. Colin's fingers felt for the niche in the high wall where he had hidden the key. He might, if he had not been so preoccupied, have wondered at the ease with which the key turned, for the secret garden had been locked up for years.

A feeling of aching nostalgia swept over him, for the place was in a similar state of wilderness as it had been when he'd first seen it sixteen years ago, the day Mary and Dickon brought him here, as a boy of ten in a wheelchair. There was the bower where he and Mary had so often sat, the entrance now almost obscured by a wisteria.

Yet he could see someone had been here recently. The grass was knee high, but the roses had been pruned and there was a semblance of order about the place. Plants were not overgrown by brambles or choked with weeds.

A wistful smile hovered round Colin's sensitive mouth. History had a habit of repeating itself. Twenty-six years ago his father, driven crazy by grief after his wife's death, had locked up the place and buried the key. The garden had remained hidden for ten years, until his cousin Mary discovered it the year she first came to Misselthwaite and brought it back to life.

She'd brought him to life too, for he shuddered to think what might have become of him had she not found him that stormy night, from which time he'd begun to grow into a normal healthy young man. It was recollections of a later time that caused him grief. She'd loved this garden, yet she'd abandoned it and him too. And it was his own fault he'd lost her.

Her spirit filled the garden. She was everywhere! The honeyed scent from the wisteria was evocative. He could see her bending over a rose to inhale its heady perfume, her cheeks flushed from her recent efforts, soft golden wisps had escaped her bun and fallen round her face. He could hear her voice calling his name, feel the warmth of her body in his arms, her soft lips against his own....

Till All The Seas Run Dry

He'd thought he was over it, all that, for he'd tried to put the past behind him and begin a new life. He should not have come, but something stronger than himself, some force he was powerless to resist had drawn him in here. Maybe the garden really did have magical properties—he'd always half believed it had. He sat down in the arbour and gave in, letting his mind drift back, thinking not of his childhood, but of a more recent time, about eight years ago, when Mary was a grown woman and he first realised he was in love with her....

Till All The Seas Run Dry

Chapter 1

Mary Lennox sat up straight, rigid with suppressed excitement. As the carriage bumped over rough roads, passing by the wild beauty of the Yorkshire moors, the memory came flooding back of that first time she'd made the long journey from India, seven years ago, in the company of Mrs Medlock, the housekeeper. How different her mood had been then, as sullen, bad-tempered and ill at ease, she'd stared out of the window at the lashing rain. Now she was seventeen, she'd just left school and she was on her way home. Her heart leapt for joy with each familiar crag and dale, for she knew the moor well, every bush and burn of it.

Not long now. It was nearly three years since she'd seen Colin and Dickon.

The carriage lurched, throwing her against her companion.

'Mercy me!' cried Lady Grantham, clasping the pearls which hung in cascades over her ample bosom, while the ostrich feathers in her hat bobbed up and down like ballerinas. 'I fear we shall be shaken to pieces.'

Mary muttered an apology, clutching her parasol in one hand, and steadying herself with the other. She had hardly spoken a word during the journey from Switzerland. For one thing she was not given to idle chatter; three years in a Swiss seminary had taught her to contain her emotions. She sat quietly now, engrossed in her own thoughts.

She was ten when she first came to Misselthwaite Manor. Her parents had died in a cholera epidemic, leaving her suddenly quite alone in the world with no family or friends to care for her except her uncle, Mr Archibald Craven, the master of Misselthwaite. Thus she was uprooted from the exotic splendour of India and thrust into the heart of the Yorkshire moor. She hadn't particularly missed her parents—she'd known very little love before she came to Misselthwaite—for she'd been left entirely in the care of an ayah. It was small wonder she'd been a spoilt, disagreeable child when she first came to England.

It had not taken her long, however, to discover that the great lonely house, miles from civilization, and its huge rambling gardens and grounds held all sorts of exciting mysteries. First there was the garden which appeared to have no door—until she found it hidden among the ivy on the wall—a garden which had been locked up for ten years. Then she'd met Dickon, a remarkable boy who could charm animals and apparently speak their language. Dickon, the boy who lived on the moor, who played on a pipe and kept rabbits and squirrels in his pockets. Her first friend in the world, he'd helped her bring the secret garden back to life.

But most mysterious of all, there was her cousin Colin.

She'd been in the house more than four months before she'd discovered him. The servants had been ordered to keep his existence hidden from her, in case she became curious, for it was feared that if he ever saw her he'd have one of his terrible tantrums. But nobody had bargained for the wilful determination of a young lady who already suspected that the strange sounds she'd heard in the night were not, as she'd been told, the howling, wuthering wind.

Then one night she'd awoken from a vivid dream to hear a wailing sound far off down the passage. It had seemed at first to be part of the dream, until at last she got out of bed and crept along the corridor, her heart thumping against her chest. And that's when she found him, a boy of her own age, in a huge four poster bed. They'd stared at each other in stricken silence, until he'd broken it with the words: 'Who are you? Are you a ghost?'

'I think we must be nearly there.' Lady Grantham's voice broke in on her thoughts. 'Isn't that the house, over there?'

At last she could see the rambling gables of the old house, nestling among the trees at the top of the next hill.

'Yes.' It came out in a sort of gasp of excitement. Her stomach became a mass of dancing butterflies. In a moment she'd see Colin and Dickon. She wondered how much they'd be altered. Colin would be finishing school this year, he was nearly eighteen, and Dickon was twenty. And it was Spring. Bulbs would be up in her garden, the birds would have started nesting and there would be riding on the moor.

'You've been very silent,' Lady Grantham observed. 'Are you feeling alright? You don't suffer from travelling malaise?'

'Oh, no!' Mary was never sick, not even on a rough sea. 'I'm sorry, I hope you don't think me rude.'

'You've a great deal to think about, I dare say. It must be exciting returning home after such a long absence. And as for me, I've slept a good deal, that is until we came upon your atrocious Yorkshire roads.'

Till All The Seas Run Dry

She'd taken an instant liking to Lady Grantham. She was Colin's godmother and as she'd been travelling in Europe she'd gone out of her way to collect Mary and bring her home.

The carriage pulled up in front of the house. Mrs Medlock came down the steps to meet them, her meticulously starched cap perched primly on her now greying hair. It was curious how small she seemed, as if she'd shrunk in the wash. The housekeeper looked at her appraisingly and with surprise. Was she, too, thinking of that first arrival seven years ago?

A moment later she was nearly bowled over by Colin's two dogs as Mr Craven came out to greet them.

'My dear Alice, how kind of you to come all this way to bring....' He stopped short on a gasp of astonishment, and stood staring at Mary.

'I know,' said Lady Grantham. 'I, too, saw the likeness. It's quite startling isn't it?'

'Mary!' Her uncle's voice wavered, but he pulled himself together and kissed her on the cheek. How well you look. The Swiss air has much improved your complexion.' He turned to her companion. 'And Alice. It was noble of you to go out of your way to collect her. A pot of tea, Medlock. In the drawing room, if you please.'

At that moment Martha, hearing the commotion, came running downstairs before Mrs Medlock could stop her. Martha, who was Dickon's elder sister, had been a very junior housemaid when Mary first came, but later she'd become her personal servant and friend.

'Miss Mary!' she cried, ignoring a glowering frown from the housekeeper. 'Eh, tha've grown into bonny lass, hasn't she, Mrs Medlock? Who'd ever have thought it?'

The look of disapproval on the housekeeper's face made Mary want to burst out laughing. She promptly compounded the apparent impropriety by throwing her arms round Martha and kissing her.

But despite this warm welcome, her heart felt heavy. Someone was missing.

'Where's Colin, Uncle Archie? I thought he'd be home for the holidays.'

'And so he should be, my dear,' Mr Craven assured her. 'He went to some house party near York, a school friend. But he said he'd be back in time to meet you.'

Lady Grantham, quick to sense her recent travelling companion's dismay, said, 'These young men are always gadding about, Archie.'

She laid a comforting hand on Mary's arm. 'Never mind, dear. I expect you're tired after the long journey. Now at least you'll have time to recover before you see him.'

But Mary was not tired. Nor did she need time to recover. She wanted to rush upstairs and change into her riding habit. She could hardly wait to get out on the moor. She was furious with Colin for not being there for her homecoming, when they had been parted for so long. And all because of some wretched house party. Then it occurred to her, with a tingle of excitement, that there was still Dickon. This was even better—she'd meet Dickon for the first time without Colin.

She demanded that Martha unpack her things immediately. 'And find my riding habit, please, Martha. I think I'll go for a ride before tea.'

Dickon was still at work, grooming Mr Craven's big stallion, Caesar. His duties had been endless today, though he'd been in no hurry to finish. Indeed he was lingering, hoping for a chance of seeing her. He knew she'd arrived because young Jack, the new stable boy had come running to tell him. He'd had to control an urge to run out there and then in the hopes of catching a glimpse of her. Then there'd been Lady Grantham's horses to attend to.

But what would she think of him now? She was grown up and nothing could ever be the same again. Not that there'd ever been anything but friendship between them, but for that one occasion....

He found himself trembling as he recalled the scene that had taken place in the secret garden before she went to Switzerland. She'd come to say goodbye, and she'd been crying.

'Will you always love me, Dickon?'

As if he wouldn't always love her, hadn't always loved her. What had begun as admiration for the lonely little girl from India had developed into love as he'd grown older.

'You will wait for me?' She'd looked at him anxiously.

She'd been out of his reach even then, she always had been, but on that miraculous day—it was three years ago now—she'd suggested that one day they might marry.

'Tha'll not want to wed me when tha grow a bit older,' he'd laughed, partly to shake himself out of the illusion. 'Th'art a lady, born and bred. Tha'll marry thy own kind.'

As soon as they were spoken he could have eaten his words, for she burst into tears. He hadn't meant to hurt her—quite the reverse; and not knowing what to say to put it right, he'd taken her in his arms

Till All The Seas Run Dry

and kissed her full on the mouth. He could still remember the sweetness of that kiss. But at that moment something dreadful had happened. The garden door had burst open and in had walked Colin. The look on his face had been terrible. He knew very well that Colin considered Mary to be his own particular property, and he had a quick temper. But he'd said nothing—just looked at them, turned very pale and fled. For several days Dickon had lived in fear of losing his place—Mr Craven had taken him on three years earlier, to do a bit of gardening and help in the stables, doubtless out of gratitude for what he'd done for Colin. The irony of it! But, by the Grace of God, the incident had been forgotten.

He had his back to the stable door when her voice startled him.

'Dickon!'

He spun round, dropped the grooming brush, almost losing his balance. Then, catching his breath he stared at her.

'Eh, Miss Mary,' he breathed.

It had been said, in the old days, that Mary was a plain child, though he'd been of a different opinion. To him she'd always had angelic qualities. But now!

Her hair, like molten gold in the evening sunlight, was plaited and caught in a net at the nape of her neck, her cheeks, a little flushed, were a rosy pink. Her riding habit fitted perfectly, leaving him in no doubt that she was no longer a little girl. She was on the threshold of womanhood and she was beautiful.

He ached to take her in his arms and kiss her as he had done three years ago, but that could never happen again. There was a definite barrier separating them now. Gone forever was the unique camaraderie they'd been able to share as two scruffy children enjoying the open air and the warmth of the sun while watching things grow in their garden. Now they stood on separate platforms, neither able to get to the other's. She'd always be out of his reach and he could never be more to her than an adoring admirer.

'Eh, tha'rt a lovely lass, Miss Mary,' he said softly. 'As I always knew tha'd be. An' a grand lady.'

Mary flushed a little. 'A grand lady, indeed,' she laughed. 'It's me, Dickon. Mary. Have I changed so much?'

'Aye tha have. Tha were bound to.'

She looked a little disconcerted and he didn't know what to say.

'Saddle Daisy for me, Dickon,' she demanded, and her voice was a touch imperious. 'I can't wait to get into the saddle again.'

'Now? But it'll be dark soon. I can't let thee go alone.'

'Then come with me.'

His heart sank. He'd just fed the horses, and he knew Mary's inclination to gallop across the moor. Also he'd groomed them all except Caesar whom he always left until last, in case Mr Craven wanted to ride. Not only would he have to do a lot of the work again, but he'd be very late home and his mother would be waiting tea for him. But for Mary...

'Right-o, Miss Mary. So long as there's no galloping, mind....'

Her face fell. 'No galloping! But....'

Dickon stood firm. He was not afraid to stand up to her, or Colin for that matter.

'I've already fed all th' horses, and gallopin' after a meal's bad for them. They get colic. Tha'd not want poor Daisy....'

Of course she wouldn't. 'Very well then, I'll restrain myself for now,' she laughed. 'But you will come with me, Dickon, won't you?'

Eagerness was written all over her lovely face. How could he fail her? 'I've to finish off here first. Then I'll saddle Daisy for thee, an' Pen for mesel' an' we'll be off.'

Mary beamed. 'Bless you, Dickon. I knew you wouldn't let me down.'

As she lay in bed that night, Mary realised she had been home for a full twelve hours and had not yet inspected her garden. It had been getting dark by the time they'd returned from their ride, and she'd had to hurry and change for dinner. She made up her mind to rectify this oversight directly after breakfast, weather permitting. She hoped Colin had not made too many changes in her absence. She liked to be consulted about that sort of thing.

To tell the truth she'd been a little disappointed by her first encounter with Dickon. They had been so close before she went away, surely nothing so mundane as class or wealth could spoil their relationship? It irked her to find that something intangible appeared to have come between them. Was it of his making? It was certainly not of hers. She was not quite sure what she had expected, but not at least to feel shy and awkward with him. She felt helpless. It was impossible for her to do anything about it without seeming forward.

It was well into the afternoon of the next day when she spotted two horsemen approaching the house. The horses were strange to her, but she recognised Colin's stance even at that distance. Then she remembered he'd written and told her his father had given him a fine black stallion for his sixteenth birthday. What had he called him? Prince, was it? But who was the other rider?

Downstairs her uncle was furious.

'Inconsiderate young bounder! Why could he not warn us? There's no room prepared, no bed aired. Medlock!' he shouted, ringing the bell for the housekeeper.

'Young men of his age are all the same, Archie,' Alice Grantham soothed. 'Impetuous and impulsive. Living for the moment. But you'd do well to get a telephone installed. One has to keep up with the times. I don't know what I'd do without mine, now.'

Mary slipped out of the house. Now she could clearly see the familiar lines of Colin's features, his face animated with pride as he demonstrated to his friend the magnificence of Misselthwaite Manor. This intrusion annoyed her. After nearly three years she had so much she wanted to tell him, but now, because of this stranger, she'd have to exercise patience.

Colin's face lit up when he saw her, and tossing his leg over Prince's head he jumped to the ground. He had a habit of dismounting in this reckless manner, specially when showing off.

'May!' It was his nickname for her. 'Oh, May, it's grand to see you. Freddie, come here and meet my cousin Mary.' He kissed her stiffly. 'This is Freddie Braithwaite, May.'

Despite his exuberance Colin seemed a trifle awkward. He was almost eighteen and she thought he'd have more *savoir faire*. She looked at him critically. His complexion was much improved. He was even quite handsome now he'd outgrown those horrid adolescent spots. He was still rather gaunt and angular, like a puppy that had outgrown its strength, and he was very tall, more than six foot. His dark hair was a mass of unruly waves that reached the nape of his neck. But it was his eyes that held one spellbound. They were agate grey, like deep pools dappled with flecks of light and framed by long black lashes. And when he smiled his mouth lifted at the corners, rendering him quite irresistible. It occurred to Mary that he could get anything he wanted out of anyone, even herself, with that smile.

She turned to his friend, Freddie, holding out her hand. This young man was shorter than Colin, with fair hair neatly parted in the middle, and blue eyes.

'Your godmother is here,' she tossed at Colin over her shoulder. 'She accompanied me from Switzerland.'

'Aunt Alice?' He always called her that, though she was not his real aunt. 'Dash it! Freddie and I were hoping to go out for the day on the moor tomorrow. But I suppose I shall be expected to entertain Aunt Alice.'

Mary was indignant. Freddie and I! What about her? He'd put himself out for his illustrious godmother, but she could rot! She was glad his plans were going to be thwarted.

'That shouldn't be difficult for you, Colin,' she said silkily. 'You could always charm the hindleg off a donkey.' Was there a hint of sarcasm in her voice or hauteur in the way she turned and sailed into the house with her nose in the air?

The smile vanished from Colin's face, and he called after her, 'I say, May. I hope you've not become too stuffy since you went to that school.'

Freddie followed, a smirk on his face. It promised to be an entertaining weekend.

Later, when she was changing for dinner, Mary looked at her reflection in the mirror. She had no illusions about her looks, but her features were similar to those of her mother, who had been known for her beauty. When she'd first come to Misselthwaite people had marvelled that such a plain child could be the offspring of a reputedly beautiful woman. She lifted the heavy coil of her hair, piling it up on the crown of her head. The colour was darker than her mother's. Hers was thick, light brown, with reddish tints. She did not make the most of it, the way she wore it. She wanted to look her prettiest this evening. There were two young men in the house. She rang the bell for Martha to come and help her.

She chose her favourite dress. It was jade green silk with mutton-chop sleeves, the colour reflected her eyes, and it showed off her well formed figure. The effect was stunning. Colin couldn't keep his eyes off her, neither could Freddie. Mr Craven's eyebrows lifted as he cast a look full of meaning in Lady Grantham's direction.

Next day Mary had a chance to get even with her cousin. Colin had been right. He was not to escape the inquisition from his godmother who had not seen him for over a year. She found Freddie kicking his heels in the rose garden. It had rained in the night and there were still a few droplets glinting in the morning sun.

'Good morning, Miss Lennox. Isn't it a lovely day? I've been admiring your garden.'

Mary inhaled a gulp of fresh air. 'I'm pretty fond of it myself,' she said. 'By the way, I think we can dispense with the formalities. You may call me Mary if you like.'

'And I'm Freddie,' he beamed. 'Well,' rubbing his hands together. 'What shall we do? I see you have a tennis court. Do you play?'

Mary looked dubious. Tennis was not her strong point, and she had no intention of making a fool of herself in front of this young man. She shook her head, pressing her foot into the ground. 'The grass is much too damp, I'm afraid.' Then the idea came to her. 'I know what we'll do. We could ride out on the moor if you like. I'd like to try Colin's horse. Daisy is a bit slow. She was fine when I was fourteen, but....' She shrugged her shoulders.

'Prince is a large horse, you know, seventeen hands, I believe.'

'You think I cannot handle him? I'm as good a rider as Colin.'

A smile tugged at the corner of Freddie's mouth. 'No doubt. But what will Colin say?'

'He won't mind. We share everything.'

'He's rather particular about his horse, though. Wouldn't let me ride him.'

But Mary refused to be put off. 'I'll go and change. Be ready in ten minutes.'

Chapter 2

'What!' Colin raged. 'You let her take Prince? How could you?'
Dickon looked surprised. 'I thought she'd ast you.'
'You know I won't let anyone else but you ride him, and I only let you because he needed exercising while I was away.'
Colin was incensed. It was bad enough that Mary had deserted him, running off with his friend. They'd been gone for hours. Unchaperoned. It was scandalous! Quite appalling behaviour from someone who had just spent three years in a Swiss convent, but to cap it all she'd taken his horse!

If she had deliberately set out to aggravate him, she could not have thought of a better way to do it. His horse was his most treasured possession, a birthday present from his father. He'd called him the Black Prince, for he was all black except for a white patch the shape of a fleur-de-lis on his forehead.

He'd been looking forward to a good ride on the moor ever since his arrival home the evening before. He'd spent the day making polite conversation, enduring a bombardment of questions from his godmother, managing, with a supreme effort, to smother a desire to yawn, consoling himself with the thought that later he'd have that desired ride, the thrill of feeling Prince's magnificent strength beneath him. But instead he'd doubtless find that Mary had ridden him hard all day and sapped his energy. If any harm came to him he'd give her a sound hiding, woman or not.

And that was another thing....

It was most disconcerting to find that Mary was now very much a woman, no longer the little girl he'd known since he was ten. He felt uncomfortable and inadequate in her company, he'd never felt like that before, at least not with her. He'd been looking forward to her return to Misselthwaite, but because he was not very good with girls, he'd brought Freddie back with him for moral support. But he was regretting it, for Freddie, it seemed, was getting on with her better than he was. And he was alone with her on the moor at this very moment.

'Which way did they go?' he demanded.

'I saw 'em go up lane as runs between Waverley's land and yours, thro' woods an' out ont' moor.' Dickon paused a moment, then added with a grin. 'If tha've a mind to go after them I'd best go wi' thee. Tha'll not find 'em else.'

Dickon always said exactly what he thought to Colin. The two had been close friends for many years and Colin accepted a forthrightness from him that he would not have tolerated from another servant.

'Alright, I could do with your company. I'll take Caesar, you take Pendragon. But hurry. It's already late.'

Colin also trusted Dickon more than anyone, even Mary. He knew he was absolutely loyal, his word his bond, and he'd supported him unconditionally when he most needed it. True there'd been times when he'd felt jealous. Mary had frequently shown a preference for Dickon who was two years older. He'd never admit how much it hurt sometimes. He'd come home from boarding school to find the two of them happily working together in the garden; she'd look up when he came in, saying, 'Oh, hello Colin!' He knew by the surprise in her voice that she'd forgotten he was coming home that day, and, after a brief greeting she'd turn her full attention to whatever she'd been doing with Dickon.

He may as well have not existed. At times he'd almost felt suicidal. But then he'd thrown himself wholeheartedly into his riding, racing across the moor on his pony without a care in the world. When he'd become proficient and begun winning cups at horse shows, Mary had wanted to compete with him. Then there'd been a fierce rivalry between them, which at least was better than being left out.

There was a heavily wooded area behind the house, beyond which the moor stretched as far as the eye could see. A small beck, a tributary of the Swale river, came off the moor and flowed towards the valley and the little village of Thwaite, which amounted to a few scattered cottages, a church, a small post office, a village hall which doubled as the school. The path ran alongside this beck, which was the boundary between the two big estates, Misselthwaite and Waverley. It seemed as if he and Dickon had been riding for several hours, but in fact it was less than one, when they met with a tired, sagging figure trudging towards them. Colin's heart sank when he saw that Freddie was alone. He spurred his horse forward.

'Where's Mary?'

Freddie looked bewildered. 'I wish I knew. I've been round and round in circles, and now I'm completely lost.'

The chill settled in the pit of Colin's stomach. He wanted to shake Freddie like a dog shakes a rabbit.

'What happened, Mr Braithwaite,' Dickon asked quietly.

Colin knew exactly what the answer would be. There was a spot on Prince's back, just behind where the saddle sat. If Mary had caught him there with the whip... He'd bolted with him on several occasions. He knew now how to control him, but the first time it happened he'd held on by the skin of his teeth. And he was much stronger than Mary.

He turned to Dickon. 'You did warn her about his sensitive spot, didn't you?'

'Aye, I did. But happen she forgot.'

Ignored, more likely, Colin thought despairingly. Mary always thought she knew better. He felt helpless. No doubt Prince would find his way home eventually but would he still have Mary on his back?

One look at Dickon's face told him he was thinking the same thing.

'If we knew where to begin I could try an' track him,' his said.

'For the love of God, Freddie.... Do try to think where you last saw them. Dickon is expert at tracking horses.' He looked at the sky. Black clouds hung ominously overhead. 'But if the tracks get washed away there'll be no chance at all.'

'I believe I might remember the place,' Freddie suggested, 'if we could go back to the stables and start from there. You see I've completely lost my sense of direction.'

It seemed a reasonable suggestion. Colin suddenly felt sorry for Freddie. It was not his fault and he did look a forlorn sight in his bedraggled state.

As it happened Freddie recognised the spot long before they got back to the stables. He described how Prince had let out a startled neigh, reared up and, with one enormous leap, bounded off at a breakneck gallop, Mary hauling on the reins and swearing at him in a most unladylike manner. He'd tried to follow, but couldn't keep up with the speed or the effortless way Prince took scrub, shrubs and ditches in his stride. He was astonished that Mary had managed to stay on his back.

'Aye, she's a grand little rider, is our Miss Mary,' said Dickon, proudly.

But Colin knew Mary couldn't keep it up for long. He imagined her lying in some ditch, injured, frightened.

'You'd better hurry back to the house and tell my father what's happened,' he said to Freddie, anxious to get on with the search. 'We'll get on faster without you.'

Till All The Seas Run Dry

Freddie winced at the last remark, but he went without a murmur.
It was an arduous task even for Dickon, tracking a horse that had jumped every obstacle that crossed his path, including ten foot wide ditches, through heather and bracken, through long, tufted grass and bog, in a race to beat the impending storm.

'It's a wonder he's not injured hissel',' he remarked, once.

'How do you know he hasn't,' said Colin, gloomily.

'If he had we'd ha' found him. But see, th' tracks are strong as ever still.'

Well that was a small comfort, at any rate.

Colin prayed fervently. He was not over religious but he had a great deal of faith in prayers. He'd found in the past that if he made an effort his were often answered. He'd been silent for the last half-hour. It was a trick he'd learned, when things got tough or he was upset or worried, to retire into himself, as a hedgehog rolls itself into a ball when danger threatens.

The rain came at last, like rods of water, thunder and lightening. The sky was black. They'd gone into a small copse for shelter and it was darker than ever in there. Dickon was about to give up when they heard the sound of a horse snorting and trampling around. Then Prince's huge form came out of the gloom to meet them.

'Prince!' cried Colin, leaping from his saddle. 'Here boy.'

But the moment of relief quickly froze as he saw that Prince's saddle was empty. He felt sick and his mouth went dry.

'Mary! Oh God! What have you done with her?' He was on his feet now, shaking the horse's reins.

'Don't you fret, Master Colin. Miss Mary's here somewhere, for sure.'

'But she could have fallen off anywhere....'

'If she had we'd ha' come across her along th' road. We followed tracks right up to this here copse.'

Colin shook his head. 'Not necessarily. Mary's not the sort to lie and wait in a ditch, even if she's hurt. She'd try to get home crawling on all fours. She could be anywhere.'

'Hush, sir. Listen.'

Then Colin heard it, a muffled sound like a sob, coming from out of the darkness.

'Mary?'

'I'm over here.' There was a movement, a rustle of leaves as she tried to get up.

Till All The Seas Run Dry

'Oh Mary!' Colin burst, dropping onto his knees beside her. 'Are you hurt?'

'My leg...' she gasped. 'I can't walk on it, and my shoulder.... I'm so relieved to see you. Are you angry with me, Colin?'

'Furious!' he said, trying to look it, but he was so overjoyed to see her he burst out laughing.

'He were fit t' kill thee a moment ago,' Dickon assured her as he and Colin lifted her to her feet. 'But like me he's right glad to find thee alive. Let's look at tha leg. Is it broke?'

'I've no idea. All I know is I can't possibly ride with it. I don't know how you're going to get me home.'

'I'll take you with me,' said Colin, firmly, before Dickon had a chance to offer. She was his, for the moment, at least. 'Caesar can carry both of us. You lead Prince, Dickon. I don't think I'd better try to ride him.'

'I tried to get back on him after I fell,' Mary told them. 'But of course I couldn't. And he wouldn't leave me. I urged him to go home so Dickon could follow his tracks and find me. But he wouldn't go. He nudged me with his nose, as if to say sorry. He's adorable, Colin.'

'You can say that, even after what he's done to you?' Colin laughed.

'It was my own fault. I shouldn't have...' She clapped her hand to her mouth. 'Freddie! I'd almost forgotten him.'

Both the boys laughed.

'Don't worry, lass,' Dickon assured her. 'He's safe indoors b' now.'

Mary was confined to bed for several days. Her leg was not broken, but she had a severe sprain and could not walk on it. Furthermore the doctor said she was suffering from shock, and she'd caught a chill. Rest was what she needed. Colin was allowed to visit her. He brought flowers and chocolates, and made her laugh. It was like the old days again.

Freddie left a few days later. He said he felt rather embarrassed about what had happened, although Colin assured him he was not to blame. He said he felt like an intruder. Mary was a terrific girl, but Colin had made it plain she was definitely 'out of bounds.'

In fact Colin was secretly grateful to Freddie, for truth be told, he was instrumental in bringing him closer to Mary. The ice had been broken, and now their friendship could flourish again. He remembered too that in his moment of distress, he'd called upon the

Till All The Seas Run Dry

Almighty, and his prayer had been answered. He should be grateful, and perhaps do more than say thank you. He made up his mind to try harder to control his temper in future.

Meanwhile Lady Grantham had a suggestion to make to Mr Craven before she returned to London.

'Regarding Mary, Archie,' she began, 'I hope you will not think it impertinent of me but have you any plans for her future?'

A puzzled frown crept over his face. 'How do you mean, her future?'

'She's scarcely a child any more, Archie. Or hadn't you noticed? It must be hard for you, having the care of a girl—specially a girl of Mary's age, without a woman to advise you.'

Mr Craven remembered Mary's appearance and behaviour that first evening, and the expression on the boys' faces. But if he had any misgivings he kept them to himself.

'In a year or so,' Alice Grantham went on. 'She'll be of marriageable age. Had you thought of that? If you keep her cooped up in this fusty old house in the middle of nowhere you'll never get her off your hands. Tell me, has she ever met any other young men but Colin? I'll warrant she hasn't. That's a recipe for disaster, Archie. Mark my words.'

Mr Craven shrugged. 'What can I do, Alice? I'm not very sociable as you know. If there are any suitable young men around here, which I doubt, I don't know them.'

'I've been thinking,' Lady Grantham announced. 'I could take her in hand if you like. She could come to me in London for the season. And if you'd like her to be presented at Court, I could sponsor her.'

'That would be most kind of you, Alice! If it's not too much trouble....'

'Of course not. I've often wished I had a daughter of my own. It would be a pleasure.'

So saying Lady Grantham took herself off back to London. She would expect Mary at the beginning of June.

Colin ragged her mercilessly, declaring they were putting her on the marriage market.

'They're hoping you'll find some rich aristocrat, May,' he teased.

'Well, they can boil their heads,' Mary retorted. 'I'm not ready for marriage yet.'

'That's probably just as well,' Colin laughed. 'No self-respecting gentleman will have you unless you learn to ride side-saddle. That split riding habit of yours is an abomination.'

'It's very fashionable in Europe,' she said indignantly. 'And anyway, I could ride side-saddle if I wanted to, but I prefer to....'

'Ride like a man,' he finished for her with a huge grin. 'My dear May, I despair of you ever becoming a lady.'

'Despair away. I don't care tuppence what you think. Nor will I marry anyone chosen for me. If I marry at all it will be someone I could love.'

'Dickon Sowerby, perhaps?'

'That's not funny, Colin.'

He laughed out loud. Then he looked at her solemnly. 'It wouldn't work, you know. You'd both be unhappy. He couldn't live up to your standard and you'd be like a fish out of water in his world.'

Mary gave him one of her grim, silent looks, eyes smouldering, lips pinched together, and he had the satisfaction of knowing he'd scored a bullseye.

'It's none of your business,' she snapped, turning her back on him. 'Go away and let me get some sleep.'

Colin smiled to himself as he ran downstairs. She had not changed so very much after all. The old nursery rhyme went round in his head.

Mistress Mary, quite contrary....

Chapter 3

As soon as she was able to hobble downstairs Mary was out in her garden. She was irritated to find that Colin had not waited for her. Well, see if she cared! She would manage on her own.

It was one of those clear, bright days that sometimes come in April after a spell of rain, bringing out a mixture of fragrances, violets, narcissi and wild hyacinths. The ivy curtain still hung over the door of the secret garden, concealing it. It had been left there deliberately and only a few people knew where the door was.

She felt a little nostalgic for the days when it was still a secret and wished she could make time stand still. But that was impossible. People altered. Colin had changed almost as much as Dickon. She sighed.

Daphne was still in flower, its delicious fragrance wafting in the air. She picked a bloom and inhaled its sweet scent. A myriad of daffodils swayed in the breeze. She could hear voices from the past whispering in the rustling trees, the old gardener, Ben Weatherstaff, who'd kept it alive all those years, climbing over the wall with his ladder despite his "rheumatics." Guilt nudged her. She'd not been to see Ben Weatherstaff for years.

There had always been a special friendship between Colin and Ben Weatherstaff, whose devotion to the late Mrs Craven had been extended, after her death, first to the upkeep of her garden, then to the welfare of her son. It was his unwitting taunt, referring to him as 'th' poor cripple,' that had prompted Colin to leap to his feet in a burst of insulted pride.

Ben Weatherstaff was crippled himself now, with arthritis and rheumatism. He'd forced himself to carry on working, anxious not to lose his post and with it his tied cottage; without a family he had nowhere else to live. If he'd had a less kind master than Mr Craven he'd have been obliged to spend his last years in some Union Workhouse, a degrading end to his life. But Mr Craven had allowed him stay in his cottage for the rest of his life, he'd even undertaken to keep it weatherproof for him, but since he was in his eighties, it was unlikely to be for much longer.

'Tha shouldna' be humpin' buckets for me, lad,' he protested, as Colin brought in a bucket of coal and laid it by the fire.

'Why not? D'you think I'm so feeble? Haven't you realised yet I'm almost as strong as Dickon. Not th' poor cripple you once said I was.'

'I never said owt of th' sort. I knew in time tha'd grow to be a big strong mon. Where's that lass, Miss Mary? I've not seen her since she were back from Switzerland?'

'She hasn't been out since the first day. Didn't you hear about her accident?'

'Aye, I heard about it. An' I can't say as I'm surprised. Always was a wilful, tetchy little lass.'

'You won't recognise her now, Ben Weatherstaff. She's a grown woman.'

'Aye, an' tha'd always a soft spot for that one, even when she were a scrawny little lass wi' pigtails.'

'Well, she hasn't got pigtails now, Ben. Just you wait till you see her.'

'If I've to wait till I see her I'll be waitin' still when I'm eight feet under ground.'

'You shall see her. I'll bring her as soon as she gets up and about. I tell you, you won't know her. She's grown into quite a pretty thing, though I'd never tell her so.'

'That's right lad, never tell a wench she looks fine. They're vain enow wi'out that.'

'What do you know about wenches, Ben Weatherstaff, an old 'bachelder' like you?'

Just then there was a knock on the door and Colin went to answer it.

'You're going to have to eat your words, Ben Weatherstaff. Here she is.'

'Ben Weatherstaff!' Mary gasped, shocked to find his condition so deteriorated since she'd last seen him. He tried to struggle to his feet.

'No, no! Don't get up,' she said, dropping on to a cushion beside his chair.

'He's just been complaining you haven't been to see him,' Colin told her. 'You didn't tell me you were getting up today.'

He laughed when he turned back to Ben Weatherstaff and saw his face.

'This in't Miss Mary!' he was muttering. 'Tha'rt....' He looked at Colin, then back to Mary again. 'It's not right, frighting an ol' man half out his wits, makin' him think he's seen a ghost. It's not right.'

'Like my mother!' Colin cried. 'You think she looks like my mother, don't you?'

The stubborn old man shook his head. 'Not wi' those eyes,' he said turning to Colin. 'They're nice eyes but they're not tha mother's. 'Tis thee has tha mother's eyes.'

'You're so lucky, going to Cambridge,' Mary said, when they were together in the secret garden. She was lying in a hammock slung between two trees. 'I wish I could.'

'You can come and visit me as soon as I'm settled.'

'I don't mean that. I want to study there, at Newnham or... What's the other one?'

'Those colleges are for blue-stockings. You'll never be a blue-stocking, May.'

'I could do literature, history or languages. I can speak several already, you know, French, German, and.... What are you laughing at?'

'Hindustani?' he chortled. 'You could translate some of the Hindu religious books like the Bhagavad Gita. Imagine you with horn-rimmed specs, carrying a pile of books under your arm. Or you might end up teaching the Hindustani songs you used to sing to me.'

She leapt to her feet and swung round to hit him but he caught her wrist before she could deliver the blow.

'You arrogant pig, Colin Craven. I hate you!'

'Hey, steady on, May! It was a joke,' he said, with a nervous laugh. 'Where's your sense of humour? And as for hating me,' he added, still gripping her wrist. 'Did you know that hate is so closely akin to love it is sometimes hard to define the difference?'

'Love! An insufferable, vain creature like you?' She never minced her words, at least not to him. She spoke through clenched teeth, wriggling to free herself from his vice-like grip. 'You're a selfish, spoilt, pampered thing. You've never been denied anything in your life. If you really wanted something badly and you couldn't have it, it might be the making of you. Then perhaps you wouldn't be such a milksop.'

He let her go suddenly and turning, walked away, unshed tears stinging his eyes. Her words had a profound affect upon him. She always got the better of him in an argument, and she had the ability to hurt him more than anyone else in the world—even more than his father, whose approval and esteem he'd spent most of his life pursuing.

That she thought he was vain and arrogant was bad enough, but for her to call him a milksop! Nobody had called him that since the school bullies had mocked him because of his long eyelashes. They'd called him a girl and a few other unmentionable names, until one day, in desperation, he'd cut off the offending eyelashes with a pair of nail scissors. Apart from making him look ridiculous for several weeks, they'd grown again longer and thicker than ever. Meanwhile his cruel persecutors continued to taunt him, daring him to prove his manhood by various hair-raising escapades. Once he was locked out after lights out and there was nothing for it but to scale the wall to the dormitory window. Inevitably he was caught, and consequently received such a thrashing he was unable to sit down for over a week. But Mary knew nothing about that episode of his life, nor did his father.

Now he wanted to get right away from her, so he took himself off for a long, solitary ride across the moor. Passing by the Sowerby cottage, he remembered he had not visited for some time. He'd been in the habit, when Mary was away in Switzerland, of calling in for a cup of tea or cocoa and a chat as he passed the door whilst riding or walking the dogs. He was fond of Mrs Sowerby who'd been like a mother to him. But, being much absorbed in Mary recently, he'd allowed these visits to lapse.

The door stood ajar so he knocked and went in. As he stepped over the threshold he heard a child sobbing, so he hesitated, reluctant to intrude. In the middle of the room stood a little girl, roughly nine years old, the same age as Mary when he first met her. Her hair was in rather scruffy pigtails, her face smudged where she'd wiped away tears with grubby hands, there were one or two patches on her dress, and her pinafore was torn. She had with her a shaggy, black mongrel, a cross between a Collie and a Labrador. She stopped crying and stared at Colin, looking a little frightened and clutching the dog's collar.

'Come in, Master Colin,' Susan Sowerby called. 'Would tha like a cup o' tea?'

'That would be most welcome, thanks, Mrs Sowerby.' His eyes went back to the child. 'Hello. What's your name?'

'Rebecca,' she said in a voice little above a whisper. 'Rebecca Parkin, sir.'

'She's Matt Parkin, the blacksmith's girl,' added Mrs Sowerby.

'This your fellow?' Colin asked, indicating the dog. 'Is he sick?'

'N-no, s-sir,' Rebecca stammered.

Till All The Seas Run Dry

'Mr Waverley says he's bin worryin' 'is sheep,' Mrs Sowerby explained. 'An' five of his pheasants has been killed—found wi' heads bitten off.'

'Sounds like a fox to me,' said Colin.

'That's what Our Dickon says. An' that's why he's gone after it.'

'But why does Waverley think it's the dog? Has your dog been on his land?' Colin asked the girl.

She began to cry again. 'Rex didn' do it, sir. He's soft as butter. Wouldn't hurt a fly, he wouldn't.' She put her arms round the dog's neck protectively, and the pet responded by trying to lick away her tears.

'Don't be afraid, child,' Colin said gently. 'I'll help you if I can, but you must tell me the whole story. This fellow looks harmless enough,' he added, stroking the dog. 'Can't imagine him ravaging anyone's sheep, but something's given Waverley that idea.'

'He ran off t'other day, when we were walking', an' he got hissel' wrong side o' fence. Couldn't find his way out. An' last year he got his foot caught in trap.'

'A gin trap?' Colin asked, grimly.

'Aye. But Dickon saved him. 'E were poorly for weeks. But now Mr Waverley says if he finds dog on 'is land again he'll shoot him.'

'I see,' said Colin slowly, already fired up to go into battle on behalf of this small girl and her dog. He knew social injustices of this sort were all too common—there were often letters in the papers and articles in Punch and other magazines—but he hadn't given it much thought because it had not touched him personally. 'Well, you stay here with Mrs Sowerby until Dickon and I return. And for God's sake don't let the dog go again.'

And he was out of the door without further ado.

'Your tea, Master Colin,' Susan Sowerby called after him. But he was already on Prince's back, riding hell for leather across the moor towards the Waverley estate.

Dickon was one of those rare beings whom everybody likes. He was particularly loved by the children whose injured pets he'd restored to life, and even some of the adults around about had taken to calling him in an emergency, for the nearest veterinary surgeon was more than twenty miles away. Colin believed he was a natural animal doctor, and had persuaded his father to excuse him from his duties in the stables whenever his expertise was needed for this purpose. But in spite of the long list of admirers, no human being can survive a whole lifetime without coming into conflict with someone.

Ted Waverley, the owner of the next door estate, had a new gamekeeper, a man whose methods of hunting down predators such as foxes and other vermin as he called them made Dickon's blood boil. He'd been on friendly terms with the previous man who'd retired a year ago. They'd shared a love of wildlife and they'd worked as a team with Dickon catching the animals and encouraging them to find their food elsewhere, leaving Waverley's pheasants in peace. They lost one or two birds but the old man would say, 'Plenty more of them, and poor old fox has his family to feed.' This amicable partnership had come to an abrupt end, however, with the arrival of Stanley Brent, a cruel man who laid gin traps which Dickon spent much of his spare time dismantling. The result was that Brent accused him of trespassing, inducing Mr Waverley to forbid him on his land.

It was a paradox that Dickon, a lover of animals, was also a crack shot with a rifle. He'd won many a prize for target shooting, but he loathed the thought of shooting an animal, specially a fox—he'd had several as pets when he was a boy. But there was little else to be done when a rogue fox had found his way in to easy pickings and wouldn't be weaned off them? Waverley's sheep had lambs, and if the old fox got one there'd be hell to pay and Rebecca's dog would get the blame.

The wily old fox came out of his lair and sniffed the air. Dickon tried desperately to suppress the surge of adrenaline, but the fox sensed danger and was gone, scurrying through the undergrowth, before he could pull the trigger. It was ironical that had his intentions been of a friendly nature the fox might have eaten out of his hand as many others had done.

A moment later a hand clasped his shoulder, startling him out of his wits, and there was Stanley Brent towering over him.

'So this is thy game, Sowerby. Poaching, is it? Tha'll come wi' me t' see landlord.'

'But I wasn'...' Dickon began. But what was the use? He'd torn it now, for who'd believe him? Caught with a gun on someone else's land, land he shouldn't have been on in the first place, lying on his belly in the undergrowth like a common poacher. Who'd believe he'd been trying to shoot a fox so that a little girl's dog would not be destroyed? Mr Craven might, but nobody else would. He could end up in prison. And even if it didn't come to that, as a convicted felon he'd lose his job; he'd never find another one around here, and his mother depended on his wages.

Brent marched him along the road, holding him by the scruff of the neck like a common thief! Then a miracle happened. They turned a corner by the woods and there in the middle of the road, standing four-square blocking their path, was Colin.

'You must be Waverley's gamekeeper. Where are you taking Mr Sowerby?'

'Caught 'im poachin', sir,' said the gamekeeper.

'Poaching? I don't believe you.'

'Beg pardon, sir? Are you tellin' me I'm a liar?'

'I'm saying you're mistaken. Dickon was not poaching. He was after the fox I saw running out of your woods just now.'

Dickon could have kissed Colin's feet.

'If you'd done your job properly,' Colin added, 'you'd have got him yourself instead of accusing a child's innocent pet of killing your birds.'

The gamekeeper went scarlet. He would doubtless have liked to answer back, but dare not, for though he might think him an arrogant young upstart, it was plain by the way he spoke, that Colin was the Quality.

'May I ask, sir, who are you?'

'I'm Colin Craven of Misselthwaite Manor,' announced that young man, pulling himself up to his full height, and Dickon was reminded of a young boy in a wheelchair, leaping to his feet to demand of old Ben Weatherstaff: "Do you know who I am?" 'And I'll have you know,' continued the young rajah, 'I've known Dickon Sowerby since I was ten, and I'm prepared to swear on my mother's grave he's never stolen anything in his life!'

'Then ye'd best see the Master, sir. Mean time Sowerby's comin' wi' me.'

Colin clenched his jaw. 'Oh, no, he's not!' he said, with grim defiance, his grey eyes glinting like steel. 'I'll see your master alright, and if you don't take your hands off my friend you'll be up before the Magistrate yourself for assault.'

The gamekeeper let go of Dickon as if he'd been a hot coal.

'And I'll take his gun,' Master Craven added.

Brent hesitated, eyeing Colin nervously, then reluctantly handed over the trophy, and casting Dickon a surly look, turned and stalked off muttering to himself.

They watched him out of sight and earshot, and Dickon breathed a sigh of relief.

'Eh, thank you, sir! If tha'd not come along then I'd ha' been for it.'

'We're not out of the woods yet, I'm afraid. You were trespassing. And I've some explaining to do. Nor is that poor dog safe yet, until we get that fox. Or...'

'We'll not catch 'im now. An' I promised that lass...'

'Don't worry, Dickon. I've a better plan. I'll tell you about it on the way home.'

The plan involved keeping Rebecca's Rex under lock and key at Misselthwaite for a few days, or until the old fox struck again.

'It's the only way to prove it isn't the dog,' he explained.

Dickon had to admit it was a brilliant idea, but young Rebecca was reluctant to give up her dear Rex.

'I'll take great care of him,' Colin promised.

But later he said to Dickon, 'I hope there won't be trouble between Rex and Rajah. He'll get on alright with the bitches, but the old boy's a bit possessive, doesn't like strange fellows sniffing around his pad.'

'I were thinking, it's odd them both being kings,' Dickon observed. 'One's called Rajah, that's a sort of king, int' it? An' t'other's a Rex.'

'So they are. But I'm afraid this is Rajah's castle and Rex'll be the "dirty rascal." I hope this is going to work. I shouldn't have lost my temper just now.'

'Tha did splendid. I were that proud o' thee.'

Colin shook his head. 'Brent could get nasty. He's bound to tell Waverley he caught you poaching on his land. And Father won't like it. He hates unpleasantness.'

'Why must you get involved in these disputes,' Mr Craven grumbled.

'But Father! What else could I do? Would you have had me sit back and allow Dickon to be arrested and sent to prison for poaching? Or see a poor dog destroyed?'

'But there's a right way and a wrong way of doing these things. All you've done is wrong-foot yourself. You could even be accused of compliance. If you'd asked me,' his father retorted scathingly. 'I'd have handled it more tactfully. I'd have persuaded Waverley to drop the case against Dickon and the dog.'

Till All The Seas Run Dry

Colin was not so sure about that, but he did not argue with his father. He looked across the table at Mary. Her face was inscrutable. He was still smarting from their last quarrel and she had not spoken to him since, so that when she looked up at him and smiled it was all the reassurance he needed.

'I'll go and see Waverley myself,' he told his father. 'And explain.'

But before he could perform this act of contrition, the gentleman himself came to the house spitting blood and fury.

'I beg your pardon, Mr Craven,' he said, ingratiatingly to Colin's father. 'I have no quarrel with you, but,' his voice rose querulously, 'my gamekeeper tells me he caught young Sowerby poaching on my land and was quite rightly about to arrest him when this young gentleman of yours prevented it.' He turned on Colin, spraying him with spittle. 'You had no right to interfere in my affairs, young man, obstructing the course of justice.'

'But it was not justice, sir....' Colin began to argue, but his father raised a hand to silence him.

'I've known young Sowerby for more than seven years,' said Mr Craven. 'And I'd stake my life on it he wouldn't dream of poaching your game.'

'Then why did he have a gun, sir? And what was he doing with it on my land?'

'I can well understand your irritation, Mr Waverley, but I understand a fox has been causing havoc with your game, and I believe it was this fox Dickon was after.'

'A fox? Why would he be chasing foxes on my land?'

'Because your gamekeeper has been threatening to have a harmless dog destroyed for doing the killing.'

'Oh, I see. He's inventing a fox to cover for his thieving. A likely story. If there'd been a fox someone would have seen him by now.'

'I can assure you,' said Mr Craven with quiet dignity. 'There certainly was a fox. My son saw it with his own eyes.'

The squire turned to Colin. 'Prepared to swear to that in Court, young man?'

Colin felt his neck and hair prickle with guilt. It was one thing to tell a white lie to the gamekeeper on impulse, but to swear to it on oath, to commit perjury... Yet to deny it would not only be to admit he'd already lied to his father and the gamekeeper, but to leave Dickon in the lurch. And how delighted Brent would be to see him discredited.

'Because that's what you'll have to do,' continued Waverley, 'if I decide to press charges against Mr Sowerby. Good day, Mr Craven.'

He turned and was about to leave when Mr Craven called him back.

'One moment, Mr Waverley. Can we talk? In private?' The squire hesitated. He obviously had a great deal of respect for Mr Craven. He wouldn't wish to fall out with him.

'As you wish, sir.'

As soon as the study door had closed on the two men, Mary turned on Colin and savaged him.

'Now look what you've done. If Dickon goes to jail for this I'll see you burn in hell.'

'But....'

'It's all your fault,' she went on before he could get a word in. 'If you hadn't put his back up none of this would have happened.'

With that she flounced out, leaving him with his mouth gaping open. Why were girls so unreasonable?

He went and found Dickon to warn him that he might still be charged with poaching.

'Tha'll speak for me, won't tha?'

'Of course, Dickon. But I hope it won't come to that.' He didn't want to burden Dickon with his own doubts. 'Don't worry.' A smile spread across his face. 'Everyone around here respects Father, and if the Magistrate is old Fielding.... He and Father were boys together.'

A few days later a cavalcade, headed by Mr Waverley himself, came to the door of the blacksmith's cottage.

'Your dog's really done it now, Parkin,' rasped Ted Waverley. 'He's had one of my lambs. Pheasants are one thing, but sheep...'

The blacksmith turned pale. 'But dog's bin up at Manor for th' last three days, sir.' Rebecca clung to her father's side and stood there trembling.

'Up at the Manor? D'you mean Misselthwaite?'

'Yes, sir. Young Mr Craven took 'im, Wednesday.'

Waverley muttered to himself, then said aloud, 'Well, they must have let him out because one of my lambs has been mauled. I'm warning you, Parkin, if I find that dog's got out I shall see that it's destroyed, and I'll hold you responsible for the lamb.'

The blacksmith laid a calming hand on his daughter's shoulder as she began to cry. If he were prosecuted, even if it didn't result in conviction, he'd be finished here in the village as a blacksmith. His whole livelihood was in jeopardy.

'With respect, sir, I think ye'd best see Master Colin.'

'Very well,' said the squire, signalling to his followers to head towards Misselthwaite Manor. 'But you'll be hearing from us.'

When Colin saw such a large group of men and horses approaching the house his heart sank, and before his father saw it, he went out to meet them.

'Good morning, Mr Waverley,' he said as his eyes swept over the men and horses now forming up in front of the house. 'What is all this about?'

'Ah, Master Craven. Just the man I want to see. I'll not mince words. Last night one of my lambs was taken, and I have reason to believe it was that dog, the one I'm told you're harbouring here, that belongs to the blacksmith.'

'But that's impossible,' he said with confidence. 'Rex has been here for the last three days.' Then he added with a smirk, 'Hasn't your gamekeeper caught that fox yet?'

Waverley shook his head. 'I doubt if a fox could kill a lamb that size. And it's very strange that nobody but you has seen this fox.'

Colin flushed. 'But it couldn't have been Rex,' he said defiantly. 'He's been here ever since that morning. That's something I can prove.'

Some of the servants had stopped what they were doing and surreptitiously gathered round them, while heads peered out of windows, all curious to see what was going on. He caught sight of Mary out of the corner of his eye.

'How do you know the dog has not got out since he's been in your charge?' said Mr Waverley suspiciously.

'One moment, sir,' said Colin. 'I'll call the housekeeper.'

'Medlock,' he whispered urgently as soon as she appeared. 'That dog hasn't been let loose in the last three days, has it?'

'Let loose!' she exclaimed aloud. 'That he has not! That animal's been the bane of my life. I've obeyed your orders to the letter, Master Colin. I've kep' him under lock and key, in my own quarters, mind. We couldn't leave him in kennel, not with the other dogs, after that fracas on the first day. Those two dogs fair moithered each other. I've been that run off my feet, taking him out on the lead to do his pennies. I'll be glad to be shot of him.'

'Good old Medlock,' Colin chuckled under his breath.

'It's no laughing matter,' said the squire, with asperity.

'Thank you, Mrs Medlock,' said Colin, straightening his face. 'You may go now.'

At that moment Mr Craven appeared having heard the commotion from his room.

'What's going on, Colin?' he demanded testily.

'My apologies for the intrusion, Mr Craven,' said Ted Waverley, his attitude altering noticeably as soon as Colin's father appeared. 'But if I'd been properly informed it wouldn't have been necessary. There's an air of conspiracy about this whole business which I don't like one bit.' He looked straight at Colin as he spoke and he felt the colour rise in his face.

Waverley sent his servants back to his estate with a message to the gamekeeper to 'get cracking and find that damned fox before it gets any more lambs.'

Colin knew the man would use one of those dreadful traps but there was nothing he could do about it.

When they'd all gone Mr Waverley said sternly. 'I'll thank you to keep out of my business in future, young Craven. As for that young friend of yours, Sowerby, you can tell him I won't be pursuing the matter of him poaching on this occasion, but if he ever sets foot on my land again, he'll be arrested for trespassing without question. Is that clear?'

Colin nodded, feeling a little deflated. Ted Waverley took his leave of Mr Craven and turned, remounted his horse and rode off.

Mr Craven turned to Colin. 'Well, son. Your attempt at being a knight in shining armour seems to have back fired on you. Your lack of tact has probably made you an enemy of Ted Waverley.' He shook his head. 'So unnecessary. Well, I hope it'll be a lesson to you.'

His father would never understand his reasons for doing what had had to be done, but he was right in one respect, Ted Waverley had been made to look a fool, and Colin would doubtless never be forgiven for that.

He went in search of Dickon to tell him the good news, he could breathe freely, at least for the present. When he reached the stables he was told Dickon had taken Mary for a ride. They'd just this moment gone. Clearly she didn't think any more of him than his father did. Her heart was cold as stone. And after all he'd done for him, was Dickon grateful? But then, it was hardly Dickon's fault that Mary preferred him.

Rex was duly restored to his rightful owner, who, if she had not been so shy, might have thrown her arms round Colin's neck.

Till All The Seas Run Dry

'Oh, sir, how can I ever thank ye for savin' our Rex,' she said, taking his hand and smothering it with kisses, then turning back to hug the dog. 'Thank ye, sir.'

So there was a brief moment of triumph after all. Whatever the cost, it was worth it to get Dickon out of serious trouble. And he'd saved the blacksmith's skin, but, most of all, he'd given this little girl the best present in the whole world.

Chapter 4

Sir Walter and Lady Grantham's house in Eaton Square was a third of the size of Misselthwaite Manor, but it was very grand. The wide hall with its marble tiled floor and elegant horseshoe staircase would lend itself perfectly to her coming out ball, Mary thought excitedly as her feet sank into a deep pile, crimson stair carpet. Crystal chandeliers, lit by electricity—they still had gas lighting at Misselthwaite—dripped from the ceiling. And the Granthams had many more servants. The butler, Bainbridge, ruled the roost, an imposing man who dominated the whole household. Even Mary was a little in awe of him. He'd stand in the hall with a big watch in his hand, his deep voice booming out.

'You have ten minutes to prepare yourself for dinner, Miss.'

She wondered what would happen if she was ever late.

London fascinated her at first. It was all the new inventions that excited her, the underground trains—there was even a moving staircase at Earl's Court—travelling in an open-topped motor bus. The streets bustled with a variety of vehicles, carts and drays, horse drawn carriages which were still used by die-hards who refused to acknowledge times were changing, alongside motorised vehicles, buses and trams that ran on rails, all jostling for the same space. It took a long time to get anywhere, but that didn't matter to Mary. She liked to observe, from the top of a bus, women tottering in skirts like drainpipes, others sporting the most amazing creations upon their heads. It would have amused Colin.

She was surprised to find herself thinking about him so much since she'd come to London. Secretly she admired the stand he'd made over Rex, though Dickon was the real hero, of course. He'd taken a very grave risk for the sake of the little girl's dog. Colin could not expect to take all the credit. But he'd shown himself to be better than the vain, selfish creature he appeared to be at times. She was sorry they'd quarrelled. She didn't like having to admit she was wrong, but she'd make it up to him as soon as she was home.

She was struck by the extreme contrasts between rich and the poor in the capital. Once they'd passed through an area where they were surrounded by abject poverty, the like of which she'd never seen in Yorkshire, and she'd been deeply shocked. She had not seen beggars, or children in rags without shoes on their feet, since she left India.

But once the novelty of the big city had worn off she began to feel rather lonely. She didn't know anyone of her own age. It was tedious having to stand perfectly still for hours while the dressmaker fitted one dress after another, or sit, holding an empty teacup with a fixed smile on her face, listening to two elderly dowagers making painfully dull conversation. If Colin were here he'd make her laugh. He always saw the funny side of things. But Colin had declared he would not come to London during the season if he were paid. And he'd been so disparaging about the "marriage market." He'd almost put her off the whole idea of the season, until Lady Grantham reassured her she would not be forced to marry anyone.

'Marriage is for life,' she'd said. 'It should be given every chance to be happy. Let's hope you make a wise choice.'

It occurred to her that if she married—even if she found the most wonderful man in the world—she'd have to leave Misselthwaite. She might even have to live in London, and, though it was an interesting place to visit she'd hate to live here.

She would have been bored to tears long before she was ever presented to the King and Queen if she had not had the good fortune to meet an old acquaintance. Constance Livingstone, who had been at school with her, was a year older, so they were not very well acquainted, but Mary greeted the girl as if they'd been bosom friends. Introductions were made and Lady Grantham invited Constance and her mama to tea the next day. Life was no longer dull. For the next two months she had a companion. Furthermore, since there were two of them, they were allowed much more freedom. But there was one rule Lady Grantham insisted upon. They must tell them exactly where they were going and when they'd be back.

Once, while walking in Kensington Gardens they saw a group of women, standing together with banners and big wide ribbons across their breasts.

'What are they doing?' Mary asked.

'Why, don't you know? They're suffragettes.'

Mary had heard talk of the women's movement, but, having spent so much time abroad recently, she knew very little about it.

'I saw Mrs Pankhurst once, about a year ago,' Connie boasted. 'I was frightfully impressed. I listened avidly to everything she said. And I think they're frightfully brave.'

She was so enthusiastic that Mary's imagination was fired, she wanted to find out more about it. When the two girls met a few days later, Constance was in a fever of excitement. She'd just heard that Christabel Pankhurst was going to be in Trafalgar Square next day, and that there was to be a demonstration.

'I don't know what I shall tell Mama but I'm determined to go,' she said. 'Why don't you come with me?'

Mary was sorely tempted. She was intrigued by everything she'd been told about the women's movement, but somehow she doubted Lady Grantham would allow them to go.

'We don't have to tell them where we're going,' said Constance.

'But I promised...' Mary began. Then, with an air of conspiracy, she said, 'Oh, well, I suppose it won't hurt, this once....'

They made up a tale that they wished to visit Peter Jones. Mary had seen some very pretty muslin that might do for a dress, if it matched her new jacket. They left the older ladies walking in St. James's Park, and agreed to meet them later at the bandstand for tea. All was well so far. They reached Trafalgar Square at the appointed time. There was a seething mass of people all gathered round a small group of women who stood near to Nelson's column.

'Which is Christabel Pankhurst?' Mary whispered in Connie's ear.

'See the three women standing together in the centre? Christabel's the tallest of them.'

They eased their way through the crowd and managed to get close enough so that Mary could see their faces quite clearly. Christabel began to speak. She was very eloquent, her speech was powerful and moving. Connie and Mary struggled to get even closer. There was a group of women round Christabel who were handing out pamphlets and sashes to wear, and answering queries. One of these women approached her and Constance. She eagerly accepted the leaflet and put on the sash.

The apparent number of supporters they had, many of them men, surprised her. As Constance was quick to point out, some of the richest and most influential families were involved. Nor was there much truth in the legend that suffragettes were all ugly, middle aged spinsters.

Suddenly there was a shout and a whistle, and a large number of police descended on the group. For some minutes Mary and Constance stood and gaped as police broke up the gathering, flaying about with their truncheons, manhandling and carrying off the women, kicking and screaming. It was a harassing and degrading scene. Mary was appalled at the violence of the police. Her whole nature screamed with righteous indignation. It was so unfair! But what could they do about it? She quickly realised that if they didn't take action immediately, she and Constance would themselves be dragged off into one of those nasty looking black vehicles.

'Connie! Quickly, we must run,' she whispered, grabbing her companion by the arm.

'Run where? Why?'

'Don't argue. There's no time. Take off that sash at once.'

Mary was panting with excitement as she took off her own sash and cast it away, then began to walk very fast, fiercely controlling an urge to run. Merging quickly into the crowd, they fought their way to the other side of the square. Once out of sight from the police they picked up their restricting skirts and ran for all they were worth back to St. James's Park.

They must have been longer than they thought, for when they reached the bandstand the band had packed up, and there was no sign of the older ladies. Mary looked at her watch.

'Heavens, look at the time! We must go home at once.'

'What, go our separate ways?'

'No, no. We must stick together of course. You'd better come with me. I expect your mama will have gone back to Eaton Square with Lady Grantham anyway. Oh, I do hope they haven't guessed where we've been.'

'Have you enough money for a cab, Mary?' Constance asked breathlessly. 'These boots are killing me.'

As always, there was never a handsome cab to be had when it was most needed, nor a motor bus, or any means of transport in sight. 'It'll have to be shanks' pony, I'm afraid,' said Mary. And what was Lady Grantham going to say?

By the time they had almost run all the way from St. James's Park to Eaton Square, they were quite exhausted, and it was well past six o'clock. A very stern-faced Bainbridge met them at the door, and Mary quaked. He raised his eyebrows with great disdain as his gaze fell upon the girls' dishevelled attire, and endeavoured to be his most intimidating.

'I think I should warn you, Miss Lennox,' he rumbled, 'that a storm is brewing above stairs. My lady has refrained from calling out the police to search for you, only because I myself reassured her that young ladies like yourself are notoriously bad time-keepers, specially when there are certain distractions in Trafalgar Square.'

Mary's heart sank.

They reached the drawing room and walked straight into a hornet nest.

It was not that they'd gone to the suffragette meeting which angered Lady Grantham. It was the fact that they had lied about it.

'How will I ever be able to trust you again. Supposing something awful had happened to you. For all we knew, you could have been attacked, or abducted.'

Mary was almost in tears. It had been a dreadful day. At the outset she had only been half interested in the suffragettes, but what she'd seen today had inspired both her support and her sympathy. She stood silently waiting for the tirade to finish.

'If I hadn't made a promise to your guardian,' Lady Grantham was saying, 'I'd cancel your ball at once. You can be thankful the invitations have already gone out. But if I have any more trouble, I shall not hesitate to send you home at once. I should have to announce that you'd been taken ill.'

Constance was ushered out of the door by her grim faced mother.

'I'm afraid Constance is a bad influence on you, Mary.' Lady Grantham said, after they'd gone. 'I shall have to keep the two of you apart for the time being. And I'm afraid that means Constance will not be able to attend the ball.'

'But why?' Mary exclaimed, breaking her silence. 'It's so unfair. It was not her fault. It was my idea. I wanted to see Christabel Pankhurst. And it won't happen again, I promise.'

The morning of the ball arrived. The house looked a picture with flowers adorning every pedestal. Mary was having breakfast with Sir Walter who had just returned from abroad. They sat at a small table in the cosy little parlour—the dining room was out of bounds this morning because the table was already being laid for the evening. She'd taken an immediate liking to the man Lady Grantham called her better half. He had a wicked sense of humour and was not averse to sharing a little joke with her at his wife's expense.

'I hear I missed a good skirmish while I was away,' he said, winking at her over a cup of coffee. 'No serious casualties, I hope? Just one or two walking wounded?'

Mary laughed. As it happened Lady Grantham's sense of fairness had prevailed—one should not be punished while the other got away

Till All The Seas Run Dry

with it—and Constance was coming tonight, after all. But before Mary could reply to her host the doorbell rang, and a few moments later they heard Lady Grantham's voice in the hall. 'Colin! What a delightful surprise.'

Her heart missed a beat. Colin had come! Colin, who'd sworn he'd be whipped rather than attend a coming out ball.

She smothered an impulse to rush out into the hall and throw her arms round his neck.

'I'm glad to see you, Colin,' she said, as soon as they were alone. 'You said you weren't coming.'

'You wanted me to come, didn't you?'

'Yes, but.... What made you change your mind?'

'Curiosity, I suppose. After I heard about your escapades with the suffragettes. Father's livid, by the way. He said you were abusing Aunt Alice's hospitality.'

'I don't want a lecture from you, thank you.'

'Well, go on, tell me what happened. Was it as bad as the papers said it was?'

'Why do you want to know? Don't say you're interested in the suffragettes.'

'Why shouldn't I be? I admire anyone who has the courage to stand up to authority. You know that. And I'm not in the least bit surprised to find you in the thick of it. You were ever a rebel.'

'But I wasn't,' Mary admitted miserably. 'I ran away like a rotten coward.'

'I'd probably have done the same thing myself. No sense in getting yourself locked up—at least until after the ball. So what happened?'

Mary told him briefly and he listened in astonishment.

'I must say they're pretty brave ladies. I admire their courage and tenacity. But isn't it rather like cutting off your nose to spite your face?'

'It seems to me they have no choice. You weren't there, Colin. You didn't see it. It was beastly the way the police were brutalising them. My blood was up, I can tell you. If they'd tried to handle me like that, I should have hit them with my umbrella, kicked their shins, and probably have been carted off in one of those dreadful Black Marias.'

'My Amazon!' cried Colin, delighted. 'You're the very spirit of British womanhood. In years to come I can see you surpassing even the Pankhursts. Let's hope you find a husband first. But what I don't understand is why they're doing all this. I mean, you women have far more freedom today than you've ever had. Why do you want to get involved in politics?'

'Why? Don't you think we have just as much right to vote as you men? Why should we be regarded as second class citizens?'

'I thought that would get you going,' he laughed. 'Who says you're second class citizens? Nobody's suggesting that women should be treated unfairly. But they should stick to what they're good at, that's all. And they don't understand politics.'

'That's a typical arrogant male attitude! And just like you, Colin Craven.'

He threw back his head and laughed. 'I love you when you're angry. But come. I didn't come all this way to pick a quarrel with you.'

'What did you come for? You still have not told me.' She gave him a saucy smile. 'Did you miss me?'

'Miss you? Don't run away with that idea. As a matter of fact Father sent me to keep an eye on you,' he said, with a smug grin. 'He's worried that the way things are going he'll never get you off his hands because nobody will have a militant young madam who has ideas above her station.'

'Why you pompous ass, Colin Craven!' she said, setting about him with a cushion.

When Lady Grantham entered the room a few minutes later, there were cushions and feathers scattered everywhere, Mary looked as if she'd been dragged through a hedge backwards, Colin's shirt was torn, his tie was askew.

'Good gracious! What on earth is going on?'

Mary thought her ball was the best bit of the season. It rated much higher than lining up to be presented to the King and Queen, and having, not only to remember how to do the proper deep curtsey gracefully, but also exactly what to say, when and when not to speak, all of which she had found quite terrifying.

But the ball! She was the centre of attraction in an ethereal dress of pale violet blue, made from delicate lawn silk, exquisitely embroidered with tiny white daisies. Candles fluttered in the chandeliers instead of the harsh electric light. She and Colin led the first dance. He looked at her with approval as they swung into the waltz, saying, 'You look terrific tonight, May. I never realised before how pretty you are. I wish we weren't first cousins.'

For a moment she was floating on air. But this adulation from her best beloved cousin was short lived. As soon as he'd done his duty he left her and went off and danced with Constance, while she was left with the rather insipid Jack Livingstone.

The Livingstones had been among the first to arrive, Constance, her mother, and brother Jack, and it was clear, from the moment she clapped eyes on him, that Constance thought Colin was the answer to a maiden's prayer. Furthermore, Mary couldn't help but notice how Mrs Livingstone was making up to him; then she remembered she'd once overheard Lady Grantham make an unguarded remark. 'Archie has so much money he doesn't know what to do with it.' What a catch Colin would be for Constance!

But before she could give it any more thought, she was swept onto the floor by one beau after another, until at last she was introduced to the Honourable William Leyton.

He was tall and handsome and he danced beautifully.

'What do you think about women's suffrage?' Mary asked, never afraid to embark upon a controversial subject. 'Are you for or against it?'

'Personally I'm inclined to sympathise with them, though my father, being a member of the House of Lords, wouldn't agree. He's had one or two brushes with them already.'

He was assured of her company for the rest of the evening.

During dinner, she was so absorbed in conversation with William she didn't notice Lady Grantham and Colin both watching her intently, Colin with a scowl on his face. And it was not until much later that she came face to face with Constance in the ladies boudoir.

'Oh, Mary, your cousin Colin is divine,' Connie whispered confidentially, with a sigh.

Mary looked at her in disgust. Her infatuation for Colin, who must be oblivious to it, was ridiculous. Connie was a nice enough girl, but she was not for Colin.

'If you knew him as well as I do you wouldn't think so,' she said, sceptically. 'He's conceited, egotistical and arrogant—hardly the qualities one might expect from a deity.'

'Oh, you would say that. You're like a sister to him. I think my brother is odious sometimes, too.'

'Well, don't expect any sympathy from me,' Mary warned, 'when he drops you like a hot potato. He's scared stiff of women and quite insensitive to their feelings. If he finds out what you think of him you won't see him for dust, believe me.'

Connie stared at her in disbelief.

'How mean of you to say such horrid things about him. And he's been saying the nicest things about you, telling me how you first met, the secret garden and all that. He thinks the world of you.'

Mary was immediately contrite. Why, indeed, had she been so spiteful about her beloved Colin? It was not like her to be so. Surely she was not jealous of Constance?

Chapter 5

Colin was down to breakfast before Mary next morning. He was feeling rather irritated about the way things were turning out. He'd come to London, against his wishes, because Mary had particularly requested it, and last night he'd had to watch her all evening gazing into the eyes of the Honourable William Leyton, whom, he now discovered, was heir to an earldom. Nor was his mood improved by the triumphant way his godmother informed him that William seemed quite taken with his cousin and wished to pursue her acquaintance.

'Aren't you going to have any breakfast, Colin?' Lady Grantham asked.

'I'm not hungry, thank you,' he said with a heavy sigh, pouring himself a black coffee.

His godmother cocked a suspicious eye at him. 'How much did you drink last night?'

That was the last straw! He'd been most abstemious about the amount of alcohol he'd consumed, knowing full well that if he overdid it his father would hear about it and there'd be hell to pay. But before he could defend himself, Mary appeared looking refreshed and lovely, having clearly had a good night's rest. He'd been kept awake by indigestion, which he put down to too much rich food. His eyes followed her as she went to the sideboard and lifted the cover off one silver salver after another.

'If it's all right with you, Aunt Alice,' he said, 'I think I'll go home tomorrow.'

The spoon hovered in Mary's hand, the only indication she'd heard what he'd said, for she didn't look at him.

'Oh,' said Lady Grantham. 'But I expected you to stay a little longer than that.'

'I hope you're not offended,' he hastened to say. 'I'll stay if you want me to.'

'No, no, dear. I wouldn't dream of insisting upon it. You must do as you please. I'm not in the least bit offended. It was good of you to come at all.'

Mary resumed serving herself, placing a large lump of black pudding on her plate.

He must have pulled a face for his godmother repeated the embarrassing question.

'Look Aunt Alice, I haven't got a hangover,' he snapped. 'I'm just tired, that's all.'

A smile hovered round Mary's mouth as she sat down, which aggravated him more than ever. There was a pregnant silence while she pushed the food around her plate pretending to eat it.

Lady Grantham broke it, saying, 'I had thought you'd enjoy escorting Mary around and about, I thought you might like to see some of the sights yourself.'

'Escorting her where? And what sights?'

'Why, the Tower of London, the Crystal Palace, Madame Tussauds....'

'I've seen all that, Aunt Alice.' She only wanted him to stay to chaperone Mary so she wouldn't have to traipse round all these places herself, and he hated sight seeing. 'Besides, it's far too hot for that sort of thing.'

'Then there's the Great Exhibition,' said his godmother, ignoring his comment about the heat. 'If you haven't seen it already, your really should.'

'To tell the truth, I find that sort of thing a dead bore.'

'A bore? Not the theatre, surely. Or dinner at Romano's? And there's the pictures?'

He made no reply but the prospect was improving a little. He looked hard at Mary who steadfastly refused to meet his eyes.

'Its only a week or so till Ascot,' his godmother commented. 'And after that there's Henley Regatta, and....'

Colin's face brightened at mention of Ascot, but he remained obtuse.

'Will I have to dress up like a clown in top hat and greys?'

'A clown. Nonsense! You'll look splendid.'

Was it that he'd willed her to look at him, or was it that Mary deliberately chose that moment to cast him one of her brightest smiles?

'Oh, very well,' he conceded. 'I'll stay—but only for a week.'

'Now you've decided to stay, Colin,' Mary said later, when they were alone. 'You'll be able to see more of Connie.'

'Why should I want to do that?'

'You could scarcely be prized away from her last night. And don't deny it. Every time I saw you dancing, it was with her.'

'I was only doing as I was told. Aunt Alice asked me to look after her. She seemed rather shy and retiring.'

'Shy and retiring! Connie!' Mary scoffed. 'Well, watch out, that's all I can say. I saw the glint in Mrs Livingstone's eyes when she heard how rich your father is.'

'That's rather uncharitable of you.'

'And as for Connie,' said Mary, ignoring his rebuke. 'You may as well know she's already a bit soft on you. Though I shouldn't tell you, insufferably conceited as you are.'

'Soft on me? What a wonderful imagination you have, May,' he retorted. 'And you're a fine one to talk. It wasn't Constance who displayed a lack of maidenly decorum last night. And if Aunt Alice wants me to play gooseberry to you and the Honourable William, she can think again.'

'Oh, so that's what's been plaguing you,' said Mary, her eyes alight with amusement. 'You're jealous because I spent a couple of hours last night talking to one man, the only one there worth talking to, incidentally. But it meant no more than that, I can assure you.'

'That's not what I was led to believe this morning. According to Aunt Alice the two of you are practically engaged. Next thing she'll be writing to Father. My dear May, you're to be congratulated! An earl, no less, at least he will be. You'd be a countess. Imagine that.'

'What a lot of balderdash!' she exclaimed indignantly. 'Can I not enjoy someone's company for one evening without people thinking it's a prelude to marriage?' She'd been about to tell him William had a stable full of thoroughbreds, and that he'd suggested a ride in Hyde Park with him one morning, an invitation she'd greeted with enthusiasm, but now felt inclined to turn down.

Truth be told it didn't need much to persuade Colin to stay a little longer. He enjoyed sparring with Mary, and while he was in her company he was never bored, even if he was obliged to go sightseeing. Nor did he heed her warning about Constance. Frankly he was flattered. He had never before been admired by a girl—except his second cousin, Eleanor, a spotty faced young wench of thirteen who'd followed him round like a lost puppy one Christmas—but that didn't count. However, here was an intelligent, attractive young lady, nearly a year older than himself, ready to fall at his feet.

He readily accepted an invitation from Mrs Livingstone to dinner and the theatre.

Till All The Seas Run Dry

And despite her reservations, Mary could not resist the opportunity to ride one of William's magnificent horses. She returned at midday, pink cheeked and exhilarated.

'It was beautiful in the park this morning,' she told Colin with relish. 'I think I might do it every morning.'

One morning a week or so later, she returned to Eaton Place to find a message from Colin. He'd gone shopping and would be back in an hour. But he was gone for five hours.

So she challenged him. 'What did you buy?'

'Buy?' A perplexed little frown creased his brow.

'You said you were shopping.'

He looked away. 'I didn't get anything.' She always knew when he was lying. 'I looked around Harrods, then I went to Kensington. I wanted to see the new garden restaurant on the roof of Derry and Toms. Have you ever been there?' She shook her head. 'I'll take you sometime. There's a magnificent view. Imagine, May, a garden right on top of the roof.' Then, with a roguish grin, 'Did you enjoy your ride this morning?'

It was not until after he'd left London and returned to Yorkshire she discovered what he'd really been up to. Constance told her the two of them had attended a suffragette rally.

'I told Mama I was going shopping with you, Mary. If she asks you will confirm it, won't you?' Constance begged.

It was a bit rich, but she had little choice but to corroborate Connie's story. To deny it would be to implicate Colin, something to be avoided at all costs. But it surprised her how much it hurt; they'd not only left her out but Colin had lied to her. She felt betrayed by both of them.

Colin wrote a week later. Evidently his conscience troubled him, for he rarely wrote her letters. In the three years she'd been away he'd only written to her twice, once to tell her about his famous horse, and once to tell her his father had agreed to let him go to Cambridge.

'...I felt so awful about it, I had to tell you the truth. But it was nothing really. Nothing so exciting as a police ambush. And I didn't see Christabel. I believe the poor thing is in prison at present. Connie is a bit of a fanatic, isn't she? I understand now what you were saying about it but I still don't think all this tying oneself to the railings and so on is necessary. Nor is it doing any good....'

Till All The Seas Run Dry

It was the beginning of August before Mary returned to Misselthwaite. She was not sorry the season was over, for she could hardly wait to be galloping across the Yorkshire moor, breathing the cool fresh air. There were things she'd miss about London, like meeting her young friends at Gunters for tea or coffee. She had not many friends of her own age in Yorkshire. And she realised that in future there'd be few opportunities, , to go to the theatre.

Mr Craven sent the brougham to meet her at the station, but when she arrived at the house there was no sign of Colin, or even of Dickon. It seemed that the two had gone fishing together. It was a pastime the two boys often shared, and one from which she was excluded.

Refusing to allow herself to be dispirited she wandered into the secret garden. A delicious fragrance of honeysuckle pervaded the air, roses, too, were in full bloom. She buried her nose in one, sucking in the heady scent. Her swing, the one Dickon had made for her, hung from the branch of a tree. She went and sat on it. How she loved this garden! A dreadful thought crossed her mind. What would become of her if Colin were to marry? He'd want to share the garden with his wife. And it would no longer be hers.

She put the notion out of her head. Such unpleasant thoughts had no place in a beautiful day like this. It was a delight to sit out in the cool air. London had been far too hot and sticky. They ought to hold the Season in the Autumn, she thought, or even in Winter.

There were footsteps the other side of the wall and a moment later the door flew open.

'May!' Colin burst in. 'I knew I'd find you here. Jack told me you were back.'

He picked her up and swung her round.

'Steady on, Colin,' she laughed. 'Where's Dickon?'

'He had to go. There was a message for him. Something about a sick animal.'

'Oh, I see.' She knew she should be pleased he was so much in demand, but somehow it irked her that Dickon could not even wait long enough to greet her.

'Aren't you pleased to see me?' said Colin. He put his hand up as if he would touch her face, but instead he removed her hat, tossing it to the ground.

'Why, Colin! That's my best hat!'

'What d'you want with a hat?' he murmured in a low voice she hardly recognised, taking her head between his hands. 'You're much prettier without one.'

His face was so close to hers, she could feel his breath on her cheek. The closeness of him sent a sudden thrill of excitement through her, yet it also frightened her.

She pushed him away gently. 'Did you catch any fish?'

He beamed, then, catching her by the hand, he said eagerly, 'Come and see.'

In his fishing bag, which he'd left outside the gate, was the biggest brown trout she'd ever seen.

'Did you catch that?'

'Aye,' he said triumphantly. 'I wiped Dickon's eye. He had one only half the size.'

Next morning Mary overslept and missed breakfast. She came downstairs to find the house deserted, but for the servants. The butler met her in the hall.

'I'm afraid breakfast has been cleared away, Miss. But if you'd like something....'

'Where's Master Colin?'

'He went out at about 9.30. He said to tell you he'd be back for lunch.'

Mary muttered something under her breath that made the austere Smithers flinch.

'Mrs Medlock told Martha not to disturb you. She said you'd be tired after the journey yesterday and the hectic life you've been living in London.'

It was true Mary knew she'd got into the habit of sleeping late in the morning whilst she'd been in London.

'If you'd like something to eat, Miss, I could arrange for a tray...'

'No, thank you, Smithers. I'm not hungry.'

With that she vanished through the door. She made her way to the stables where she found Dickon mucking out. He turned when he heard her voice.

'Good morning, Miss Mary,' he said airily. 'What can I do for thee?'

She was still feeling a little annoyed with him for avoiding her the day before, so there was a slight edge to her voice when she spoke. 'Have you seen Colin today?'

'Aye. He said he were going to Ravensfell. I think he were planning' an early morning swim,' he grinned. 'It being such a fine day, and that.'

She knew Ravensfell well. It had been one of their favourite haunts in summers past. It was there that the river plunged a hundred feet into a deep ravine with high cliffs on either side. There was only one way down to it, a rocky, slippery path that could only be safely attempted in summer. In winter it was far too dangerous. As children they used to bathe there for it was well sheltered on three sides.

'Saddle Pendragon for me, will you, Dickon. I'm going to change.'

After her experience with Prince, she was taking no chances. Mr Craven's horse, Caesar, though a more exciting ride, could be just as unpredictable. But Pendragon was an old gelding who'd been an inhabitant of Misselthwaite stable for as long as she could remember, a gentle, steady ride.

'That's right, tha'll be safe wi' Pendragon. I'd come wi' thee but I've that much work to do....' He turned, but she'd gone.

Dickon sighed. How beautiful she was. Even more so in that lovely flowing dress she was wearing this morning. His heart had almost stopped at the sight of her standing there, framed in the doorway, holding a wide-brimmed hat with flowers on it in one hand, like one of them pictures he'd seen on calendars. For some reason he didn't know why she seemed annoyed with him. What had he done?

Mary found Colin's horse tethered to a tree near the top of the crag, quietly grazing. His ears went back when he saw them, but he continued nibbling. She could already hear the roar of the waterfall, as she dismounted and tied Pendragon to another tree, a discreet distance from Prince. She climbed to the top of the crag and felt her way along the path until the cascade came into view.

She stood still, looking down into the ravine and she caught her breath. It was indeed a beautiful sight, the sunlight making the water droplets sparkle like diamonds, forming a brilliant rainbow. But it was not that which made her gasp. There, standing poised on a rock, looking into the deep pool, was Colin, and he was stark naked.

Because of the distance between them, he seemed to her a little unreal, like a naiad or water sprite. The spray from the waterfall whirling around him like white mist gave him an ethereal appearance, so that she did not feel embarrassed. She watched as he dived into the pool, swam around and clambered out onto the rocks the other side, unable to drag her eyes off him. She felt a little like an intruder, all the same, and wondered whether she ought to warn him of her presence, or simply wait until he'd finished his swim and put his clothes on again. If he was not, after all, aware of being watched....

At that moment he looked straight up at her. She had not realised she was so conspicuous, her figure standing out clearly against the skyline. But judging by the nonchalant way he waved to her, picked up his clothes and began dragging them over his wet body, it was clear he was unperturbed by her presence.

'Come on down,' he shouted, pulling on his trousers. 'I don't suppose you've brought a picnic with you?'

Summer gave way to autumn, the trees in the park began to change colour, making a panorama of golden yellows, reds and dark greens. Squirrels scurried about gathering as many nuts as they could find, often squabbling over each other's store. The wind whipped Mary's hair in her face, lifting her hat, so she was obliged to hold on to it, and twigs from broken branches crackled under her feet. Like the seasons, her emotions were undergoing constant change.

For a long time she had considered herself in love with Dickon. He had been her first love, and she'd thought of him constantly while she was in Switzerland. She still had a deep affection for him, but he seemed to have become too remote. She knew now she could not marry him. She hated to admit Colin had been right, but she knew she couldn't tolerate living in the rough conditions of a cottage like the Sowerby's.

And then there was Colin....

She had never thought of Colin in romantic terms before. It was absurd, she kept telling herself, to imagine she was falling in love with a boy she'd known since she was ten, and had always regarded as a rather tiresome brother. Or worse—that some deep depravity in her made it impossible to forget the vision of him swimming in the altogether?

On her eighteenth birthday Mr Craven had a surprise for her. He led her to the stables where Dickon held the bridle of a pure white mare with beautiful lines and a soft silky coat.

'Isn't she lovely, May?' Colin said. 'What shall you call her?'

'Snowdrop,' she said, without hesitation. 'They're the very first spring flowers, and you know how I love the Spring.'

'Snow White would go better with the Black Prince,' Colin suggested.

Till All The Seas Run Dry

But Mary wouldn't change her mind, so Snowdrop it remained. They took the horses out on the moor almost every day. Nobody thought it remarkable that they were allowed so much freedom, so much time alone together. It didn't occur to Mr Craven to provide Mary with a chaperone while Colin was around to protect her. As far as he was concerned they were like siblings. The possibility that they might develop anything more than fraternal feelings for each other never entered his head.

It began in small ways, touching, hand seeking hand as they sat side by side in church. For a long time nothing was said, but they both knew. Then one day while they were in the secret garden he came up behind her and caught her round the waist. He bent his head and kissed her gently in the nape of her neck, while his hand impudently cupped her breast.

'Colin!'

Her body stiffened and she tried to pull away, but he turned her round to face him.

'Why so prim, my Mary May?'

Her heart was pounding so that she could scarcely breathe. His fingers touched her cheek, brushing away a strand of hair. She felt him tremble and her senses reeled.

He gently but firmly lifted her chin. 'You want me to kiss you. I know you do. As much as I want to do it.'

He had a most disconcerting way of reading her thoughts. Their lips met so softly at first, a butterfly's touch. Then he drew her closer, kissing her more deeply, until she felt his tongue touch hers, igniting a flame inside her which left her breathless.

'I love you, May!' The words echoed in her heart. 'I've always loved you. And you love me. Admit that you love me.'

She did love him. At any rate it was not infatuation, she knew him far too well for that, nor was it something that had suddenly happened. Whether she liked it or not she'd been falling in love with him for some time.

'Oh, Colin, this is madness,' she said weakly. 'We're first cousins.'

'So what?' His fingers were in her hair, pulling out the pins, letting it fall loose round her face and shoulders. 'You look lovely with your hair down, like a wild creature.' He kissed her nose, eyes and mouth.

'We shouldn't be doing this,' she managed to say, trying again to drag herself away.

'Why not?'

'I don't know. It...just...seems...wrong, that's all.' It seemed a feeble argument but she could not explain her misgivings. She'd been too close to him, she supposed. 'We're more than cousins, more like brother and sister.'

'It's not incest,' he laughed, 'if that's what's bothering you. Look, forget we're cousins.'

She was drowning, fighting to stay afloat.

'I can't. Oh, Colin, how is this all going to end?'

'End! It's scarcely begun. Listen,' taking her face between his hands. 'You can't cross a bridge before you come to it. It's foolish to try.'

'It's even more foolish to try to cross a river that has no bridge.'

'Oh, my sweet, practical Mary. What a pessimist you are,' he said, laughing. Then he kissed her again.

'Be serious, Colin. Your father will never let us marry. You know he won't. And if he finds out about us he'll send me away again, I know he will.' The words burst from her in a tirade of passion.

'Then we'd better make sure he doesn't find out.'

He put an arm round her and led her to the arbour in the corner of the garden, sat down and pulled her on to his knee. The scent of late roses mingled with elderflower hung in the air.

'It'll be our secret,' he said. The idea pleased him. He liked secrets, especially the ones he shared with Mary. It was reminiscent of the secret garden. 'Only this time we tell no-one, not even Dickon.'

Chapter 6

Keeping the thing secret made it all the more exciting, like living dangerously, and Mary soon gave up trying to fight it. She knew she'd loved Colin from the very beginning. Why else had she bothered with an imperious, tyrannical boy who threw a tantrum at the least provocation? She could as well have left him and returned to her garden and Dickon, indeed she'd often wondered why she hadn't. It was not as if she'd done it because she felt sorry for him. In those days she'd been far too selfish to make such a sacrifice. Yet he'd inspired the first unselfish thoughts she ever had. From the day they'd met her world had begun to revolve around him instead of herself, his recovery had become of paramount importance. In a flash of perception she saw that it was not Dickon, much as she loved him, nor yet the secret garden that had brought about the change in her. It was Colin.

Therefore her feelings for him now were simply a part of growing up, one kind of love replacing another. Because she'd always loved him it was inevitable, as night follows day, that she'd grow to love him as a woman loves a man.

And as for Colin... He knew intuitively, despite what he'd said to Mary, that his father would never consent to their marriage, fond though he was of her. And he had no wish to defy his father, or to lose the parental esteem he'd worked so hard to earn, and which had been denied him in the early years of his life, leaving deep scars. But now he had another *raison d'être*. Mary. He wanted to believe the two of them were inextricably bound together. It was a clash of ideals he tried to put out of his mind. His miraculous recovery in the secret garden had made him an optimist. Had he not once said he'd live forever and ever?

The moor was their refuge. It was so gloriously wild, empty and mysterious, parts of it so remote they saw no other human being, and they loved it like their own souls. It was a part of them, its moods sometimes reflecting their own. And that autumn it seemed more beautiful to them than ever before.

Christmas came. Hot rum punch round a blazing log fire, sneaked kisses under the mistletoe, lingering a little longer than perhaps was quite safe, a furtive glance to make sure no one was around. Singing carols in the village while the snow fell on their heads, Colin's arms round Mary to keep her warm. The stars, brighter in their eyes than in the sky. The Christmas tree, lit with candles from head to foot, a tradition introduced by the late queen. And all their little gifts to each other, some hidden in secret corners, to be opened.

Colin gave Mary a fur muff, white with black spots on it, and a hat to match.

'To keep you warm this winter, May.' Then he whispered in her ear, 'Though I'd prefer to do that myself.'

In spite of her absorption in Colin, Mary did not forget Dickon. The last thing she wanted was to hurt his feelings in any way, but he'd made in plain enough he was no longer in love with her, and she was glad of that. She was convinced he was capable of better things. He'd refused Colin's offer to pay for him to get proper veterinary qualifications. He wouldn't accept charity, even from Colin. Nor could he afford the luxury of studying; his mother needed the wages he was bringing home, she still had four mouths to feed.

'And anyhow, you know me, Miss Mary. Book learning's not for me. I like to be out an' about wi' Mother Nature, not cooped up indoors.'

'Maybe one day he'll change his mind,' Colin said.

But Dickon could not foresee a time when he'd want to leave his Yorkshire home. He'd seen his friends drift away, seeking their fortune in the big cities only to return disillusioned and penniless. Some had even starved to death on the streets, others had gone down the mines, a soul destroying job in his opinion, and an unhealthy one. It had killed his father.

And he liked working at Misselthwaite. He could see Mary every day. He thought she looked quite radiant these days, her eyes sparkled, her hair had a lustre about it and her cheeks were always slightly flushed. Clearly she was a young woman in love. But not with him. He knew, he'd always known, she could never be his, that sooner or later she'd turn to Colin. The two were born for each other. But that didn't prevent his heart from aching, because she had loved him once. To him she was an angel—untouchable, and in a way he wanted her to remain on her pedestal. He didn't want to discover she had clay feet.

And they were still friends, that was the important thing, and she'd begun to confide in him recently. That pleased him, even if he had to listen to her telling him how much she loved Colin.

His mother, seeing them together so much, became concerned.

'Don't tha go falling in love wi' her,' she warned.
'No chance that, Ma,' he laughed. 'Miss Mary's not for me, I know that.' He'd never admit, even to his mother, how he really felt.

'I don't know what's to be done about her an' Master Colin,' she sighed. 'There's no denyin' how they feel about each other.'

Dickon's eyes opened wide. Mary had confided in him but as far as he knew she'd told nobody else. 'Howd' tha ken, Mother? It's supposed to be a secret.'

'That pair an' their secrets,' she laughed. 'Well, it's no secret to me. Plain as pikestaff, it is.' She picked up the bucket of potatoes Dickon had just brought in and emptied it into the sink. 'Poor wee bairns,' she sighed.

'Poor bairns! Why? They're happy as pigs in muck.'

'Now, mebbe. But where's th' future. What if Mr Craven finds out?'

'What if he does? Happen he knows already.'

'What, an' he lets 'em out alone ont' moor every day?'

Dickon shrugged and grinned. 'Well, they're almost old enow to get wed.'

'He'll never let them wed. He's more like to turn her out.'

'Turn her out! Why? Mr Craven thinks th' world of Miss Mary.'

'Ay, but she's like a daughter to him. He'll not let her wed his son.'

'Why not? Plenty o' cousins get wed. Only two year ago Matt Dougal married his cousin Katy, over Scarborough way, remember? Our Sarah Ann was bridesmaid.'

'But they'd not been brought up together like our Colin and Mary. Mr Craven spoke of adopting her once. Said so to me when she first came. Ast if I thought it were good idea.'

'He ast thee?'

'Ay, in them days he'd a mind to speak t' me about th' two young uns. He'd no one else to talk to, see.'

'An' what did tha tell 'im?' Dickon asked, inordinately amused by the notion of Mr Craven asking his mother's advice.

'I said it were a father's love she needed, not 'is name.'

'Eh, that's it!' said Dickon. 'He didn't. If he'd adopted her she'd be called Miss Craven, not Miss Lennox.'

'Ay,' said his mother thoughtfully. 'So she would. All th' same he won't be happy about it.'

Till All The Seas Run Dry

Spring came and the first pussy willows burst into bud. Colin picked some and gave them to Mary. Willow catkins and winter jasmine gave way to forsythia, snowdrops and crocuses were out in profusion in the garden, and soon primroses and violets began to appear in the hedgerows. A few bracken shoots were popping up in the long grass. Small animals, awaking from hibernation, started to scurry around making their nests among them. Love was in the air.

Mary never told Colin she loved him. She thought she didn't need to. They had only to look at each other to know what the other was thinking, and they'd often laugh together when nothing had been said, which was most disconcerting for those around them.

When the weather was fine they'd spend the whole day out on the moor, taking a picnic with them. After an exhilarating ride, they'd dismount and let the horses graze while they lay in the sun in each other's arms, tickling each other with long grasses, or dangling their feet in a stream. Mary remarked once that the horses were in love too.

'See,' she said, 'how their noses come together while they're grazing. Look, Colin, they're kissing.'

'He tries to boss her around. He's a bully,' Colin commented.

'They do say animals copy their masters,' she teased.

She jumped up and ran away, but he caught her, bringing her to the ground, laughing and squealing.

Innocent as they both were, Mary soon discovered in herself a deep sensuality. She loved to run her hands through his thick dark hair, to open up his shirt and kiss his naked chest. While the heather came out on the moor, they grew up together. By the end of September he knew every inch of her body, he'd seen her breasts, touched them and kissed them, as they lay together in the long grass. Yet she shrank from the ultimate, knowing intuitively that if she gave him everything he wanted, he'd no longer value it or her.

Dickon lay on his back gazing at the sky, the white puffy clouds scudding by. It was one of his favourite pastimes, to go out on the moor early in the morning and just lie on the ground listening to Nature. He was lying there enjoying the warmth of the sun when a pert young voice made him start.

'Well, I never, Master Dickon! So this is what tha does on tha day off.'

He squinted at the figure above him. She was a pretty thing, though not very old—at a guess she was still at school. But she was full grown all the same, for he could see the fullness of her breasts through her clothes.

'And who might you be?' he asked.

'Molly Pine's me name. I've seen thee ridin' out wi' th' young mistress from Misselthwaite. An' I've heard tell of thee, too. Most folks ken Dickon Sowerby.'

'So I'm famous, am I?' Dickon grinned, sitting up. 'What've tha heard about me? Nowt bad, I hope.'

The schoolgirl come young woman giggled.

'Nowt bad, o' course. Can I sit wi' thee an' talk a bit?'

'Aye, there's no law as says tha can't.' He patted the ground beside him and she sat down.

'I've heard tha can charm birds an' wild animals, get 'em eating out o' tha hand.'

She smelt of lavender and he discovered to his consternation his pulse was beating faster.

'Aye, sometimes,' he said.

'Go on then,' she said, peeping at him from under a fringe of black eyelashes. 'Let us see how 'tis done.'

'I doubt it'd work wi' thee sat beside me. Most wild animals are main shy.'

'I could hide,' she suggested, 'behind that bush.'

He shook his head. 'That'd be no good. They'd soon smell thee.'

She moved closer to him and he was conscious of a sharp sensation in the pit of his stomach. He'd never felt such unadulterated physical attraction before. It was quite different from what he felt for Mary. This, he suspected, had more to do with lust than love. And she looked so very young. He must be wary.

'How old are you?' he asked.

'Just turned fourteen.'

He whistled through his teeth. 'Is that all? Well, shouldn't tha be at school today?'

She threw her head back and laughed. 'Aye, but I'm abscondin''

'Absconding, is it? That's a long word for a little lass like thee. Does it happen often, this absconding?'

All of a sudden her face became grave. 'Eh, tha'll not tell me Ma, Master Dickon? I'll be in sore strife.'

'If I'm found talking to thee when tha should be at school I'll be th' one in sore strife when tha Dad catches up wi' me.'

'Tha'll get no trouble from him,' she grinned. 'Me Da's dead.'

'I'm sorry to hear it.'

'Oh, it's all right. He died a long while back.'

'Did he now. Well, what I'd like to know is why a young lass like thee's wanderin' about moor, taking up wi' strange men? Your Ma'll be after me, never mind teachers, if I don't get thee t' school pretty damn quick.'

He rose to his feet, but she was too quick for him, darting off, swift as a hind. The chase was a game to her. He realised this to his dismay as soon as he caught her, and that he had played right into her hands. Once captive she went limp in his arms. He felt her heart flutter against his chest and his own pulse began to race. She wound her arms round his neck and he had to force himself to remember she was only fourteen.

'A kiss, Master Dickon!' she exclaimed triumphantly, revealing a row of white teeth. 'Give us a kiss, an' I'll do as I'm told like a good girl.'

That summer Ravensfell became as special to Colin and Mary as the secret garden itself. They went there often. It was during their last visit, one unusually hot day in early September, that something significant happened. The waterfall was quieter than it had been the day Mary had watched Colin swimming, for the autumn rains had not yet begun. There was not a breath of wind, no cooling spray, and the water looked cool and deliciously tempting.

'If only we'd thought to bring our bathing costumes,' Mary remarked. 'I could really do with a swim.'

'I don't know about you, but I'm going in anyway,' Colin announced springing to his feet and beginning to remove his clothes.

'You're not... going in naked?'

'Why not?' he grinned. 'Aren't you going to join me?' Then, raising one eyebrow, he added, 'You could, of course, keep your under clothes on if you want to.'

Mary shook her head. 'I'll stay here.'

'What are you afraid of, sweetheart?' he laughed. 'D'you think I'd take advantage of you?' Then he looked at her solemnly. 'Cross my heart I won't touch you.'

She turned her head away, trembling at his words, and he shrugged, removed the last vestige of clothing and jumped into the water.

'Ah, that's better,' he sighed as he splashed around. 'You must come in, May. This water is ripping!'

The heat was sweltering, and Colin looked as if he was really enjoying the cool water. He clambered out onto the rocks the other side of the pool, and she dared to look at him, as he had his back to her. He's like a Greek god, she thought, watching the muscles in his thighs and buttocks ripple as he stepped over the stones. And to think he was once so thin and scrawny. He went and sat under the waterfall.

'Oh, this is magic,' he moaned with delight.

Mary could stand it no longer. She'd been hot enough before, but watching Colin in that lovely cool water....

'If I do,' she began, hesitantly. 'Promise you won't look.'

'Tell you what. I'll keep my eyes covered until you're in the water.'

She began hurriedly to undress down to her underwear, then she hesitated. She could swim in them, as he'd suggested, but then she'd have to go home in wet clothes. Decisively she discarded them and put one foot in the pool. In contrast to the heat of the air, the water was icy cold. She was not prepared to plunge in as Colin had done, so she began to walk in at a shallower place, the water swirling and splashing round her legs.

Colin looked up.

'Colin! You promised not to look.'

'But I thought... I heard....' He broke off, overcome by the vision before his eyes. The water was only up to her knees. 'Oh, God, you're so beautiful!'

She tried to cover herself with her hands, saying reproachfully, 'You promised, Colin.'

He plunged his head under the water to shut out the unbearable temptation, and Mary slid the rest of the way in until she was in the deep part of the pool. Colin tried desperately to keep to his promise not to touch her, and for some time he succeeded, keeping a discreet distance from her. But once she came so close to him, her delicious little breast peeping tantalisingly above the water.

Before he could stop himself one hand flew out to touch it, and the other entwined itself around her waist.

'Colin!' she said in a breathless whisper. 'No touching, remember.'

But she didn't try to get away from him. The sensation was so erotic, the cold water against her skin in direct contrast to the warm melting inside her body.... He kissed her, drawing her close against him. She knew she should resist, but what with struggling to stay on her feet as the water swirled around her legs, and Colin's arms around her making her tremble, and she was melting inside... How could she resist him when she really wanted him to do whatever he wanted to her?

'It's alright, darling, I won't hurt you,' he whispered, kissing her, while his hands caressed her back, bottom and thighs. 'Oh, God, Mary, I want you so much!'

Whether it was his words or the feel of his nakedness against her own, brought Mary to her senses, sheer panic overcame desire, and she struggled frantically.

'Colin! No, no! Stop! You swore you wouldn't...'

'It's all right,' he said, letting her go suddenly. 'I was not going to do anything. But you're right. I did promise not to touch you, and I'm sorry.'

He covered his face with his hand. 'You'd better get dressed quickly. I won't look. I'm sorry, truly I am. I didn't realise quite how desirable you are.'

They went home in silence. He was more shaken than she was by what had almost happened that day, for it made him realise he did not have himself as well under control as he thought. Though he'd denied it, he could not, in truth, be certain he would not have gone further if she had not prevented it. He was even less confident about the outcome should the temptation ever arise again. And if they must wait a further two and a half years....

'I think we should be married without delay,' he suggested when they were alone a few days later. 'We could elope to Scotland. What do you say?'

'But Colin....' She looked at him doubtfully. 'It hasn't been legal to marry at Gretna Green for 50 years.'

'I know that. But if we're married, even if it's not strictly a true marriage, and it's consummated, do you really believe Father would refuse to let us make it legal?'

'Present him with a *fait accompli*? Is that what you mean to do? Colin, he'll be outraged!' But it sounded like an exciting adventure all the same.

Colin shrugged, his mouth curling up in a smile.

'But I don't think he'd kill us. And he'll soon get over it. He's quite fond of you. I believe he'll be pleased if he cared to admit it.'

'How will we get away?'

'We cannot go together from here, that's true. But I'll be off to Cambridge in two weeks' time. We'll arrange to meet somewhere.'

Mary's heart sank at mention of him leaving. 'Must you remind me of that?'

'You'll need an alibi,' he said. 'What about Constance?'

'Connie! Of course. I could pretend she'd asked me to stay with her. She owes it to me anyway. I lied for her more than once when I was in London and she wanted to go off to her suffragette meetings.'

'Be careful, though. Remember Aunt Alice and her mama are acquainted.'

'I don't think there's much of a threat from that quarter. I believe Lady Grantham saw through Mrs Livingstone and I don't think she liked her very much. I'm fairly certain they never meet now.'

'We'll need a witness. But we can't ask Dickon. It wouldn't be fair to involve him.'

'Nor Martha,' Mary agreed. 'I'd hate to be the cause of either of them losing a job.'

'In fact, it would be best if neither of them knew anything about it. I expect I shall be able to find someone in Cambridge. We'll meet at Darlington and go on together from there. And afterwards....' He kissed her tenderly, his hand on her breast. 'We'll find a nice quiet little hotel in Northumberland, or maybe the Lake District. Would you like that?'

Like it! To Mary it sounded like Paradise. The very thought of spending a whole weekend with Colin, as man and wife, in a little country hotel made her bones melt and turned her legs to jelly. But first there was an obstacle course to be overcome.

'I'll write to Connie, today.'

Chapter 7

The day came when Colin must leave for Cambridge. It was Autumn again and the trees in the park were a gay patchwork of colours. It was on such a day a year ago that it had all begun. Mary felt desolate until she received his first letter. It was not a love letter. It didn't need to be, for it was perfectly plain to her, reading between the lines, that she meant far more to him than words could express. He seemed to know intimately what she was thinking and doing so that it seemed as if they were not parted at all. And he wrote to her so often that she hardly had time to digest one letter before another arrived.

'Cambridge is magic, May,' he wrote. 'A mixture of ancient tradition and majesty. I can't wait for you to visit. It's hard to describe the atmosphere here in mere words. And then there's the river which runs right under our window. Punting is a favourite pastime here, specially in the summer. Punts are flat bottomed boats, propelled along by a pole which often gets stuck in the mud, causing the operator to lose his balance. I've just been watching some students larking around in one which they've managed to upset completely. Rather chilly, this time of year, I would think, but they seem to be taking it in remarkably good spirit.

'I'm sharing a room with a fellow called Bertie Higginbotham. "What an extraordinary name," I can hear you say. He's a good sort, a bit eccentric, he wears a monocle. But then, some people think I'm eccentric, I suppose. Most of us here have our little quirks....'

The letter, describing the college, his lodging, his fellow undergraduates, the professors, tutors and all their little idiosyncrasies, was ten pages long, written on both sides. He was bursting with enthusiasm. For Colin, going to Cambridge was fulfilling a dream. He'd once vowed his life would be spent 'making scientific discoveries.' Mary was quite envious, especially when he told her he'd met some girls from Newnham, the ladies' college. She wished more than ever she could go to Cambridge herself, and not just because Colin was there.

She'd heard nothing from Constance, and it was some weeks since she'd written to her, then just as she was beginning to lose heart a letter arrived.

'Delighted to be of help,' Connie wrote. 'That's what friends are for, isn't it? After all you did the same for me in a similar situation. Though nothing quite so exciting as an elopement! How romantic! Unfortunately I've never found a fellow willing to elope with me, or I might have been tempted. All the same, my dear Mary, I do hope you know what you're doing. I'm eaten with curiosity to know who you're running off with?'

Then she rushed on in a fever to tell Mary all her news. 'My dear, so much has happened to me since our somewhat inglorious flight from Trafalgar Square that day—can it only be just over a year ago? I am now a fully active member of the WSPU (Women's Social & Political Union) in case you don't know what it stands for. Mama has given up trying to stop me being a suffragette, and now I get a lot more freedom. I have recently met a wonderful man called Frederick Lawrence. Like your Colin he's wealthy and well educated, Eton and Cambridge, and he comes from a good family. He's very dedicated, and has already spent a great deal of his fortune building homes for poor and disadvantaged women, which will be run by his partner Emmeline Pethick. I've already offered my help as much as I can, and spend much of my spare time running errands for dear Freddie....'

She'd obviously abandoned her passion for Colin in favour of this Freddie Lawrence, who's name cropped up a great many times during the rest of the letter. Mary wondered how Emmeline Pethick felt about it. Poor Constance, was she destined always to be the bridesmaid, never the blushing bride? It was also clear that Constance's mother had completely lost control of her. She was blandly talking about the WSPU's plans to lobby Parliament next week. Mary hoped she knew what she was doing.

****

'You must have been blind, Archie, if you've not noticed, before now, that those two are in love,' said Alice Grantham, handing her guest a cup of tea.

'Truth is, Alice, I couldn't believe it at first. They've always been very close, you know. Inseparable as children. And they fight, sometimes, like cat and dog,' Mr Craven added, recalling some of the verbal sparring he'd witnessed quite recently.

'Some husbands and wives fight like cat and dog, too. You ask Walter. That merely means they feel so much at ease with each other they don't need to pull punches.'

'I suppose, truthfully, I didn't want to believe it. So I kept telling myself it was absurd to think it was anything but platonic affection.'

'So what made you suspect any more than that? Not simply the arrival of a handful of letters from Colin?'

'More than twenty letters in just over a month! And in general Colin's a most infrequent letter writer. When he was at school I'd be lucky to get one letter a term from him, and Mary complained bitterly she heard so little from him when she was in Switzerland.'

It was not simply the letters, some of which Mary had read out to him, long passages that had seemed innocuous enough. He'd never underestimated the strength of the affection between them, but recently there'd been signs of a very different kind of love between his son and his niece. He was not sure what to make of it, and there was nobody else he could talk to. Alice had offered support whenever a problem arose concerning Mary, so as he happened to be in London, it seemed a perfect opportunity to spend a convivial sojourn with the Granthams before returning to Yorkshire.

'Well,' said his hostess. 'It was clear to me when they were here last year. He couldn't keep his eyes off her, and he was quite piqued when she danced all evening with William Leyton. He tried to hide his feelings, but he couldn't fool me.'

'If you saw what was happening then, why on earth didn't you warn me, Alice?'

She shrugged. 'I didn't think I needed to. You'd only to see them together. And I did warn you, if you remember, about keeping Mary insulated. It appears it was already too late.'

'Too late. You mean, Mary...'

'Mary may be a little cleverer than Colin at hiding her feelings, but it was clear she wasn't interested in anyone else. Why, even Walter remarked how her face lit up when she heard me greet him in the hall—and he's not one notice that sort of thing as a rule.'

'But they're so young. I can't believe it's anything more than calf love.'

'Don't fool yourself, Archie. Those two are growing up fast. Their emotions and passions have already begun to develop.'

'But don't you realise what this means, Alice?'

'I admit I had hopes of William Leyton, but I'm afraid Mary had eyes for nobody but Colin...'

'What worries me, Alice,' Mr Craven interrupted in a voice of doom, 'is that they've spent so much time alone together for... well, for the best part of a year.'

Till All The Seas Run Dry

Lady Grantham sat up, slopping her tea into the saucer. 'What! Out on the moor, unchaperoned?'

'Certainly. But don't you see. They've always been like siblings. I never thought... It didn't occur to me....'

'Is she still a virgin, do you think?' she whispered breathlessly.

'Good God! I should hope so!' Mr Craven took out his handkerchief and mopped his brow. 'Of course she is. She's as innocent as a new born lamb.'

'I wouldn't count on it.'

'And as for Colin, I'm not sure he'd know what to do.'

'He'd know,' she nodded vehemently. 'For the Lord's sake, Archie, it's doing what comes naturally. Think back to your own youth. Did you have to be told, at the age of eighteen or nineteen, what to do?'

'What should I do, Alice? I can't let them marry. Even if they were not so closely related, they're far too young....'

'Well, they won't see so much of each other now that Colin is at Cambridge. Maybe you should find something for Mary to do. I could keep her here, if it would be any help, but I'm afraid London doesn't seem to suit her. She's very much a country girl.'

'No, I couldn't impose upon you like that. And Mary being in London would not be at all satisfactory. Yet I don't want to send her off to be a governess in an English house. If I could find some congenial family in France, or even Germany, she speaks both languages quite well, it would be ideal, and might benefit them both. She'd improve her French, and if there were children, she could teach them some English. But I'm not sure where to begin.'

'Ah! I do believe I have the solution. My friend the Marquise de Bergerac wrote to me only a few weeks ago asking if I knew of a suitable English girl for just such a position. Would you like me to write and suggest Mary?'

'I should be most grateful if you would, Alice. Forgive me for asking, but is there another cup in that pot?'

'Oh, Lord,' she said. 'I'm forgetting my manners. Of course there is.' She filled his cup and handed it back to him.

Silence fell between them. Alice Grantham studied her companion. Colin was very like him, she thought, though he had not got his father's unfortunate crooked shoulder. But Archibald Craven had been good looking in his younger days for all that. He was tall, like Colin, clean shaven and his hair was greying at the temples, which added distinction to his looks. They were alike in temperament too, intense, passionate, loyal. Archibald Craven had never looked at another woman either before or since his wife's death.

'By the way, Archie,' she began thoughtfully. 'What if they feel the same way about each other in a few years' time? Would you still have strong objections to them marrying?'

He got up from his chair and went to the window. He stretched his long lanky body, hunched his shoulders and leaning on the windowsill, gazed out along the street below. He was so long answering she thought he'd forgotten the question.

'Would you mind very much if they married eventually, Archie?'

He shook his head. 'No, no. They'll grow out of this infatuation. Once they're away from each other, meet other people, see the world a bit, find out what life's all about. Colin will meet plenty of other girls at Cambridge. He'll soon forget about Mary.'

'But supposing he doesn't. Supposing, even after he's met lots of other girls, he still loves Mary and wants to marry her?' She looked at him steadily until he was forced to meet her eyes.

'I don't know, Alice,' he said at last. 'I wouldn't want them to be unhappy, but I can't say I'd like it. It would not seem right to me. And I certainly wouldn't encourage it.'

'It's not incest, Archie,' she said softly. 'If that's what bothers you.'

'Not technically, nor legally I suppose, but.... Good God, Alice, don't you realise I might have adopted her as my own daughter. I very nearly did.'

Later that evening, replete after a five course meal, the three of them sat in front of a warm fire, making inroads into a bottle of port. Sir Walter liked his port, and Lady Grantham liked talking. She was holding the stage. The port was making Mr Craven feel sleepy. He was not the only one. His host was struggling to keep awake, too, and had, once or twice, begun to snore. Alice Grantham was expounding the qualities, or otherwise, of the suffragette movement, a subject very much on everyone's lips these days.

'I'm afraid they have lost an awful lot of sympathy since all this trouble started. If they had continued with peaceful demonstrations I think a great many more people would support them....' At that moment a gentle snort came from the direction of the sofa. 'Walter!'

Her husband awoke with a start. 'I'm sorry, m' dear.'

'As I was saying,' she resumed, glaring at him. 'I should have joined them myself, yes I would, Walter. Don't look so disbelieving.

Speaking of which, Archie, you'd be wise to keep Mary away from that Livingstone girl. Her poor mother came here in despair the other day. Constance had been arrested. I suppose she thought I had some influence, and might be able to get her out of prison....'

Archibald Craven sat bolt upright, suddenly wide awake.

'What did you say?'

'Constance Livingstone. You remember her, Archie. A school friend of Mary's....

'Yes, yes, I know that. In prison, did you say?'

'Yes. Why? You look very agitated, Archie.'

'When did this happen?'

'You mean, when did her mother come and see me?'

'No, when was she arrested?'

'I've no idea, but I believe it was something to do with that effort of theirs, that dreadful scene they created in the House of Commons last month. She was convicted and sent to prison two or three weeks ago. But I cannot imagine what I'm supposed to do about it....'

'Is she still in prison?' his voice boomed.

'I believe so, but there's nothing we can do.... Heavens! What's the matter, Archie? You've gone as white as a sheet.'

Mr Craven stood up. 'I'm afraid I'm going to have to leave you, Alice. I'm extremely sorry, but this is a matter of the utmost urgency.'

'Leave? This minute? But....'

He looked at his watch. 'If I can get to Kings Cross in 50 minutes I could still catch the night train and be home in time. D'you think your man could get me there in time, Alice?'

****

There was a hive of activity in Mary's bedroom at Misselthwaite, and an air of suppressed excitement.

'Eh, I hope you know what you're doing, Miss Mary,' cried Martha, all of a pother. 'What if it all goes wrong?'

'What could possibly go wrong, Martha? Stop fussing. And do keep your voice down. We don't want to be overheard. I'm supposed to be going to London, remember, to visit my friend Miss Livingstone.'

She congratulated herself on how smoothly their plans had been executed. It was most fortuitous that Mr Craven was away from home for a few days. She had been on tenterhooks for weeks, afraid he might find out and put a stop to it. It had all been so easy,

Constance's invitation, and her guardian giving her permission to go to London for a few days, before he went away. And finally, Dickon being available to take her to the station in the brougham.

'Everything's going according to plan.'

'But if th' master won't let tha get wed proper like. If there's a "just cause or implement....'

'Impediment, Martha,' Mary corrected. 'There won't be. What possible impediment could there be? And if he won't give his consent, we'll simply have to wait 'til we're both twenty one.'

'What if tha get pregnant?'

'Hush Martha! Mrs Medlock might hear you. I don't suppose I will, not after one weekend. But if I do, it would be even more reason for Mr Craven to give his consent.'

Martha threw up her hands in horror. 'Eh, Miss Mary! Tha'll be th' death o' me.'

'Look, Martha,' said Mary patiently. 'You're not going to stop me, whatever you say. So why don't you give me your blessing and wish me well.'

'Eh, but I hope tha'll not repent it.'

'Why should I? Colin and I have always loved each other. I can't believe it's really happening. I've been walking around on air for the last few days.'

'I remember th' day after tha first met. There was me, in a fair fever, afraid I'd lose me place for letting thee find him, afraid he'd raise th' roof wi' his tantrums, but I'd no need to fret, had I? Tha'd already bewitched him.'

'I think he bewitched me too, truth be told,' Mary smiled. 'I changed after I met him.'

'Aye, so tha did,' Martha agreed. 'A right little madam tha were, too, when tha first came. Well, I hope you'll be very happy.'

At that moment they heard a carriage come rumbling at great speed up the drive, pulling up outside the door with a loud commotion.

'Make ready, Miss Mary. That mun be our Dickon, though he shouldn't be driving so reckless, I'm sure.' She went to the window and looking out, she let out an exclamation, and her hands flew to her face.

'Why, it's th' Master. We wasn't expecting him hack 'til Monday.'

Chapter 8

Another train pulled into the station. Colin watched anxiously as the passengers began to alight, searching up and down the platform for Mary. But there was no sign of her on this train either. It was the fifth, or was it the sixth train he'd waited for.

Doors were slammed, a whistle blew, and the passengers dwindled away as the train pulled out, leaving Colin and his companion alone on the platform. A biting wind cut across the large expanse of tangled railway lines. Bertie Higginbotham hitched the collar of his great coat up round his ears and hunched his shoulders.

'Let's face it, old chap,' he said. 'It's been a wasted journey. She's obviously not coming. Even if her departure was delayed or she got on the wrong train, she's had time to travel to Edinburgh and back by now. Perhaps she's had second thoughts.'

'Never!' Colin spoke almost savagely, anxiety making him irritable. 'Mary wouldn't do that to me. She's not one of those flighty females.'

'I never said she was, but she might have decided that eloping was too precarious a business. Women are usually more sensible about these things.'

'Are you saying I'm not sensible? That it wasn't sensible to marry her?'

Bertie put a reassuring hand on his friend's shoulder. 'I wasn't deriding you in any way, my friend. If I'd thought it was quite lunatic I wouldn't have agreed to come with you. I'm merely suggesting, if we want to avoid getting pneumonia, we should call it a day, and get the next train back to Cambridge. Then tonight we can go out and get very drunk.'

So saying, he tucked his arm in Colin's and pulled him towards the station master's office. 'Let's go and find out when's the next train south.'

'I'm sorry, my dear,' said Mr Craven, gravely. 'I'm afraid it's out of the question. I cannot let you marry Colin.'

Mary saw that he was adamant, confirming her worst fears. And now she was sure to be sent away to "get over it," without even the chance to say good-bye. And heaven knew how long they would be parted for.

'It's not as bad as all that,' her guardian said, gently. He was not an unkind man, and he was sensitive to her acute distress. 'There's many more fish in the sea as ever came out of it. And you are young yet. You've hardly given yourself a chance. Who knows, you may even meet a young Frenchman who'll sweep you off your feet.'

He looked at her sadly. Alice Grantham was probably right. It was obvious she really loved Colin, and the attachment was far deeper than he'd ever imagined. To tell the truth he'd thought at first they were planning an illicit weekend together in Cambridge. He had not anticipated that they were actually preparing to tie the knot permanently. And whilst he was relieved Colin's intentions towards Mary were at least honourable, he was also aware that this had more serious implications.

He studied her closely. Mary was very much a Lennox. By the strange vagaries of nature she was more like his late wife than her own mother. That Mary reminded him so strongly of his dear departed had always tugged at his heart, and had invoked in him a softness towards her that he had not felt even for Colin, his own son. But this likeness to Colin's mother was a stark reminder of their close relationship. There was a theory being voiced abroad nowadays that interbreeding caused deformities and other disabilities in the offspring. Indeed it was widely thought to be the reason for the degeneration of the Hanovers, culminating in the madness of George III.

And yet he had no wish to destroy her happiness, but that would not be necessary, surely. She'd get over it. Hadn't she once been rather fond of the Sowerby boy? Highly unsuitable, too, but at least she'd grown out of it. She'd grow out of her infatuation for Colin too.

See,' he said, putting an arm round her shoulder. 'You must begin to look forward. I'm told Madame de Bergerac has a very warm, kind and sympathetic nature, and the children are sweet things. Even so, if it doesn't work out, if you're unhappy with these people, I shall not force you to stay, if that's any consolation to you. I should not like you to be miserable. We'll find somewhere else for you to go.' He was thinking, now, more of the future, after France. 'Maybe you have some ambitions of your own.'

Hope sprang into Mary's eyes. 'Oh, Uncle Archie, do you really mean that, because I've always wanted....' She broke off, biting her lip.

Till All The Seas Run Dry

He waited. 'Well?'

'C-could I go to university like Colin? Not necessarily Cambridge,' she added hastily, 'though there is a ladies' college there. But somewhere...else...perhaps?' Seeing his face she trailed off.

'My dear child!' He shook his head. Mary at university! While Colin was at Cambridge! Did she think he was born yesterday? If it was too far away for Colin to reach her, he would be unable to keep an eye on her himself. And he was very old fashioned in his ideas about educating women.

'I should not have put such doubts in your mind. Of course you'll be happy in the south of France. And I'm sure you can make a success of it. You've had a good education. You can cope with teaching English to two young children under five. You can teach them to read, and a few simple sums.'

'How long must I stay there?' she asked, thinking she'd be away for Christmas, all by herself among strangers. Unshed tears stung her eyes. It was all too reminiscent of when she first went to Switzerland. How homesick, frightened and lonely she'd felt. And now she must go through it all again.

'I'd expect you to remain with the de Bergeracs for two years at least, longer if it's going to be of benefit to you.'

Her heart sank. It was an interminable time to be parted from Colin. Would he still love her after such a time? It didn't enter her head she might no longer love him. 'Will I be able to come home to visit occasionally?'

'That depends on Madame de Bergerac. Once you are established in the family, I dare say she'd allow you to come home for special occasions, like Colin's twenty-first birthday, or your own.'

Or Colin's wedding! The thought sprang into her mind, and the blood drained from her head making her feel faint and dizzy. For now it was crystal clear that as soon as she was gone all the loveliest girls in England would be sought for Colin's acquaintance. Mr Craven would leave no stone unturned in persuading him to fall in love with someone more suitable. If he were far less susceptible, Colin would find it hard to resist such inducement. At the same time it hit her like a blow that she had never really told him how much she loved him. She'd taken it for granted he knew. The instinct of self-preservation, always strong in her, had made her hold back, afraid to lay naked her heart. It was he with his generous spirit who'd loved her wholeheartedly. And now that she hadn't turned up.... All the unspoken words of love, the things she might have said to assure him, came into her mind to taunt her.

Her throat ached with suppressed misery. 'I must see him before I go,' the words squeezed out of her, the tears overflowed, spilling down her cheeks. 'Please, Uncle Archie?'

Chapter 9

'Father, I'd like you to meet Miss Charlotte Denzel-Fitch.'

Mr Craven found himself looking into a pair of cat's eyes. She was the most exquisitely beautiful young woman he'd ever seen. Her skin was like alabaster, a smooth clear complexion, her hair was jet black, and luxuriant, and her figure made the Venus de Milo look fat and clumsy. But those eyes....

'Father?'

He might have been there to this day if Colin had not recalled him. He cleared his throat and held out his hand.

'How do you do, Miss Denzel-Fitch.'

Left alone to reflect, Mr Craven tried to analyse his first impression of the girl Colin had brought home for his inspection. For some reason he didn't like her. She had a foreign look about her, and with a name like that she was probably of German extraction, maybe Bohemian. But there was something else, yes, something in those eyes. Something elusive, maybe even devious, that made him feel he could not trust her. Maybe it was too early to judge, after such a brief encounter. He must simply hope she didn't mean very much to Colin, although Colin, who'd never been short of feminine admirers, had never actually brought one home before.

He'd given up trying to control his son's choice in women. For almost three years since Mary left, he hadn't looked at another woman, he'd begun to despair of him ever getting over her. His intractable son had shown no interest in any of the acceptable young ladies he'd produced for him. He had plenty of female companions among his friends in Cambridge, groups of them, of mixed gender, went off skiing together in Switzerland or Austria in the winter. And in summer the same thing, camping out in tents. Heaven knew what went on. And during the term they were in and out of each other's rooms with no decorum whatsoever. All very libertarian, nothing like it was in his day. Thank God he'd had the sense to send Mary away to France. He'd never have had a moment's peace of mind with her at university.

'Well, Papa, what do you think?'

Mr Craven jumped. He'd been so deep in thought he'd not heard Colin come in.

'Think? What about?'

'Charlotte, what do you think of her?'

'I don't know,' Mr Craven said slowly. 'But you're not serious, are you? I mean, you're not thinking of marrying her, surely?'

'You don't like her, do you?'

'I'd want to know her better. How well do you know her? And for how long?'

Colin shrugged. 'Does that matter? You told me once that when you met Mother you knew immediately.' His voice was teasing. 'How do you know I don't?'

Mr Craven was cynical. 'You mean you were instantly bewitched. My dear boy, you're infatuated!'

'That's what you said about Mary. It's what you always say. If I'd chosen to marry one of the insipid "ladies of quality" you produced for me you'd have said it was love at first sight, as you said it was with you and Mother.'

'I may have been wrong about Mary,' Mr Craven admitted sadly. 'At least I know she loved you and was not simply out to feather her own nest.'

Colin looked aghast. 'You think Charlotte's after my money!' Then he laughed. 'Oh, but then, you think they're all after my money.'

Mr Craven shrugged. 'It's always a hazard when one has it.'

'Then I'd never trust anyone. I'm not going to be like that. Like you!'

With that he left of the room. Life was full of irony, Mr Craven thought. Colin was now well over the so called age of discretion, being twenty-two. He could do nothing to prevent it if he set his mind to marrying this girl. He would simply have to stand by and watch the son to whom he'd never been a very good father, ruin his life and happiness. At the same time it struck him forcibly that three years ago he had prevented a marriage which, though not ideal, might at least have been happy.

It was time Mary came home.

****

Mary stood gazing out over the parapet, the outer wall of the chateau, deep in thought. Hundreds of feet below the river wove its way through woodland, twisting and turning like a silver ribbon, glistening in the sunlight of a Spring morning. It was so beautiful she could hardly bear to leave it. The view, the chateau with its little pointed turrets, which reminded her of a fairy tale palace, perched high on the cliff overlooking the Dordogne.

It was hard to believe that in less than a week's time she would be back in England. Hard to imagine waking up to find herself in Misselthwaite Manor, instead of in her little room in the chateau. It was well over three years since she'd left.

Nobody had expected her to be away so long, not even her uncle. She had been about to go home for Colin's twenty-first birthday party when the Marquis de Bergerac became seriously ill, and they needed her to take care of the children so Madame could give her full attention to her husband. The Marquis never recovered. He died, leaving his poor wife bereft, and Mary had to delay her departure yet again. She could not have left the poor lady who had been devoted to her husband, at such a time, nor the children who needed her more than ever. Young Gerard, at seven years old, suddenly inherited the title, and had the burden of being the head of the family unexpectedly thrust upon him. That was more than a year ago. Now Gerard had a tutor and Annette was to go to school. Mary had received a letter from her uncle requesting her to return home as soon as she could be spared.

She missed the dear old Marquis. He had none of the arrogance all too often attributed to the French aristocracy. And if there was any trace of it in Madame it was outweighed by her indubitable charm. She was a friendly, vivacious little person, and her husband's quiet sense of humour had been a perfect foil for her rather volatile nature. His gentleness and compassion had been like a steady hand on the helm in a rough sea.

Mary's life in France had not been without drama. Her passion for Gilles—a little involuntary shudder shook her at the thought of him. The attraction had been intense, almost violent. It had taken every ounce of will she possessed to resist his attempts to seduce her. She knew it couldn't last—such passion was sure to burn out—but then she discovered he had no intentions of marrying her. How could he when he already had a wife! She shuddered again. He'd never loved her, he only wanted her body. He'd very nearly ruined her life. It still twisted her inside to think of her humiliation. She'd felt cheap, ashamed, though she'd done nothing wrong other than loving him. She thought she'd never get over it.

It was the Marquis, sick as he was, who'd comforted her, without being told, for she'd told nobody of her shame. But she didn't have to tell him. Somehow he knew. Aching tears welled at the thought of his kindness. He'd been like a father to her. Why could she not feel the same affection for her uncle? Mr Craven had always been rather remote, unapproachable. She could not imagine crying on his shoulder.

And she had got over Gilles, just as she had got over being parted from Colin. But it had taught her a sharp lesson about men. They were simply not to be trusted.

She thought of Colin. It all seemed so long ago, like another life, their youthful love. Her uncle had been right to intervene. Now that she was older and wiser, she realised they'd been far too young to take such a momentous step. Clearly she, at least, had not been ready for marriage. She'd been shocked at the ease with which she'd fallen for Gilles. She'd meant to be faithful to Colin. Yet it was not entirely her fault that his image had faded in her mind. It was he who'd ceased writing first. His letters had gradually become less ardent, then less frequent, until recently she was lucky to hear from him once or twice a year. But now that it loomed imminent, she was a little apprehensive about the prospect of seeing him again.

****

'But Charlie, you agreed to come with me to the ball.'

'As I recall,' said Charlotte grimly. 'I said I wasn't sure, because I'd already half promised to go with someone else.'

'Who?' Colin felt a stab of jealousy.

'Never mind who, Colin. But you mustn't take me for granted, that's all.'

'Well, this is a fine time to tell me. I've already bought tickets.'

'I'm sorry to say this, Colin, but you're not my only admirer, you know.' She raised her eyes to his, their lids weighed down by long black lashes. 'And we're not engaged or anything.'

'So you keep reminding me,' he said curtly.

'Never mind,' she purred, putting her hand seductively on his cheek. 'I'm sure you'll find someone else, an attractive man like you.'

With that tantalising remark she sailed off, looking paralyzingly lovely, and, espying another admirer, hailed him.

'Hello, Tommy. How jolly to see you.'

Tommy Sutcliffe looked elated. They linked arms and went off together. Colin stood staring miserably after them, when a voice behind him startled him.

'My lady disdain! It grieves me to see you make an ass of yourself, old chap.' He turned to find Bertie Higginbotham at his elbow. 'You'll never get any joy out of that one.'

'Oh, Bertie. What am I to do?'

'Are you really asking me? Forget her. That's the best advice I can give you.'

'No, I don't mean about Charlotte. I mean the ball. I'm stuck without a partner for the May ball for the first time ever. Imagine, Bertie, me with nobody to go with.'

'It mightn't be a bad thing, if it helped get that creature out of your system, to forego the ball for once. That wench'll be the ruin of you, believe me. There's a name for her kind.'

'Yes, so you've said before.' He was walking very fast and Bertie was having a job to keep up with him.

'I don't mean that sort of name. There's another that's very apt. What is it? Oh, yes, I know. It's a siren. Charlotte is a siren, Colin. A very dangerous creature.'

'I know you don't like her, Bertie. And I know why.'

'You think it's sour grapes, because she's never come after me. It's little wonder,' he laughed. 'When there are charming, handsome fellows like yourself, and wealthy with it, what chance has a dull fellow like me, poor as a church mouse, nothing much to look at....'

'Oh, shut up, Bertie.'

'There's a little ditty going around in my head. D'you want to hear it?'

'Not particularly.'

An hour or so later, Colin returned to his rooms to find a note pinned to his door.

'Charlotte Denzel-Fitch is a witch, witch, witch,

She's a fortune-hunting, callous little bitch, bitch, bitch.'

He tore it off, screwed it up and threw it in the waste-paper basket.

'Damn Bertie!' he muttered.

Colin straightened his back, closed the bonnet and patted his prize possession. He was proud of his motor car, a silver Daimler he'd bought with part of his inheritance on becoming twenty-one. He spent a great deal of his spare time tinkering with it, always trying to improve its performance.

Bertie Higginbotham came round the corner on his bicycle, whistling. He'd been whistling the same tune for a month. It was an annoying habit he had.

'Hello, Colin. Still up to your armpits in motor oil, I see. Will you be coming to Francis' party on Saturday?'

Colin shook his head. 'Not this weekend. I'm off home. Mary's arriving from France.'

Bertie's face brightened.

'Your cousin Mary? The same young lady we waited five hours for on that platform at Darlington? I'd like to meet that young woman. Will she come and visit you, d'you think?'

'I hope so, if my father let's her. Or else you must come to us in the summer.'

'I'd like that enormously. I say,' he added as an idea struck him. 'Why don't you ask Mary to the May ball?'

'That's not a bad idea, Higginbotham. Sometimes, just sometimes, you have brilliant ideas. It would kill two birds with one stone; first, it would give me a reason to invite Mary here, and Father'd be more inclined to allow it, and second, it would teach Charlotte a lesson. I'll show that little minx she can't twist me round her little finger.'

'Bravo!' cried Bertie, delighted. 'Ho-ho! I'd like to see her face when you walk in with another lady on your arm. Is she beautiful? Your cousin Mary?'

Colin considered. 'Nothing like as beautiful as Charlotte, I'm afraid.'

'Well, she must be something quite special if you were thinking of marrying her once.'

'I was very young. She was my first love. Calf love, of course, on reflection.'

'All the same, I'm looking forward to meeting her. Have you finished fiddling with that machine? Coming for a pint?'

Colin shook his head. 'No time, I'm afraid. I must go and clean up, then get ready to leave. I've a long drive ahead of me.'

'I say,' said Bertie. 'You're not surely thinking of driving all the way to Yorkshire in this bone rattler? Why not go on the train? It'd be much quicker.'

Colin pulled himself up to his full height. He was used to Bertie's rude remarks about Charlotte, but such slander about his pride and joy....

'If you complain about my motor car you'll never get another ride in her. Since when has she ever let you down?'

'Don't say you've forgotten the time we broke down on the way back from that party over at Royston, and had to walk nine miles in the pitch dark. And it rained. Then you had to walk the nine miles back next day to go and fix it. And what about the time....'

'Oh, shut up, Higginbotham. I haven't time to argue with you.'

He was not to be put off. It might be quicker by train, but he'd waited nearly a year for the opportunity to meet Mary at the station in his motor car.

****

Mary alighted from the train clutching the small portmanteau she'd brought with her. The large trunk carrying the rest of her belongings was to follow. She was feeling fatigued from the long journey and thought longingly of a hot bath and her own bed at Misselthwaite. When she caught sight of Colin her heart missed a beat. He look fresh, clean and strikingly handsome—she had forgotten how handsome he was—in his striped blazer and straw boater. She felt travel worn and weary, her face was pale from lack of sleep, and she wished there'd been time to freshen up before they met. At that moment the train hissed, letting off smutty steam which enveloped her in an added layer of grime.

Colin was coming towards her.

'Mary?' He hesitated for a moment, then advanced, taking her in his arms in a brotherly bear hug. 'I can hardly believe I'm really seeing you, after all these years. D'you realise it's the longest time we've ever been apart?' He picked up her bag, taking her arm with his free hand. 'Come, I've something to show you.'

He looked much the same, a few years older, of course, and he was more mature, poised and self assured. She'd expected that. She knew she'd altered herself. But there was, about him, a sort of reserve, something indefinable, and it frightened her. He was a stranger.

The Daimler stood, in all it's glory, waiting for them just outside the station. She knew he had a car. The few letters he'd written recently had been full of it, and these machines were not new to her— the marquis had owned a fleet of them. But she had to confess that Colin's Daimler really was rather grand. It was built on similar lines to Mr Craven's old carriage, the back being completely covered in, and it was a very dashing silver grey with black runners and fenders.

'Oh, Colin, it's beautiful!'

She could feel the pride emanating from him as he opened the door for her, and helped her to her seat. He got out a blanket from the boot to wrap round her legs and a scarf to put round her head. How thoughtful of him.

She waited while he struggled with the starting crank, she knew these machines could be temperamental, but Colin was short of patience. A few choice oaths rang in the air, and the corners of Mary's mouth twitched irrepressibly. Perhaps he was not so changed after all.

Goggles, hat, overcoat were all thrown off, and sleeves rolled up. The car's bonnet was flung open and Colin's head disappeared into the body of the engine. To her amusement she heard him scolding the engine, as if it was a person.

'Dammit!' he shouted. 'What the dickens is the matter with you? You brought me all the way from Cambridge without any of this nonsense. Why play me up now? If Bertie Higginbotham hears of this I'll never live it down. And neither will you.'

By now she was shaking with laughter. She remembered well how he used to talk to Prince in the same vein when he misbehaved. A dark cloud loomed ominously above and she felt a splash on her hand. Another oath emitted from Colin, and he emerged from behind the bonnet, his face smudged with grease. She suppressed an urge to laugh out loud.

'You'd better get inside,' he said, flinging the door open and indicating the back of the car which was covered in. 'There's no sense in you getting soaked. I'm sorry about this.'

'It's alright, Colin,' she sighed wearily. 'There's no problem.'

She sank thankfully into the upholstered back seat thinking this latest toy must have cost him a small fortune. She was just dozing off when she was awakened by the bonnet being slammed down.

'Now!' Colin swore at his car, 'You'd better start alright this time, or upon my word I'll abandon you right here on the side of the road and leave you to rot! D'you hear?'

And it was as if the vehicle understood exactly what its master had said, for the next time he tried to crank her up, she grunted, spluttered and started like a bird. By now it was pouring with rain, Colin's hair and clothes were dripping wet, and he was covered in oil. Mary felt sorry for him. He poked his head through the window.

'I'll have you home in a tick now, May. Sorry about the delay.'

Till All The Seas Run Dry

Mr Craven was delighted to see her. She couldn't remember when he'd made her feel so welcome. She wished she had not felt so tired so that she might have enjoyed all the attention, for the two men seemed to be vying with each other to spoil her. She had a strong suspicion Colin had something on his mind, that he wanted to tell her something, but whenever they were alone he fidgeted and there was an awkward silence.

She was so tired she could scarcely drag herself upstairs.

It was delicious to be back in her own bed in her own room at home in Misselthwaite, with the familiar smell of wax polish and scented geraniums. The last three years seemed to roll back, and it was as if she'd only been away a short time. Everything was exactly as she'd left it. Colin had not altered very much after all. She'd imagined it. He was impetuous as ever, with the same inimitable charm and wicked sense of humour. He still bragged and swore and apologised afterwards. He was still loveable, laughable, sincere and wonderful.

It was she who had changed.

She had just fallen into a deep and restful slumber when there was a tap on the door. At first she didn't know what had awakened her. Then the rap came again, more insistently.

'Martha? Is that you?'

The door creaked and opened and a head peeped round it.

'No, it's me,' a voice said, apologetically.

'Colin! What on earth....?'

'Forgive me, May,' he said sheepishly, coming into the room. 'I know this is not very conventional, but I simply have to talk to you. I cannot sleep until I get it off my chest.'

'Are you mad!' She couldn't reach her wrap which was hanging behind the door so she pulled the bedclothes tighter round her neck.

'It's all right,' he laughed nervously. 'I haven't come for that,'

'I should hope not!' She hadn't meant to sound so indignant.

'I.... I've something I must tell you...myself...before anyone else does. I'd meant to tell you in the car, but....' he shrugged. 'And tomorrow I go back to Cambridge.'

'Won't it wait till the morning?'

'I have to leave early to get back to Cambridge, and there mightn't be a chance.... You saw how it was tonight.'

She waited several seconds, looking at him, her eyes growing accustomed to the dark so that she could see his features more clearly. He looked anxious and embarrassed.

'Well? What is this momentous bit of news that can't wait?'

He remained silent, standing on one leg, then on the other. 'Come and sit down,' she invited, patting the bed beside her, 'and tell me what's worrying you.' She spoke in a tone she might have used to soothe him in the old days when he was a boy.

'I've a confession to make,' he blurted out suddenly. 'You see, there's...someone....'

'Another woman,' she supplied, and he nodded, sinking back into silence.

He sat on the very edge of the bed and she took his hand. He didn't look at her. He was trying to tell her he'd been with a woman, she thought, full of worldly wisdom she didn't have. Well, he was twenty-two, and a young man. Young men must sow their wild oats. Where had she heard that? Madame de Bergerac had once tried to explain where men differed from women in that respect.

'There's no need to feel guilty about it,' she laughed uneasily. 'I've been away long enough, I didn't expect....'

'You didn't expect me to be faithful?' He seemed surprised.

'Well, three years is a long time...for a man. I mean....' This was embarrassing, she was glad it was dark. 'I'd be surprised if there was no other woman in all that time.'

'You don't mind, then?' he exclaimed jubilantly, then rushed on to explain, 'You see, I thought you might still consider us to be engaged.'

'Engaged?' She was taken off her guard. Had he believed they were still engaged? Her hand shook inside his at the thought of her own involvement with Gilles. 'No, not really. It was a long time ago and we were very young.'

'My thoughts exactly.' His relief was obvious. 'So you don't mind calling it off?'

'No, no.' What else could she say?

'You see, there's this girl, the most beautiful I've ever seen, and I'm crazy about her.... Oh, I should have known you'd be all right about it, but I was afraid of hurting you, that you might still.... You are a dear, my dearest cos' in fact, the best friend I've got. Three years is a long time to be apart, but I've been feeling awkward since I picked you up. Silly, isn't it?'

He was rattling on. A cold sensation crept over Mary. She understood it all now. Colin wanted to be relieved of his obligation to her because there was another woman—not simply the sowing of wild oats, but another woman he loved—loved more than her. Why did it hurt so much? Why, when she had half expected it?

'I'm glad you're happy,' she said, letting go of his hand. 'Now let me get some sleep?'

She wanted him to leave the room. Indeed she couldn't bear his proximity any longer. She had not thought she could feel the pain of rejection so soon after Gilles—she realised now that the Frenchman had meant nothing to her after all, it had been her pride only that was hurt. But this was worse, much worse. She'd never have believed anything could hurt so much. It was a different kind of hurt, a dreadful feeling that she'd lost something very precious.

'Anyway, it's just as well,' he said as he got up to go. 'Father was right to stop us, you know. You and I shouldn't marry. There's scientific evidence, I've discovered since I've been at Cambridge, that the offspring of first cousins can turn out...well, not quite right.'

It was the twist of the knife. He crept out of the room.

'Goodnight May,' he whispered upon reaching the door. 'And thanks.'

The door closed behind him.

Thanks for what? For disturbing my sleep to tell me you no longer love me? This is no time to discover you still love him, she scolded herself fiercely. For now she knew she did and always had. It was no childish illusion after all, but a deep and lasting love. The only youthful thing about it was that it couldn't last the test of so long apart. And so she'd lost him.

The tears came easily, wetting the pillow, just as they had done when the marquis died. At length, because she was dropping with fatigue, she fell asleep.

Chapter 10

There was a profusion of colour in the garden that day in early May, the grass seemed greener than ever, and her senses were bombarded with delicious fragrances. It was all the more poignant because the secret garden, which had once been her consolation, her refuge in times of trouble, had now become her bane, magnifying her heartache. Every scent, every flower, every corner of it awakened a memory, not only of Colin, but of her childhood. It represented a time when she was intensely happy.

Nor could she escape these memories by going elsewhere. Even a walk in the woods where the bluebells formed a violet carpet as far as the eye could see, invoked a vivid picture of Colin, as a boy of twelve, carrying an armful of bluebells, stumbling, almost dropping his load, and singing:

> *"Bluebells I've gathered,*
> *Take them and be true.*
> *When I'm a man, my plan,*
> *Will be to marry you...."*

Her throat contracted, her eyes ached and stung with tears. If she'd written more often, might she have kept the flame alive? Or if they'd met in the mean time, if she'd come home for a visit, would it have made any difference? And was it too late now? Was it?

Colin had left early that day. He said he had a long drive back to Cambridge. She was relieved to see him go. The effort of pretending she didn't care, pretending, under her uncle's inquisitive eye, nothing was amiss, was an unbearable strain. But now that he'd gone a great sadness descended on her. It was a bright, glorious day with an arched blue sky, yet the warmth of the sun was lost on her, she felt cold. Gone was the warm feeling of the evening before when they were making a fuss of her. Had this attention been prompted by guilt?

She heard a whistling noise behind her and turned to see Dickon talking to the birds in his inimitable way. His joy at seeing her was undisguised, making her heart ache anew that anyone should be so glad to see her. She felt regret that she had been so engrossed in her own misery that she had not given him a thought. At another time she would have sought him out long before now. She chided herself for thinking the world revolved round Colin. She'd survived without him for more than three years. Surely she could do so again? She must snap out of it. The pain would ease as time went by, and life would go on.

'Hello, Dickon,' she said, with an attempt at a cheerful smile.

It was hard to fool Dickon who could sense when people were unhappy, in the same way as he knew when an animal was sick or frightened.

'Eh, Miss Mary. Why art hiding away in this damp place?'

'I like the woods at this time of year. The bluebells are lovely.'

'Oh, aye, they're fine. But tha'rt shivering. Tha'll catch tha death sitting on damp tree trunk.' He looked at her suspiciously, then suddenly spoke out boldly. 'Tha've been weeping. Come, tell us what's upset thee.'

'I'm not upset, Dickon. It's the cold wind, it makes my eyes water,' she lied. She tried to escape him, but he caught both her hands and held them captive.

'Aye, I know. Tha'rt like a poor wee bird wi' a broken wing that tries to hide from harm's way. But I'll not let thee get harmed,' he said, his voice soft and gentle, laying his hand on her cheek. 'I don't like to see thee hurt.'

Her eyes filled with tears, and it was all she could do to hold them back, to resist throwing herself into his arms and weeping on his shoulder, as she would have done in the old days.

From that day Dickon watched her like a hawk, making a point, whenever he was off duty, of seeking her out. As far as he was concerned she needed love and tenderness like the roses and fruit trees in the secret garden, like the injured animals he'd rescued and made his pets. Like them she was hurt, and he had a shrewd idea who'd hurt her. He supposed that Colin's affairs were none of his business, but if he hurt Mary....

He didn't like the vain, callous female Colin had brought home last Christmas.

'It won't last,' his mother had assured him. 'Mester Colin'll see sense, right enow. Soon as Miss Mary's home, tha'll see.'

Ben Weatherstaff had agreed.

'He's bewitched,' the old man had said in disgust. 'Stuck up prig she is, too. An' if I know owt, she's no breeding neither. She'll not do for th' mistress of Misselthwaite.'

'What d' tha ken about breeding, Ben Weatherstaff?' Dickon laughed.

Till All The Seas Run Dry

'I ken more 'n you think,' said the old man stubbornly. 'Not as there's much a body can do. He'll not listen to th' likes o' thee an me. There's only one lass as can, if she's a mind to, an' that's Miss Mary.'

Dickon smiled. Ben Weatherstaff rarely paid Mary a compliment. Indeed he had little time for women at all. Colin would come round. As soon as he saw Mary alongside that other female he'd be back at her feet, begging forgiveness.

The letter was there on the hall table. Mary's heart leapt into her mouth as soon as she saw the unmistakably familiar handwriting. She ran into the garden to read it, ripping the envelop open as she went.

'My dear May,' it ran. 'I can't think what possessed me to forget. I meant to mention when I was home, that in three weeks' time, at the beginning of June, the May Week celebrations begin here. You always said you'd like to visit Cambridge and this would be an excellent time to come. May Week is enormous fun, and at the end of it there is a ball here at Trinity. I would very much like you to come to it, and I'd like you to meet some of my friends here. Let me know as soon as possible if you can come....'

She went in to breakfast and found Mr Craven there having his. He looked up from his paper when she sat down.

'There was a letter for you this morning. Did you get it?'

'Yes,' she said breathlessly, her heart racing as she felt the letter in her pocket. Then she thought she may as well tell him. 'I'm invited to a May ball, in four weeks' time.'

She saw to her surprise a look of approval, and there was even some eagerness in his voice when he asked, 'Shall you go, d'you think?'

'I...don't know,' she said, holding the coffee pot poised over her cup. 'I thought I might like to.'

'Splendid! I'm delighted Colin's asked you. You've never been to Cambridge, have you? You ought to see it, at least. And everyone seems to enjoy the May balls. They're the highlight of the year, I believe. Never been to one myself. Not my cup of tea.'

She looked at him in amazement. He was not usually so chatty, particularly at breakfast time, and he was being positively enthusiastic about her going to Cambridge.

'Why don't you go a little earlier, for May Week itself. Did Colin explain to you what that is? They have races on the river. The colleges all compete, and I gather there's much jollification. I think you'd enjoy it. Leave your accommodation to me. I'll arrange it.'

This was incredible. He was encouraging her to spend more time with Colin, he who'd been at pains to keep them apart. Could it be that he thought, now that she was older she'd outgrown all that, or was it because he knew it was safe, that Colin's heart was engaged elsewhere?

His voice intruded on her thoughts. 'As a matter of fact, I want to talk to you about Colin. He always spurns my advice, whereas he might listen to you....'

Were her ears deceiving her? Incredible! Her uncle, confiding in her, about Colin.

'It was his idea to stay on at Cambridge after he got his degree, doing what, I cannot imagine. I suggested he might consider taking a commission in the army, or something useful like that.'

She was tempted to remind him that Colin was a grown man, not a schoolboy, but she held her tongue.

'Perhaps he thinks he is doing something useful at Cambridge,' she said. 'He always wanted to be a scientist.'

'Oh, I don't mind him staying at Cambridge if that's what he wants. It's the people he associates with. He's not a good judge of character like you.'

If that's what he thought it was as well he knew nothing about Gilles, she thought. But she could not help feeling immensely pleased that he had such a high opinion of her.

'He's very fond of you. You could be such a good influence on him.'

'I don't know about that,' she laughed, trying to sound light-hearted. 'I'm afraid we've grown apart. I don't know what you think I can do.'

Mr Craven looked at her sharply. 'He's always admired you. He greatly values your opinions. You should not underestimate yourself. You know,' he added, with a smile, patting her hand across the table. 'You've grown into a very attractive young woman, Mary, if I may say so. You're so modest, I don't suppose a little flattery will go amiss.'

It was so unusual for him to flatter her, she began to wonder what he was after.

'I'm sure you'll be much admired at Cambridge. What are you now? Twenty-one? It's high time you thought about settling down.'

Till All The Seas Run Dry

So that was it. He wanted her off his hands and he saw some young man at Cambridge as the last hope. Yet she was perplexed. A moment ago he'd complained about Colin's lack of taste in friends, now he was encouraging her to choose a husband from among them. Or, could it be that he didn't care for the new woman in Colin's life and hoped she'd knock some sense into him? It was an interesting position to be in, but not one she relished.

'So,' said her guardian. 'It's settled then. You'll go for the whole of May Week, then to the ball afterwards. I'll write off immediately and book your accommodation. I'm sure you'll have a wonderful time. And who knows what may come of it.'

The last remark was addressed more to himself than to her.

****

When Colin saw Charlotte a week or so later, she was all sweetness and light. But this was typical of her capricious nature. Having snubbed him and been perfectly beastly one day, she'd be all over him the next, and vice versa. He was getting used to it. In fact he enjoyed it. It was an exciting game, like Russian roulette, though he'd never be insane enough to play that game. Charlotte was the most exciting thing that had ever happened to him. No other woman stirred his senses to such a pitch, or stimulated his wits so much. She was maddening, passionate, sensuous, cruel, bewitching and infuriating all at once.

'Oh, Colin, you'll be pleased to hear I will come with you to the ball, after all.'

'Well, it's too late now, Charlie. I've invited someone else.'

Her jaw dropped. 'But you can't!'

'Why not? You said you wouldn't come with me.'

'No, I didn't. I said I didn't think I could. But I've changed all my plans now just to please you,' she pouted her full lips. 'But if you don't want to take me, I can easily find someone else.'

'Now don't try blackmail on me, young lady,' said Colin, a finger under her chin.

She shrugged her lovely shoulders, and turned limpid eyes on him. 'Blackmail! But I wouldn't dream of it.'

'Oh, wouldn't you?' he laughed, drawing her close and kissing her.

'Who is she? Who have you asked instead of me, you horrid man.'

'My cousin Mary.'

'Your cousin?' Her face brightened. 'Oh, well, that's no problem. Bertie could take your cousin. I'm sure you could persuade him, specially if you offer to get the tickets.'

'If you're so keen on Bertie coming,' he chuckled. 'Why not get him to take you?'

'Colin, you're a devil,' she laughed, gently tapping him on the cheek in a mock slap. 'You know how Bertie and I simply love each other.'

'But I can't expect poor Mary to go with a complete stranger. But I have the solution. I'll get two more tickets, as you suggest, and we'll go as a four.'

Charlotte looked dubious. He knew she didn't really want Bertie anywhere near her. And it was not quite what he'd had in mind, either, since one of his reasons for inviting Mary had been to make her jealous, to teach her a lesson for teasing him so.

'If you insist,' she said. 'But don't expect me to speak to Bertie.'

It was not until afterwards that Colin realised he'd once again been outmanoeuvred.

****

Determined to keep her independence as much as possible, Mary got a fly from the station and asked to be set down at the little hotel where Mr Craven had arranged for her to stay. She had some money of her own, so she would not need to ask Colin for anything. After she had settled into her room she wandered down to the riverside.

Colin was right, the beginning of June was a delightful time to visit Cambridge. The banks of the river were covered with fallen blossom, and weeping willows, adorned in their early summer plumage had a fresh yellow green hue. It was more beautiful than she'd expected. Though Colin had described it to her, she had not imagined the quiet majesty of the ancient buildings, the atmosphere of timeless dignity and tradition, nor the tranquillity of the river Cam flowing silently through it. She'd never been to Venice, but she was strongly reminded of some pictures she'd seen of it.

She sat for some time watching a pair of swans with a small brood of signets. Their squawks echoing across the water was the only sound which broke the silence, until suddenly the great towering buildings seemed to burst, issuing forth hoards of chattering, laughing students. In minutes the whole place was teeming with people, some on foot, some on bicycles, even on the river, boats appeared from nowhere.

She wandered back to the High Street. The town centre, where a moment before there had been only a few people going silently about their business, had now been transformed into a bustling market town. Students gathered in small groups, thronging into cafes, hailing each other. There were bicycles and all sorts of vehicles besides, clogging up the narrow cobbled streets. She walked towards the bridge, and she was about to ask someone which of these massive buildings was Trinity College when her attention was diverted so that she didn't see the silver Daimler. Colin stopped the car bang in the middle of the road, opened the door and jumped out.

'Mary!' he shouted. 'Why didn't you tell me? I wasn't expecting you until next week.'

At the sound of his voice her heart contracted painfully. Why did he still have this affect on her?

'Hey Colin,' came a slow drawl from within the car. 'You can't stop here. You're causing a traffic jam.'

Horns were blaring and people were shouting, but Colin took no notice.

'Bertie, this is my cousin Mary.' He took her by the arm. 'May, come and meet a chap who's been my closest friend all the time I've been here.'

She looked at the bemonocled gentleman sitting in the passenger seat of Colin's car and thought she already knew him. Colin had described him so well in his letters. She saw that he'd rolled back the car roof as it was a sunny day. Bertie jumped out and took her hand.

'My word,' he said, 'I quite understand now why Colin was prepared to wait five hours at Darlington station.'

'Very charming, thank you,' said Mary demurely. 'Colin, I think you should move the car from the middle of the road before there's an ugly scene. The man behind you looks fit to burst a blood vessel.'

'Get in then,' He opened the door for her with a sweeping bow. 'Madam, thy carriage awaits.'

'Where are we going?' she asked, after a moment.

'Where would you like to go? Bertie and I were just off for some light refreshment. I have a savage thirst.'

'Why do you go everywhere in the car. You hardly need to. Everyone else seems to walk here, or cycle, and the town's full of cafes. You should leave your car at home where you need it.'

'Bravo Mary!' cried Bertie. 'You're quite right, he's as idle as sin now that he has the motor. Never walks anywhere. Now, I have a bicycle....'

'And ride with me in the motor car most of the time....'

'If you want the truth,' Bertie put in, ignoring his friend's last quip. 'Your cousin is an appalling show off. That's why he keeps his motor car here.'

'Absolute rubbish!'

Mary laughed. She was enjoying this friendly bantering and Colin was in the best of humour.

'The real reason,' he explained, 'is that after three years of pedestrian activity.... You see, when I was an undergraduate I couldn't keep my motor here, so after three years on foot with all its limitations I grew tired of the pubs in town and had a yen for pastures new.'

'But I'd prefer the boring places in town,' said Mary. 'And I want to see your college.'

'Bravo again! Colin, I like your cousin,' said Bertie. 'She's got you taped.'

'You shall see everything,' said Colin. 'All in good time.'

Mary was happy again. Perhaps, after all, the future was not so bleak. Colin would get over this infatuation and things would be normal again. They had a cup of tea in one of the cafes, then she was given a grand tour of Cambridge, finishing up at Trinity College.

'Where are your things?' Colin asked suddenly, in the middle of all this.

'At the White Hart Hotel, where I'm staying.'

'Are you? That's Father's favourite place. Not that he comes here much.'

'Yes, he arranged it for me.' It was surprising how much satisfaction it gave her to be able to say that.

'Oh, did he? But I've made arrangements for you to stay with some people I know here, Professor Mainwaring and his wife. But I suppose, if you're settled there, you may as well stay. It would be more convenient in a way. The Mainwarings live a little way out of town. I must send our apologies to Mrs Mainwaring.'

Mary was relieved she was not staying out of town where she'd be at Colin's beck and call. That evening she was introduced to some of his other friends including Mr Prendergast, his old tutor when he was an undergraduate.

'Where have you been hiding this charming young lady, Colin? Why have we not met before?'

'Mary's been in France for three and a half years, sir.'

'More's the pity,' said Mr Prendergast, and Mary sensed he was not merely flattering her. But she must not keep looking for allies.

Bertie joined them later for dinner in one of the little restaurants in town. It was her idea to invite him for she wanted to make sure she and Colin were not alone. She had a dread of him confiding in her. She didn't want to know about the woman who'd stolen his heart.

It was Bertie who called for her next morning.

'Colin asked me to escort you to the river,' he said. 'To watch his race.'

'Yes, he told me he was in the races today. It's nice of you to come for me. I'd quite expected to find my own way.'

But there was something on Bertie's mind, and he was one of those people who liked to get things off his chest as soon as possible.

'As a matter of fact, there's something else he hasn't told you. I think it's a pretty poor show myself, and I told him so, but there it is. He wants me to escort you to....' his usually pale complexion took on a high colour. 'To the ball next Saturday.'

A stab of pain went through her and her heart did a somersault.

'You see,' Bertie went on, becoming more and more embarrassed. 'It's rather awkward because he asked Charlotte first, but she turned him down. Now, apparently she's changed her mind. We're all going together.'

Oh, no, not that! Mary's heart cried. She said nothing, but her step faltered and Bertie swiftly caught her arm. So that was her name, was it—Charlotte? And now she must see them together, watch Colin with another woman, and pretend she didn't care!

'I hope you don't mind coming with me,' Bertie ventured as Mary's step quickened to such an extent he'd almost to run to keep up with her. She was reminded of her manners.

'Mind? Of course not. I'd be delighted to have your company. Please forgive me for being so ungracious as not to say so at once.'

But it was not only for the ball she must endure this torture. They walked along the river bank, fighting their way through the crowds that had already gathered to watch the races. It took some time to find Colin, and when they did, Bertie pointed him out some distance away, he was standing laughing among a group of his friends, and hanging on his arm, rather possessively, was a beautiful sprite-like female with jet black hair.

Mary's heart contracted painfully.

'Is that her?' As if she needed to ask.

The tone in her voice made Bertie glance at her sharply.

'Yes, that's Charlotte the...' he broke off, clearly stifling an impulse to give her a less flattering name. 'Her name's Charlotte Denzel-Fitch.'

Chapter 11

The weather was fine the first Sunday and they went punting, the sky a clear blue, broken only by a few puffy white clouds. A gentle breeze rippling the water from time to time was a welcome break from the heat. Floating down the river, the only sound to be heard was the gentle swish of the water passing under the boat, and the cluck of a moorhen as it dived in among the reeds. It should have been idyllic. It would have been, Mary thought, had she been here with Colin three years ago when they were in love.

Most of the afternoon Colin and Bertie had been taking it in turns to steer the boat.

'Let me try, Colin,' Charlotte insisted. 'You did promise to teach me, remember.'

'Come on, then, Charlie, hop up here. Everyone else move down a bit to balance the boat, please.'

Charlotte scrambled up on the tailboard with him. Why did he always do her bidding? She had him twisted round her little finger, Mary thought bitterly. She looked away in disgust when he put the pole into Charlotte's hand and his own arms round her, to show her how to use it. It seemed as if they were deliberately taunting her.

She and Charlotte had been daggers drawn from the outset, each determined to discredit the other in Colin's eyes. Only Mary was a poor match for Charlotte who was an expert at being spiteful in the most subtle, covert way.

She couldn't look at Colin. There was a familiar dreamy expression on his face when he looked at Charlotte—the same look that a few years ago had been reserved only for herself. But it was impossible to pretend it was not happening. She should never have agreed to come. And there was another week before the ball.

She couldn't think of a credible reason for leaving. The last thing she wanted was that Colin should know he'd hurt her, and if she went home so soon he'd guess why. No feeble excuse, like she was unwell, or she was running out of money, would convince him. He knew her too well. And how would she explain to her uncle? She was trapped.

She was suddenly impatient with herself. Why had she let him get under her skin? If she could only forget that they'd ever been sweethearts and simply look upon him as a friend, she'd be able to reason with him without him thinking she was jealous. It was crystal clear to her that Charlotte was the most false creature she'd ever met. She was completely self-centred—Mary recognised that particular fault, having had it herself once, a long time ago, when she first came from India. But, she suspected, that was the least of it, for she sensed in Charlotte a cold, calculating heart, unable to love anyone but herself. Why was Colin so blind? It was as if he was under some enchantment.

Charlotte was not very competent, the boat was lurching precariously, and they were laughing a lot. It would not take much to tip them into the water, she thought mischievously. Charlotte's ethereal white lawn muslin dress with the blue bows on it would be ruined. It was very tempting. Colin had clean white trousers on, his striped blazer and his straw boater, with his team colours, his blues. He'd be livid. She caught Bertie's eye and he began to giggle. Had he guessed what was in her mind? Next thing they were both shaking with suppressed mirth, so that when it happened, Mary was not sure whether she'd done it, or Bertie had, or it had simply been an accident.

Charlotte screamed as she fell in, dragging Colin with her, then she came up coughing and spluttering. How sweet, revenge, Mary thought, watching her struggling, her skirt tangled round her legs, almost drowning. There was much scrambling and heaving to get them back in the boat, which almost overturned completely, casting them all into the murky water. Charlotte did indeed look like a drowned rat, and Mary wanted to burst out laughing again. She felt a spasm of guilt, though, when she saw that Colin's clothes were covered in green slime from the river. Would it ever come out?

Nobody was laughing now. Charlotte's teeth were chattering and Colin's sense of humour failed him completely. 'For God's sake let's get ashore. I must get Charlotte home before she dies of pneumonia.'

But it was a hot day. And anyway, Mary wished she would die of pneumonia. At that moment she caught Colin's eye, and the look he gave her made her feel about the size of a mouse. Did he suspect her? If so, heaven help her!

'Bravo Mary!' Bertie said, when Colin and Charlotte had gone. 'I've been longing to do something of the sort but haven't quite mustered the courage.'

'I didn't mean to do it. I was laughing so much, thinking how funny it'd be if it happened, and it did.'

'You willed it, in other words,' he laughed. 'And, by golly, it was funny.'

Mary felt cheered. He was amused, at least. 'I'm afraid Colin's furious!'

'Wouldn't you be? His best blazer, ruined.'

'And Charlotte's dress.'

'Who cares about that. The little wench got her just deserts. But I must confess, I do feel a little sorry for Colin, and not just because his clothes are ruined.'

'Does he intend to marry her?'

Bertie shrugged. 'I'm not in his confidence as far as Charlotte's concerned, but I hope not. I only hope he'll come to his senses in time.' He glanced at her astutely. 'How would you feel about it if he did? I hope you don't mind me mentioning it, but I know you almost married him yourself once. I remember waiting at Darlington for nearly five hours in a biting wind.'

'It all seems a long time ago,' she said, carefully evading his question. 'I gather you don't like Charlotte much, either.'

'You're right about that. But Colin will tell you that's because she doesn't like me, but if you ask me she'll make his life a misery. She's spoilt, vain, and utterly selfish. She can be a perfect bitch sometimes, forgive my language, she'll not stick a tooth in flirting with other men, even in front of him. I've seen her do it. In short, she's a jezebel.'

'Why does he tolerate it?'

'Don't ask me. I've tried, I keep trying, to make him see what she is, but he won't listen. He thinks everyone else here admires her, but in fact there's only one thing they admire about her. She's...forgive me for speaking plainly...a seductive nymph.'

'Oh dear!' Mary clenched her hands together until her knuckles were white. 'If he won't listen to you I doubt if he'll listen to me.'

'I was rather hoping he would, in fact, for I believe he still loves you, though he may not realise it at the moment. Are you still in love with him?'

'No!' The denial was a little too emphatic, and he looked at her quizzically.

'He needs someone like you, Mary,' he said, placing his hand reassuringly over hers as it lay on his arm. 'Don't give up hope. You're showing her up, I believe. That's why she doesn't like you. She's a little afraid of you.'

'I'm sorry, Charlie, I'll buy you a new dress,' said Colin as he drove her home wrapped in a blanket.

'She did it!' Charlotte spat vindictively, her teeth chattering. 'I saw her do it.'

'Who Mary?'

'Yes. Didn't you see her?'

Colin suspected as much himself, but he loyally defended his cousin. 'Nonsense, it was an accident. I know Mary can be a little frivolous at times, but I doubt if she'd countenance quite such an irresponsible prank.'

'A prank, indeed! She did it deliberately to humiliate me.'

'Oh, no! You're imagining it. I know Mary well, and she has no malice whatever in her nature.'

Charlotte's lip curled. 'You'd be surprised what a woman will do when she's jealous. Remember what Byron said, "Hell hath no fury like a woman scorned."

'That wasn't Byron. It was William Congreve.'

'I couldn't care less who wrote those words, and I don't want a lecture in English Literature. The fact remains that Mary is jealous.'

'Of you?' he laughed. 'Oh, no, my dear, there you're quite wrong. She's my cousin.'

'But she's been more to you than that. I've heard that you were about to elope with her once when your father found out and stopped it.'

'Who told you that?' Colin asked, dismayed. 'It was Bertie, wasn't it?'

'No, not Bertie,' she said, scornfully. 'He wouldn't tell me anything like that. I'm not saying who.'

'Dammit! You are an infuriating little witch sometimes.'

'Really, Colin, don't swear at me like that.'

'Anyway, Mary can't be jealous, not now. Why, that was years ago.'

There was something in the tone of his voice that made Charlotte glance up sharply. 'Do you care? She doesn't mean anything to you any more.... Or does she?'

'No. At least, not in that way. But I'm still fond of her, I wouldn't like to hurt her.'

'Well, you'd better make up your mind, Colin, dear,' she said with silky sarcasm. 'Because I have no intentions of playing second fiddle to her.'

By this time they had reached her house. He jumped down from the driving seat, came round to her side, and opened the door for her.

'Well, you've nothing to worry about, my love. You know I'm crazy about you.'

She pushed past him and flew up the front steps of her house. He followed her to the door, adding, 'And Mary is no more to me than a devoted sister.'

She turned to him before stepping inside. 'I'm not in the least bit worried, Colin. You're not indispensable, you know. I've plenty of other strings to my bow.'

'Shall I call for you later?'

'No, don't bother. I've seen enough of you for one day.'

The door shut in his face, leaving him standing on the doorstep.

'Damn you, Charlotte!' he shouted, kicking the door. 'Damn! Damn! Damn!'

He got back in his car and drove off at great speed, muttering, 'God preserve me from bloody women!'

After a long soak in a hot bath, a hair wash and a shave, Colin's humour had improved a little. He took his blazer and trousers to the laundry, and then went round to see Bertie.

'What are we doing tonight?' his friend asked.

'I don't care, so long as it doesn't involve any women. I'm through with the wretches.'

Bertie threw back his head and laughed. 'Had a row with Charlotte, have you?'

Colin didn't answer. He could usually counter Bertie's gibes with witticisms of his own but his humour, after Charlotte's handling of him, was in shreds.

'What about Mary?' asked Bertie.

'I'm not too enchanted with her, either, at the moment. I've a sneaking feeling she had something to do with our ducking this afternoon.'

Bertie chuckled. 'It was rather funny, Colin. You should have seen yourself.'

And Colin, because he had an irrepressible sense of humour, laughed in spite of himself.

'Charlotte's seething. Hardly surprising. The little minx nearly drowned us, and ruined my best blazer, to boot. The laundry weren't sure they'd be able to get all the stains out.'

'You didn't tell Charlotte it was Mary?'

'Of course I didn't. What do you take me for? As a matter of fact I defended her. I told Charlotte she was imagining it.'

'Ah! A very clear picture is emerging. I see now why Charlotte became a pussy cat and scratched you. It must be flattering, women fighting over you. You must tell me how it feels, one day.'

'D'you think they're both jealous?' Colin's mouth broadened into a grin.

'Don't get a swelled head, old man. I was being facetious.'

****

That Sunday in Thwaite village church the vicar gave a particularly bombastic sermon, all about the sins of the flesh, the evils of lust and fornication. Molly Pine would never forget it. Everyone knew who it was aimed at. That poor girl Lucy Styles—she who had born a child out of wedlock—standing there, all eyes upon her, alone because nobody would stand by her, not even her own father, as if she stood in the dock like one condemned. Her head was bent in shame, her cheeks sodden with tears. It was rumoured the father was young Waverley, though his family denied it, of course. Lucy had lost her position in the house as soon as they discovered her condition. It was no use expecting any help from the likes of them. The rich always closed ranks in those situations. Molly would make sure nothing like that ever happened to her. She knew exactly what she wanted, and she was going to get it.

****

Although it had given her some satisfaction at the time, Mary began to wonder if it had really been worth humiliating Charlotte, for now Colin scarcely spoke to her, and when he did he was coldly polite. She would rather have had a flaming row with him and cleared the air as they always used to before she went away. It was as if they were strangers. She saw very little of him during the days that followed. He made excuses, he had a lot of work to do, or he was involved in the races. If she did see him he was with Charlotte. He seemed to have plenty of time to chase her.

Bertie called for her every afternoon, introduced her to his friends and amused her by composing witty rhymes about Colin and Charlotte. But she spent a great deal of time alone, wandering round the town, sitting in cafes drinking coffee or tea.

All Bertie's attempts to bring about a reconciliation between her and Colin failed. On Saturday afternoon he arranged a punting party, but Colin excused himself, saying he'd a lot of work to catch up, owing to the recent races. Everyone in Cambridge seemed to be out on the water that day, there were punts milling around everywhere. There were five others in their boat, and Mary was squeezed between two girls. They were all in high spirits.

They passed a punt tied up under a willow tree, the branches of which partially hid it from sight. Mary's view was further obscured by Bertie who sat squarely in front of her, but she gathered from the barracking of the other men that the occupants were a courting couple.

'Trust you, Craven?' one of them shouted. 'to find a pretty girl and a punt all to yourself. Some people have all the luck!'

Everyone was laughing, all except Bertie, who shot her an anxious, apologetic look. Her heart was racing, almost suffocating her, and she felt sick. It was as she'd suspected. Colin was with Charlotte. He'd lied to her. She didn't want to see them. She looked deep into the swirling dark water, and wished it would swallow her up. She wanted to hide so Charlotte would not have the satisfaction of seeing her humiliation. But Colin had seen her....

'What's the matter with you, Colin?' Charlotte complained. 'You've been in a filthy mood ever since you saw Mary in that other boat.'

'If you don't understand, Charlie, you must be exceedingly insensitive, that's all I can say. I told her I was working. Oh, I knew I shouldn't have let you talk me into this.'

'Well, thanks. I thought you could do with some relaxation, you've been working so hard lately, I've hardly seen you. Anyway, who cares what Mary thinks?'

'I do. I don't want her to think I'm a liar.'

'You seem to be more concerned about your cousin's feelings than you are about mine. And frankly, Colin, I'm getting a little bored with it. If you're still in love with her, say so, and we'll call it a day.'

'Don't be so absurd. I don't have to be in love with her to care whether I offend her. But then, you don't care who you offend.'

'Take that back at once, or I'll never speak to you again.' Her high cheek bones were tinged with pink and her dark eyes glittered. She was magnificent when she was angry!

'Then you'll miss coming to the ball,' he teased.

'Don't think I'd care if I missed it,' she said, acidly. 'I'll never go to anything with you—ever again!'

'Oh, come now, Charlie. This is no way to end an idyllic affair.' His lips quivered in suppressed amusement. He was growing accustomed to her fits of pique and learning to handle them.

'Idyllic!' It was always his humour that got to her in the end. She managed to keep a straight face for about five seconds, then burst into laughter. 'Oh, Colin, you're incorrigible.'

Mary got back to her hotel that evening to find a bouquet of flowers and a note from Colin. "I'm sorry," it said, "I had truly intended to work this afternoon, but Charlie can be quite persuasive when she wants to be. Have dinner with me tonight?"

It was tempting to accept the olive branch, but her pride would not let her. She could not allow him to treat her the same way as Charlotte treated him. She sent a note back to his rooms saying she had made other arrangements for the evening.

There was no further opportunity to make friends, for the next afternoon, Sunday, an important event took place. There were no races that day, and Colin had told Bertie he was going up in a balloon. He was excited, for the owner was letting him take it up himself for the first time. Down by the river news of the ascent was buzzing through the crowd.

'They're taking off in a field about a mile from here, at about two o'clock,' one girl told Mary. 'Will you be coming to watch it? We're all going. Bertie you'll come, won't you?'

'It's Fulton-Jones' balloon,' Bertie told Mary. 'Colin goes up with him quite often, he's been giving him lessons. He should ask if he could take you. That's if you'd like it.'

Mary didn't say anything but it was the last thing she would have wanted. She was terrified of height. 'Have you done it yourself,' she asked Bertie.

'No, no! Not me! I'm afraid I'm a dreadful coward. And I'm quite certain that if the good Lord had intended us to fly he'd have given us wings. But Colin's a dare-devil. No fear at all, or none he'll admit to. He's intrigued with the motorised variety as well. I wouldn't be a bit surprised if he has a go at that if he gets half a chance.'

A crowd was gathering in the field where the balloon was supposed to take off. Mary hung on to Bertie. She had a sudden frightful notion that because she had not made up her quarrel with Colin something awful was going to happen, and she began to feel quite panicky about it.

'It's a bad omen,' she told Bertie.

'Fiddlesticks!,' he said, patting her hand. 'Nothing's going to happen, I assure you. He's been up lots of times before, and Fulton-Jones is a very experienced aviator.'

All the same, Mary dragged on his arm to get closer, close enough to shout some encouraging thing to Colin. She pushed her way through the crowd. She hadn't told Bertie but she'd seen a dreadful accident with a balloon once, in France. It was a young honeymoon couple. The thing had gone up in flames, and the poor young couple had perished, before the very eyes of all their friends.

She could see him now, he was getting into the basket. Another man, whom Mary guessed to be the owner, was standing talking to him, but he did not get in with him. With a sinking feeling she realised Colin was going up on his own. Fulton-Jones was giving him last minute instructions. Just at that moment another figure, a woman, lifted her skirts and ran up to the basket. Mary realised with a shock it was Charlotte. She was going to kiss him goodbye. No she was not, she was standing there arguing with him. Mary could not hear what she said, but she heard Colin's reply.

'No, Charlie. I'm not taking you this time. It's the first time on my own, and you'll be a liability.'

'I don't care!' she shouted, stamping her foot. 'If you're going to die, I want to be with you. If you won't take me, I'll never speak to you again. And I mean it this time, Colin.'

Mary couldn't believe her ears. She was blackmailing him into putting at risk her own life as well as his, jeopardising the safety of what was already a hazardous expedition. Reluctantly she had to admire her courage, though she hated her for doing it.

'Why, you little witch,' Colin laughed. He looked at the owner. 'What d'you think, Henry?'

Henry Fulton-Jones shrugged. 'It's up to you, old chap. I've got confidence in you as a pilot. It's a question of whether you think she'll do as she's told.'

'Right,' said Colin, opening the door of the basket for her. 'The first sign of insurrection from you, Madam, and you'll be out in lieu of a sandbag.'

Henry Fulton-Jones laughed and Charlotte stepped into the basket with Colin, such a look of triumph on her face. A gasp went through the crowd. 'He's taking her up with him!'

The guys holding it down were released, Colin threw out several sandbags, turned up the flame and the balloon took off. Mary felt sick. Bertie put a hand under her elbow for support. Still she hadn't said goodbye to Colin, he'd probably not even seen her, and she was with him. The sight of them there together was a vivid reminder of that honeymoon couple.

'Well, Charlie, here we are, flying together. What do you think?' He emptied another sandbag and they floated higher. 'Isn't this magic?' he said, putting his arm round her. 'Don't hold on so tight, darling. Relax.' he said, gently easing her hand away from the rail which she was clutching as if her life depended upon it, and kissing her neck below the ear.

'Pay attention, Colin,' she said nervously. 'There's a wood ahead of us.'

'You want to go up a little,' he laughed, nonchalantly emptying another sandbag, whereupon they rose ten feet. 'Well, that's alright. One thing about Cambridgeshire, there are not many hills to worry about. You should try it in Derbyshire, or the Yorkshire fells. What's the matter? You look pale, my darling.'

'How do we get down again? When we've disposed of all the sandbags?'

'It's easy. Just turn off the burners. Shall I demonstrate,' he turned them down a little and the balloon fell ten feet.

'That's enough, Colin!'

'Why, Charlotte, my love, you said just now you wanted to die with me. Have you lost your nerve already?'

She looked at him, his lips were quivering, his eyes were dancing and he was obviously enjoying every minute of her predicament. He was completely confident himself, he knew what he was doing, and he loved flying. She had not imagined how terrifying it would be. She'd watched people go up in balloons and thought it would be an exciting thing to do. And she'd particularly wanted to go with him today because she knew Mary would be watching. It had almost been worth it, to see the look on her face when she stepped into the basket with Colin.

And she had another motive for coming with him today.

'Don't you love it,' he said, exultantly. 'Don't you think it's the most amazing, magnificent sensation you've ever experienced? Floating up here above the trees, in the silence. Listen to the silence, up here with the birds. Look, there's one now, keeping pace with us. Is it a hawk or a kestrel? I thought it was so brave of you to come with me. I want you to enjoy it,' he added, taking her face between his hands and kissing her on the mouth.

His enthusiasm, his sheer pleasure, began to infect her.

'I am enjoying it, Colin,' she said, giving him one of her rare smiles. When Charlotte smiled at him, he felt the earth move. 'I'm enjoying being up here with you.'

He was exhilarated. To Colin, flying was the ultimate pleasure— it beat skiing, even making love. It gave him a wonderful feeling of freedom, of omniscience, watching the land slip by beneath him, the small houses and even tinier people. And today, he was in control. The world was his, and beside him, this beautiful woman, who loved him, who'd said she'd die with him.

'Charlie,' he exclaimed, bursting with happiness. 'If you're happy to die with me....'

'I didn't say I was happy about it, Colin. Who'd be happy to die.'

'Very well then, prepared.... If you're prepared to die with me, why not live with me. Why not become my wife?' He looked at her earnestly now. 'Charlie?'

She smiled, enigmatically. That was her other motive for doing this flight with him.

Chapter 12

'Charlotte didn't want me to tell you, not until it's official. But I said I must tell you and Father before anyone else. Well, aren't you glad for me, May?'

Mary could scarcely speak. She was thankful she was sitting down, or she'd probably have fallen down.

'I can't believe it! Why didn't you tell me?'

'I'm telling you now,' he laughed. 'Or did you expect me to ask your permission? Would you ask mine if you wanted to marry a fellow?'

Would she have asked, or even told him about it, if Gilles had asked her to marry him?

'You don't like her, do you? That's the problem. I sensed it from the outset, though I'd hoped you two might be friends. I've been wanting to talk to you, but....'

'If I thought,' she began cautiously, anxious not to give away her feelings, 'she was the right girl for you. Or that she even cared for you....'

'Cared for me? Of course she does. She loves me. She was even prepared to die with me. But of course you didn't hear her say that.'

'Oh, yes, I heard it. It was clever of her. She is clever, Colin, that's the trouble.'

'I know. You've been talking to Bertie. He's poisoned your mind against her.'

'Nonsense! I'm quite capable of forming my own opinions. It's easier for people who are not involved to see things more clearly, and I can see plainly she doesn't love you.'

'What makes you think so?'

'Call it intuition, call it what you like, but I can tell by the way she treats you, the way she speaks to you. If you ask me it's your money she's after. You're a good catch for any girl....'

'I seem to have heard all this before.' His voice was chilling. 'The words were almost identical. Only then it was Constance Livingstone who was after my money.'

Mary closed her eyes. She might have known he'd say something like that the minute she tried to reason with him.

Then his face softened. 'I don't want to hurt you, May, but sooner or later I'm bound to marry, and ....'

'You think I'm jealous!'

A smile twisted his face. 'Well, aren't you? Not even a tiny little bit?'

'You're insufferable.'

'I know,' he agreed. 'It was a beastly thing to say. But you said some pretty rotten things about Charlotte. And we've always been frank with each other, haven't we? You're the one person in the world I know I can speak my mind to.'

'Can't you speak your mind to Charlotte? If you're going to be married, you should be able to open your heart to her?'

'You're being absurd.'

'Am I? Isn't it true to say you can't love someone until you really know them?'

She was not to know his father had made a similar observation. He looked at her in stunned silence.

'I'm not jealous, Colin. I don't particularly care for her, but if I could believe she really loves you, and that she'd make you happy, I'd make the best of it.'

'Would you? Well, then, why don't you give her a chance? Look May, if you thought things were going to be the same as they were between you and me....'

'Of course I didn't,' she said, defiantly. 'D'you think I've been pining after you for the last three years? Let me disabuse you on that point, at least. As a matter of fact I was very much in love with a Frenchman who let me down badly.' She had not intended to tell him about Gilles, but she could not allow him to think he'd hurt her. 'That is precisely why I'm able to recognise that Charlotte is using you. If you marry her you'll be hurt. I can see it coming. But disbelieve me if you like.'

He was silent, and when she looked up she found he was staring at her, a strange look on his face she could not quite define.

'I'm sorry you've been hurt, May,' he said, after a while, and his voice was gentle. 'I wish you'd told me before about your Frenchman. But you're wrong about Charlie. I happen to know, you see, that she does love me. But don't let's quarrel over it,' he said, holding out his hand to her.

'As you wish,' Mary shrugged. 'I don't care a fig what you do with your life, as long as you don't come crying to me when it all goes horribly wrong, which it will. You never listen, so I don't know why I bother giving you advice.'

'Will you never leave off trying to mother me, May?' he laughed. He looked at his watch. 'Oh, lord, I must be off. I didn't notice the time. I've got a lecture in five minutes.' He picked up his gown and mortarboard and went to the door where he turned, remembering something else. 'I almost forgot.... We're invited to drinks before the ball, with Mr Prendergast, in his rooms. Bertie will call for you at 7.30.'

Mary left the next day. She simply couldn't face going to a ball with Charlotte and Colin. Why on earth had he bothered to ask her? She'd seen precious little of him the whole time she'd been there. Nor could she bring herself to seek him out to tell him—for one thing she couldn't face the inevitable interrogation. So she wrote him a letter excusing herself.

'Please forgive my untimely flight. The evening promises little for me. Bertie doesn't dance, he tells me, and you.... Well, I'm afraid the role of gooseberry to you and Charlotte would not suit me at all. And don't imagine I made this decision as a result of what you told me yesterday. The truth is I've been looking for an excuse to cry off.

I know you've been preoccupied, and not just with Charlotte, but don't worry, Bertie has looked after me very well. He is a dear. Say good-bye and thank him for me. Cambridge is magnificent, far more than I'd imagined, and May Week has been fun....'

She was relieved to get home to Misselthwaite, though she had to face endless questions from her uncle, who wanted to know how she'd got on. How was Colin? What did she think of Cambridge? Did she enjoy the ball.

'I didn't stay for it?'

'What? I thought you were home earlier than I'd expected. But why did you not stay for it? I thought that was the principal reason for going. You're not ill, are you?'

'No, Uncle, I'm not ill.'

'You do look a bit pale.'

'That's because I didn't sleep very well last night. I tossed and turned a great deal.'

'But why did you come back? Why?'

She was silent for so long he asked her another question.

'I take it you were not very impressed with Cambridge?'

'Oh, yes, I thought it was wonderful. I'm quite envious of Colin.'

Her guardian sat in a chair opposite her, his elbows on the arms, and the tips of his fingers pressed together. The posture was typical of him.

'Tell me,' he asked. 'Did you meet a girl by the name of Charlotte?'

'Yes.' Her pulse quickened.

'Did you form an opinion?'

What should she do? Should she steel a march on Colin by breaking the news of his engagement before he did?

'He's asked her to marry him.'

It was as if he became a statue, his hands stopped in mid air, so still did he sit. She too. They were like a tableau, staring at each other.

'Oh!' he said, coming to again. 'Oh, lord! Is that why you left?'

'I don't want to talk about it,' she said, getting up from her chair and going towards the door. 'I don't suppose I should have told you. Colin wanted to tell you himself, but I think it's only fair to warn you. It's not official yet. He's still to ask her parents' permission.' She left the room.

Mr Craven buried his head in his hands and groaned. 'Oh, Colin, Colin. What in the world have you done?'

It was of cold comfort that Mr Craven clearly thought little of Charlotte, for what could he do about it? It was ironical that, after all these years, he regarded her as an ally. It was no good wishing she could put the clock back. She must learn to live with the eroding pain of jealousy.

She went to find Dickon. He'd cheer her up, he always did. But when she found him he was not alone. The new kitchen maid, the one Mrs Loomis had helping her temporarily, was with him. What was her name? Polly or Molly? As soon as she saw her, the girl blushed to the roots of her hair.

'If you've finished your duties,' said Mary, icily, 'You'd better change and go home.'

'Yes, 'm,' The maid did a hasty little bob and fled.

She looked at Dickon, and felt the stirrings of suspicion. Could he be interested in this new addition to the household?—a pretty creature but hardly Dickon's type. Yet it was clear there was something between them, for the atmosphere was charged. She was surprised at her own reaction. If he was engaged in a flirtation with one of the maids was it any business of hers?

She put the incident out of her mind but for some inexplicable reason she felt inhibited in Dickon's company after that. She found she could no longer confide in him, nor talk to him about Colin and Charlotte. She put a wall round herself and withdrew, keeping her grief inside.

Colin was put out when he got Mary's note. Why had she said nothing about going home yesterday? Could she not have waited to say goodbye? Why was she behaving so childishly? He was disappointed. He'd expected support from her, for he was afraid his news would not go down very well with his father. The fact that he'd seen so little of her weighed heavily on his conscience, and he regretted cutting short their conversation that morning after breaking the news to her of his engagement. Had he been a little insensitive? Surely she didn't think, just because he was in love with Charlotte, he was no longer fond of her? It was, after all, possible to love more than one person.

And why had it given him such a shock to discover she'd been in love with another man? He'd felt as if he'd been struck.

Bertie's comments, when told she'd gone home, did not help.

'You know,' he said. 'when I first met Mary I thought she might make you see sense. I know you scorn my opinion, but she's worth ten of Charlotte, and if you can't see it, you're an even bigger fool than I thought you were. Pity you didn't take her up in that balloon.'

What could he do to make amends now that she'd gone? He always found talking easier than writing letters. He could gauge her mood by her voice. It was at times like this he wished there was a telephone at home, but his father had steadfastly refused to have one installed. Colin secretly believed it was because he was afraid of the new-fangled machines. He didn't like cars either. Thank God he hadn't had such scruples or old fashioned ideas when it came to improving the plumbing in the house.

So there was no way of communicating with Mary except by post.

And what could he say in a letter? It was wonderful seeing you.... But he had not seen much of her as she'd pointed out. It was no good apologising. I'm sorry I neglected you.... It sounded so insincere. That's why he hated letter writing. Letters were too easily misconstrued. Yet he'd never had any difficulty writing to Mary before. In the past it had never mattered what he'd said, she'd have understood. So what was different now?

As for Charlotte.... Now that Mary had gone, in spite of their engagement, she'd begun to play him up again, teasing, flirting with other fellows. The evening they'd become engaged, she'd been loving, sweet and adorable. He'd been walking on air. But then her capriciousness was part of her charm. She drove him mad! She was exciting, amusing and tantalising all at once.

Last night he'd had a vivid dream. He had them from time to time, though not as often now as when he was a boy. His mother had come to him in a scolding mood. 'You were ever a hothead, Colin,' she'd said. 'And now you've done the most insane thing you ever did in your life. The consequences will be hideous. Be warned!'

She was a powerful ghost whenever she'd tried to influence him. In the days, before Mary came, she frequently haunted him. She'd come out of her portrait, stand by his bed and tell him to get up and walk. Once she had picked him up, carried him to the window and thrown him out of it. He'd expected to be quite dashed to pieces on the paving stones of the terrace below, but to his astonishment he'd found himself floating gently to the ground only to land softly back in his bed.

Mary decided that the only way to get Colin out of her system was to make a clean break from the past, so she set about sorting out her drawers, throwing away the memorabilia she'd collected through the years. This proved a harder task than she'd anticipated. She came across Colin's letters to her when she was in France. It was unlike her to be sentimental but she had kept them all, wrapped in a pink ribbon. She picked one at random and read it.

'It's so long since I heard from you.... I still think of you all the time, and miss you dreadfully. If only we could see each other. Could you not be spared for just one week? Father's still trying to find me a wife. Last time I was home he gave a huge reception for me. I was bombarded with females of every shape and size. Not one appealed! I guess I still love you...Why don't you write. If I don't hear from you soon, I think I'll go mad....'

She had not answered that letter. It was dated November 1909. At that time she'd been too taken up with her passion for Gilles to write to Colin, or even to give him a thought. Could she blame him now for being blinded by his passion for Charlotte?

After a while a sort of numb acceptance dulled her senses. She must find something to do, something she could become completely absorbed in. It was no good sitting here surrounded by living memories, with an uncle who was becoming more cantankerous with each day that passed. To stay here and stagnate would be almost worse than being in Cambridge with Colin and Charlotte. She went to see Susan Sowerby.

Dickon's mother did things around the village. She was the midwife, the helping hand, the one who comforted the bereaved and visited the sick. She'd try to right an injustice if she could, or attempt to heal a rift that had torn a family apart. Mary had always admired her. She wouldn't mind taking on some of her duties. No doubt there'd be some among the villagers who'd think she was interfering. She was a young girl like her, and from the big house, and they were proud. Some might think she was being patronising. But attitudes were changing. There'd come a day, quite soon she suspected, when class barriers would be broken down, and all men would fight for a common cause. Thoughts like this slipped into her mind from time to time. But when she found Mrs Sowerby in tears she realised that day was a long way off.

'Tis poor wee Lucy Styles,' she sighed. 'She's done away wi' hersel'. I did what I could, Miss Mary. I pleaded wi' her pa, and th' parson too.'

Mary had been away when the scandal had broken, but she knew about it. It was discussed all over the village—Lucy Styles, the girl who'd had a baby—young Waverley's by-blow, it was rumoured, though the squire's family distanced themselves from it. The poor girl had lost her job and would have been cast out onto the street had not Mrs Sowerby intervened, for her father had declared she was unfit to be his daughter. She'd been branded a bad girl and nobody but Mrs Sowerby and one or two others would speak to her. Mary had heard, too, about that dreadful humiliating sermon. No wonder the girl was suicidal.

'After all that, bairn only lived a few hours. Died of starvation poor thing, if you ask me. An' I think it were th' last straw, him saying he'd not have it buried in his churchyard, because it were born out o' wedlock....'

'The sanctimonious hypocrite,' muttered Mary bitterly.

'He's supposed to be a man of God!'

'Man of God, indeed!' Mary retorted, her face pink with anger. 'He's not fit to call himself a vicar. Can you see old Reverend Williams behaving like that?'

Susan Sowerby shook her head sadly.

'I miss him,' said Mary. 'He really was a man of God, though I think he'd prefer to be thought of as a man of the people. D'you remember the children's parties he used to give in his house every Christmas? All the children in the village were invited, whoever they were. Your tribe all went, and so did we. And carol singing. We got rum punch and mince pies at his house afterwards.'

'Aye, love, them were th' good times.' She patted Mary's knee. By coincidence the sofa they were sitting on had once belonged to Reverend Williams, who'd given it to Mrs Sowerby because he said he had no use for it and she could do with a decent sofa.

'Meanwhile David Waverley gets off scot-free. And you can bet he insisted it was her duty to please him.'

'Nobbut knows for sure 'twas his bairn, Miss Mary. 'Tis only rumours.'

'You know what they say, "No smoke without fire"? But he's no more to blame than his father, or her father, come to that.'

'He's th' worst! An unnatural father, that Bernard Styles.'

'I think the vicar's the worst. Have you been to see them, the Styles, I mean?'

Susan Sowerby shook her head. 'I couldn't, Miss Mary. I couldn't show sympathy, not when I still feel so unforgiving.' Her face crumpled and she began to weep again.

'But what about Mrs Styles?' Mary pointed out. 'She needs support even if her husband doesn't deserve it. I'll go and see her, if you like.'

She went for Mrs Styles' sake. Bernard Styles was a stiff necked man who'd probably resent it, but she couldn't care less about him. However, she changed her attitude when she saw him. As soon as she entered the house, her anger was swallowed up in pity. Mrs Styles looked pale, with dark rings under eyes that were swollen from weeping. But it was the state of Mr Styles that affected her most. He sat holding his head in his hands, rocking backwards and forwards, crying like a child.

'E's been like that for three days now, ever since....' sobbed Mrs Styles. 'Says it's all 'is fault. She'd be here now if he hadn't....' she gulped, fighting back tears.... 'if he'd been a good, loving father. Says he'll never forgive hissel''

Mary went to him and put her hand on his shoulder. He didn't appear to mind her, if he even noticed it was her. She squeezed his shoulder a little and the gentle pressure seemed to have an effect, for he stopped rocking so much. She took his head in her arms and just held him for a while. Nothing was said, not a word spoken, but love and kindness was given and received.

The incident made a lasting impression on Mary. She never forgot it, or the terrible lessen the poor man had learned. And it certainly put her own troubles into perspective.

She was not so forgiving of the vicar though when, a week or so later, her uncle returned from church on Sunday with a message.

'He wants to know why you don't attend church. You've only been once since you came back from France.'

'Does he now? Well, you can tell him I'm following Our Lord's advice. He said: "Be not as the Scribes and Pharisees who get their reward from being thought holy."'

Mr Craven looked shocked. 'My dear child!' he exclaimed. 'What in the world's brought on this spirit of rebellion?'

'I don't like hypocrisy, Uncle, specially in someone who's supposed to be our spiritual leader. To see him being so obsequious towards you and Ted Waverley makes me feel sick.'

'Does this have anything to do with that poor girl Lucy Styles? I agree he was a little hard on her, but....'

'Hard on her! He was abominable. He should have been supporting her as the old vicar would have done. There's not enough tolerance in this world, not enough fellow feeling,' she declared. 'Everyone is so critical of everyone else but themselves.'

'But why vent all your wrath against the unfortunate vicar. If you want someone to blame for Lucy's death, try that father of hers.'

Mary shook her head. 'Oh, no! He's the least of the protagonists. And the poor man's suffered terribly for what he did. No. The leaders of society are to blame. It's a matter of attitudes, Uncle, prejudices, perpetrated by people like your precious parson. If they were not so condemning, if there had not been that stigma, Styles would not have acted like that.'

Mr Craven stared at her in astonishment as she went on, pacing the floor. 'It's the rich, particularly the men, who think they can do as they please so long as they keep up an appearance of respectability. They ignore all the Commandments except the eleventh, "Thou shalt not be found out."' Seeing the look on his face, she added, 'I don't mean you, Uncle.'

'You've got very modern ideas, my dear, and you're beginning to sound like those wretched suffragettes in London. But whatever you do please don't stir up trouble around here. I've lived peacefully with my neighbours all my life and I've no wish to fall out with them now because of the wild, turbulent nature of my niece.'

'Thank you, Uncle Archie. You've helped me make an important decision.'

Mr Craven cocked an enquiring eyebrow in her direction.

'Yes,' said Mary. 'I know now what I must do with my life. I shall go to London, and join the suffragettes.'

Mr Craven groaned, covering his eyes with his hands.

Dickon tried to persuade her to change her mind. He must have known things had not gone well for her in Cambridge, though she had not spoken of it, and he could not know about Colin's engagement for it was not yet official. Yet he was not altogether surprised to here of her plans to leave Misselthwaite.

'Don't go, Miss Mary. There's enough of them suffrigits in Lon'on already. Tha've been doing a grand job here. What'll us poor folks do wi'out thee?'

'It's nice of you to say so, but it's not me they need. Your mother does more for them than I do. And anyway, I can't stay here, not now....'

'Are tha running away?'

Was it running away? Should she stay here and help the people she loved instead of running off to help people in London who meant nothing to her? Then she remembered how it hurt to see Colin and Charlotte together in Cambridge. Cambridge was one thing, but she thought of the secret garden, of riding on the moor, of Ravensfell—all sacred to her. Could she endure to watch him enjoying these things with Charlotte?

'I must go, Dickon. I'm going to London so as to make something of my life. I couldn't stay here as a hanger on. Surely you can understand that.'

He laid both hands on her shoulders, forcing her to look at him. 'It's not like thee t' give up. You're the fighting kind, you are. Tha'rt made of far finer stuff than that there witch woman. Don't let her win, Miss Mary.'

Her eyes filled with tears. 'It's too late. She's won already. He's going to marry her.'

She had not heard from Constance since she was in France. She wondered what had become of her friend. The women were attracting much publicity nowadays. Holloway was full of them. They went on hunger strike and were being force fed. As far as she knew none had yet died in gaol, but it must be a harrowing experience. Yet if God required it of her....

She was clearly not destined for marriage, though she would have liked to have had children. But one could not have them without being married.

Then something else happened which hastened her decision to leave.

It was Martha who told her that Dickon was to be married to Molly Pine.

Shock knocked the wind out of her lungs. Dickon! *Et tu Brute?*

'He never told me... I'd no idea he was in love...'

She thought of that pert little miss she'd seen him flirting with the other day, and she was conscious of a pain in her chest. It was something she could not identify.

'I don't know about that, Miss Mary. He dun't say much about his feelings. A dark horse is our Dickon.'

'But isn't it rather sudden?'

'Sudden! Hardly. She's been after our Dickon for three years, since she were fourteen and still at school.' Martha's voice was scornful.

'She probably thinks she's in love with him,' Mary muttered, remembering how she herself had chased Dickon when she was fourteen.

'Love!' Martha scoffed. 'I doubt if that scheming little whatnot has ever been in love wi' anyone but herself.' She bent her head confidentially towards Mary and dropped her voice. 'You may as well know, Miss Mary, since everyone else will soon enough. She's expecting.... Says it's his. And our Dickon, being a decent lad, says he'll wed her.'

A baby! The idea that Dickon may have got someone pregnant was inconceivable. She couldn't imagine him making love to a woman he wasn't married to. But why should she expect him to be perfect? He was, after all, human. And if, as seemed likely, this girl had thrown herself at him....

Oh, Dickon, Dickon! What have you done?

She tried to rationalise her emotions. Why did this news make her so miserable? If Dickon had found love at last she should be happy for him. She'd always believed he loved her, and he was not capricious like Colin. Of the three of them he was the least fickle with his affections. But she had no right to demand his fidelity, when she'd turned away from him herself. She'd made her choice. That Colin had let her down should not concern Dickon. She'd be the worst kind of dog-in-a-manger if she resented his happiness. But would he be happy with this girl, or had he been trapped?

'I'll speak to him,' she told Martha.

'Eh, Miss Mary, don't say owt about bairn. He'll be that vexed wi' me for tellin' thee.'

But it was not so easy to avoid mentioning it. She felt uneasy about the whole thing. What if Dickon, in his typical way, was being noble? And what if the child was not his? There was one question she simply must ask him, even if it sounded silly.

His mouth twisted in a half smile. "Course, I love her, Miss Mary. Else why'd I be getting wed?'

'It's just that it's a bit of a surprise,' she shrugged. 'I had no idea....'

He gave an embarrassed laugh. 'Have I to tell thee everything as goes on in my life?'

Had they become such strangers, she thought sadly, that he could not tell her how he really felt, and she could not voice her fears for him? She tried to meet his eyes but he kept them fixed upon some aspect of the floor.

'You're not marrying her because you feel responsible for...?' It had slipped out before she realised what she was saying.

He looked up suddenly, frowning. 'Who've tha been talking to? What's been said?'

It was too late for caution. She took a deep breath and launched herself.

'I'm not being nosy, Dickon, but I wouldn't like to see you ruin your life because of a false sense of obligation...' She broke off as another ugly thought slid into her mind. What if Molly Pine was not pregnant at all? It was not unheard of for a certain kind of woman to play that trick, and Martha had said the girl was determined to catch him. She remembered Mrs Loomis complaining about her slovenly ways, saying she'd only taken her on for her mother's sake. 'Poor as church mice they are,' she'd said. Maybe she thought she'd escape from poverty by marrying Dickon.

'Are you certain she's pregnant?' she asked without thinking. 'If you want a doctor to look at her, I'll pay for it. I could get...'

She bit her lip, but it was too late. This time she really had gone too far. His face hardened and, for the first time in her life, she saw anger in his blue eyes. He took her by the shoulders and shook her, not hard, but firmly.

'Don't you meddle, Miss Mary. This is my business, an' I'll handle it mesel'. I don't want you bringing in doctors an' that, or telling me what to do.'

She felt the blood rush to her face. 'I'm so sorry, Dickon. I didn't mean…'

His face softened. He could not be angry with her for long. 'Aye, I know tha meant no harm. But I can look after mesel' tha ken, I don't need thee to defend me.'

Truth be told, her outburst troubled him more than she would ever know, not so much because he resented her interference. He still loved her, in a pure, unselfish sort of way, and he didn't want her thinking badly of him, but he'd realised three years ago that she could never be his, and then Molly had come into his life. His feelings for Molly, he suspected, had more to do with lust than love. That she was a flirt, he knew well enough, but he refused to believe she was as bad as some people, including his own sister, made out. There'd been other men in her life, he knew, but he'd been the first. In the beginning she'd chased the life out of him, she'd followed him everywhere, dallying on the way home from school, waiting for him to finish work and take her home on the bar of his bike. She was hard to resist. Then she'd gone off with Sam Potter, and for a while he'd been consumed with jealousy. A couple of weeks ago he'd found her in tears and she'd told him she was pregnant, and the child she was carrying would need a father. He'd never forget Lucy Styles, the sight of whose pale face and frail body would haunt him for the rest of his life. He could not let that happen to Molly.

And Mary would soon be leaving. It was no use him trying to stop her, and then she'd no longer be part of his life. He must forget her.

Indeed Mary's departure came sooner than either of them expected. A week or so later Mr Craven announced that Colin would be coming home in ten days time, bringing Charlotte with him, and Mary was spurred into immediate action. She must leave for London before the end of the week.

'Do you think Lady Grantham would have me to stay, until I can find Constance?'

Mr Craven was horrified. 'You're not serious about this suffragette business are you?'

'Of course I am. I'm going to join Constance and the Pethick Lawrences in their work with the poor. So,' she added with a mischievous twinkle. 'You can tell your precious vicar, when he asks why I'm not in church, that I'm in London, doing the Lord's work.'

Chapter 13

'My dear Mr Craven, or should I say Colin, since you are soon to be my son-in-law?' said Mrs Denzel-Fitch, shaking his hand and fixing him with her hypnotic eyes. 'I'm delighted to welcome you as part of our family.'

She may as well have said, *Will you come into my parlour said the spider to the fly.* For as he looked into her eyes, they were shaped like Charlotte's, but her features were coarser, he had an uncomfortable feeling about his future mother-in-law.

'Have you a date in mind for the wedding?' she asked. 'May I suggest Easter? Such a lovely time of year to be married, don't you think?'

Why did she remind him of Shylock? He could almost see her rubbing her hands together.

'I shall have to speak to my father first,' he said hastily. 'If it suits you, I should like to have Charlie...Charlotte visit Misselthwaite again before we make an official announcement.'

Mrs Denzel-Fitch's face fell, but she quickly recovered her composure. 'Why, certainly, my dear, as you wish.'

****

Lady Grantham made Mary welcome in London.

'Leonie de Bergerac tells me you were a great support to her when her husband died,' she said. 'I'm so glad you got on so well with them.'

'I was very fond of the whole family, and I felt an acute loss myself when he died.'

'Shall you go and see them again?'

It was a temptation to forget everything and go back to France, but Mary had set her hand to the plough.

'Perhaps I will sometime. But for now there is something else I must do. There are so many social injustices....'

'You would not be the first young thing who wanted to change the world, but you can't do it single handed. And I'm afraid the WSPU is a hopeless cause. Those Pankhursts have made so much trouble, but I suppose, if you are to get it out of your system you may as well get on with it. I'm afraid I have not kept up with the

Livingstones. The last I heard of Constance she was living somewhere in the East End with the Pethick Lawrences. I rather think her mother has washed her hands of her.'

'I heard that Emmeline Pethick and Frederick Lawrence had married. I'm afraid poor Connie was in love with him.'

'She does seem rather unlucky in love, doesn't she?'

Mary looked at her sharply. 'So you knew how she felt about Colin?'

'My dear I knew far more than you realised. By the way, it may interest you to know that William Leyton was married in June. I think he was quite badly smitten with you, you know.'

'I hope I didn't hurt him. I didn't mean to!'

'I'm sure you didn't. But that's life, isn't it? We can't always have the one we want.' It was an unfortunate remark, and, seeing the look on Mary's face she changed the subject quickly. 'I suppose if you must get involved with the suffragettes you couldn't do better than join the Pethick Lawrence's. They, at least, are doing something worthwhile. But I warn you, Mary, you've never seen a real slum. It might come as a nasty shock to you.'

****

Charlotte was relieved to find Mary absent when she and Colin arrived at Misselthwaite. Confident though she was of her hold over Colin, she was forced to admit she found Mary a little intimidating. It was the way she had of looking at her as if she could see her naked soul. It was unnerving, as was her obvious influence over Colin. She would not tolerate her living with them once they were married, but of course she dare not say so now. It irritated her that Colin was so concerned about her safety in London. If Mary wanted to be a suffragette, let her be.

She didn't understand why Colin liked being at Misselthwaite so much. He was not interested in going to Scarborough or York. And he seemed to prefer horse riding to driving his car. She hated horse riding. She was frightened of the horses, particularly that dreadful stallion of Colin's. She wouldn't even ride Mary's mare, Snowdrop. The only one she felt at all comfortable on was the old horse, Pendragon, but given half a chance Prince would bully him, so she was obliged to keep her distance from Colin. It all seemed such a dreadful waste of time.

However Colin didn't force her to go riding with him. As soon as he realised she didn't like it he simply went off on his own leaving her alone with Mr Craven who, for the most part, shut himself away in his study and ignored her.

She endured the boredom for as long as she could, aware that she should make some effort. Then after three weeks she announced she had to get home because 'poor Mama' was ill and couldn't cope without her. Thus, attributing to herself the role of dutiful daughter, she left.

'I couldn't stay a moment longer in that ghastly old house with all those impertinent servants,' she told her mother. 'There's a dreadful housemaid called Martha, who is so disrespectful. She won't do anything I tell her without asking Colin first. She'll have to go.'

'Steady on! You can't start dismissing the servants.'

'Why not? When I'm mistress of the house I can do what I like.'

'Well, wait and see. I expect Martha will dance to a different tune once you and Colin are married and she knows you are her mistress.'

'And as for that Dickon in the stables,' Charlotte continued, as if she had not been listening. 'He's worse than Martha. He even speaks to Colin in a familiar way, and Colin never redresses him for it. Indeed he seems to like it. He says they've been friends for most his life. But you can't be friends with a servant. Colin has no idea how to treat the working class. He took me once to a shack on the estate where an old gardener lived, and, would you believe it, he actually carried buckets of coal for him. I ask you, the future master of Misselthwaite humping coal for an old servant!'

Mrs Denzel-Fitch became seriously alarmed. 'For heaven's sake, Charlotte! I hope you have not been behaving badly. Is that the real reason why you've come home early?'

'Of course not, Mama. I've been as good as gold.'

****

Colin was having serious doubts about marrying Charlotte. The interview with Mrs Denzel-Fitch had made him feel most uncomfortable, though he suspected that the seeds of doubt had been sewn even before that. And now that he was back in Misselthwaite, surrounded by those people and things that mattered most to him it seemed clear that Charlotte simply didn't fit in. She belonged to his life in Cambridge, not his home....

He found himself thinking of Mary, remembering, with a wave of nostalgia, that summer when they had been so much in love. He always thought of her more when he was at home. She was so much a part of it. Could he still be a little in love with her? Her presence did not excite him, nor cause his pulse to race, as did Charlotte's, her smile did not produce a whirlwind, or make him feel as if he was walking on air, but...but....

He could not imagine life without her. Already it felt a little empty with her absence. It had given him a warm feeling of security to know she was back in the country. She was a tower of strength, always, and a good friend. Was it possible she still loved him? Could they recapture the magic? He shook his head. First love, like the first flowers of spring, so sweet, so innocent, yet over so soon. It could not be the same again. Why then did he regret it?

His thoughts returned to Charlotte. Was he really in love with her? Would she make him a good wife? She inspired in him an all consuming passion. But was that love? She drove him crazy. She was exciting, tantalising, her wit, her charm, her very presence ignited a fire inside him. In a flash of perception he saw that such a fire might destroy him. But could he give her up?

She'd attempted to put a wedge between himself and Mary—he'd never forgive her for that. Indeed she may even have succeeded, for Mary had deserted him. Surely she'd come back when she'd had enough of the slums of London, or would she?

With a wave of remorse he realised she might not. That he'd offended her too deeply. He must find her and bring her back whether Charlotte liked it or not.

He had to drive eight miles to the nearest town to find a National Telephone Co. kiosk where he telephoned his godmother.

'Where in heaven's name are you, Colin?' Lady Grantham bellowed down the line, trying to ram the receiver further into her ear. 'It sounds as if you're speaking from Timbuktu. I can't hear a word you're saying.'

'There's no need to shout, Aunt Alice, I can hear you quite well,' said Colin, holding the receiver away from his ear. 'Is Mary still with you?'

'I'm afraid not.'

'Oh, dash it! D'you know where she is?'

'Speak up!'

'Do you know where she is?'

'I've no idea, but I believe she's living with Constance somewhere in the East End. She promised to write and let me know her address, but I've had no word for six weeks.'

Colin muttered an oath.

'What was that?'

Till All The Seas Run Dry

'Nothing. Please don't shout, Aunt Alice. You're deafening me.'

'Where are you speaking from? Has Archie got a telephone at last?'

'No, I'm in a public kiosk.'

'It sounds like it. The line's terrible.'

'I can hear you clear as a bell, Aunt Alice.'

'What was that about a swell?'

'Oh, never mind. Can I come and stay?' he shouted each word separately.

'Certainly. But I don't promise you'll find Mary. When shall you come?'

'Tomorrow, if that's all right. I'll get the 11.10 from York. Meet me at King's Cross.'

Lady Grantham met him at the station in her new chauffeur driven Bentley. As they drove past a less salutary area he was suddenly reminded that Mary was this very moment somewhere in one of the most poverty-stricken districts of London.

'I must find her, Aunt Alice.'

'Who, Mary? If you're hoping to dissuade her from what she's doing, I don't hold out much hope, but you will make these hasty decisions.' She cast him a sideways glance, then added, 'I hope you don't mind me asking, but I'm most curious to know why you are chasing around after Mary. I heard you were about to marry another young lady.'

'Who told you that?'

'Your father, of course, though he seems none too happy about it.'

Colin was silent. Charlotte was a sore point at the moment.

'Em, I know there's safety in numbers and all that, but your reputation, you know....'

'What are you talking about, Aunt Alice?' he said irritably. 'Mary is my cousin.'

'But this Charlotte, I understand, is staying with you....'

'Not any more. She's gone home.'

'Oh!' Lady Grantham's face brightened. 'Are we to understand, then, the engagement is off?'

'No, it isn't. But it's not officially on yet either. Look, Aunt Alice, what is this, the Spanish Inquisition?'

'Oooh, Colin, you're the most non-committal young man I've ever met.'

She was silent for a moment, and Colin dared to close his eyes. He was just nodding off when undaunted, she tapped him on the knee.

'What about Mary? You haven't explained yet, why you're chasing her about?'

'My dear Aunt Alice,' he sighed. 'Would you kindly refrain from jumping to conclusions. I'm concerned about her, that's all.'

'Very well then, I won't tease you any more. By the way, it's time you dropped the "aunt". You're not a schoolboy any more.'

'I'll try to remember...Alice.'

'That's better. Being called 'aunt' by you makes me feel so old. Tell me, what are your plans? You're very welcome to stay as long as you like, but shouldn't you be returning to Cambridge soon?'

'The term begins early October. Oh, it's all right,' he added seeing the dismayed look on her face. 'I won't inflict myself on you for as long as that, Aunt...I mean Alice. Once I find Mary I intend to take her home with me.'

'I see. And what if, assuming you find her, she refuses to go with you?'

'She won't refuse to go with me.'

'You're very sure of yourself. I wouldn't mind making you a wager.'

'What sort of wager?'

'£100 you won't manage to persuade her to give up what she's doing and go back to Yorkshire with you, before you have to return to Cambridge. What do you say?'

'What are you trying to do, Aunt Alice, ruin me?'

'Alice! Alice! Alice!' she said, beating a tattoo on his knee. 'Oh, go on,' she urged, nudging him with her elbow. 'You've got lots of money to lose.'

'Who says I'm going to lose. Make it fifty pounds and you're on.'

'Done!' said the lady, offering him her hand. 'Only don't tell Walter, he doesn't approve of gambling.'

Colin found the Pethick Lawrence's house at last. Instead of a bell there was a large brass knocker in the shape of a lion on the door. He knocked and waited. In a few moments a woman, carrying a baby under her arm opened up a crack, leaving the door held by a heavy chain, and looked at him suspiciously.

'Mrs Lawrence?' he enquired.

Till All The Seas Run Dry

'No, she ain't in, nor Mr Lawrence, neither. Who might you be, sir?'

'I'm Colin Craven, and I'm looking for my cousin Miss Mary Lennox. D'you happen to know where I can find her?'

The girl shrugged. 'I know her. She lives with Miss Livingstone, but where that is....' The anxious look lifted from her face, and she took the chain off the door, having evidently assured herself he was not going to hit her over the head with a bottle. 'Excuse me,' she said. 'Can't be too careful around here. You can come in if you like and wait till Mr and Mrs Pethick Lawrence return.'

'Would they know where Miss Lennox lives?'

''Course they would. They see her almost every day.' She thought for a moment. 'You might find 'em at the soup kitchen, down Pimlico Lane. Miss Lennox and Miss Livingstone work there, serving 'ot meals to them what's got no home.'

'Is it far from here?' Colin asked eagerly. 'Can you tell me where I can find this soup kitchen?'

The girl frowned. 'I don't rightly know exactly where it is, I've never been there. I stay indoors and 'elp with the children. If you'd rather, you can wait, in there,' she said, pointing to a large room, the door of which stood ajar. He could see several women sitting sewing, some using machines. One of them had a small child on her knee. He remembered what Alice Grantham had told him, that the Pethick-Lawrences had started a dressmaking business for the benefit of the less fortunate. Apparently they were not all fallen women by any means. Some were victims of rape or some other abuse, or had run away from men who'd beaten them up, and some had had husbands who'd left them, usually penniless, with at least one child to care for.

'What time will the Pethick-Lawrences be in?' he asked, looking at his watch.

The girl shrugged. 'Could be any time. They often don't come home till eight of an evening.' The baby wriggled in her arms and began to squeal. 'Excuse me, sir, I must....'

'Attend to your baby. Of course.'

'He's not mine,' she said. 'Though 'e might be, cos I look after 'im. His poor mother died giving birth to 'im. It 'appens all the time. We all muck in and 'elp each other care for the children.' The baby's cries became deafening, then another one started somewhere else and one of the women ran out of the big room.

'Off you go,' said Colin. 'Don't worry about me. I think I'll come back later.'

Till All The Seas Run Dry

He went away wondering at the generosity of the Pethick Lawrences, who'd turned their house into a refuge for poor and homeless women. This was very different from the secure, comfortable world Colin was used to. And there was Frederick Lawrence who might have been his mirror image, with the same background as himself, a wealthy family, an education at Eton, a degree at Cambridge.

Only a few hundred yards from the Pethick Lawrence's house it seemed to Colin like another world. The streets were littered with rubbish of every kind, and there was a stench of drains, stale urine and even worse coming from the canal. He suspected it was an open sewer. He shuddered as a huge rat ran almost under his feet, and quickened his step, afraid to stand still, in case he might catch some dreadful plague or disease. He'd heard about the slums of London, but his imagination had not stretched to anything like the reality.

In one street where the houses were all dilapidated, washing hung from almost every window, and he imagined that each room was occupied by a whole family. Ragged, bare-footed children played hop-scotch on the pavement, but as soon as they spotted Colin they were round him like wasps round a jam jar.

'Please sir!' 'Me Ma ain't got no money for bread. Ain't had nuffin' to eat this week!'

It was true, they all looked half starved, but it was more likely they were exaggerating, and Colin only had a limited amount of change. He threw it into the middle of the road, and they all scrambled and fought over it. He'd like to have given them more but he knew he'd be pestered to death if he did. He felt in his breast pocket and was thankful he had not been robbed of his wallet, watch and chain.

A little further down the street there was a brawl going on, grown men fighting, some dispute outside the pub. No sense getting involved with that. It was amazing, he reflected, how men could allow their wives and children to starve, yet they'd always manage to find enough for a pint in the pub. Colin turned back towards the river. This was no place to be about on foot, and alone. But there was a fat chance of finding a cab around here. The cabby who'd brought him to the Pethick Lawrence's house obviously thought he was crazy.

'Sure this is the right place, sir?' he'd asked incredulously.

He heard more shouting, followed by screaming, and turning a corner he encountered a man holding a small boy by the scruff of the neck, shaking him as if he were a dog.

Till All The Seas Run Dry

'You little beggar! I'll give yer the hidin' yer deserve.' He had a stick with which he began beating the child. 'I've seen yer, nickin' things off of my stall, yer little tealeaf.'

All the time he was beating the child, a tiny scrap of a thing, as if he might kill him. The boy's legs were already cut from the brutal knobbed stick. For what? Stealing food off a stall when he was starving? Colin could not bear to stand by and do nothing about it.

'Hey, you! Stop that!' he shouted.

But the man took no notice, whether he heard him or not, for he continued to chastise the boy. Colin went closer, shouting louder.

'Stop it, I say! Stop beating that child.'

The man looked up and stared at him in disbelief.

'Who the 'eck are you?' he swore. 'Mind your own bleedin' business.' And he went to resume the punishment, but the child, taking advantage of this distraction had managed to escape, and was running off down the road, apparently quite unscathed by the thrashing he'd just received.

The man looked at him accusingly. 'There! Now look what you've done,' he said, looking as though he might set about Colin with the stick. 'That little blighter's been nickin' things from my stall for weeks. Always the best things, mind. I've been waiting to catch up wiv' 'im, but 'e's always too quick for me. Then, tonight I get him, and 'oo should come along and spoil it all....'

'Why did you not report it to the police?'

'The law?' said the barrow man scornfully. 'What are vey goin' to do 'bout it. As if they ever catch 'em.'

'But there's no need to beat him to death. You might have killed him.'

'Ran off, didn't he? As if nuffin' 'ad 'appened. And I'm the one 'oo's 'ad me stuff nicked.'

'How much has he stolen from you?'

'Why d'you ask?' The barrow man became ingratiating, as if he saw a chance to make profit out of this gullible fool. 'Finkin' of payin' me back? Well, you're a right sucker, I'll be bound. Tell yer what. If yer stick around 'ere long, yer'll 'ave nuffin' left, not even the clo'es yer stand in.'

Chapter 14

Colin went back to the Lawrence's house feeling pleased with himself. After all he'd managed to prevent a rough bully from beating up a poor child. But when he told Frederick Lawrence the tale it did not get the reception he'd hoped for.

'I'm afraid there's little one can do in these cases,' said Lawrence, looking solemn. 'It's usually better not to interfere.'

Bereft of speech, Colin's jaw dropped.

'You see, the boy was very young,' his host explained. 'It may even have been his first offence.'

Colin knew it wasn't, according to the barrow man, but he kept it to himself.

'I know it sounds hard, but if he'd been severely beaten at this stage, he might have learned a lesson and been saved from a life of crime. But, because of your intervention….' Lawrence shrugged. 'He'll be pleased with himself. He got away with it. He'll probably do it again. Undoubtedly. Then he'll move on to less petty crimes, he'll start picking pockets, and finally he'll grow up to be one of the big criminals. Might even end up being hanged.'

Colin groaned. 'I thought I was doing the right thing.'

'Of course you did.' Frederick Lawrence's grey eyes softened. 'And I'd probably have done the same thing myself when I first began this work. It's a natural reaction. And you must not blame yourself, or dwell on it. There are so many of them, boys like that. It's impossible to help all. One can but do one's best.'

He thought of Oliver Twist, imagining Frederick Lawrence as a sort of Mr Brownlow.

At that moment a lady entered the room, and he knew, even before her husband announced it, exactly who she was. She was not very tall, and of slight build, but she had a presence about her, as if she was not one to be trifled with.

'Emmeline, this is Colin Craven.'

'Ah, yes,' she said, taking his hand in a firm grasp. 'You came earlier. Annie told me. And you're looking for Mary. Did you say you're her cousin?'

'That's right. But she's more like a sister to me.' He was not sure why he'd said that.

'And you want to see her? It's a little late,' Lawrence said, looking at his watch. 'Can we put him up, my dear?' he added, turning to his wife.

'There's a small attic room. Or you can have the sofa, if you prefer it,' she said, with a smile.

'You evidently think I should not go to Mary's house tonight.'

'It's not that,' Frederick Lawrence laughed. 'It would be perfectly respectable, I'm sure, but this is no area for anyone to walk alone at night, and dressed as you are....'

'Don't worry about me. I'll be all right.'

Lawrence shrugged. 'I know the district well, I never go about after dark, at least not unaccompanied. The streets are full of thieves and pick-pockets, vagrants and vagabonds.'

Colin thought, with reference to pick-pockets, of the ragged children he'd seen playing hop-scotch earlier, of the young boy who'd robbed the barrowman. Surely he could handle creatures like that? And drunks.... He'd seen plenty of them in Cambridge, and provided one kept out of their way.... He'd been waiting all day to see Mary, and now that he was so close to where she lived, he had no wish to wait until morning.

'How far is it from here?'

'About fifteen minutes' walk away, but....'

Colin was impatient. 'I hope you don't think me rude, but I'd rather go now.'

'If you insist,' said his host with a shrug, getting up to see him out. After he'd given him directions he said, 'Well, it's been a pleasure meeting you. Give my love to Cambridge, I'm fond of the place,' he added wistfully.

He closed the door after Colin and turned to his wife. 'That young man was in a very great hurry. I wonder if I should really have let him go? I think I'll call Constable Sherwood.'

The streets, which had been busy a couple of hours before, were now almost deserted, and dark. There were no oil lamps as there were in the well-to-do parts of Belgravia. He took out his torch and looked at his directions. Second turning on the right, fourth on the left. He hurried on, counting the turnings. It was so dark he couldn't see the broken paving stones, and he tripped up several times. It was a miracle he didn't sprain his ankle. Was this the left turn he should take? It was strange how his footsteps seemed to echo, or was it an echo? Was there someone following him?

With his torch he was able to make out the name of the street. It was not the one he wanted. Had he gone one too many or one too few. He was thus deliberating when he heard loud laughter and shouting quite close by, and footsteps, coming towards him. Next moment a group of very scruffy looking youths appeared in front of him. Colin quickly turned and started walking back the way he'd come, controlling a desire to quicken his step, but they'd already spotted him, for he heard one of them say,

'Hush, lads, stop yer natterin'. D'yer see what I see. Rich pickings if I ain't mistaken.'

'Cor, yeah! C'm on, Stan, let's get 'im.'

'Steady, lads,' the first man said, dropping his voice to little above a whisper. 'No rush. Fan out, and go quiet, like. Don't want to frighten our bird, now, do we? Don't want 'im t' fly off.'

Colin's heart was pounding. He had not heard all that the men said to each other, but he'd heard enough. He ducked down the next street he came to, without bothering to check if it was the one he wanted. He strongly resisted an urge to run, and tried to walk as quietly as he could, hoping they wouldn't hear his footsteps, and not daring to look behind him. But he found to his dismay that the street he was in came to a dead end. And if he went back the way he'd come he was likely to encounter his pursuers. He stood still and listened, he could hear their voices, but it was hard to tell where the sound was coming from. He thought their footsteps were receding and began to breathe more easily. His eyes were growing accustomed to the dark and he saw there was another turning to the left, further up the street. But now he was completely lost. Perhaps it was a way out, but to his horror, two of the ruffians suddenly appeared in front of him, and he turned round to find the other two behind him.

They quickly surrounded him.

'So, what 'ave we 'ere,' said the leader, the one they called Stan. 'A rich gen'lman, an' I'm not mistaken, by the way 'e's dressed.'

Colin felt sick to the pit of his stomach.

''And it over, sir. Yer wallet. Let's see it.'

'Get out of my way,' said Colin, fear making him angry. 'If I don't turn up in a few minutes my friends will call the police.'

They all burst out laughing.

'The police,' one man sneered, trying to mimic his speech. 'Ear that, lads, says 'is friends'll call in the law.'

They all laughed and closed in on Colin, backing him against the wall.

'Let's cut the cackle, shall we,' said one man, the biggest, bringing his fist into Colin's belly. He doubled up, winded, but two hands under his armpits heaved him up again.

'Had enough, 'av yer?' said Stan.

Colin lashed out with his feet, kicking one of them in the groin.

'So yer want a fight, do yer?' the man growled. 'Well, lads, fink we'd better teach the posh party a lesson.'

It all happened so quickly that later Colin could not remember the details very well at all. He heard the crunch as a fist smashed into his jaw, throwing his head back. Then blows came from all directions, winding him, blinding him, bringing him to the ground. Once he was down they started kicking him. He thought every bone in his body must be broken. He even thought his end had come. At length, through a haze of pain, half conscious, he heard Stan's voice.

'That's enough, lads. Don't want te kill 'im. 'E's not werf swinging for.'

'Shhhh!' another one whispered. 'Someone's coming! The law!'

Left lying on the ground, half conscious, Colin heard their footsteps retreating and others advancing. He was unable to move, unable to see, half blinded by the blood that poured from a gash on his forehead. Someone was bending over him.

'Oh, my God!' It was a voice he'd heard before, recently. Not the police after all. 'I should never have let him go out alone, inexperienced as he is, and dressed like that. The poor fellow was a sitting duck.'

Colin opened his mouth to speak. He wanted to tell Frederick Lawrence he was still alive, but no sound came out. Then he lost consciousness.

'Well, Mary,' Constance yawned. 'I don't know about you, but I'm for bed. D'you realise it's after midnight?'

Just then there was a loud banging on the door.

'Good lord!' she exclaimed. 'At this time of night! Who on earth could it be.'

'Don't answer it, Connie. Is the chain on the door?'

'I could try and see who it is....' Connie said, going to the window and drawing the curtain an inch, just enough to peep through into the street, but she could not quite see round to the front door. 'Dare I open the window, d'you think?'

The banging came again, accompanied by a familiar male voice from the other side of the door. 'For the Lord's sake, will one of you women open this door.'

'Freddie!'

She ran and opened the door.

'Where's Mary?' he demanded, coming inside. 'I must speak to her.'

Mary's heart sank, for what dreadful news would bring Frederick Lawrence to their house at this time of night? 'What is it, Frederick,' she said, breathlessly.

'It's your cousin Colin. He's been set upon by a gang of thieves and badly beaten. We've got him at home. Emmeline's taking care of him, and we've called the doctor. But I thought you should know as soon as possible.'

'How badly hurt is he?' Mary's stomach was churning in a most unpleasant way. One look at Frederick's face told her how serious it was.

'It's not good, I'm afraid,' he said. 'To tell you the truth, Mary, I don't know if he's going to survive.'

It was as if she'd been stabbed in the heart. She closed her eyes. Not Colin! Not her dearest love—near to death? But why? What was he doing here? He was supposed to be at home with Charlotte. She felt giddy, as if she'd been on a roller-coaster. Frederick stepped forward and took her arm.

'Come and sit down,' he said gently.

Connie took her other arm and they eased her into a chair.

'Put your head between your knees, Mary.' It was Connie who spoke. 'Stay with her, Freddie. I'll go and make her a cup of hot, sweet tea.'

When Colin came to, he found himself in a strange place. He could only open one eye fully, and when he tried to turn his head it caused him quite a lot of pain. Indeed he could scarcely move at all. A lamp burned low beside his bed, and there were voices outside the door, one of which he recognised as Emmeline Lawrence's.

'I'm afraid you can't question him until the doctor has seen him. Besides, he has not gained consciousness since he was brought in last night.'

'But if we're to have any chance of catching these villains....'

'I'm sorry, but I can't help that. Mr Craven's welfare must come first. He's very sick. We don't know if he'll live.'

'That's the whole point. If he dies, I shall be carrying out a murder investigation....'

Colin drifted off to sleep again, content that he was safe in the Pethick Lawrence's house. Would they tell Mary? He desperately wanted to see her, specially if he was going to die. What seemed like a moment later he was woken by a commotion downstairs, banging on the door, followed by the clatter of running feet.

'It may be the doctor. Open the door, Annie,' someone shouted.

'Oh, Freddie, thank God you're back,' Emmeline Pethick Lawrence's voice echoed downstairs. 'And Mary!'

'She insisted upon coming with me. Wouldn't be persuaded to wait until morning.'

'Where is he?' Colin heard Mary's voice and his heart leapt. 'Quickly, tell me! Is he all right?'

'My dear, there's no change, I'm afraid. He's still unconscious.'

'Oh, dear God! Let me see him.'

Her obvious concern warmed each ailing cockle in Colin's heart. He could hear her running upstairs without waiting for an answer.

'I must warn you, Mary,' Emmeline panted after her. 'He looks quite a sight. Pray do not be shocked.'

Before she'd finished the sentence the door burst open and Mary flew to Colin's side.

'Colin! Oh, Colin!'

He wanted to tell her he was all right but he couldn't make anything work. All that came out was a moan.

'Emmeline,' Mary called over her shoulder. 'I think he's coming round. Thank God! My poor Colin.' She took his hand in hers and kissed it.

He began to lose consciousness, though he fought it. He didn't want to go. He tried to hold on to Mary, he wanted so much to speak to her. Yet it was a relief to escape his pain-ridden body. He seemed to slide easily out of the top of his head, and then stood looking dispassionately at his body lying on the bed. What a ghastly sight, he thought. His face was unrecognisable. Mary sat beside the bed, she was in tears. He wanted to comfort her, to tell her he was still there, but he couldn't make her hear. Yet he was reluctant to return to his body, it was such a relief to be free of pain. He saw Mary get up and run out of the room.

Now he found himself floating out of the window, flying over the rooftops, and in moments he was back at Misselthwaite, flying over the terrace, the lawns and into the secret garden. Mary was bending over the rose bed. He went to gather her in his arms, but she turned round and it was not Mary. It was his mother.

'Colin! What have you done?' she said in a voice full of reproach.

'I was attacked, Mother. You can't be angry with me about that.'

'Oh, I'm not talking about that,' she said irritably. 'I meant, allowing yourself to be beguiled by that female. It'll have dire consequences, mark my words.'

'But we're not married yet....'

'Do you think she'll let you go so easily? I'm afraid you're in for a shock, Colin. Well,' she sighed. 'You've made your bed, now you must lie on it.'

And before he could answer, she disappeared, and when he turned round Charlotte was there looking her most seductive, in his favourite dress. She beckoned to him and he had to follow. She led him into a church where her mother and an army of relatives all started closing in on him. He tried to get up off the ground, but he couldn't, and finding he couldn't move, he began to panic. They bound him hand and foot, tied to a pillar. He tried to call for help but no sound came.

'Mary!' All that came out was a hoarse whisper.

'Yes, dear, I'm here.' It was her voice, but where was she? She was not in his dream. Only Charlotte now—all the others had gone—stood and laughed at him as he struggled to free himself of the bonds, the more he struggled the tighter they became, until they cut into his flesh. She had a whip in her hand, and she began to thrash him with it. She was like a fiend. The pain seared through his body until he writhed and groaned.

'It's all right, love,' said Mary's gentle voice, soothing, while a cool sponge was put on his forehead. The weight on his chest was terrible. He was back in bed now, back in that ravaged tortured body, and Mary was bathing his head.

'He's delirious,' she said to someone beside her. 'Is that doctor never coming?'

His mouth was dry as a bone. 'Water,' he managed to gasp.

'What was that, dearest?' Mary bent her head down to his lips.

He must have made her understand for, to his great relief, his head was gently lifted and a cup of cool water was offered to his parched lips.

After that he heard only snippets of whispered conversation.

'...Freddie fears...internal injuries...kicked in the kidneys...tell the doctor....'

The whispering went on intermingled with his dreams, such weird, fantastic dreams. He was in Greece with his mother and Mary. They were in some temple, his mother was a priestess, and he and Mary were getting married. He felt intensely happy, until the dream changed. Another woman—she looked a bit like Charlotte—seduced him, and Mary found them in bed together. She ran from the room, and he ran after her, searching, searching, but when he found her she was dead. She, his own true love, dead, and it was his fault. He wept, overwhelmed by grief and pain such as he'd never known in real life. Then he came back into his body, sobbing.

'Hush dearest,' It was Mary's voice. He tried to speak, to reach out and take her hand, but he couldn't. He was drifting off again....

And now the scene had changed completely, and they were all dressed in Elizabethan clothes. Mary was there again, but this time she was married to Dickon, or someone who looked like him, only this Dickon was someone important, a nobleman or a knight. He ached with love for the woman who could never be his, eaten with jealousy. Next thing he knew he was in a small boat in a very rough sea...a severe storm...he was drowning...drowning....

'The doctor's here,' someone said, bringing him back to painful consciousness.

A cold hand felt his forehead.

'...Very high temperature...' a gruff voice said. '...Better examine him. Is one of you a nurse? ...Need some help....'

Colin was vaguely aware of being turned over and prodded by cold hands. He heard the doctor tell the women to watch out for blood in his urine.

'We could take him into hospital, but if you can manage, he'd be better off here.'

Mary said, 'I'll take care of him.'

'Well, if you're worried about it, let me know.'

And that was the last lucid thing Colin remembered before he trailed off into oblivion for several days, only conscious occasionally of gentle hands tending him.

Night and day Mary sat by his bed, sometimes weeping, sometimes praying, despairing, hoping, until she was dropping with exhaustion. The doctor had said the worst danger was dehydration. She must get him to drink, a difficult enough task when he was half conscious, but for the most part he was not there at all.

She'd been told he'd been looking for her, that he'd been on his way to her house when he was attacked. But as to why he had come, or what had become of Charlotte, she had no idea. It occurred to her to write a quick note to her uncle. She'd never be forgiven if Colin died and he'd not been informed of his son's critical state. Also Lady Grantham, who probably already knew he was in London, and may have been expecting him.

She was right about Lady Grantham, who was on the telephone as soon as she heard. She knew something bad had happened and she'd been frantic with worry. Was he all right? Should she come and see him, or should she wait until he was over the crisis? Had Mary told Archie? Yes, yes, yes. He must have the best Harley Street doctor. She'd send one to see him immediately, and she'd pay the bill of course. Mary tried to tell her it was unnecessary because the Lawrence's had faith in their doctor, who'd been to see him every day.

Apart from these little excursions to the telephone, she never left Colin's side. Her guardian came down from Yorkshire. He came over with Lady Grantham to see Colin, who was oblivious of his visit. But he did not stay in the house. He went back to Belgravia with Lady Grantham. Mary thought this a little strange, but then she'd forgotten his abhorrence of sickness. She should have remembered the peculiar way he behaved when Colin was chronically ill as a child. But he was anxious, all the same, for he telephoned every day, sometimes twice to see if there was any sign of improvement or otherwise.

Then one evening she noticed beads of sweat on Colin's upper lip, and his head felt damp and cool. Merciful Lord, his temperature was down to normal, he was breathing evenly and sleeping restfully.

'Emmeline!' she called, in triumphal excitement. 'Come quickly!'

Emmeline came running and panting up the stairs. 'What is it?'

'Look,' Mary cried. 'I think he's going to be all right.'

'Yes, the crisis is over. He's on the mend. Now you go to your own room and get a good night's rest. I'll call you when he wakes up.'

Colin awoke next morning feeling almost whole again. He was still very sore, still covered in bruises, and his eye was half closed, but apart from that....

Emmeline Pethick Lawrence came into the room, drew back the curtains and said,

'I'm so glad you're feeling better. We've all been extremely worried about you.'

'Where's Mary?'

'Having a well deserved rest, poor thing. She hasn't left your side for fifteen days.'

'Have I been here as long as that?'

'Two weeks ago Freddie brought you here, more dead than alive. You've been very ill ever since. There's a detective who wants to question you. He's called several times. I keep sending him away. Do you feel strong enough to answer his questions yet?'

'I don't remember very much, but he's welcome to try me.'

'Are you feeling hungry? Could you manage some porridge?'

He should feel hungry, he thought, if he'd eaten nothing for a fortnight. But eating, even porridge, proved a difficult and painful business. Mary came and sat with him.

'It's a relief to see you sitting up. Last night we knew you were going to recover. Your temperature had fallen and you were sleeping peacefully. None of that shouting and fighting.'

'Was I doing that?'

She giggled. 'You seemed to be fighting the battle of Waterloo single handed. At first we thought you were fighting off the villains who attacked you, then you began to jabber in another language, and you kept calling me by different names. It was most odd.'

'Really?' Colin frowned, trying to recollect his strange dreams. 'I seem to have made rather an idiot of myself, and caused you all a lot of trouble.'

'It wasn't your fault you were attacked.'

'In a way it was. If I hadn't been so dashed cock sure of myself, I'd have taken Frederick's advice and waited till morning. But you know me. Patience is no virtue of mine.'

'I'm curious to know what you were doing in London in the first place?'

'I came to find you, to try to persuade you to come home. I had a wager with Aunt Alice....' His hand flew to his mouth. 'Oh Lord, May! You'd better get a message to her immediately to tell her I'm alive and well—as well as can be expected, at any rate.'

'She already knows. Emmeline telephoned her as soon as we saw you were better. Your father's been staying with her.' She said nothing about returning to Misselthwaite.

'Father? Here in London?'

'Yes. They've been to see you a couple of times already.'

Alice Grantham came to see him that very afternoon. She arrived soon after the doctor had been and pronounced him to be on the mend.

'Well, well, Colin,' she said. 'I've heard of people using many and varied ploys in order to win bets, but this just about takes the cake.'

'Oh, lord!' Colin groaned. 'Don't make me laugh. It hurts.'

'Your father sends his love. He wasn't feeling very well himself today, but he's very relieved to hear you're on the mend. He suggests you go home as soon as you're fit to travel and spend some time there recuperating. I think we should inform Cambridge too.'

'Mary's already done so, bless her.'

'That girl's too good for you, you know.'

He remained in bed, slowly recovering his strength. In the mean time he had a stream of visitors, including Constance Livingstone who's comments about his black eye, and how it improved his looks, reduced him to tears of laughter.

'Stop, I beg you. You've no idea how painful it is to laugh.'

Frederick Lawrence popped his head in to find no less than five women round his bed.

'He's not as handsome as that,' he laughed. 'D'you think, if I acquired a black eye, I'd attract such a bevy of beautiful ladies? Colin, the police think they've caught two out of the four who attacked you. When you feel strong enough, could you go and identify them?'

But really the only person Colin wanted by his bedside was Mary, and since he'd begun to recover he'd seen little of her. She no longer slept in the house, and only visited him when she happened to be there for another reason. She'd given him no opportunity to speak to her, they'd never been alone together. His heart ached for the old fellowship between them. She seemed distant and aloof. He listened for her step on the stair and his heart lifted when he heard her voice. And when she was in the room his eyes followed her, unconsciously. He was up, sitting in a chair the next time she came, with Constance. When she went to leave, he called her back.

'Stay and talk to me a while, May.'

She and Constance exchanged glances, and Constance left the room.

'You will come home with me, won't you?' he asked eagerly.

'Just so you can claim £50 from your poor godmother?' she remarked cynically.

'The bet's not important. It's....' Could he admit he'd made a mistake over Charlotte and wanted her back? 'I don't like you living in these parts, two women on your own. It's dangerous. If it's charity work you're after there's plenty of that at home.'

'But I'm quite happy here, Colin. For the first time there is a purpose to my life. Why should I give it up just for some whim of yours?'

'It's not a whim. May....' He stretched out his hand to her, but a sharp stab of pain made him wince, falling back against the cushions with a grunt. She looked at him sharply.

'You shouldn't still be in that sort of pain—unless you've a broken rib.'

'Only when I move a certain way. It's nothing. I'll be back to normal in a week or two. We'll be able to ride together on the moor, visit all the old haunts. You'd like that, wouldn't you? It'll be like old times.'

'You seem to have forgotten one small detail,' she said, her voice full of bitterness. 'You happen to be engaged to be married.'

'Is that any reason for you to desert your home and everything?'

'That's rich, coming from you,' she said, pulling her hand out of his. She got up and went to the window, her back was turned to him so he couldn't see her face. 'Haven't you learnt yet, you can't keep your cake and eat it? What do you expect of me, that I should remain at Misselthwaite, a dependent relative, until I'm an old maid....'

'No!' His denial was quite violent. 'That shall not happen to you. I won't let it.'

She laughed, 'Dear Colin. You remind me of a small boy I once knew who thought he owned the world, a young rajah! Do grow up. What, pray, could you do to prevent it?'

She was right. He was in no position to make demands upon her. And why should he expect her to trust him? The path between them was already littered with his broken promises.

'Besides,' she added. 'I'm afraid I couldn't live with Charlotte.'

'Very well then,' he said, resignation in his voice. 'I understand you don't want to come home to live, but couldn't you come for a respite? Charlotte isn't there now, you know.'

She sighed wearily. 'I'll think about it. Because you're sick, I might accompany you home, but if I do I'll stay no more than a few days.'

He sighed raggedly. He'd been a perfect cad. And now it was no good thinking he could take her in his arms and expect her to forgive him. Once again, as in the past apparently, he'd blown his chance of happiness. His eyes filled with tears which he wiped away furiously with the back of his hand. It was physical weakness, he told himself, glad Mary had her back to him and couldn't see his unmanly tears.

'Perhaps it would have been better if those fellows had done for me,' he said gloomily.

'Now you're being idiotic!' she scolded, turning on him. 'Really Colin, why must you be so dramatic? You're a most capricious creature! What am I to do with you?' she sighed.

Chapter 15

Mary felt wretched. She was not usually so indecisive, but she'd been severely hurt already by Colin, and she still felt terribly vulnerable. But it had been a dreadful shock, finding him in that state, then sitting up with him, night after night, anxious, unable to eat or sleep, wondering if he'd live, and if he did, whether he'd be permanently damaged in some way. The sheer relief, when he regained consciousness and began to recover, had been overwhelming. It had been a great strain, and she was exhausted, and it was very tempting to go with him. But if she did, she knew she'd be tempted to stay, and if she stayed she knew exactly what would happen.

She discussed it with Emmeline.

'He's in a weak condition, physically. I feel I should accompany him on the journey.'

'I quite agree,' said Emmeline. 'If you hadn't, I was going to suggest it myself. And don't be in too much of a rush to come back.'

Mary shook her head. 'I won't be staying away long. A week, no more.'

How could she explain to Emmeline she was afraid of getting involved with Colin?

Emmeline looked at her gravely. 'You're not being fair to yourself, Mary. You need the rest as much as Colin. You're looking washed out. Why not stay a couple of months—till Christmas, if you like. Indeed, you don't have to come back at all, if he wants you to stay....'

'Of course I'll come back.'

'There's no need, on our account, at least.' She glanced towards the room Colin was in. 'I watched you, when he was ill, I saw the way you cared for him.' Her keen eyes pierced Mary's soul. 'I know a woman in love when I see one.' Mary shook her head. 'And what's more, he's in love with you. Oh, yes, he is.'

'No he's not,' Mary said, sadly. 'He may be fond of me but he's not in love with me, he's engaged to marry someone else.' She didn't go into details about their past attachment.

'Is he? Well, you astound me!' said Emmeline. 'But if anything should happen to make you change you mind, don't sacrifice your happiness for your work here. It's not worth it.

'How can you say that? You, who are so dedicated?'

'I was fortunate in Freddie,' she said with a wry smile. 'He and I are driven by the same motivation. But if he hadn't shared my views when I met and fell in love with him, I'm not sure I should have stuck to it either.'

So Mary went home to Misselthwaite with Colin, and of course she stayed, much more than a week. There was pressure on her from all sides, not just Colin's. Mr Craven, Dickon and Mrs Sowerby. In the end it was a relief to give in. And she hadn't spent Christmas at home for four years. Yes, she'd stay until the new year.

Meanwhile Colin recovered from his injuries and his scars went, all but a small one just above his left eyebrow, which would probably remain with him for the rest of his life, his health and strength were gradually restored. He'd become very thoughtful since his attack, and a little subdued. He never mentioned Charlotte, or his engagement. Nor did she want to talk about it. But she could not forget it. It hung over and between them like a black cloud.

But Colin's optimism was infectious. She must accept the inevitable, she told herself, Colin would marry Charlotte and she'd go back to London. Meanwhile she was drawn to him like a moth to a flame. She even began to enjoy herself.

Dickon was pleased to see her too. He was pleased to see her with Colin again, and began to hope they'd stay together as they ought to be. He had mixed feelings about his own marriage. Molly fulfilled at least one of her wifely duties, she more than satisfied him sexually. She was exciting and inventive, and grew daily more voluptuous. And morally she appeared to have turned over a new leaf since their marriage, for it seemed she was faithful to him. She was also a good cook when she put her mind to it. But she was lazy and slovenly about the house. She was untidy, and often left the dirty dishes from one meal to the next.

Just as Colin decided he was fit to return to Cambridge, tragedy struck.

In the middle of one stormy night, Mary awoke suddenly. At first she thought it was the howling wind that had awakened her, it whistled and wuthered through the eaves of the old house and rattled the windows. But as she lay awake it came again, the most blood curdling sound she'd ever heard. Was it a horse in pain?

She was out of bed in seconds, pulling on her dressing-gown and grabbing a blanket to wrap round her. It was cold outside. The autumn wind was biting, but the thought of what she was going to find when she reached the stables drove everything else from her mind.

Dickon who'd reacted faster than she had, was already there. It was Prince. He was lying in a pool of blood on the ground in the stable yard, a great gash down one of his flanks, and both his front legs were at a sickly angle. It was easy to see what had happened. He'd broken down the door of his own stall, and attempted to jump the wall which divided two sections of the stables. But why? Dickon was talking to him, soothing.

'Seems he were trying' to get at Snowdrop,' he explained. 'We keep 'em apart when we think she's coming' into season. But he knows. He's th' canny one.'

'I'll get Colin,' she gasped, and ran towards the house, almost colliding with him.

'What is it?' Then he saw the look on her face, 'Oh, God! It's not Prince, is it?'

She nodded, putting her hand on his arm. She wanted to shield him from the horror. But he pushed past her and ran to the stables. When he saw the state of his horse the blood drained from his face.

'Oh, God!' he cried, falling on his knees beside the stricken animal.

Dickon gripped his arm. 'Try to keep calm, Master Colin. I could try an' save him, but....' There was little conviction in his voice.

Colin shook his head in anguish. Prince's eyes were rolling horribly. He could never bear to see animals in pain, and when it was his own beloved Prince.... And there was nothing even Dickon could do for him.

'My poor fellow,' he said gently, stroking the silky neck, now all damp with sweat.

Prince looked up at him pathetically, as if he was pleading for him to do something. He was so trusting, Colin's throat constricted painfully and tears welled up in his eyes. He swallowed hard, pressing his clenched fists to his eyes. Dickon put a hand on his shoulder.

'I think 'tis best if we made an end. I'll do it if tha like.'

'No, no. I must,' he gasped, 'if I can bring myself to. Mary?'

'Yes, love?' She came to his side, and laid her hand on his.

'Get my gun.'

'Oh, no!' she gasped, and her hand flew to her mouth.

Till All The Seas Run Dry

'Don't make it impossible for me,' he snapped. 'For God's sake, do as I ask, and be quick about it.' He shook her hand away, impatiently.

She looked pleadingly at Dickon who nodded sadly.

'Aye, let's put him out o' his misery, Miss Mary.'

She wanted to protest, to urge Dickon to try to save him, to suggest that they should get the vet who might give him a drug to ease the pain, but she went obediently, the tears streaming down her face, already wet from the rain. For in her heart she knew that if Colin had made such a courageous decision, it was not for her to try to put him off. Common sense told her it was no use him driving fifteen miles to the nearest horse doctor, who, when he got here could do nothing. A gust of wind whipped her hair stingingly across her face.

She came back with the gun as quickly as she could but by that time she could see that Colin had begun to lose his nerve. He was shaking violently.

'Will I do it for thee?' Dickon asked him, gently.

'No!' he said, gripping the gun, gritting his teeth and closing his eyes. He must do it himself, and it must be done in one shot.

He took the safety catch off, and Prince's ears twitched backwards.

Mary could not bear to look. She put her hands over her ears, but she could not blot out the sound of the gun going off. Then she heard Colin vomit.

She went to put her arms round him, but he flung away from her. He was like a wild man, shivering, sobbing like a child. Yet she'd never admired him so much, for she knew the courage he'd had to muster. Never had she loved him so much or felt such sympathy for him.

He quickly recovered his self-control and apologised.

'It's alright, I understand,' she said gently.

'Take him back inside, Miss Mary,' Dickon suggested. 'I'll finish off here.'

'Come on, dear,' she said, taking Colin's arm, feeling some resistance.

'You go back to bed, yourself. I'll stay and help Dickon.'

'Wi' respect, sir, tha'll do nowt of th' sort,' said Dickon, firmly. 'I'll get young Jack to help me in th' morning,' he said covering up the carcass. Mary was surprised to hear a note of irritation in his voice—Dickon, who was usually so placid. Then, looking at his face, she realised suddenly that he too was near to tears. He loved that horse just as Colin did, and the effort of controlling himself must be a great strain. Colin seemed to understand. He put an arm round her, and, for the first time in that terrible night, she felt the tension ebb from his body.

Strangely the wind had dropped, the storm passed, though the air was damp and chill. Dawn was beginning to break in the distant eastern sky. She went with him to his room. It seemed the most natural thing to do. He didn't have to ask her. She knew he wanted her to stay with him. They sat on the bed together, and he put his head in his hands.

'It's all my fault,' he said. She couldn't see his face but she could hear the tremor in his voice and knew he was near to tears.

'How can it be your fault?' She began stroking his back between his shoulder blades.

'Father said I should have him gelded, but I didn't listen. I thought it would dampen his spirit, make him go to fat like Pendragon.'

'And so it might have done. He had a good life. But why didn't you let them breed?'

'We did. Snowdrop's already had three foals sired by him, while you were in France. Last time, about nine months ago, she was not at all well. We nearly lost her. We didn't tell you because we thought it might upset you, but Father said we simply couldn't risk it again.'

'Well, you did the right thing then. And he apparently enjoyed himself.' There was a hint of amusement in her voice, in spite of the circumstances. 'So don't blame yourself.'

'It wouldn't have been fair to try to keep him alive. If I'd let Dickon try, it'd only have prolonged the agony, and even if he'd miraculously recovered he'd never have been the same again. But I can't believe it, my Prince, gone, my constant friend and companion these last seven years.' His voice broke and she heard a shuddering sigh.

'I know,' she said, taking him in her arms as if he were a child and holding him tight.

'I'm going to miss him dreadfully. All the time when you were away, I had him. And what will Snowdrop do?'

Mary found herself thinking of all the happy times, the four of them together, specially that year when she first had Snowdrop. She was almost in tears herself.

She heard Colin say, 'I remember you once said that if I lost something, or someone that meant a lot to me, it might be the making of me.'

'Don't think of that now. It was unkind of me to say it.'

'It was probably true, though. But if you leave again.... Must you go back to London, May? If you do, there'll be nothing for me to come home for. I shan't come home at all.'

'Now you're being absurd. What about your poor father.'

'What about him? He doesn't need me. He's never cared very much about me.'

'That's not true!' she said furiously. 'Now you're wallowing in self-pity. Pull yourself together.' She heard a sharp intake of breath, and, regretting her outburst, she added more gently, 'Don't worry, I won't desert you.'

'You won't go back to London then?'

Emmeline had said, If he wants you to stay....

'I'll stay as long as you want me to.' But she was thinking he would not want her to stay once he was married.

'You'll stay with me tonight, won't you, dearest?'

Dearest! He hadn't called her that for years! And what was he asking her to do?

When she hesitated, he added, 'Oh, you needn't worry. You're quite safe. I'm in no mood for that. All I need is some sleep. It would be a comfort just to have you stay with me.'

Of course she would. She'd not leave him.

They got into bed together and snuggled up, cuddling each other like the forlorn babes in the wood.

'You're so good to me, May, my dearest friend,' he said, kissing her on the mouth. He was still shivering. 'What would I have done without you?'

'I'm sure you'd have coped quite well,' she said. 'You've had a bad shock. Now get some rest and it'll be better in the morning.'

Exhausted though she was, both physically and emotionally, she didn't sleep straight away. His body so close to hers, so intimate, stirred her senses, keeping her very much awake. Also his arm, tight round her, kept her pinioned down so that she could not move without disturbing him, and when she tried to extract herself from this position he held her more closely. She felt the curve of his body, his manhood against her thigh, and began to tremble. She lay there for some time, desire mounting in her like a volcano that's about to erupt.

She must have transmitted her feelings to him, for he lifted the arm which held her prisoner, running his hand over her body, her breasts, her belly, her thigh. A moment later he was feeling for the hem of her night dress, pulling it up. His hands were on her naked skin. A warm, yearning sensation crept up from her loins, melting her bones.

It was going to happen. This time she'd let it, she did not want to resist him. Her heart was so full of love she wanted to give herself to him, regardless of the consequences. She didn't consider that afterwards she'd be cast aside, her maidenhood defiled, while he married Charlotte. She loved him so much, all she wanted was for him to make love to her.

He slipped her night dress over her head, then threw off his own night shirt. When he came back to her, taking her in his arms, his naked chest pressed against her breasts, and the contact sent a thrill of delight through her. They were naked together. It was like that time by the waterfall, only this was much more intimate. All the years of yearning for this moment and it had come so suddenly and unexpectedly. And now she burned with a fever of desire and trembled from head to foot. He took her swiftly, his passion too urgent to contain. He took her silently, no words or endearments whispered in her ear. The pain when he entered her initially passed, and she was floating on wave upon wave of sensuous pleasure. She had often tried to imagine what it was like, but this was not like anything she'd dreamed of.

When it was over he lay still for some minutes, his body half covering hers. She wanted him to remain there forever and she experienced a sense of loss when he withdrew.

'I didn't mean it to happen,' he said, apologetically. 'But I suddenly wanted you so much. I'm sorry. I hope you won't hate me for it?'

'Hate you? I could never hate you,' she said softly. She couldn't tell him yet how much she loved him. She still felt far too vulnerable.

'My darling May, I love you,' he said, stroking her cheek with the back of his hand. 'You're so different....' He checked himself.

Different? A pang of jealousy stabbed at her heart as she realised he was thinking of Charlotte. Why did the ogre of Charlotte always have to appear to spoil her happiness.

'No, don't turn away from me, my love,' he said softly, as if he read her mind. *'C'est toi que j'aime.'*

Those words—the very same Gilles had used. And how false they had been. Empty words spoken in the heat of passion. It was no use thinking he loved her. It was Charlotte he'd asked to marry him, she he was in love with, to whom he was betrothed. He'd called her his dearest friend. There was a world of difference between loving and being in love.

'I think I should go back to my own room now.'

'No!' His voice was quite vehement. 'You said you'd stay with me. If you go I'll start thinking about Prince. I shall not be able to sleep.'

He put his arm round her again, possessively. 'Why are you in such a hurry to escape me? Didn't I please you just now?' His lips traced a tortuous route from her throat to her nipple, teasing it with his tongue and teeth. 'In that case I'd better try again.'

She woke to find herself still in his arms. Through the crack in the curtains, the sun cast a shaft of light across the room, a bright day after the storm the night before. She marvelled that they'd slept so soundly, so closely wrapped in each other's arms. Only once before in her life had she tried to share a bed—in India, with her mother—and she remembered that neither of them had slept a wink. But after last night.... Her body was suffused with warm remembrance. She'd never been a prig, but she was astonished at her own sensuality. Nobody had told her it was like that. She'd been led to believe that only men enjoyed love-making, that for a woman it was nothing more than a wifely duty. Was it lack of modesty on her part, or did others derive the same giddy pleasure from it as she had when he'd made love to her the second time?

She looked around the room. His mother's portrait staring down at them made her blush. Then she caught sight of his clock and her heart leapt into her mouth. It was eight thirty in the morning. The servants! Had they noticed she was not in her own room? Could she get back without anyone seeing her. It wouldn't do for anyone to find her here!

'Colin, I must go,' she whispered in his ear.

He grunted, hardly stirring, as she got out of bed and dragged on her dressing-gown. There was a secret passage they'd discovered as children which ran from Colin's room direct to the centre of the house, but she still had a way to go for her room was in the east wing. She slunk along the corridors, hiding in a doorway each time she heard voices along the passage, her heart in her mouth all the while.

When she got back to her room she found Martha, with a cup of tea in her hand, looking dubiously at her empty bed.

'Eh, Miss Mary! Thank heaven tha've come, I've been waiting for thee. Your tea's stone cold now. I'd best get another cup.'

'It's alright, Martha,' she said, breathlessly. 'I don't want any tea, thank you.' She was about to say she'd been having a bath when Martha further confounded her.

'I heard th' rumpus in th' night wi' that poor horse, Miss Mary, an' I came to see if tha were alright.' She didn't need to say any more. Mary felt herself blush to the roots of her hair, the blood in her face and neck so hot it prickled.

'I was only...I was trying to comfort him, I....'

'I know, Miss Mary. Nob'dy thinks badly o' thee. Not like that other one.'

'What other one, Martha? Do you mean Miss Charlotte?'

'Aye,' said Martha, a grim look on her face. 'She's no good, that one.'

The maid hurried from the room, and Mary was thankful it was only Martha, whose loyalty she knew she could count on. But she was appalled by the hint that Colin may have slept with Charlotte. Was that what he meant by 'you're so different'? And even if he had not. If people thought such dreadful things about Charlotte, whom he'd asked to marry him, what might they think of her? She'd gone to bed with him, knowing what might happen. She'd put up no resistance. She'd even invited it. With a stab of conscience she remembered Madame de Bergerac's warning not to be seduced by a man before marriage, even if he claimed to have *'toutes les ideés modernes,'* and that it would make no odds to his feelings for her. 'In truth, every man wants his bride to come to him pure and virginal on her wedding night.'

What had she done?

What had seemed like a miracle had suddenly become shameful. And yet....

She was still warm from his loving. She could never forget how tender he had been. He had not behaved like a man who'd merely satisfied his lust, even a need to be comforted. And she could not blame him. He had never misled her, he'd made it perfectly clear they could not be married. But now it hurt more than ever, for she realised she was more deeply in love, and far more vulnerable. Furthermore, she knew it would be impossible to resist him in future.

She had little chance to gauge his feeling during the next few days for she saw little of him, and when she did, he was silent and withdrawn. She knew he was upset but why didn't he let her share his grief? Hadn't she always been there for him, to comfort him?

It was Dickon she found herself comforting. He was standing staring at Prince's empty stall, the tears running down his rugged cheeks, tears he hastily dried with the back of his hand as soon as he saw her coming. He said he felt responsible for losing the horse, if only he'd done this or that. She could not take away his grief but she tried to ease his regrets.

'Don't blame yourself, Dickon. There was nothing you could have done. Colin knows that too.'

'How is Master Colin? It were good tha were with him last night, Miss Mary.' He looked at her so intently, she wondered if he knew. She blushed and dropped her eyes.

'He's hardly spoken to me since,' she said. 'I think he's avoiding me.'

'Don't be upset, Miss Mary. I reckon he thinks he made a fool of hissel'. He thinks it were cowardly, bawling like that.'

'Cowardly! He was far from that. I could never have done what he did? Could you?'

'I offered, but to tell th' truth, I were main glad I didn't have to. And I don't think it's unmanly to weep when tha lose someone dear, but I didn't go to public school. Tell him he were brave, Miss Mary. You find him an' tell him.'

'And tell him you love him,' he might also have added. But hadn't she already told him that in the best way a woman could? She'd given him the most precious gift she had, and now she was afraid he despised her for it.

She couldn't get used the fact that Dickon was a married man.

'How's your wife?' she asked him.

'She's well and getting bigger,' he said with a wink.

But it was what he didn't say that worried Mary.

She'd heard that Susan Sowerby was not on the best of terms with her new daughter-in-law, that Molly used her pregnancy as an excuse for sitting around all day expecting Dickon to wait on her hand and foot. But Dickon being a loyal soul refused to be drawn.

Her heart ached for him. It seemed that the two people she loved most in the world were doomed to be tied to women who'd make their lives a misery. What of the friendship nurtured in the secret garden that bound the three of them together? Would it be forgotten?

And she who'd had the love of both of them would end up with neither, wasting away, a lonely old woman. What a mess they'd made of their lives.

The truth was Colin wanted to be alone for he had a great deal on his mind. He sat on a large stone watching the water tumbling over the pebbles in the beck. It was cloudy and torrential after the storm. The salmon would be running, he thought absently. If he'd been in the mood he'd have rushed to get his fishing rod. The last few days had been the most traumatic in his life, and his emotions were in turmoil. In Prince he'd lost, not only his horse and his friend, but a whole era of his life. Nothing would be the same again. All the memories, the times he and Mary....

And Mary!

Why had she suddenly decided to give herself to him? Did she really love him or was it out of pity? Heaven forbid that it should be the latter! His conscience troubled him. Mary's sweet innocence had been violated and it was he who'd done it! While Charlotte, who'd promised much and given nothing, who'd teased and tormented him, had not only kept her honour intact, but had extorted a promise of marriage from him. He knew now that, cousin or not, it was Mary he wanted to marry. He should have done it years ago.

At any rate he would not desert her, but it was not going to be easy. Neither Charlotte nor her family would let him go without fierce retribution, he was well aware of that.

He heard the click of the little wicket gate behind him and turned to see young Rebecca Parkin, walking her Rex. She sat beside him and put her small hand in his.

'Me Da told me about your poor Prince, sir. I were that sorry to hear it.'

Colin squeezed the little hand in his, and fought to contain the tears that welled up in his eyes. He was her hero. No hero worth his salt shed tears.

'Thank you for your concern, Rebecca,' he gulped. 'And how's my old friend Rex?' He fondled the dog's ear. His muzzle was going grey now.

'He's right fine, thank ye, sir. I saw thee, driving through village in tha motor car,' she went on to explain. 'An' I thought I might find thee here.'

'So you came looking for me? I'm touched.'

His throat constricted again. This girl who was fast developing into a young woman, it was five years since he'd rescued her dog from destruction, probably understood better than anyone what it would mean to lose a beloved pet.

He arrived late for dinner that evening, mumbled an apology to his father, and sat down opposite Mary. She hardly dared to look at him, half afraid she might see contempt in his eyes. But the warmth she saw there made her fizzle down to her toes. His eyes burned into hers across the table, turning her insides to jelly.

She declined coffee after dinner and went out onto the veranda, wrapping her thick woollen shawl tightly round her. It was a cold, still night in late October and the moon had just risen. After a few minutes she heard his footsteps behind her. She knew it was him, she always recognised his step. His hand on her waist, his breath on her neck sent a shaft of pleasurable pain through her whole body, making her shudder involuntarily.

'Why are you angry with me, May?'

'I'm not. I....'

'Then why avoid me?'

'I thought you were avoiding me!'

'Why would I avoid you, when I need you so much?' His arm tightened round her waist and he kissed her neck just below the ear. 'We need each other, May. You know we do. I'm afraid I must leave soon. I've been away from Cambridge far too long, it's high time I went back. I'd like to take you with me, but....' He was nibbling her ear, sending shivers down her spine. 'In all fairness, I should speak to Charlotte first. Let's make the most of our time together. Come to my room tonight?'

'No, Colin, I can't....' she gasped.

'Why, my love,' he laughed, turning her round and lifting her chin. She could see the corners of his mouth quivering irrepressibly. 'Isn't it a little late for such prudishness? Anyway I didn't think you cared for all that respectability and convention. But fear not, my intentions are honourable, I shall make you my wife as soon as possible.'

'Your wife! But.... Look, you don't have to marry me just because we....'

'For God's sake!' he exploded, 'Is that what you think? That I'm only asking you because I feel guilty?'

'What about Charlotte?'

He shrugged. 'I'm not married to her yet,' he declared. 'And I've no intentions of ever being so. Look, I know I've got a hell of a cheek asking you to be patient after the way I've treated you, but I think I should speak to Charlotte first. It's the only decent way to go on.'

'You've certainly got a nerve,' Mary agreed. 'What makes you think I'd marry a man who's cast me aside, become engaged to someone else, then broken it off again all in the space of a few months? The despoiling of your reputation needs no assistance from Charlotte, I can tell you!'

'I might have known you'd say that,' he groaned. 'I'm a reformed character, May.'

'Reformed into what?' she laughed, then added more gently. 'I'm delighted you've seen sense over Charlotte, and you're right not to marry her if you can get out of it, but....'

'But what? What the devil must I do to convince you? I know what I must do,' he said, snatching her into his arms and kissing her deeply. 'I'll show you how much I want you, need you. I'll give you a little taster of how it will be when we're married....'

'Don't be absurd, Colin,' she said, struggling to keep her equilibrium. He was fondling her breast, his fingers seeking her nipple, driving all sensible thought from her mind....

'You're mine,' he said, his voice deep with passion. 'We're already married in the eyes of God. You do realise that, my darling, don't you?'

It was true, she reasoned to herself, already feeling weak at the knees. And if he really did want to marry her....

'I suppose I may as well be hung for a sheep as a lamb. But this time,' she warned, 'you can do the prowling around the passages in the dead of night.'

'Of course,' he said, kissing her again. '*Ça va sans dire.*'

Chapter 16

Colin would have delayed his departure indefinitely, for since they'd become lovers it was an even greater effort to tear himself away from Mary. But when he arrived down to breakfast next morning, still warm from her bed, there was news from Cambridge that prompted him to leave in a hurry.

Unable to sleep again after leaving her and returning to his own room in the early hours of the morning, he'd arisen and come downstairs to find two letters waiting for him on the hall table. One had flowery writing he didn't immediately recognise, the other was in Bertie's scribbled hand. He opened this one first.

'…If you're fit enough, my dear fellow, I think, in your own interests, you should get back here as soon as possible. I'm relieved to hear you've "got over" your infatuation for Charlotte, but I'm afraid it won't be as easy as you think to get out of it. Oh, my dear friend, if only you'd listened to us all before. But, no! I promised not to say "I told you so."

How is dear Mary? Pray do give her my kindest regards. You could do a lot worse than to marry her, you know. But I'm afraid you may have to escape to a desert island in order to do so. The prognosis here could scarcely be worse.

From what I hear, they, (I refer to Charlotte's family as well as herself) are sharpening their knives. I suspect that should you try to "escape" nothing short of a pound of flesh, and that of the deadliest kind, will do. Meanwhile you can be sure she'll save her own reputation at your expense, and come out of it smelling of roses, leaving you to stink of the cesspool. I think she already suspects you of infidelity and is determined to get her revenge. I overheard a conversation the other day which made my blood boil, but I could say nothing to defend you. So you'd be well advised to return hastily while you've still got a reputation to defend….'

He turned to the other letter, already guessing who it was from.

'My dear Colin,

I'm sorry to hear you've been ill, but that is really no excuse for not writing. We have been waiting for the last three months to hear from you. Charlotte is beginning to think she is deserted, since she's had no word from you since she left your house in August. It seems a strange way to behave towards your betrothed.

I, too, am anxious to know when we are to begin planning the wedding. I need at least four months notice to make arrangements, clothes to be made, invitations to be sent. Surely you are not going to leave all this to chance? In view of your silence I propose to take matters into my own hands, and suggest Easter Saturday as a provisional date for the wedding. If this does not suit you, please write immediately to one of us suggesting an alternative....'

He told his father during breakfast time, he'd have to leave straight away.

'How would you feel, Father, if I told you I intend to marry Mary?' he threw in, by way of testing the ground. 'Could I count on your support this time?'

Mr Craven almost choked over his porridge.

'But I thought you were engaged to that other female?'

'In a moment of insanity, which I now regret, I did ask her, but I intend to break it off as soon as I get back to Cambridge. Don't look so shocked, Papa, that scheming little witch never loved me. It won't break her heart. Only her pride might be wounded a little. Meanwhile I'd appreciate it if you'd back me up.'

'I'm not pulling your chestnuts out of the fire for you, Colin,' Mr Craven rumbled.

'I'm not asking you to, Father.'

'What does Mary say?'

'Mary? Why she's as keen as mustard,' said Colin, crossing his fingers under the table, knowing full well Mary had not actually agreed to marry him.

'Really? You surprise me, I must say, after the way you've treated her. To tell the truth, Colin, I'm amazed she still loves you. If I was her I'd tell you to jump in the lake.'

'No need to rub my nose in it, Papa.' He refrained from pointing out that if he had not sent her away in the first place, they'd no doubt be married already. 'What I want to know is will we get your blessing?'

Mr Craven looked at him solemnly. 'Well, at least we know Mary would be good for you. She's a fine girl. The very best. And she understands you better than anyone—better than I. And I guarantee, as far as one can, you won't find another who'll love you as well. But there's no rush, is there?'

'I want Mary and I to be married at Christmas. It's all right, we don't want too much fuss—just a small family affair. And it'll save you the expense of a large wedding.'

'Why the unseemly haste?' Mr Craven exclaimed, horrified by the thought of a hurried, hole in the corner marriage. 'People will think you have to get married,' he added, eyeing his son suspiciously. Any whiff of scandal was abhorrent to him. 'Besides, our friends and relations will feel cheated if they're deprived of a grand wedding. They'll think I don't approve. And what's all this nonsense about saving expense. Who d'you think I am? Ebenezer Scrooge!'

Colin couldn't help laughing at his father's indignation.

'I must say I'm glad you've come to your senses regarding that other creature. She wouldn't do at all. It was quite clear what she was after. But you'll have to get rid of her before you can marry Mary, and that won't be easy, I'm afraid.'

'I know,' said Colin, aware of the letters in his pocket. 'For that reason I must ask you not to say anything yet to anyone, not even Mary, until I've settled things with Charlotte.'

He packed hastily, sorted out his papers and things, left a few instructions and said goodbye to Dickon. Finally he went to find Mary to take his leave of her.

'I've come to say goodbye, sweetheart,' he said taking her in his arms.

Her face fell. 'Goodbye! This minute?'

'I'm afraid so. News came from Cambridge this morning. I must get back.'

Her eyes opened wide. 'Not bad news, I hope?'

'Nothing you need worry your pretty head over, my darling.' he said evasively. 'I must go now or I shall be benighted. It gets dark so dashed early these days.' He took her in his arms and kissed her, not caring who saw.

'You look lovely this morning, dearest. Quite radiant,' he said, stroking her cheek with his thumb. 'I'll try to come home one weekend soon. And I'll write as soon as I can.'

He arranged a drinks party in his rooms at Trinity, by way of telling everyone he was back. He invited all his friends, including Rupert Brooke, who was fast becoming famous as a poet and playwright, Mr Prendergast, his old tutor, and of course Bertie. It would have been successful but for the arrival of one uninvited guest.

She stood on the doorstep in the dress he'd bought her to replace the one that was ruined when they fell in the river. He looked at her dispassionately, seeing her for the first time as she really was. She was like a Dresden china doll he thought, exquisitely beautiful to look at, but hard and cold. If she had an inkling he was having second thoughts about marrying her, she showed no sign of it. They stared at each other, eyes locked, for some seconds before either spoke. For the first time he saw in hers the contempt behind the "come hither", and realised with a flash of anger that she'd always despised his susceptibility.

'Come in, Charlotte,' he said in a harsh voice, adding under his breath, 'Could you not have waited until you were invited. I need to speak to you, alone.'

'That's alright, darling,' she said clearly, loud enough so everyone could hear. 'We can be alone after everyone else has gone.' Then, lowering her voice she added, 'Anyway, you ought to have invited me. We are, after all, engaged to be married.'

Colin sighed heavily. This was a bad start. And if an unpleasant scene were to be avoided he'd have to tread softly.

'I'd no idea you were going to be here this year,' he lied.

'Then you should be pleasantly surprised to see me, shouldn't you?' She looked critically at the scar on his face, adding, 'That scar looks quite horrid. It ruins your looks. What a pity.'

Nobody else but Charlotte would make such an unkind remark, he thought, disliking her more than ever. It was incredible to think this was the woman who'd once been able to excite him to fever pitch.

The minute she set foot inside the room full of people out came a different personality, like a chameleon. Why was she not an actress, he wondered, she could have a brilliant career on the stage. For the whole of the party she acted the perfect hostess, handing round trays of things to eat, chatting affably to everyone, hanging on his arm, as if to make the point that they were a couple. She knew she could get away with it because Colin would not make a scene in public.

It was not until the last of the guests, with the exception of Bertie, had gone that she made to leave herself. Colin held her back.

'Charlotte, we must talk. We can't just let things drift on. We have to discuss it.'

She looked at him coldly. 'Discuss what, Colin?'

Why, when faced with the direct challenge, did he become paralysed like a rabbit dazzled by a bright light in the dark, unable to speak? Charlotte's mouth twisted in a cynical smile, and she shrugged, laughing as she walked off, 'When you've decided what you want to discuss with me, Colin, you must let me know.'

When she'd gone he turned to Bertie who'd remained behind.

'Dammit, Bertie, I couldn't say it. I couldn't tell her it was over. What am I to do. Her mother's going ahead with arrangements for an Easter Wedding. I feel like a stoat in a trap.'

'Well, they can hardly have a wedding without a bridegroom,' said Bertie. 'But you must make the situation clear to everyone here, including Charlotte. Take the bull by the horns, old man.'

'Oh, well,' said Colin, with a sigh. 'One good thing's come out of it. You'll be glad to hear I'm cured, Bertie. Completely! She means nothing to me any more. Nothing at all!'

However "taking the bull by the horns" proved an almost impossible task, for Charlotte had become as slippery as an eel, and twice as elusive.

'She's avoiding me,' he complained to Bertie. 'Each time I go round to her lodging I'm told she's out, or she's resting and doesn't wish to be disturbed. She'll wait until I'm surrounded by a group of friends to appear, like a genie out of a bottle, throwing her arms around my neck, but as soon as there's an opportunity for us to be alone she disappears again, as if by magic. D'you know, Bertie, I'm beginning to think she really is a witch.'

Bertie suggested he wrote her a letter.

'But I can't break off an engagement by letter. That's a cowardly thing to do.'

'Let's face it,' Bertie shrugged. 'You're going to get a bloody nose whatever you do. And the longer it goes on the worse it'll be.

'Then I shall have to resort to your suggestion of the desert island, shan't I? Or do you think the Yorkshire moor would be remote enough?'

'Would you throw your reputation to the wind? Give up Cambridge—everything? It's meant so much to you.'

'For Mary?' Colin scarcely hesitated. 'Yes I would.'

Until this moment he had not stopped to analyse it. Suddenly he realised he'd give up everything for Mary, she meant more to him than life itself. But so far he'd given her nothing but pain. She, who'd given him so much ever since he'd known her. He wanted to tell her. He began a letter.

'...Could it be true, that by some miracle you are mine? That we are as man and wife? Or was I dreaming? I ache to hold you in my arms again, to hear you whisper words of love in my ear. Lying alone in my bed at night, if I stretch my imagination I can feel your warm and tender body next to mine, smell the sweet scent of your hair on my pillow....'

Of course he could not send such a letter. If it fell into the wrong hands.... He screwed it up. He'd have to be patient. First... Yes, first he had other matters to settle.

He tried once more to see Charlotte. Somehow it went against the grain to write a letter declaring their engagement off. But why should he have such scruples? If it was the other way around she wouldn't care two hoots. He made up his mind he'd sit on the doorstep until she either came in or out. He took several blankets, preparing for a long vigil. But when he got there he was told that Miss Charlotte had left only the day before, and gone home to her parents' house in Gloucestershire, and would not be back before Christmas.

He broke into a cold sweat at the thought of following her to Gloucestershire, facing, not only Charlotte, but her parents as well. It would be like walking into a lions' den at meal time. And unlike Daniel, who had the Lord's protection, he'd be a Roman sacrifice!

He'd take Bertie's advice, after all.

It took hours and tons of discarded paper, before he was satisfied that he'd explained, as tactfully as he could, that he'd made a mistake, and that it was better if he and Charlotte did not get married.

****

Mary waited anxiously for news of Colin. Each morning she'd rush downstairs to inspect the letter rack only to find a handful of official letters for Mr Craven. Old doubts wormed their way back into her mind. Did he really want to marry her, or was he doing it to appease his conscience?

She'd written to Constance and to Emmeline to tell them she would not be going back there. Constance would want to find someone else to share her flat. Emmeline wrote back.

'I'm delighted to hear things have worked out so well with you and Colin. I knew it would, mark you. Who but I told you he was in love with you? I'm relieved he's asked you to marry him, or you might have been tempted to have an affair with him.' It was uncanny how perceptive the woman was!

'It happens too often, these days, and men think they can get away with it... I've heard some of them talk about women being their equal—and they are the worst offenders—but woe betide the woman who takes him at his word and shares his bed. I've seen it happen time and again, as you well know. Women are sorely tried these days....'

She was hearing Madame de Bergerac all over again.

'I don't think they mean to be beastly. It's just that underneath their avowed liberalism there's a puritanical streak. They're afraid that if a girl can be seduced once, she could as easily be taken by someone else and she might become wayward. I know how they think from talking to Freddie. Men are hunters, and the chase is more exciting than the kill.

'Dear me, I've just re-read this letter and it sounds horribly like a lecture. Take no heed, my dear. I hasten to add, before you become too disillusioned, none of it applies to marriage....'

Disillusioned? She was devastated. She'd said nothing in her letter to Emmeline about the intimacy between herself and Colin, only that he had asked her to marry him, yet she had put her finger immediately on the pulse. She was an amazing woman.

But her comments stabbed at Mary's conscience, even twisting the knife a little. Colin was no different from any other man. Had he already lost respect for her? Was that why he was taking his time about confronting Charlotte?

Then one morning the long awaited letter arrived.

'...I can hardly believe it, that you are mine. Did it really happen? Already it's like a dream. I can't think what took me so long, or why I've been so blind. When I got back here I found, in my jacket pocket, a handkerchief of yours. It smells of you, so I sleep with it under my pillow. I wish I could exchange it for its owner!

'It seems like a lifetime since I left you. I've delayed writing, hoping to have better news, but the fact is I haven't managed to see C. yet. I think she's avoiding me.'

The letter ended with a P.S. 'Have you read *Room with a View* by E. M. Forster? I'll send you a copy, also a signed copy of Rupert's latest book of poems.'

****

Charlotte let out a squeal of rage when she opened Colin's letter. 'How dare he! He won't get away with this!' she spat venomously. 'If he thinks he can drop me and marry that trollop of a cousin of his, he's got another guess coming.'

It wasn't that she cared about Colin. She didn't want him any more—there were bigger fish in the sea than Colin Craven—and since his illness he'd become staid and dull. She was bored with him. But he'd had the audacity to break it off, depriving her of that pleasure. He'd committed the atrocity of wounding her pride. If she had been queen of some exotic country in times gone by she'd have had him boiled in oil, and Mary too. Or better still she'd make her watch Colin die first, knowing the same fate awaited her afterwards. But as it was she could do nothing. She was not a queen and England was a civilized country.

But wait. There was a way....

A slow smile crept over her face as she thought of how she would get her revenge on both Colin and Mary, and a wicked plan began to form in her devious little mind. She tore up his letter into tiny little bits and threw them into the fire. She would carry on as if nothing had happened. Who was to say she'd ever received his letter? The post was not always to be relied upon. All she had to do now was to wait for the net to close around her erstwhile lover.

****

Mary looked despondently out of the window. Why did she have a feeling of foreboding? She should be deliriously happy. Only this morning she'd had a letter from Colin saying he'd be home in just over two weeks.

It had been a loving letter, but for some reason she had an uncomfortable feeling he was not telling her everything? He'd escaped from Charlotte's clutches, it seemed, with remarkable ease, far too easily in fact. She felt his letter in her pocket, and got it out to read again. Already she knew it by heart.

'...I've found the most delightful cottage in a village a little way out of Cambridge. It has a pretty little garden. I think you'll love it. Tomorrow I shall visit my solicitor with a view to purchasing it. I can't believe I shall see you again so soon. It seems as though we've been parted for years, but it's only because time drags for me here without you....'

He scarcely gave it a chance to drag. Indeed he seemed set upon filling it with reckless, thrilling adventure?

'There's a fellow here who's building a proper aeroplane. I've offered to give him a hand in the hopes that I might get a crack at a test flight some time....'

He was crazy! Now he was trying to kill himself!

Impetuous, impossible and utterly incurable, dear Colin. Being married to him would be like lying on a bed of roses, the flowers delicious and sweet, but the thorns.... He'd be demanding, possessive, draining her of every ounce of love she had to give. It would be like having a husband and child all in one. He'd take her for granted, knowing she'd always love him. She knew him too well. Yet she knew she couldn't live without him.

The rain beat relentlessly against the window pane. It hadn't stopped for the last three days and she'd been unable to get out in the garden. Perhaps that was why she felt depressed.

She hated being stuck in the house, whatever the time of year.

Outside she heard the unmistakable sound of a motor car crunching on the drive, and her heart lurched. Not many people round here had motor cars. But there was no reason to expect Colin so soon. It turned out to be one of those stumpy vehicles favoured by doctors, but it did not belong to their doctor. Looking down from her bedroom window, she couldn't see the face of the man who got out of the car. Then she heard her uncle greet him in the hall.

'Geoffrey! This is a surprise. Do come in.'

Geoffrey Craven, who was her uncle's first cousin, had been the doctor who'd attended Colin during his long illness as a child. Colin had always disliked him, maintaining that he'd deliberately kept him from recovering because he wanted him to die, so that he and his family would inherit Misselthwaite. Mary had always thought that idea was a little uncharitable, though there was no love lost between her and the doctor either.

She peeped over the banister, hoping he hadn't seen her. He was a short fat man, with a silly little goat's beard, compared with her uncle who was tall and lean and always looked distinguished. The doctor was always slightly scruffy, and wore a harassed look.

'May I ask what you've come all this way for, Geoffrey?'

'I need to speak to you, Archie. In private. Is there anywhere we can....'

'Come into my study.'

She waited until the two men were out of sight. She really did not want to meet the doctor if she could avoid it. She'd been waiting all morning to get outside, and now it had stopped raining at last. She had to pass the study to get to the cloakroom where boots and coats were kept, so she tiptoed past the door, which she found to be slightly ajar, so as not to be heard. She was about to hurry past when the following words stopped her in her track.

'I hope Colin's not still thinking of marrying Mary.' It was the doctor who spoke.

Mr Craven shrugged. 'Don't ask me. He doesn't confide in me these days.'

'But you wouldn't allow it, Archie, surely?'

'I couldn't stop him if I wanted to. He's an adult, now. And anyway, what is it to you, Geoffrey? Unless,' Mr Craven laughed softly. 'You're aspiring to marry him off to your daughter Eleanor.'

Mary remembered Colin telling her, years ago, about how the doe-eyed Eleanor had chased him, and that her father had encouraged it. If Geoffrey Craven had ever cherished a secret hope that his family might inherit Misselthwaite, it was surely revived when his daughter showed signs of affectionate feelings towards her cousin.

'That's not funny, Archie. Oh, I know she was sweet on him, but I never took it seriously, and with such a taint in the family....'

'A taint in our family? You're exaggerating, you old fool.'

'May I remind you,' the doctor warned, 'Gertrude Lennox is also related to Colin. She is your wife's cousin, Archie, in case you'd forgotten. But don't worry, she's too distant to affect Colin, so long as he marries fresh blood. I discussed all this with you a long time ago, remember, when Colin wanted to run off with Mary. You told me then you'd never allow them to marry.'

'That was years ago. And I stopped it more because they were so young than for any other reason. But if they want to marry now....'

'Tush! You could influence Colin. Look, you asked me about Gertrude because, I imagine, you are concerned. Well, I'm telling you, and my opinion has not changed in the last four years. Archie, it's well established now in medical circles, that any hereditary weakness is ten times more likely to come out in the offspring of closely related couples. And there isn't a closer relationship, at least not within the law, than first cousins. Did you know, by the way,' he added, with relish, 'Mabel and Gertrude's parents were also first cousins?'

There was a pregnant silence. Then her uncle spoke.

'You've been busy in your investigations, Geoffrey,' said Mr Craven sardonically. 'Oh very well, I'll write to Colin. It's right he should be told. But I'd like to get one thing clear. Are you sure this dementia Gertrude's suffering from is hereditary? Couldn't it simply be senility? She is, after all, seventy.'

The doctor shook his head. 'I'm afraid not. She has all the symptoms of congenital dementia. She's been getting steadily worse for the last ten to fifteen years. I've had to arrange for her to be committed. Mabel was against it, but I know she finds it increasingly difficult to cope with her. A few weeks ago, she was found wandering along the beach in her nightdress, singing at the top of her voice, at midnight! But that's not the worst. There was the incident when she chased the cook round and round the kitchen table brandishing a carving knife, and cackling like a hag. Needless to say the cook left immediately. Poor Mabel!'

At that moment Mary heard footsteps in the hall. It wouldn't do to be found eaves-dropping. She hastily put on her boots, hat and coat and hurried out into the garden, taking great gulps of fresh air. She must sit down. She felt suddenly very sick. It must be the shock.

Did Colin know about this mad cousin? If only he was here to talk to. Would he still want to marry her? Was there really any danger to their children? Perhaps they could avoid having them. She knew that was possible, but she loved children and wanted them very much. She pondered over this. Did she still want to marry him? Yes! Without hesitation, she'd marry him whatever the risk, if the choice were hers alone. But Colin would want an heir, and so would his father, for Misselthwaite.

There was that queasy feeling again. What was it? It came and went. She could barely face meals, yet she felt better when she'd eaten. And it was worse first thing in the morning. She'd go to her room and lie down. And later, when she felt better, she'd write to Colin.

Chapter 17

'My dear fellow, I should be honoured to be your best man,' said Bertie. 'But are you sure you want to risk it?'

'Risk it? What d'you mean?'

'It's just that I'm a superstitious old devil,' Bertie chuckled. 'Thought, after what happened last time you and Mary tried to get married…. Don't want to be a Jonas.'

'It wasn't your fault it didn't come off last time. Besides, there's nobody else, except Dickon. But you'd look better among the stuffy old relations. There's only one thing that bothers me. There's been a resounding silence from Charlotte since I wrote to her. I can't believe she's accepted defeat just like that.'

'What if she hasn't had your letter? Can't always depend on the post, you know.'

There was a gentle tap on the door and a pink faced young undergraduate poked his head round it and addressed Colin.

'Excuse me, sir, but Mr Prendergast sent me to tell you he'd like a word with you at your convenience.'

Colin looked at Bertie, who said, 'You'd better go now. I'm off anyway.'

When he entered his tutor's study, Dick Prendergast stood with his back to him, gazing out of the window. Just before he turned to face him, Colin's eye caught a glimpse of an embossed card sitting on his desk. Though he couldn't read the words very well upside down, the flowery writing was unmistakable, and his stomach turned six somersaults.

'Colin,' said Mr Prendergast, with a huge twinkle in his eye. 'Determined to be married, I see. But you'd better make up your mind, my dear fellow, whether it's to be Mary at Christmas or Charlotte at Easter. For clearly you cannot marry 'em both.'

'Oh, God,' Colin muttered, going red in the face.

'I don't think He'll help you. He's not keen on bigamy. Seems you're in rather a mess.'

His spirits were not improved when, on his way back to his rooms he was hailed from across the road by Rupert Brooke.

'Hey, Colin. Just had an invitation to your wedding at Easter. But you told me you'd ended it with Charlotte.'

He wondered how many more invitations had been handed out. It was his own fault. Mrs Denzel-Fitch had said she'd go ahead with plans if she didn't hear from him. He should have written to her as well as Charlotte. But what was the little witch playing at? She must have had his letter. He didn't harbour the same mistrust of the postal system as Bertie. There was nothing for it but to leave immediately for Gloucestershire. And please God might he have the protection afforded to Daniel.

At the same time as Colin was racing towards Gloucestershire, Mary was writing to him from Misselthwaite, telling him about the doctor's visit and mad cousin Gertrude.

'I realise this may raise a question about our marriage,' she wrote. 'And I must know how you feel, how you really feel. Whether or not we have children—at first you might decide against it, but then later you may change your mind. And then, should we risk it, and your son turned out to be an imbecile, how would you feel? I know how you'd feel. You'd blame me, oh yes you would, and you'd hate me for it.

'I've always been afraid that if I loved you too much, I'd lose you. At the same time I couldn't bear to think that one day you might hate me. And I can't help wondering why, if God intends us to marry, He has put so many obstacles in our way.

'It's just as well you're coming home next weekend, for we have much to talk about...'

If only she could shake off this perpetual feeling of nausea. It must be her nerves. She must pull herself together.

She'd scarcely posted the letter when she received one from Colin saying he'd have to postpone his weekend home for a couple of weeks. There was something important he must do, and it meant he must be elsewhere that weekend. She was disappointed but not unduly alarmed, until, a day later, two letters arrived, both written in the same flowery handwriting. One was addressed to her, the other was for her uncle.

'D'you recognise the writing?' she asked him as she handed Mr Craven his.

He shook his head. 'Never seen it before.'

'Mine feels like a card. Perhaps it's an invitation from our neighbour, the new owner of Lodbury Hall.' She tore it open, then let out something between a yelp and a gasp when she saw what it was.

An invitation to Colin's wedding! To Charlotte!

Till All The Seas Run Dry

'It's a mistake,' she gasped, disbelief being the only emotion she could register at first.

Mr Craven, when he saw her reaction, reached for his and opened it. His hand flew to his mouth and he sat staring at it, speechless, for some moments. There was a letter included in his, which he handed to her in grave silence.

'Dear Mr Craven,' it read. 'I've written to Colin confirming that his marriage with Charlotte will take place on Easter Saturday as we agreed. And since I have had no reply from him to the contrary, I have sent the first batch of invitations and begun making arrangements. I've enclosed a list of guests whom I propose to invite, and I'd appreciate it if you'd let me know if there are any members of your family missing from the list, or any other friends you would have included....'

She could not read any more for the words began to dance around the page. There was a loud ringing in her head, and a feeling of nausea, the room heaved as if she was in a rough sea. *"I've written to Colin confirming that his marriage with Charlotte will take place on Easter Saturday as we agreed...."*

'Are you alright, my dear?' Mr Craven's voice sounded a long way off.

She couldn't answer, she could neither speak nor move. She knew she was about to pass out for the first time in her life, and a moment later she slithered onto the floor.

'Dear me!' Mr Craven exclaimed, jumping up from his chair and bending over her.

She came to, to find herself on her bed. She had a vague recollection of being carried upstairs, but with consciousness a sinking feeling in her stomach brought her back to reality. Someone was bending over her, Martha this time, looking anxious.

'I've brought you a cup of strong, sweet tea, Miss Mary. Mrs Loomis says 'tis th' best thing for shock.'

Her tongue stuck to the roof of her mouth but she managed to say, 'Thank you, Martha.'

'Mr Craven's that worrit about you. He carried you upstairs hissen an' laid you down on bed.'

She remembered now why she'd fainted and the full recollection of that dreadful invitation, and in particularly the letter, hit her stomach, curdling the tea.

'Quick, Martha! A basin!'

Fortunately Martha's reactions were quick enough to save the bed linen.

She still couldn't believe Colin had reneged on her, yet a woman like Mrs Denzel-Fitch wouldn't lie, surely? If Colin had intended to break off his engagement to Charlotte, why had he not answered that vital letter? She remembered his letter to her, a loving letter, telling her about the pretty house and so on. Would he have said all that if he meant to marry Charlotte? Yet if something had gone wrong why had he not mentioned it? It simply didn't make sense.

'We must send him a telegram, Martha.' She scribbled a message on a piece of paper.

INVITATION ARRIVED FROM CHARLOTTE'S MOTHER STOP LET ME KNOW AT ONCE WHAT'S GOING ON

Martha bicycled to the post office and dutifully sent off the telegram. She couldn't believe, either, that Colin intended to desert Mary. She knew full well what had been going on between them, and if her suspicions were correct Mary was in serious trouble. She couldn't blame the mistress. She'd watched her eating her heart out for him for the last six months or more, probably longer than that, for she didn't believe she'd forgotten him while she was away in France. And she knew what it was like to love a man like that.

She thought with an aching heart of Will Daley, whose memory was still so dear to her. She'd almost succumbed, as Mary had, before he'd gone off to fight for Queen and country and never returned. After she'd heard of his death at the siege of Mafeking she wished she'd given herself to him. She was certain he'd have married her, had he come back from South Africa, but now she had nothing but the memory of what might have been.

But Colin was not off to war, and she wanted to believe he was honourable. She'd grown fond of the young master who'd improved so much since Mary had come into his life. He owed everything he was to her. How could he forsake her now?

If he knew she was pregnant he'd give up that strumpet, surely? He should never have got tangled with such a spoiled, pampered creature. She wondered if Mary was aware of her condition. Should she tell her? Should she tell him? She thought about rewording the telegram in such a way as to make him come home, but she was not clever like that, not with words. And the mistress might be angry. If she lost her place for being so bold, what would her mother do? Mother needed the wages she brought home to live on.

She'd like to have talked to her mother about it. Mother was discretion itself, she'd be able to help the mistress. But how and when could she visit her. Her next day off—she only had one a month—was not for another ten days.

Mary waited anxiously for a reply to her telegram, but the days passed. She remembered the interview she'd overheard between the doctor and her uncle regarding cousin Gertrude, and the letter she'd written expressing her own doubts. A cold sensation engulfed her. Could it have been her letter that had influenced his decision? No. There had not been time. Then another unwelcome thought crossed her mind. What if Mr Craven had already warned Colin? He'd evidently discussed the dangers before with the doctor. She suddenly remembered a remark Colin had once made, '...*we should not marry, you and I ... scientific evidence that children born to close relations....*' Had the prospect of imbecile children put him off? In that case why had he not been honest with her about it? Why had he not written? And why had Mr Craven said nothing about it?

There were more shocks in store, for a day or two later she received another letter, this time from Charlotte herself.

'Dear Mary, ...I feel a little awkward about this, but I think I ought to tell you that Colin is here with us, and he doesn't want to write to you himself. He says he couldn't put it well in a letter, so he'd rather tell you when he next sees you. But I don't think that's fair. I know if it was me, I'd want to know straight away. In any case, you must be wondering why he has not come home this weekend. The fact is he came here to talk to me, to make a confession about his little indiscretion with you. Doubtless he thought I wouldn't forgive him, but of course I have. How could I not? And incidentally I forgive you too.

'He thinks he ought to marry you, he feels obligated, but I told him he shouldn't. I hope you don't mind me saying this but if it was me, I wouldn't want a man to marry me out of obligation. He doesn't love you, Mary, at least not in that way. He told me, he loves me.

'The wedding is to be at Easter. Well, you must know that by now—no doubt you've received the invitation. Mother is determined it shall be a splendid affair....'

She didn't faint this time, but she felt very cold and began to shiver violently. It occurred to her that Charlotte might have made it all up, though it was almost too vindictive, even for her. But this last hope perished when later that evening, she received a reply to her telegram, which verified Charlotte's letter, inasmuch as it confirmed Colin's whereabouts.

It said: COLIN VISITING CHARLOTTE STOP DONT WORRY ALL FOR BEST BERTIE.

If Colin was with her, even Charlotte, were she the most compulsive liar in the world, would not have dared to write such a letter unless it was in part true. She could only conclude that he was a weak willed, moral coward, who'd changed his mind about marrying her because of the congenital madness, and faced with the inevitable pressure from Charlotte and her family, had taken the line of least resistance. In any case she was well rid of him. How could she marry anyone so pliable? She wanted to die. She lay on her bed listlessly, unable to eat or sleep.

Mr Craven became anxious about her. 'I don't know what to do,' he told Mrs Medlock. 'She must be tempted to eat something, anything. Tell Mrs Loomis to put her mind to it. I can't think what's got into Colin,' he muttered more to himself. 'I've never felt so ashamed of him. And yet it's so unlike him….' He shook his head.

'Tha mun eat, Miss Mary,' Martha coaxed. 'I've brought some nice soup. Mrs Loomis made it special. If tha don't eat tha'll get so weak th' bairn inside thee'll die.'

Mary, who'd appeared to be lifeless, jumped up at mention of the word 'bairn.'

'What! But I'm not….' she gasped breathlessly. But she knew Martha was right. It had not occurred to her before, but she realised on reflection that her monthly visitor was well overdue. Indeed she had not had one since Colin had left. Why on earth had she not noticed? And as Martha hastened to explain the sickness she'd been suffering from for the last fortnight and the fainting were all symptoms of her condition.

It took a few minutes for the full implications of her situation to sink in. She was going to have a baby, and she was not married! And now Colin had deserted her. A stark vision of poor Lucy Styles, head bent, penitent, in tears, sprang vividly to mind. What if people were to hear about her condition, people like Bartholomew or Waverley?

The thought made her break into a cold sweat. Oh God! What on earth was she to do?

This fear of discovery concentrated her mind and drove away her previous apathy. She must get away—right away from here to somewhere where nobody knew her. That ruled out most of the places she first thought of. It was no good thinking she could go to London, though Emmeline and Constance would almost certainly offer her support. But if Lady Grantham should hear of it...! And it would be the first place Colin would look for her. And she did not want him to find her. The last thing she wanted was to trap him into marriage, particularly in view of Gertrude.

Neither could she go to France. How could she face Madame de Bergerac? She was a kind and understanding lady, but Mary could not endure for her to know. No. She must find a refuge where nobody would think of looking for her, and where her true identity would not be discovered, where she could begin a new life.

If Martha had guessed about her condition whom else might? Though, as her personal maid, she had intimate knowledge of her. Martha wouldn't betray her. Heaven be praised Mr Craven thought her 'sickness' was due to the shock she'd had. But she did not have much time. He'd already suggested calling the doctor.

'Martha!' She tried to get up off the bed, but the room went dark and she felt giddy. It was weakness, of course, from lack of food. This would not do. Martha was right, she must eat for the sake of the baby.

'Yes, Miss Mary?'

'You must promise not to tell a living soul about this, Martha. And I must leave here as soon as possible. We must devise a plan.'

'Aye, Miss Mary, tha can trust me for sure. But... Would tha mind Mother knowing? She knows more about bairns than me.'

Mary thought for a moment. Susan Sowerby was the nearest she had to a mother, she didn't doubt she'd be sympathetic, and it would be comforting to have her warm and loving shoulder to cry on, but what would that good woman think of her? And what could she do practically? What had she been able to do for Lucy Styles?

She shook her head. 'I'm sure your mother would be most discreet, but I'd rather you didn't tell anyone.'

'Mother'll not tell a living soul, Miss Mary. An' she can help thee. She knows all about th' herbs tha can take to...'

'I'm not getting rid of this baby, Martha, if that's what you're suggesting.'

'Of course not, Miss Mary, if tha've a mind to keep it. I were only trying to help.'

'I know,' said Mary, gently, holding out her hand to the girl. 'And I'm so grateful to you. I don't know what I'd do without you. We must be careful, Martha. I don't want you to lose your place.'

After the initial shock had worn off, a bitter aching regret swept over her. If she and Colin had been married, how wonderful it would be to discover she was carrying his child—that his seed was strong in her. She could feel his life in her! A little miracle. The notion that she would not be losing him entirely, that she'd still have a part of him in his child, invigorated her, and she began eating properly again quite soon she was looking better.

Martha suggested that if she was set upon keeping the baby it was even more important to let her family help and shelter her. She was sure her sister 'Lizabeth Ellen, who lived in Scarborough, would help, and our Dickon....

'I'd rather you didn't tell Dickon,' Mary said.

Martha looked hurt. 'Don't tha trust him, Miss Mary? Our Dickon loves thee, he'd never let thee down.'

'But I don't want him to be disgusted with me. I feel so ashamed, Martha.'

'There's no need, Miss Mary. It in't your fault. If it's anyone's it's Master Colin's.'

'Hush Martha! Someone might hear. That's where you're wrong. Men are such silly, weak creatures when it comes to sex, it's up to us women to keep it under control. And I've failed miserably. I've no intentions of involving your family in my misfortune. I have a plan of my own anyway. I can't tell it you, then you won't be tempted to tell anyone after I've gone. Now don't look so downcast, Martha. The world is not going to end because I'm leaving.'

'I want to go with thee, Miss Mary.'

'What, and never see your family again? Besides, I won't be able to afford to keep you.'

Martha broke down in tears.

'Oh, Martha,' said Mary, taking her in her arms.

It was dull and overcast the day she and Dickon said goodbye. They'd arranged to meet in the secret garden. She looked wistfully into his eyes, those clear blue eyes she'd known since her very beginnings, it seemed. She'd been so busy making plans and carrying them out, it hadn't sunk in until this moment, that she would never see him again, or any of them.

Dickon thought it was the worst day of his life. It was a travesty, his beloved Mary, in this situation through no fault of her own and he, powerless to help her. He'd married Molly to protect her and her child, out of the kindness and generosity of his heart, and now here was Mary in the same predicament, and he could do nothing for her. He could not bear to think of her, alone and vulnerable, with the shame of an illegitimate child to bear. She would never know, for he could never tell her, how much he loved her. If he'd been free he'd have gladly taken care of her, called her child his own. But now it was too late.

He looked at her hands, so small and slender, smooth and fine, compared with his large rough ones in which they lay. He stroked the backs of hers with his thumbs, and he felt something warm and wet fall on one of his. Then seeing that she was in tears, he put his arms round her and kissed her gently on both cheeks, tasting the salt tears. She wept as if the river had finally burst its banks, burying her face in his chest. To his supreme joy she responded to his caresses, whispering his name so lovingly in his ear, and he held her until her weeping subsided.

He stroked her face, wiping away the tears, and kissed her again. 'If I were free....'

She put her fingers on his lips to silence him. 'Wishing won't change anything.'

'I'd never let thee go. Never let thee out o' my sight.'

'I'll never forget you, Dickon. And I'll always love you. Remember that.'

It was all he could do when he put her on the train, watched it draw away until it passed out of sight, not to give way to the tears that made his throat and eyes ache, not to jump on the train and go with her. She looked so small, so alone, so defenceless as she stood at the window of the railway carriage waving to him....

Only when he could no longer see the train, when he heard, from far in the distance, its whistle blow, did Dickon close his eyes, letting the tears spill over and roll down his cheeks.

Chapter 18

Once Colin had managed to extricate himself from the clutches of the Denzel-Fitch family, he made for home as fast as possible. He knew he'd have a lot of explaining to do, both to Mary and his father. If Charlotte went ahead and sued him for breach of promise, as she was threatening to do, his father would be furious—he was allergic to scandal—and Colin would have to sell everything that was his to pay for it. He'd be finished at Cambridge, of course. Better to leave now before he was thrown out. Maybe Bertie's suggestion of a desert island was not such a bad idea after all. Or else he could join the army, which was what his father had wanted him to do in the first place. Yet he was confident that Mary, as soon as she realised what a sacrifice he'd made, would fall forgivingly into his arms.

But when he reached Misselthwaite he found his father was preoccupied with something much more serious than a little scandal. He was greeted by pandemonium as soon as he entered the house. There was a detective interviewing all the servants, and Martha was in floods of tears.

'What on earth's going on?' he demanded of Mrs Medlock. 'Where's my father? And where's Miss Mary?'

'Oh, sir,' said the housekeeper in a hushed voice. 'Your father's lying down. Please don't disturb him. He's been unwell ever since....' she broke off, wringing her hands. 'And as for Miss Mary, why she's the cause of it all. She's disappeared, sir!'

A sickening thought sprang into Colin's mind. Mary had gone riding and not returned. She'd had an accident or she was lost on the moor, though the latter was unlikely.

'Don't be absurd, Medlock. How can she have disappeared. You mean she's gone away without telling anyone where she was going?'

'I wish it were as simple as that, sir. But it's not. It was that note she sent your father. But you'd better speak to that detective. He'll explain.'

A detective! A chill ran down his spine. Why had a detective been called in? Unless....

'I don't know, sir. That's what I'm trying to find out,' said the detective tersely. 'Who did you say you are? Oh, yes, you're the son, aren't you. How d'you do, Detective Inspector Manson, at your service, sir.'

Colin was stunned. He wanted to ask a million questions but all he could do was blurt out, 'You...you don't think my cousin is...dead....'

'I don't know, sir. We haven't found her yet. But her disappearance, the circumstances, and the tone of the letter she left your father....'

'That letter. Can I see it.'

'I can't let you have it, I'm afraid, sir. It's the only lead we've got. Maybe after the Inquest....'

'An inquest! Surely you don't suspect....'

'Suicide? It seems likely, sir, but until we find a body....'

'Suicide! But that's absurd!' Icy fingers twisted his guts. This was not really happening. It must be one of his ghastly nightmares. 'Why on earth would she kill herself?'

The detective shrugged, looking at him curiously. 'I was hoping you might be able to answer that one, sir. But until we find her we're not ruling out anything, abduction, murder or accident.'

Colin put a hand against the door frame to steady himself. Nothing made sense. He went to find Martha. The girl was distraught, sobbing and crying, and he got very little sense out of her.

'I don't kn...know, sir,' she stammered. 'I know nothing.'

'But why does everyone think...? I'm sorry, Martha,' he added, seeing the anguished expression on the maid's face. 'I know this must be painful for you. It's painful for me, too, God dammit! But please....' he clenched his fists in an effort to control a rising hysteria. He must be patient. He'd get nothing out of her if he lost his temper. 'D'you know what was in the note she wrote my father? Why has he called the police?'

'It were a farewell note, one as you'd write if you knew you'd never see a body again. An' she left all sorts o' instructions. Oh, Master Colin it were like as if it were her Will. An' she didn' turn up at Scarborough....'

'Scarborough? Why was she going there?'

'We tried to help her but she wouldn't let us. She said she had plans of her own, but I never thought....' She clapped her hand over her mouth as if she thought she'd said too much.

'Martha, I'm trying very hard, but I don't understand why she was running away in the first place? Mary and I were to be married....'

Till All The Seas Run Dry

To his horror this last remark drew a howl of misery from the maid. This was getting him nowhere so he gave up and went to find Dickon.

He wondered why Dickon was so hostile. He might have been hurt had he not been so anxious to get to the bottom of Mary's disappearance. But at least he was able to piece together a few more bits of the puzzle. Dickon had apparently been the last person to see her when he'd put her on the train to Scarborough. She was to have spent a day or two with his sister while she made travelling arrangements for the continent. Dickon thought she was heading for France, but he didn't know for sure, and she'd never arrived at Scarborough. His brother-in-law, Dan Thornton had met every train for the rest of that day.

'I still don't understand,' Colin persisted. 'Why was she leaving?'

Dickon looked at him coldly, and his voice was cutting. 'You sh'd know, sir. It's plain enow, I'd ha' thought.'

'You think it's my fault, don't you? Why? Didn't she tell you I'd asked her to marry me? That I've broken off my engagement to Charlotte?'

A puzzled frown flickered across Dickon's brow, but the condemnation was still in his eyes when he said, 'Everyone thought you'd changed your mind, what with invitations to weddin', your weddin' with Miss Charlotte? An' then Miss Mary got a letter from Miss Charlotte telling her tha'd made up wi' her an' wedding were to go on as planned.'

Colin closed his eyes. 'Oh, no! Oh, dear God!'

So Charlotte had had the final word. She'd stabbed him in the back.

After all he'd been through he'd lost Mary. She'd gone, she might even be dead. And he'd missed her by a matter of days. Couldn't she have waited? Didn't she know he loved her? A sudden memory flashed into his mind—the dream he'd had when he was delirious, Mary killing herself after finding him with another woman. It had been a confused dream, about a different time and place, but now it occurred to him, with a shock, it might have been a premonition. But surely she didn't think.... His throat constricted, his eyes ached with unshed tears, his head reeled.

The next two days became a living nightmare. The police found, in the river, not far from the station next up the line to Scarborough, some of the clothes she'd been wearing the day she left. There was no

Till All The Seas Run Dry

sign of her body, which mystified them, but finding these things prompted them to pursue the search in earnest, and the investigations went on for months.

Colin refused to believe she was dead. Not his brave, his wonderful Mary. She was somewhere, hiding from him and from all of them. But where?

****

Ben Weatherstaff was dying. Not that the old boy minded that very much for he was well into his nineties (nobody knew exactly how old Ben Weatherstaff was, not even Ben Weatherstaff) and he reckoned he'd had enough of this world and was ready for the next. And he'd been asking for Colin.

But the young master was too busy writing letters to people who could not help him, to realise the seriousness of Ben Weatherstaff's condition, or to find time to visit him. He was off to France in search of Mary, he'd visit him as soon as he got back. He believed, in any case, that the old boy was indestructible. Ben Weatherstaff had been ill before and had recovered. So all Dickon's urgent messages went unheeded.

'He's not coming, is he? Th' young master?' Ben Weatherstaff asked Dickon sadly.

'I'm sure he'll come, soon as he can. He's main fond o' thee.' But his voice lacked conviction.

The old man had been getting progressively frailer for some time, and now he was finally confined to bed with a chest infection which was getting no better. Susan Sowerby reckoned it had turned into pneumonia.

'Nay, he's other things on his mind. He's not found her yet, Miss Mary? Have tha heard?'

Dickon shook his head sadly. 'They found her things, week or so ago, int river.'

'Do tha think she's dead?' Ben asked anxiously, wheezing noisily.

'Nay, not our Mary. Not my brave little lass. I reckon she threw 'em clo'es int river on purpose to make 'em think that.'

'Does he know she's wi' child?'

Dickon stared at him in astonishment. 'How d' tha ken?'

'Never mind that. Does he ken, Master Colin? 'Tis his bairn.'

'I don't think so. But it's no use telling him now. There's nowt he can do about it.'

'She were main lovely, th' little lass. I never dreamed she'd grow up like that.' His voice rasped, and Dickon suspected it was not just his bad chest. 'She came to see me—she found time—before she left.'

Was that how he knew? Dickon didn't ask, but he doubted if Mary would have told Ben Weatherstaff when she had not told him, and she was scared of people finding out. It always mystified him where Ben Weatherstaff got his information from. He seemed to know everything that went on, though he could hardly walk and never left his cottage these days. His mind was as bright as a twenty year old.

'Tha'rt not afeared, Ben Weatherstaff? Of dying, I mean?'

'What me! Feared o' dyin'?' He tried to laugh but his chest crackled alarmingly. 'Nay! I sh'd ha' been long gone be now. I'm fed up of this life. Its time I were off.'

'Tha've had a good innings.' Dickon patted him gently on the shoulder.

'Aye, but now I'm ready for a rest. Look at me! Bedridden, useless, can't hardly put one foot afore t'other. I've overstayed me time. But I wish...I wish, afore I go, Master Colin'd come in here like he used to, wi' his Miss Mary.' He was struggling with tears now.

'If tha've a mind to it, a prayer or two 'd not go amiss,' suggested Dickon. 'Do tha know any prayers, Ben Weatherstaff?'

It would not be a bad idea, Dickon reflected, if the old boy was about to meet his Maker. He looked at his watch. He'd been longer than he'd intended. There was someone coming to see him in an hour's time, about a stray kitten found half starved to death, and Molly would be badgering him to get the shopping first. His days off were always busy.

'I'll be off now, Ben Weatherstaff. I'll get your stout while I'm at shop.'

No reply came from the bed so Dickon slipped out.

When he'd gone Ben Weatherstaff lay back on the pillows. Colin and Mary were very much on his mind. He'd never been a great one for praying and was seldom seen inside a church, but he closed his eyes and put his mind to it. But he found himself drifting off....

Soon he was floating several feet above the bed. It was quite a pleasant feeling, and he was breathing easily for the first time for months. Suddenly he was aware that he was not alone. There was a lady in the room with him. She was coming towards him.

He was startled to discover it was Colin's mother, but he was not afraid. She put her hands out to him and called his name.

'Mrs Craven, Ma'am,' he tried to say, but nothing came out. 'Where is Miss Mary?'

'Never mind about Mary,' came Mrs Craven's lilting voice, apparently reading his thoughts. 'It's you I've come for, Ben Weatherstaff. Your time is up.' And she put her hands out to him and he felt himself being pulled....

There was a blackout, and he had the sensation of rushing through a dark tunnel very fast. Next moment he found himself standing beside her, not in that dark, dingy room, but in a grass glade. The sun shone, the grass was very green, and there were all manner of flowers, and bright, bright colours. He looked around and found to his immense joy he was in the secret garden, not as it was now, but looking more beautiful than he'd ever seen it.

But something still troubled him.... Oh, yes, the young couple he'd left behind.

'Mrs Craven, would tha do summit else for me, Ma'am? Spare a thought for poor Master Colin. Miss Mary were his whole life.'

She laughed softly. 'Mary's not dead, Ben Weatherstaff.'

His face brightened. 'Then tha could send her back to him?'

She looked at him rather sadly. 'I'm afraid that's not possible. I cannot influence what happens on earth. All I can say is nothing can sever the bonds of true love, not even death. Love is worth more than all the gold on earth, it's the foundation of all goodness. Without it a person's soul will wilt and die. It's like water to a plant, it makes it grow and blossom. The one who's been mean and selfish all his life may become kind and generous when he finds someone to care for. There's a turning point.

'But wi' respect, ma'am, i'n't there another side of love? I've seen folks do rotten things, husbands beat their wives, them as they're s'posed to love. It's why I stayed a bachelder. An' folks have killed in th' name o' love, out o' jealousy.'

'That's not love, Ben Weatherstaff,' she laughed. 'It's passion, the root of all evil.'

'I thought money were th' root of all evil.'

'Not so much the money itself, more the love of it, because it provokes greed and envy, and everything unpleasant. It's all part of passion, ache to have. Passion and love are opposite ends of the spectrum. But I didn't come here to lecture you. In time you'll understand. Now you may rest awhile. I'll come for you later and show you the work we do here. You see, there are people, those less fortunate than us, who need our help.'

Ben Weatherstaff's face broke into a smile. 'Master Colin and Miss Mary?'

She shook her head. 'They're on earth. I'm afraid we can't help them, not yet. Our work is here with the poor souls who are lost. But in a way you're right. It was because of your unselfish prayer that I was able to help you. Colin has forgotten about prayer for the time being and is giving in to despair. When he remembers it I might be able to help him. Straighten up, Ben Weatherstaff. There's no need to stoop like that any more.'

****

It was Christmas and a full month since Mary's disappearance. It ought to have been a joyful occasion, they were to have been married. Nothing worse could happen to him now, Colin reflected, as he wandered aimlessly round the grounds. He'd come home in order to patch things up with his father, or try to. They'd quarrelled pointlessly, each blaming the other for Mary's disappearance.

He was furious with his father for listening to Dr. Craven. The man was the bane of his life! He'd disliked the doctor, and with good reason, when he was a child, but he'd never wished him any actual ill. But if ever he caught up with him now he'd probably kill him. He warned his father that unless he wished to see his son charged with homicide he'd better keep the doctor out of his way. That whole business about Gertrude was poppy-cock, of course. Everyone knew she was a dipsomaniac. Poor Mabel had been trying to cover it up for years. The old hag had bottles hidden everywhere. It had all come out, of course, when they came to take her away to the asylum.

Mr Craven told him it was his own fault.

'You should never have got mixed up with that vixen, Charlotte, in the first place. What an appalling mess it all is.'

He refused to give up hope of finding Mary. His recovery from his childish illness had turned him into an optimist. He couldn't believe she was dead.

He'd searched all over Europe and written copious letters in an attempt to find her. Neither Constance Livingstone nor Emmeline Pethick Lawrence could help him. He'd visited Madame de Bergerac where he'd learned all about her involvement with Gilles du Pré. Madame was adamant Mary would never go near the man again. He was very taken with the marquise and her two children, and was not surprised Mary was so fond of them. The kind lady made him promise not to give up trying to find her, and to keep her informed of his progress.

From there he'd gone to Switzerland to the convent where Mary had been at school. It was a last ditch hope, that someone might know if Mary had had any close friends she may have turned to. Constance had not been able to help him. Nor could the nuns. They shook their heads sadly. The Mother Superior, a formidable lady whose grey eyes seemed to penetrate one's soul, told him Mary was an independent young madam, very much a loner, though she did have an admirable tendency to defend the underdog, but close friends.... She shrugged. Run away from home had she? Well, she was not altogether surprised. Mary was always a rebel, averse to discipline, difficult to control, very difficult.

He came away wishing he'd not been near the place, since his enquiries had done nothing for Mary's reputation in the convent.

He was dispirited. All this useless travelling, together with a long drawn out legal wrangle with the Denzel-Fitch family, had drained all his resources. He could cheerfully wring Charlotte's neck.

He'd spent most of his inheritance from his mother's Will. He'd even had to sell his car.

'At least I haven't asked you for anything, Father.'

'Tush!' Mr Craven muttered. He didn't like being made to feel mean, but he hoped it would be a lesson to Colin. 'You'll have to earn an honest living, now, instead of playing games at university,' said he tersely. 'Perhaps you'll reconsider joining a regiment as I suggested before. But I don't suppose they'll want you in the Guards after all this scandal.'

'I wouldn't want to be in the Guards, Father. I've already decided I'm joining the Royal Engineers.'

Mr Craven lifted his eyes to the ceiling. The Royal Engineers were not considered to be out of the top drawer, at least not in his day. But Colin had a good reason for choosing the R.E. It was the only corps or regiment that had, as one of its supplementary branches, a ballooning unit. His mania for flying was exceeded only by his obsession about finding Mary.

He didn't care what people said, or that he was the subject of gossip in polite drawingrooms around the place. Some likened him to the Duke of Hamilton, who, legend has it, courted one lady, was betrothed to another and married a third. Hence the reel, Hamilton House. Others called him the dashing white sergeant because he'd been engaged to two women at the same time, then not married either of them. He was talked about below stairs as well.

'He's looking old before his time,' said Mrs Medlock to her friend Betty Barlow. 'And if you ask me he's going exactly the same way as his father before him. He'll end up shutting himself up like he did.'

Indeed he'd followed his father's example in one respect. He'd locked up the secret garden and hidden the key. It held memories that were far too painful, and not only of Mary. Dear old Ben Weatherstaff had passed away. Another friend, whom he'd failed, who's pleas for him to visit had gone unheeded. By the time he'd realised how ill he was it was too late.

He went through the little wicket gate which led to the bluebell wood. How often had he kissed her over this gate, how often had they gathered bluebells, returning with armfuls to the house, Mrs Medlock declaring there were not enough vases to hold them.

There was Dickon, too. That was the unkindest cut of all—the one person with whom he might have shared his grief, his closest friend other than Mary herself—had chosen to ostracise him. He'd tried to reason with him to no avail.

'Why are you punishing me, Dickon.'

'If you don't ken, I'll not bother telling you,' was all he'd say.

It was unlike Dickon to be so unforgiving, and it hurt more than anything.

Thinking of Dickon, he passed by the paddock and there the saddest sight of all met his eyes, for there, looking as forlorn as he felt, was Snowdrop. She came to the fence, braying gently, and bent her head. Was it his fancy or did he see tears in her eyes?

'You're lonely too, aren't you?' he said, stroking her velvet nose. In response she nuzzled him, nibbling his ear with her lips. He put his arms round her neck, patting her, then he buried his face in her mane, as if she were a friend whose shoulder he could cry on. 'We'll go for a romp on the moor later,' he said. That's if he could bring himself to do it.

He made up his mind not to come home again, not until he'd found Mary. And if he never found her.... He would not be like his father, he'd make a new life for himself.

Chapter 19

Mary's first months of exile in Switzerland were not without incident. She'd taken on a new identity hoping to remain incognito, Mary Lennox was dead, now she was Mary Drummond, widow, from Richmond in Yorkshire. It was a familiar location, reducing the risk of being caught out due to lack of geographical knowledge, yet nobody was likely to connect her with Mary Lennox of Misselthwaite Manor, or so she hoped. The story she invented was that her husband had been killed in a climbing accident, and, since she'd fallen out with her family by marrying him, she could not go home now, so she remained in Switzerland with her school friend, Maxine Steinberger.

But she could not stay in Zurich with her friend's parents for long. There was a large British community in that city and sooner or later she might be recognised. Apart from that, her condition would undoubtedly invite comment, once it became apparent. Already she had seen a couple of women exchanging knowing looks when she'd been introduced as Mrs Drummond, recently widowed. No doubt they thought the worst of her, living in Madame Steinberger's house as she was. If they knew she was expecting a baby too....

Madame Steinberger, once a courtesan of considerable beauty, whose marriage to the wealthy Count von Steinberger, had elevated her to a position of great influence and restored her respectability. Indeed the highest in the land, in Europe even, had been guests in her house. Her parties were very popular with Swiss and foreigners, the Austrian and German nobility, ambassadors from all over Europe.

These house parties were as notorious as those in similar English houses. It was well known in certain houses the sleeping arrangements were discreetly designed to accommodate, not only known liaisons, but also Lotharios who could not enjoy a weekend unless wives unaccompanied by their husbands were available along the same landing!

Mary remembered Colin telling her he'd once been to such a house party. She'd have been badly placed in such a situation without a husband at all if it was not for Madame's personal protection. For, despite her own reputation, Madame Steinberger was a fierce custodian, protecting her own young like a tigress. What was acceptable for her guests was forbidden her daughter. Maxine was not allowed to stay up later than midnight. She was not allowed to go out with anyone unchaperoned—even though she was twenty-one. She was packed off to Lake Constance to stay with her aunt for the season. In fact it was jokingly suggested that she wore a chastity belt of which Madame herself held the key, and if anyone wished to court her they'd have to confront the formidable lady first.

She could not, of course, afford the same protection to Mary, since she was supposed to be a widow, and was therefore experienced—no girlish virgin. In the eyes of fashionable European society she'd be deemed to be fair game. So it was decided that the best way to protect her was to hide both the girls away in the Steinberger's alpine retreat. But before these plans could be carried out something happened which might have caused Mary's immediate exposure, and which was to have repercussions later on.

That she was near to tears a great deal of the time during those first weeks did not arouse speculation. After all she was a widow whose husband had been recently and tragically killed. In fact the pathetic figure she cut gave authenticity to her story.

Christmas was the worst. She was homesick as well as being grief-stricken about Colin. And seeing the English boys from the Embassy who swarmed around Maxine only made matters worse. They were all in love with Maxine. She was certainly very beautiful. She had long, silky black hair, a clear soft complexion and eyes like sapphires. She was vivacious, too, and her broken English quite delighted the young bucks. They were all invited to spend Christmas with the Steinbergers—Madame's idea, to make Christmas a little livelier for Mary.

There was one young man called Basil Crawford who, despite his desire to make his mark with Maxine, took time to sit with Mary and try to cheer her up. He sat down beside her on the floor and proceeded to try to draw her out.

'Tell me about yourself, Mrs Drummond. How did you come to be here?'

'Maxine and I are old friends. We went to school together.'

'But you're not the same age, are you?' Mary found his obvious disbelief galling.

'I am a year or two older. But we are still good friends.'

'All the same, I'd have thought, at a time like this, you'd want to be in the bosom of your own family. Have you no parents, brothers or sisters?'

Mary shook her head. 'My parents died when I was ten.'

Till All The Seas Run Dry

'But you must have some family.'

'I fell out with my guardian,' she explained. 'He didn't approve of my marriage.'

'Oh, I see.'

After an awkward silence he resumed the conversation this time talking about himself.

'I'm lucky in that respect, if you can call it lucky. Mine's a rather large family. There are seven of us. I spent much of my childhood in India.'

'India!' Mary exclaimed, without thinking. 'I was born there.' What harm could there be in talking about things that happened so long ago, she thought.

'Really?' The young man was delighted. At last he'd found some common ground. 'Well, that's a coincidence. So was I. Do you remember much about it?'

'Quite a lot. I lived there until I was ten, when my parents died in a cholera epidemic.'

Another silence. She almost felt sorry for the young man who was trying so hard to cheer her up, and the conversation kept coming back to death. But now he was looking at her curiously.

'And that was when you came to live in Yorkshire,' he said slowly.

'Yes, Richmond,' said Mary, hurriedly changing the subject back to India. 'Why were you in India? Was your father stationed there, in the army, or the foreign office?'

'No, no,' he laughed. 'Far from it. He was a clergyman, a missionary.'

'Oh!' She was taken aback. She'd been thinking for some time there was something vaguely familiar about the young man's features, and now a bell rang loudly in her mind. 'Where about did you live?'

'It was a place called Sengalhi, in the hills, a beautiful place. Our bungalow was always overcrowded, and not simply because there were seven of us. My parents were always taking in strays, women and children. The house was always full of children.'

'Natives?' Mary asked tentatively, her suspicions growing by the minute.

'No, no,' Basil laughed. 'They were British. People used to send their children to the hills for health reasons at certain times of the year to escape from the heat and disease of the cities. And once, during the mutiny, the house was full of refugees. Fortunately we had a large garden in which we could roam freely. There was a temple tree, I remember, its bell-like, creamy flowers had an unforgettable fragrance. I used to love to climb it. Being the youngest it was the only way I could gain an advantage over the others. Once at the top I was king of all I surveyed. Why are you looking at me in that strange way?'

Now the last bit of the puzzle fitted into place and she could see the whole picture.

'Basil Crawford,' she muttered under her breath. 'Of course.' She was not sure whether it was his account of the overcrowded bungalow, filled with children from the heat and disease ridden cities, or if it was mention of the tree with the exquisitely fragrant cream coloured flowers, but a vivid recollection came back to her. She pictured the house belonging to the clergyman and his large family where she'd been taken after her parents died, until she was brought home on the boat to go and live at Misselthwaite. Her life had gone full circle.

'Have we met before, Mrs Drummond?'

'No, I don't think so,' she said hastily, her heart pounding like a drum. But her heightened colour belied her denial. Well she remembered gathering the divinely scented flowers, sometimes called frangipani, which formed a creamy carpet beneath the tree he called a temple tree, planting them in the ground to form a garden of her own. It was the beginning of her interest in gardens, and the boy, with freckles and a cheeky turned up nose, up the tree, taunting her, singing, Mistress Mary, quite contrary!

And this was the boy! She glanced furtively at his features again. Yes, it could be. And to meet him here, in her present predicament....

'Mary,' he said, half to himself. He must have heard Maxine and Madame Steinberger calling her by that name. 'Are you sure we haven't met before?'

What could she say? How could she put him off the scent?

'I remember you,' he said suddenly. 'You came to stay with us yourself for a bit. You're Mary Lennox, aren't you?' His blue eyes bore into her.

Mary shook her head, turning scarlet. 'No!' The heat in her cheeks told her they were ablaze. She began to rise from her seat, following an impulse to run from the room, but almost immediately she pulled herself together. It was no good behaving like that. It would only make him suspect she had something to hide, if he didn't already. She'd simply have to admit to the truth and brazen it out. At least he knew nothing about the Cravens or Misselthwaite.

'Yes,' she said, with a little nervous laugh, not daring to look at him.

He began to chuckle. 'I thought so. Well, imagine that. Meeting you again, and here of all places. What a small world it is. You know, what brought it to mind was when you said about your parents dying in that cholera epidemic. I remember how surprised we all were that you survived it, but now I come to think of it, you were a rather lonely sort of girl. Didn't want company. I remember you putting those flowers on sticks and planting them in the soil. I knew they wouldn't grow, but you thought they would.'

'You were a very rude boy,' she said. 'You made fun of me.'

'I know,' he admitted, 'But I tried to be friendly at first, but you told me to go away. You were a bit stuck up, you know. But I think we've both changed since then.'

She peeped up to find him looking at her, his smile so warm and friendly she was forced to smile back.

'Shall we call a truce,' he grinned, holding out his hand to her.

'By all means,' she said, taking the hand he offered. 'And you may call me Mary in future.'

'I say, folks, you cannot imagine,' he announced to the others. 'I've just discovered Mrs Drummond and I are old friends. We met thirteen years ago, in India. Isn't it incredible?'

'Friends! You were no friend of mine. You were a perfectly horrid small boy. You called me Mistress Mary, quite contrary!'

There were hoots of laughter from the assembled company.

The next day was Christmas Day. There was an English church in Zurich, and Basil and his friends thought it would cheer Mary up and make her feel at home if she accompanied them to the morning service. She felt so homesick she was tempted. It would be nice to hear the Christmas service spoken in English. The fact that she had already bumped into one old associate should, perhaps have been a warning to her, but she would surely not meet anyone else—not on Christmas Day in church.

As she sat in the pew with five young men from the British Embassy she became aware that someone was staring at her. She looked round involuntarily and espied a young man whose face was familiar. Where had she seen that face before? She felt the colour rise in her cheeks. She'd run away to Switzerland to hide from the past, but she began to think she'd be less conspicuous if she'd stayed in

Scarborough. She forced herself not to look round again for the rest of the service, though she could feel his eyes boring into her back.

After the service she got hemmed in and was unable to escape before she came face to face with the man she was trying to avoid meeting.

'Excuse me,' he said. 'It is Miss Lennox, is it not? You are Colin Craven's cousin?'

She felt the blood rush to her face and turned to Basil for inspiration, though what she thought he'd do.... He'd probably verify her identity, and all would be lost.

'You may not remember me,' the stranger pursued, 'but we met in Cambridge. Last May, I believe it was.'

'You must be mistaken,' she said, trying to simulate a blank expression, and trying to keep her voice as light as she could, at the same time digging her fingers into Basil's arm warningly. 'Those names mean nothing to me. And I've never been to Cambridge in my life. I'm afraid you've mistaken me for someone else.'

'You have the wrong person, I'm afraid,' said Basil, taking the hint with remarkable sensitivity, and coming swiftly to her rescue, for which she gratefully squeezed his arm. 'This lady is my wife, and I've never heard of those names either.'

Great Heaven! What was he saying?

'My apologies,' said the suave gentleman, whose name completely escaped Mary.

'My dear Mrs Drummond,' said another voice from behind her. She turned to find Mrs Somerville, whom she'd met in Maxine's house, at her elbow. She prayed fervently that the little lady would not also greet Basil by his name. 'A very happy Christmas to you. Do you spend it here at Zurich with the Steinberger's? Shall we see you at their New Year party? I hear you and Maxine will be moving to the Alps soon.'

'Yes, we are...all spending Christmas together,' Mary stammered a trifle breathlessly, hoping desperately that the fellow from Cambridge had by this time moved out of earshot. This was simply dreadful! She should never have come.

Once alone in the cab with Basil, for the others had decided to walk round the lake before lunch, Mary heaved a sigh of relief and collapsed into a state of helpless giggles.

'I gather that fellow was *persona non grata*,' Basil chuckled. 'May I ask who he is?'

'Oh, just an acquaintance. But why did you claim me as your wife?'

'I thought it was what you wanted me to do. But since I've stuck my neck out, I'd appreciate an explanation. What if I was to bump into that fellow again....'

Mary's face fell. 'Oh, I hope you don't. It could have awkward consequences. But you won't tell anyone who I am, will you? It's a matter of life and death. Mary Lennox doesn't exist any more. You've never heard of her. Please, Basil, promise.'

She was speaking earnestly, almost feverishly, and he was confounded.

'Look, I don't in the least mind playing your little games, but since I've already perjured myself for you, will you please explain what this is all about? Who is that fellow to whom I've lied through my teeth? You know, you're really not being very fair to me, Mary.'

'I honestly can't remember his name, but the fact is...' She paused, considering. She'd have to tell him something, that was certain, but how much? She had a strong feeling he was completely trustworthy. Strange that she had disliked him so much as a small boy in India, yet here she was placing her life in his hands, or almost.

'Why did you lie for me just then?' she asked, changing the subject. 'You didn't have to.'

'To tell you the truth,' he said, giving her one of his warm smiles, 'I don't know why I did it. Let's say, there's an air of conspiracy about this whole thing, and I love mysteries. And then, well, I sensed an appeal, a cry for help, as it were. And finally....' he hesitated, as if searching for the right words. 'I think Mary Drummond is such an improvement on the Mary Lennox I met in India thirteen years ago, that if you wish to bury the latter, then I'm happy to assist you. Long live Mary Drummond! I like her.'

'Thank you, Basil,' said Mary, when she'd stopped laughing. 'That's the nicest thing anyone has said to me for a long time. And I wish I could tell you everything, but I can't. It's not that I don't trust you. I do, entirely, now. It's just... It's just....'

'Never mind. I'll simply have to take it on trust, and follow my leader,' he said giving her a mock salute. 'In the secret service we don't question orders, we simply carry them out.'

'Well, I'll try not to lead you into any severe scrapes,' she said.

'You know, you are a very mysterious woman, Mrs Drummond. I've never met anybody quite like you and I'm intrigued.'

Early in the New Year Mary and Maxine moved to the Steinberger's alpine retreat, to await the arrival of Mary's baby. It was a delightful chalet high up in the mountains, near a small village called Alpenstuck.

Maxine's brother Rudi had been running the place as a guesthouse, or, to be more precise, he had filled it up with his young friends, but he was forced to change his way of life, wild parties and the like, when the girls moved in. Rudi had been told nothing about Mary's circumstances. He didn't know she was expecting a child. All he knew was she was a young widow whose husband had been tragically killed in a climbing accident, that she'd come to them because she was penniless and estranged from her family. Rudi knew all about accidents in the mountains. He ran the local team of mountain rescuers with their St. Bernard's dogs. He looked at Mary sympathetically. He would take care of her, such a pretty young widow.

Mary was nervous that he'd ask too many questions about the accident. But he didn't. He was not a bit like Maxine, and Mary wondered at their being brother and sister. His appearance and manners were those of a rough yokel, but on further inspection his features were not coarse, though he'd none of Maxine's obvious breeding, and Mary quickly realised he was one of Madame's little "mistakes" before she was married. It was probably for that reason he'd been banished to the mountains.

Before she left again for Zurich, Madame Steinberger took Mary on one side.

'I have been so anxious to get you away from Zurich before your condition became too obvious, I have not had time to discuss with you, what we are to do after baby's arrival. I sink ve should discuss it now. I shall make enquiries about a possible home for the baby.'

'A home for my baby? But, Madame....'

'You are not thinking of keeping it?'

'Why not?' Mary's heart felt like lead.

'But you can't! Your circumstances. It's out of the question. Now, I know a great many people, and I'm sure I can find the perfect parents for your child. There are lots of people who'd give anything to have children of their own, but can't. What's the matter, child? Surely you did not expect to keep it yourself?'

'Can't I stay here with my baby. I'd be alright with Rudi to protect me. And I can work. I could teach English, and French, too.

Didn't I see a school in the village? Oh, please, Madame, let me keep my baby.'

'Rudi!' she scoffed. 'He knows nothing about children. And you can't stay here with him, at least not on your own, and Maxine will not want to stay here forever. If I could have found a suitable husband for you…. But there was not time, and it was not possible for you to remain any longer in Zurich. No, no, this is the best way, I assure you.'

'You can't…take my child from me…. It's against the law,' said Mary in desperation.

'What do you know about Swiss law?' Madame was angry now. 'I'm doing this for your own good, you stupid girl. You have no idea what it means to be an unmarried mother. I do. I know exactly the sort of hardship that lies ahead of you if you insist upon this stubborn, stupid course of action. You little fool! What do you think would have become of me if I had not met my husband, if I had not made him fall so helplessly in love with me he cared nothing for scandal. Oh, yes, there was a big scandal. It's all been forgotten now, but at the time…. And you…I don't wish to be rude, Mary, but you have neither the wit nor the beauty to pull it off, I'm afraid. And don't think anyone's going to believe your story about a dead husband. Not even Rudi, when he discovers you're pregnant, will believe that.

'And what about the child. Do you think he'll thank you when he's labelled a bastard? When he's a social outcast? Look at poor Rudi. He can never be anything but a peasant, while his sister's hand is sought after by the sons of the highest in the land. And he's lucky by comparison. At least I have the means to make him comfortable. You and your child will doubtless end up as beggars. Think about it.'

With that she stalked off, tossing over her shoulder. 'You should be thankful I have not sent you to a convent for unmarried mothers.' Mary was left shaken and in tears.

Rudi found her a while later. He was uncertain of his English, which was very rough, so he spoke to her in German. 'Hey, *was makt es*? What's the matter? Oh, I know. I don't need to ask.' Then he had an idea. 'I know what. Come with me, I have something to show you. Come'

He took her hand and led her into a stable and showed her a calf that had just been born. 'Have you ever seen one so small?'

'Oh, it's darling!' she said.

The sight of the tiny thing, wobbly on its pins, having just got to its feet for the first time, reminded her so much of her own wee babe who was to be given away to strangers, that the tears sprang to her eyes, and it was all she could do not to begin weeping again.

Within a very short time it became apparent that Rudi had taken a shine to Mary. In many ways he reminded her of Dickon, though nobody was quite like Dickon, and none could replace him in her heart. But he seemed to have a similar gentle nature, close to the earth, and with a love of animals. The little calf thrived while Mary observed, and Rudi taught her to tend to the animals, to milk the cows, and as the Spring came she would go with him when he lead the herd to pasture and collected it again at sunset. The sunsets were breathtaking.

She loved the mountains. It gave her an enormous feeling of excitement each morning when she awoke to the sound of the cock crowing, to step outside and take great gulps of fine, clear mountain air, to see, all around her the high snowy peaks. How beautiful it was!

'You know, my brother is in love with you,' Maxine announced one morning.

'Oh, I hardly think so,' said Mary, going a gentle shade of pink.

'Oh, yes, he is,' her friend insisted. 'I can tell by the way he looks at you, by the way he appears every morning after breakfast, looking for you. Usually we don't see him until lunch time, and then only because he's hungry. I tell you, he's what do you say in English, head in heels in love?'

'Head over heels.'

'That's it. He's head over heels in love with you, Mary.'

What a pity she could not return it. If only she could for her baby's sake—her pregnancy was quite obvious now, yet it had apparently not shocked Rudi in the least. Whether or not he believed her story, he did not seem to mind that she was carrying another man's child, nor that her belly was swelling in an unshapely way. If he asked her to marry him it would solve all her problems about keeping the baby. Her little one would be assured of a secure home and two parents. But could she do that? Could she?

She had no doubt he'd make a kind and loving husband. In fact, he'd probably spoil her to death. But she knew what marriage meant, and much as she liked Rudi, the thought of doing with him what she had done with Colin.... It would be like being a prostitute, she thought with an involuntary shudder, and it suddenly occurred to her that all the women who married men they were not in love with, whether for expediency, or because it was arranged by their parents, would have to brace themselves for this.

Till All The Seas Run Dry

But Mary was not of that disposition. To her the whole idea filled her with revulsion. Yet what was the alternative? As time went by she became more and more determined to keep her child no matter what the consequences. The utter, unspeakable joy she experienced when she first felt her baby move inside her was indescribable. How could she possibly give him/her away to strangers. And yet she could see the sense in Madame Steinberger's argument. And now that Rudi had so unashamedly fallen in love with her it was not possible to contemplate staying here for any length of time, unless she married him, even if Maxine stayed. And she could not expect the girl to do that. She had her own life to lead.

There were other alternatives. She could abandon the whole scheme and write to her uncle. She wouldn't even have to return to England. She could simply explain the situation and why she'd left the country. He'd appreciate that. All she needed was enough money to continue to live in exile without having to impose on the Steinbergers. He might be grateful enough to oblige her since she'd gone to so much trouble to avoid a scandal. On the other hand he might not. He was much more likely to insist that Colin married her. And that would be intolerable. There was only one thing worse than having to submit to a man one felt no desire for. Colin, if forced to marry her against his will and when he was in love with someone else would soon despise her. That's if he was not already married to Charlotte.

Madame Steinberger wrote to her saying she'd found the perfect parents for her baby, a young German couple who were desperate for a child. They'd been trying to have one for eight years without success, and now the doctor had advised the woman she couldn't have them. Mary would be well advised to agree to this exchange. The Engelbergs were a delightful couple and would make devoted parents. She must think of her child, she must not be selfish. 'Don't you think I know how you feel?' the letter ran. 'Have I not been a mother myself?'

Mary felt hemmed in. She had nobody to talk to, she was surrounded by people with biased views. Maxine would follow her mother, she always did, and Rudi wanted her to marry him. How she missed Martha. Faced with the most important decision in her life, she had never felt more alone.

****

'Dickon!' Molly's shrill voice got on his nerves. 'Go to shop for me and get some ciggies will yer?'

'Tha shouldn' be smokin'—not in your condition.'

Would he feel so resentful, he wondered, if it was not for Mary? If he hadn't failed her because he was already married to Molly? If she had married Colin as she ought... If he'd been free to marry her himself he might have saved her. But he must put such wicked thoughts out of his mind. Molly was his wife, and he'd promised to love and cherish her.

On the whole he tried to be a good husband, telling himself things would be different when the baby came. He refused to believe it was not his child she was carrying, in spite of what his mother and Martha said.

'Anyhow, I'm off fishing,' he said, picking up his rod and bag and walking towards the door.

'Get me ciggies first, Dick. There's a good lad.'

That did it. He hated being called Dick.

'It'll do thee no good, smoking. Better to go wi'out.'

With that he left, shutting the door firmly behind him.

He no longer looked forward to his days off. When they were first wed they'd often have a good laugh together, but she was no fun any more. She was always badgering him to get her things, lying there like a stuffed elephant. He was worried about the size of her. She looked as if she was carrying triplets or even quads. Bawdy jokes were put about in the pub, folks were laying bets and he was congratulated on his virility!

If she took more exercise instead of lying on sofa, loafing.... He was sick of making excuses for her when his mother and sisters complained about her laziness.

He preferred to be working—his hours in the stables were getting longer and longer, and if there was not enough there to keep him occupied he put in extra time in the secret garden. The secret garden needed his attention. Colin had locked it up again, but he knew where the key was hidden.

He felt sorry for Colin. He'd been angry enough with him at the time, but the poor fellow had paid for what he'd done. He was grieving, that was obvious, and there was no denying he loved Mary. But he doubted if their friendship would ever be the same again. That magic—the three of them in the secret garden—could never be recaptured—not without Mary. She was the nucleus that held them together. Colin seldom came home these days anyway. He was too busy inventing flying machines and playing with balloons, and, truth be told, he probably found being at Misselthwaite far too painful.

He got home late that evening, tired and hungry. There was no meal prepared for him so he had to set about getting it for himself. There was nothing unusual about that. He often had to get his own meals except when his mother left something out for them. Molly did little cooking these days. That night he slept on the sofa. There was not much room in the double bed—it was not much bigger than a single—with Molly in her condition. She'd be more comfortable and he'd get some peace.

Next morning she pleaded with him to stay at home.

'Don't go, Dickie. Don't leave me....'

'I've got to, you silly woman.'

'I feel poorly, and me back hurts. Can't you stop home today?'

He hesitated. She did look a bit seedy, but she was always saying she felt poorly. He'd come to realise it was an excuse to lie around and do nothing.

'How can I? I had me day off yesterday. There'll be loads of work today.' He wanted to say it was because she was too heavy, she ate too much and smoked too much. If she'd a proper diet... 'I'll get Mother to come round and be with thee.'

He called in at his mother's house on the way to the manor.

'She must be near her time,' said Susan Sowerby. 'By th' size of her she ought to be. You go on off, son, an' don't worry. I'll watch out for her.'

Now it happened that Dickon was somewhat preoccupied that day with the birth of a foal, and there was nobody else Mr Craven trusted to stay with the mare. So there was not much he could do about it when his youngest sister, Ellie, came running to tell him Molly's baby had started.

'It's all right. Mam can manage,' his sister assured him.

'I'll come soon as I can,' he said, indicating the mare. 'I should think mare'll produce foal quicker than our Molly can produce bairn,' he laughed.

However, because there were complications with the mare, it was well after dark before he got away. As soon as he'd cleaned up and made her comfortable, and made a hay bed for the little foal, he hurried home as fast as his bike would carry him.

Till All The Seas Run Dry

He found the lower half of the house in darkness and he knew intuitively something bad had happened. Susan Sowerby greeted him with a sombre face and his heart sank.

'What is it? Molly?'

She shook her head. 'She's all right, but only just. But we lost bairn. I'm so sorry.'

He mounted the stairs two at a time. Molly lay on the bed looking more dead than alive, her cheeks were white, her eyes sunken. Guilt, for all his uncharitable thoughts, swept over him. Followed by an overwhelming sense of compassion.

'Molly!' He fell on his knees beside her bed and took her hand. It felt icy cold.

'Dickon.' It came out in a hoarse whisper and he realised she'd probably screamed until she'd lost her voice. While he'd been thinking the worst of her she'd been going through hell, and after all that the child was dead. He felt ashamed. He put his hand on her brow and found it, too, was cold, and damp with sweat. At the same time he noticed his knee felt wet, and looking down he saw to his horror a great puddle of blood emerging from under the bed.

He leapt up, crying out, 'She's bleeding to death!'

He ran downstairs and within minutes he was on his bike, peddling like fury, praying he could find the doctor and get him to her in time.

The doctor came as soon as he could, but it was no good. Within an hour he emerged from the room, shaking his head sadly.

Dickon fell back against the wall, and stood there staring into space. He'd worked hard to save the mare and her foal that day, but he'd failed to save Molly. He, who knew when an animal was in pain, had not noticed his own wife was in labour. He'd neglected her and now she was dead. The feeling of guilt was almost suffocating.

'Come and sit down, lad.' said his mother gently.

'It were my fault,' he said, holding his head between his hands, afraid that if he didn't it might explode. 'I killed her.'

'What utter nonsense!' Susan Sowerby exclaimed. 'You did more for that lass than anyone.' Then her voice softened and she put her arms round him and held him close. 'Nob'dy could ha' saved her. Bairn were too much for her. Tha' mustn't blame tha'sel' son.'

But there was little anyone could say to console him. All he could think of was his callousness, his harsh words about her slovenly habits, her smoking, her laziness, and no excuse, telling himself she had driven him to it, could absolve his conscience. He would be haunted by it for the rest of his life. How could he ever forgive himself?

Chapter 20

Spring came in the mountains, the snow began to melt away in the valley, and everywhere the little edelweiss appeared like white stars. Soon other flowers followed and the valley sprang into life, and it seemed to Mary as if her baby jumped for joy because of it.

As the infant grew inside her she dismissed any thought of parting with him, marriage with Rudi became more and more acceptable, being by far the lesser evil. She'd overcome her aversion, she told herself, she'd simply have to. Rudi was fascinated by her baby. He liked to lay his hands on her belly, feeling the movement, the life inside her. She didn't mind this. It was when he wanted to kiss her on the mouth, his breath which often smelt of beer and cigarettes on her face, his hand behind her head so that she felt trapped, suffocating....

Oh, Lord, would she ever be able to endure it? And the other— the more intimate side of marriage? But what else could she do? Accept charity from Colin and his father? She'd rather die!

Her heart ached whenever she thought of Colin. She tried not to, she wanted to forget him, forget everything about her former life. But how could she forget when she was carrying his child?

She had moments of extreme apprehension about the birth. What if something went wrong? She refused to even contemplate the possibility that something might be wrong with the child. Dr. Craven was talking through his hat. But if she lost the baby as well as Colin.... The thought filled her with horror. At times like this she missed him more than ever. She could have done with the comfort of his arms around her, enveloping her in his love. He had loved her once, hadn't he? Did he think she was a woman of easy virtue? Was that why he'd deserted her and gone back to Charlotte? She supposed they'd be married by now.

She must not be bitter. She must remember the good times and be glad she'd had them. She had a whole new future ahead of her, with her child. She'd marry Rudi if she had to, but not before the baby was born. He'd probably have the courtesy to leave her alone while she was pregnant, but if he did not, if he insisted upon consummating the marriage straight away... It would be a violation of the foetus, a risk she was not prepared to take.

Rudi was a strange mixture. He had no refinement in his manners, and he wore the clothes of any other yokel or farm hand, yet his fine features indicated a man with breeding.

'Do you know who your father was, Rudi?' she asked him once.

'No,' he shrugged. 'My mother never told me.'

'Don't you want to know?'

'Of course I do.'

'Then make her tell you. You have a right to know.'

'You don't know Mutter,' he said bitterly. 'You can't make her do anything she doesn't want to.'

'Perhaps your father was someone really important. You have the features of an aristocrat. Where did you get the name Bergmann from? Was it your mother's former name?'

'No. It's an assumed name. I chose it myself. I love the mountains, you see. I didn't have to stay here. I could have gone to university, there was never a shortage of money, but I prefer this kind of life. Nobody tells me what to do, though Mother often tries. But I do as I please. Now I don't tell her about my plans. That way she can't interfere.'

It struck her suddenly that, kind as he appeared to be, he had a stubborn, arrogant streak in him. He'd do exactly as he pleased regardless of anyone else's wishes. He was not really like Dickon after all. No wonder he and his mother were so often at odds. There was in her an arrogance, a ruthless determination to have her own way. She was not one to be crossed, and Rudi had a bit of that in him, Mary thought with a little involuntary shudder.

And she soon discovered another unwelcome aspect to Rudi's character.

There was, attached to the chalet, and a little apart from it, a log cabin which was sometimes used as an annex when the chalet was full. He'd been fitting it out with a view to making it their home once they were married, and preparing it for her confinement.

'I've made a cradle for ze baby,' he told her proudly. 'I shall fix it here by ze bed, *Ja*?' He was more confident now about speaking in English. 'Zen I can help wiz ze baby when it wakes in ze night'

'Oh, Rudi,' she laughed. 'You don't know one end of a baby from the other.'

She made a joke of it in order to hide her true feelings, for the thought of him sharing such intimacy with her and the baby filled her with dread. But he didn't laugh.

'Don't you want me to help you? he demanded, looking hurt. 'I want to share things with you. I thought that was what we were getting married for.'

All too frequently she hurt him with her casual, unthinking jests, and he'd sulk for the rest of the day. He seldom understood her frivolous remarks or shared her jokes, and soon she realised he had little or no sense of humour. How could she live with a humourless man? It wrenched her heart to recall how easily she and Colin used to banter.

Time flew by and soon it was June. In the valley the snow had all gone, though up by the chalet there were still a few large clumps of icy rock which stubbornly refused to thaw. And the peaks which rose on all sides were still heavily laden. Today it was bright and sunny, the air was crystal clear, and the snowy peaks glistened in the sunlight.

Rudi had taken the goats up the mountain path this morning. He'd promised her that as soon as the snow cleared sufficiently, and there was no longer a risk of avalanches he would take her up there, but this morning he'd said she was too heavy with child. What he really meant, she thought petulantly, was that she was getting too slow. She'd hold him up. Well she'd show him what stuff she was made of. Besides, the doctor had told her she must take exercise or she would get overweight. A little gentle walk on a day like this would do her the world of good. She'd take her time. She saw which way he went, she could see the goats heads bobbing up and down, and she could hear their bells.

She panted a little in her exertions, and stopped many times to catch her breath and admire the view. And what a magnificent view it was! Far, far below she could hear the tinkle of cow bells rising from the valley. That and the goats' bells, a little above her, were the only sounds to be heard up there. The silence was eerie. It was so quiet one could just discern a creaking sound—it was the snow shifting on the mountains, Rudi had told her once, and when there was an avalanche you could hear it for miles, like the rumble of far off thunder.

She could no longer see the goats, they were too far ahead of her, but she could still hear them. How far up this mountain did Rudi intend to lead them? Much further up and they'd reach the snowline and run out of pasture. She sat down on a rock to rest and took deep breaths, filling her lungs with the clear, thin air. How peaceful it was up here. She could understand what the old shepherd meant when he'd said he loved being on the mountains for he felt nearer to Heaven.

A mist appeared from nowhere, blotting out the sun, and the air felt damp and cold suddenly. With a spasm of fear she remembered she'd been told about the mists which could gather quickly and without warning. It was the reason why Rudi had said she should not go up the mountain alone. She got up and went to go back the way she'd come, but the mist swirled around, becoming rapidly denser. Where on earth was Rudi? She called out to him, he'd taught her to yodel a little, if only she could remember the codes. But the only reply she got was the echo of her own voice and the creaking mountains.

The fog was thickening by the minute and soon she could see no more than a few feet in front of her, so she kept her eyes to her feet, treading carefully step by step. She felt disorientated, uncertain which way to turn, but who could tell how long it might be before the mist dispersed. And what if she couldn't find her way down the mountain before dark? Such imaginings chased each other around her mind. Her heart was beating wildly, and because of the silence she could almost hear it. And now she was shivering with cold.

By now the fog was so dense she could scarcely see her feet at all, so she was reduced to feeling her way. The path had become unaccountably rougher, she found herself staggering over great big stones. This was surely not the way she'd come. Then to her dismay it petered out altogether and she was confronted by rock on one side and empty void on the other. Now she was really frightened. Carefully she turned to go back, clinging to the rocks on her left, imagining there was a sheer drop on her right where she could see nothing at all. She cried out for help, but this time it was not Rudi's name on her lips, but Colin's, like a child cries for it's mother when it's frightened or in pain. In a state of panic she slipped and fell—and went on falling....

****

At precisely the moment she fell, over a thousand miles away, Colin, who was learning to fly an aeroplane, saw it in a flash of perception. The vision caused him to lose control of the craft for an instant and it went into a spin, but he managed by the skin of his teeth to pull the plane clear.

His instructor bellowed, 'For Christ's sake! What the ... are you doing, Craven?'

But how could he explain to his down to earth flying instructor that he'd just seen the person he cared most for in the whole world, someone he supposed to be already dead, fall off a cliff? He didn't understand it himself, but this fellow would simply think he was mad.

'You can't afford to lose concentration for one moment in this game.' His tutor's voice was stern. 'If you do that sort of thing I wouldn't give tuppence for your chances of survival as a pilot, and you certainly won't get your Aero Club certificate.'

The R.A.C.A. certificate was a qualification Colin needed to be accepted as a pilot in the newly formed Royal Flying Corps. He desperately wanted to be a pilot. He'd joined the Royal Engineers for the sole purpose, the flying battalion which later became the exclusive "corps", being a part of it. And after months of gruelling training at Farnborough and Laffans Plain he'd passed his fitness tests and obtained the consent of the military authorities to learn to fly, he could not allow himself to fail now.

He'd tried to put thoughts of Mary from his mind, but it was impossible when she haunted him at unexpected moments like this, when she dominated his dreams at night, his imagination by day. He didn't know if she was dead or alive. So what did it mean? He never knew whether or not to take his visions seriously. Was it all delusion, the ravings of his tormented soul? But what if something dreadful had happened to her? Yet even if she were alive and needed his help, what could he do about it? He hadn't a clue where she was.

****

Rudi got back to the chalet for lunch to be met by an anxious, accusing Maxine.

'Where's Mary? Didn't you take her with you up the mountain this morning?'

Her brother shook his head. 'I told her she's too heavily pregnant to climb mountains.'

Maxine sighed impatiently. 'But Lotti says she saw her follow you up the goat path about half an hour after you left. I thought you'd arranged to meet her at the berger's hut, and when she didn't come back... I've been so worried. I didn't know whether to go and look for her myself or what. And here you come, sauntering in here, demanding your lunch....'

'It's not my fault,' her brother retorted, breaking off a large piece of bread and dunking it in his soup. 'If Mary doesn't do as she's told. When we're married she'd better not be so disobedient!'

'Don't you care that she might be lost on the mountain? That she might be injured? Even dead? I thought you loved her.'

'I do love her,' said Rudi, stung. 'But there's no need to get so hysterical. She's only been gone a few hours and it is after all summer. If she kept to the path she'll come to no harm, it's a good track, wide and firm, and she can't have gone far in her condition. If she's lost Jager'll soon find her, won't you, boy.'

'Then stop eating!' cried Maxine, snatching the bowl of soup away before he could get the first spoonful to his mouth. 'Call together the mountain rescue team at once and go and find her. *Dummkopf*!' she added, clipping his ear.

She rang the bell for the maid.

'Put Herr Bergemann's dinner back in the oven, Lotti. He's going out again.'

****

Mary's firstborn arrived six weeks early, on 30th June. Her fall had induced labour. Recollections of the accident and how she'd been rescued from the mountain side were vague and shadowy. She'd been aware, through a haze of semi-consciousness, of Rudi's St. Bernard, Jager, licking her face, then barking above her for what seemed hours, then of men milling around with ropes, hauling her onto a stretcher and carrying her down the mountain. And all the time the pain had been like nothing she'd ever experienced before.

Miraculously she had not even broken any bones. She'd landed on a grassy slope and begun to roll, but her descent had been stopped by rocks and bushes. She was covered in cuts and bruises, but otherwise unharmed. The birth was a nightmare, the worst ordeal of her life, and she was surrounded by strangers. She'd never felt so frightened, so alone, so vulnerable. She clung to the bedpost in an agony that lasted forty eight hours. They wouldn't let Maxine in to see her, not that she'd have wanted the poor girl to see her like that, or hear her screams. It might have frightened her out of her wits. It was as well the baby was rather small, otherwise they might neither of them have survived. It is said that history repeats itself; indeed the birth of his son was remarkably similar to Colin's own, and at one moment the outcome might have been the same. She was a long time recovering from it.

She was in a weakened condition due to much loss of blood, susceptible to infection. The doctor advised her to remain in bed for several weeks.

When she came out of her stupor several days later, she was frantic about the baby. Apart from the moment of birth, when she'd heard, as she floated away into unconsciousness on a cloud of joy and relief, his vital cries, she had not seen him. And despite both Maxine and the midwife's assurances.

'Please,' she begged the sister. 'Let me see my baby.'

'Oh, haven't you seen him yet, *liebchen*? I'll bring him to you right away.'

The moment her son was put into her arms and she felt the warmth of his small body against her own, she discovered a kind of love she had never felt for any living soul, not even Colin. There was no question of parting with him now. He was hers, her very own little miracle. She examined his tiny hand, firmly gripping her forefinger, each minute finger so perfectly formed, his little feet, his ears.

'You're so beautiful!' she crowed, kissing him.

His eyes, which had been tightly shut, opened and he began to cry. To her joy she saw, fleetingly, a strong resemblance to Colin. Then he screwed up his face and screamed loudly.

'He's probably hungry,' said the midwife. 'I'd better take him back to the wet nurse.'

'But I can feed him myself.'

'Do you want to feed him yourself? But I thought...'

'Of course I do.'

A deep suspicion began to cloud her joy. It was all happening, just as she'd feared, they were trying to wean her baby away from her.

She experienced a thrill of pleasure as her baby latched on to her breast and sucked greedily, kneading her with his little fists.

She could not have known how much her child would mean to her, and the fact that he was also a part of Colin made him all the more precious. How wonderful it would have been to share the joy of parenthood with him. Yet she missed him less, so taken up with the child was she. It was as if her love for him had culminated in her love for their son.

She was settled in the log cabin, which Rudi had only just finished refurbishing. After a week or so Frau Finkel went, and she was left with Rudi, who vowed to respect her privacy until they were married. He would sleep on the floor in front of the door, like a bodyguard, protecting her. But she felt uneasy, and asked to be moved back into the chalet with Maxine.

'But you don't want to share a room with Maxine now you have the baby. And the other rooms are all taken. We're expecting visitors. No, no, it's better you stay here.' The appraising, almost hungry look

Till All The Seas Run Dry

in his eyes as they rested on her now slim figure and breasts swollen with mother's milk, frightened her. 'Anyway we'll be married soon.'
She felt like a caged bird.

The baby, she called him Tom, was still very delicate, and Mary found in the days that followed he was not thriving as well as she'd hoped he might. What she did not realise, when she sent the wet nurse away was that she had been supplementing his feed. Frau Finkel, the wily old midwife, while trying to keep her happy, knew that he could not thrive on what she was giving him. And now, because he was losing weight she began to fret. Anxiety about the future too, the constant reminder that she would soon have to fulfil her side of the bargain for keeping him, preyed on her mind to such an extent that her milk supply began to wane.

Rudi had a habit of walking in when she was feeding him, and the lustful way he'd look at her, his eyes roving impudently over her full breasts, made her feel threatened, even though he always apologised and left the room, and as yet he had not touched her.

Madame Steinberger arrived from Zurich, and she was furious to find that all her instructions had been disobeyed. She was to have been present at the birth. Why had nobody told her about it? And where was the wet nurse?

When she learned that Mary had sent her away and was feeding the infant herself she was incensed. 'Now it will be impossible to take the child away from his mother,' she raged at Maxine.

Maxine attempted to pacify her. 'But Mama, there is no need. The baby will have a father. Rudi and Mary are to be married.'

'What? Why was I not told about this? All the arrangements have been made with the Engelbergs, I can't let them down. Where is Rudi? Tell him I want to speak to him. Now!'

'I don't know, Mama,' said Maxine, with a sigh. 'But he'll be back soon for his tea.'

'Is Mary so desperate to keep her child as to persuade a gullible fool like Rudi to marry her?'

'Oh, no, Mutti, it's not like that. Rudi adores her. He wants to marry her.'

'But she doesn't love him.' There was a cynical ring to the countess's voice.

'I'm sure she does,' said Maxine, but she sounded unconvinced. After a moment she added, 'Or she wouldn't have agreed to marry him. She doesn't have to get married. She's a respectable widow.'

The cynical courtesan looked at her daughter. It seemed a pity to destroy her innocence. 'Do you really believe all that about a husband and a mountain accident?' Maxine's eyes opened wider. 'Yes, I see that you do.'

'But why should it not be true, her story?'

'My darling, you are so naive you will believe anything.'

'And you, Mama, are so cynical you will believe nothing.'

'Anyway,' said the countess. 'I still think it would be best for all concerned to go ahead with the adoption. Such a marriage has little chance of happiness, believe me. You've no idea, any of you, what an unhappy marriage can be like.'

'Mama?'

'Oh, don't go reading anything into that. But I do know that nothing hurts more than loving someone who doesn't care for you.'

Later that evening Mary heard Rudi and his mother having a heated argument. Their voices were raised from time to time, specially Rudi's, and she could hear they were talking about her. They spoke in the *Schweizerdeutsch* dialect instead of the *Hochdeutsch* the countess usually insisted upon, probably because they imagined she wouldn't understand.

'I don't need your advice about who I should marry, Mutter.'

'You fool! Can't you see the girl doesn't love you, that she's only making use of you?'

'I see that you must always interfere. Well, I'm fed up with it. It's my life!'

Mary closed her eyes. Grateful though she was to Rudi for taking her part, she knew the countess was right. She was using him. But what else could she do? If only she didn't have to marry him. She cradled little Tom in her arms holding him close.

'You're mine,' she whispered, stroking his downy head. 'My very own, and nobody shall take you away from me, nobody. If only we could get away from here, from all these hostile people. We're between the devil and the deep blue sea, you and I.'

She slept fitfully that night, and, beset by fears that someone might sneak in and kidnap him, she kept her hand on Tom's cradle all night.

In the days that followed her health deteriorated rapidly. She'd never really recovered from the birth, and now she was exhausted, trying to care for the baby, who kept her awake at night with his crying. And when she did sleep she'd wake up in a muck sweat, haunted by garish nightmares. By the end of a week she was very ill indeed with a raging fever.

Madame Steinberger felt her forehead.

'You'd better stay in bed today and rest,' she soothed. 'I'll take care of the baby.'

'But I have to feed him,' Mary rasped.

Madame Steinberger looked at her dubiously. 'You don't have anything to feed him on. You shouldn't have sent the wet nurse away. A small baby needs regular feeding and constant care and attention, and you are in no condition to cope. Besides, you may have an infection. You wouldn't want to pass it on to him, would you?' She turned to Maxine who'd just entered the room. 'Do you know where the woman lives? Can you fetch her back?'

Mary clung to the cradle on the point of tears. 'Please, don't take him away from me,' she begged Maxine.

'Do you want him to die of starvation?' cried Madame.

'But I have been feeding him...up till now....'

'And now the little you had for him has gone,' said her mentor cruelly. 'He's not been thriving as he ought. Now, Mary, don't behave like a ninny.'

'Nobody's going to take him away, Mary,' said Maxine, kindlier than her mother. 'Couldn't we give him a bottle, Mama? Then we can keep him here and Mary will be happy.'

'I suppose we could try him on goat's milk,' said Madame. 'It's the nearest to human milk. But they don't all take to it, and he may not. I still say he'd be better off with the wet nurse.' She raised her eyes to the ceiling. 'This place is far too cold at night for a newly born baby,' she complained. 'I can't imagine what Rudi was thinking of, putting you in here.' She looked at Tom more closely, then put her hand on his head. 'Look, he's cold as stone. He'll die of cold before long, if not starvation.'

Mary sat up, leaned over the cradle and put her hand against his cheek, and finding Madame had not exaggerated, the chill closed round her heart. Then she saw to her horror he was shaking, his eyes rolling alarmingly. 'What's the matter with him?' she cried in terror.

'He's having a small convulsion,' said Madame 'Premature baby's are apt to have them. But being in this cold room with you hasn't helped. Call the doctor, Maxine.' She lifted him carefully, wrapping him up in tight bundle. 'On second thoughts, I think I'd better take him myself. Tell Rudi to get the gig immediately.'

A terrible fear gripped Mary. For some reason she felt uncomfortable about Madame, as if she couldn't trust her. She struggled to raise herself up out of bed.

'I'll come with you,' she said.

'You'll do no such thing,' snapped Madame. 'You'll stay right here, in bed.'

'But he's my baby,' she pleaded, a feeling of despair welling up inside her.

'You don't trust me, do you?' said the countess, with disarming frankness. 'Look, I know he's your baby, and he means the world to you. I'm a mother, too, you know. But, if he is not got quickly to the doctor.... And you are in no condition, with a high fever, to go anywhere at the moment. Be sensible, Mary.'

It all sounded so plausible, and yet she could not dismiss the dreadful fear that she would never see Tom again. Maxine called from downstairs to say the gig was ready and Madame hurried out of the room carrying that most precious of parcels. Mary sank into the pillows and wept as if her heart would break.

Chapter 21

Mary was ill for several weeks with a very high fever, drifting in a state of semi-consciousness. She awoke one morning to find Rudi sitting by her bed. He'd brought her a bunch of flowers, but they looked a little limp because he'd held them in his hand so long.

'Are you feeling better,' he asked anxiously.

She made no reply, her eyes fixed on the bedraggled flowers.

'I've brought you some flowers. I should put zem in water. Zey are dead almost.'

His English was improving, but her mind was not on flowers, or his English, and before he could leave the room she stopped him.

'Tom! Where is he?' she asked in a hoarse whisper. He turned and looked at her and the expression on his face struck terror into her heart. 'What's happened? Tell me, at once!'

'Don't get over excited,' he said, gently. 'You'll put your temperature up again.'

'He's dead, isn't he?' She had no idea what made her realise it, quite suddenly, and the look of pity in his eyes confirmed it. 'I knew it! I knew I'd never see him again.'

Her anguish touched his heart and he took her in his arms, trying to cradle her from the pain. 'Don't cry, *liebchen*. We'll be married soon, then we'll have other babies. As many as you want.'

Mary shook her head. She had no intentions of marrying him now, and the last thing she wanted was to have babies with him. She could hardly bear him to touch her, but she couldn't tell him either. She was not ready to face conflict yet. 'Leave me alone, Rudi,' she said, pushing him away.

As if he'd been stung he let her go and stood there for a moment, a stunned expression on his face, watching her, her face buried in the pillows, her whole body shaking with silent convulsive sobs. Then he hurried out of the room.

Later on Madame came. 'I'm sorry, my dear. The hospital did everything they could.'

'I don't understand,' said Mary in a flat toneless voice. She felt dead, washed out, having cried until she had no more tears to shed. Grief, deep and searing, worse than anything she'd suffered before, even losing Colin, had drained her of energy. 'Was it my fault? But I thought he was doing so well….'

'It's no use blaming anyone,' said the countess, 'least of all yourself.

'What was wrong with him? When did he die, and why?'

Madame looked uneasy and when she answered she didn't look at her.

'I don't know. I took him to the hospital straight away when he had those convulsions. I think there was something wrong with him. You could not have done anything about it. He just went into decline. He didn't live longer than about a week. I'm so sorry, my dear.'

Mary's heart wrenched in anguish. The thought of her Tom, her own beautiful, lovely little baby, lying there all alone in that hospital, with no one to cuddle or console him. If she'd had any tears left in her body she'd have begun to weep all over again. Why couldn't she have died, too? She had nothing at all left to live for now. She looked at the cradle Rudi had made, the fluffy ball made by Maxine hanging from its hood. How could the sight of such things cause so much pain?

'I know it hurts terribly now,' said Madame, laying a hand over hers. 'But it will pass, I promise you that. Give yourself something else to think about. What about a holiday in Italy? Maxine could go with you for company. It would do you both good.' She had no enthusiasm for the idea, and what would she do for money? She was broke. 'Or,' said Madame Steinberger thoughtfully. 'You could go home. What's to stop you now?'

Go home! See Dickon, Martha, Susan Sowerby, even her uncle, and Colin…. Colin! It was certainly tempting. And after all she had nothing to hide now. But then there'd be Charlotte—Charlotte to grind her nose in all that she'd lost! The thought of being at Misselthwaite with the two of them, seeing them together….

'I can't….' she said.

'I imagine you have your own reasons, but if it's Rudi you're thinking of…. There's no need for you to marry him now. You don't love him, do you? It would have been a marriage of convenience, *nicht wahr?*'

Mary said nothing. It was no use lying about it.

'Well, now there is no need,' said Madame. 'You won't have to marry him. I'll speak to Rudi. I'll explain to him.'

Mary bit her lip. It was tempting, an easy way out of the situation, to let his mother do the talking for her, release her from her

Till All The Seas Run Dry

commitment, avoid the conflict, but she knew Rudi would be hurt and it would be moral cowardice on her part.

'No, let me talk to him myself.'

Madame looked at her, eyebrows raised.

'As you please,' she said, getting up from the chair by the bed. 'But do it soon. And let me know what you decide to do. I don't mean to be heartless but if you're not going to marry him, the sooner you leave here the better it will be for both of you.'

She wanted to be rid of her, Mary thought miserably. She'd got rid of her offspring, now she wanted to see the back of her too, so that she'd no longer be a threat to her son, or a burden to her family.

'I'll find somewhere else to go,' she said, turning her head away. She might go to France, dear Madame de Bergerac.... But how would she get there without any money? And she would not ask Madame Steinberger to help her.

'I'll be returning to Zurich tomorrow,' said Madame at the door. 'Unless you've other plans, you and Maxine had better join me there as soon as you're fit to travel.'

It was a further two weeks before Mary was herself again, physically at least. Her mental scars would take a great deal longer to heal, if they ever would at all. Her chief need was to earn a living, almost all the money she'd had when she left England had gone. She could teach in the local school, she'd already spoken to the head master there, but she couldn't stay in Alpenstuck now. Nor would she accept any more charity from the Steinbergers. So where should she turn? She remembered Basil Crawford at the British Embassy. He'd once told her the embassy were often asked to recommend British citizens to fill certain posts.

A few days after his mother left for Zurich Rudi came to her and suggested they should be married without further delay. She tried to be as gentle with him as she could be.

'Rudi,' she said, holding out her hand to him. 'Come and sit down. We must talk.'

Instead of sitting on the bed he knelt beside it, taking both of her hands and kissing them reverently. And then he heard her say,

'I don't know how to tell you this but...I can't marry you, Rudi.'

He looked up in shocked astonishment.

'It wouldn't work,' she continued. 'We'd neither of us be happy. Truth is, I like you very much, Rudi, but I'm not in love with you. I know I shouldn't have agreed to marry you.'

'So,' he said bitterly. 'Mutter was right. You only wanted a father for your child.'

'Not entirely. I thought I could make you happy, but now I realise I'd only make you miserable. Forgive me,' she pleaded, dropping a quick kiss on his brow.

'Why should I?' he rasped, breathing heavily, his anger thinly veiled. 'You think you can cast me off like an old coat, *nicht*? You're a jezebel, a.... How could you do this? All this time I've waited patiently until after the baby. I could have insisted we got married before.... I could have made you mine. I wish I had, then you'd have to marry me!'

He was on his feet, trembling with suppressed rage and frustration and for one ghastly moment she thought he was going to rape her. She wished she had not said anything, not while she was alone with him here. She should have waited until she was up and about, back in the chalet with Maxine and the servants.

'Listen Rudi,' she said, edging back further into the pillows and pulling the covers tightly round herself. 'Let's be rational about this. You don't surely want to be married to someone who does not return your feelings?'

Maxine was out, and it was Lotti's day off—she could not have picked a worse day. If she screamed there was nobody to hear her. Physically he was a powerful man, it would be useless to resist, and who knew what he might do if he lost his temper. The molten look in his eyes, a mixture of anger and naked desire, sent a chill through her veins.

But to her relief nothing else happened. He didn't touch her. Whether or not he had ever intended to or whether he changed his mind, she would never know.

'You're right. You're not worth it, a woman like you,' he said derisively, turning sharply and leaving of the room.

The next day Mary moved back into the chalet to share a room with Maxine.

Two weeks later the girls had an unexpected visitor.

'There's a gentleman to see you and Mrs Drummond,' Lotti announced in mysterious tones. 'An Englishman.'

Mary's heart almost stopped, though why on earth she should think it was Colin.... Maxine got up and ran to greet the visitor, and she heard her voice outside.

'Basil Crawford. What are you doing here? How did you find us?'

Basil! Of course! She'd almost forgotten she'd written to him. It seemed like a lifetime ago after all that had happened. But she had not expected him to come in person, all the way from Zurich!

'I couldn't resist coming,' he explained, taking Maxine's hand and pressing it to his lips, then holding out his hand to her. 'I've been trying in vain to find you for the last six months or more.' She saw the look in his eyes when they rested on Maxine and remembered his tender feelings for the girl. 'But your whereabouts has been an astonishingly well kept secret. Is there anywhere reasonably cheap in the village I can stay? I'm due a few days' leave, and I don't have to be back at the embassy until next week.'

'You can stay here,' said Maxine, promptly. 'If you don't mind sleeping in ze attic room. Or I could let you have Rudi's room and make him sleep in ze garret.' She looked doubtful about this. Rudi had been rather surly lately.

'What about the log cabin,' Mary suggested tentatively.

'Of course! I'd forgotten about zat. It's a good idea.' And she ran off to tell Lotti to make the bed up and air the place.

Rudi greeted Basil's visit with suspicion. He'd been sulking ever since the scene with Mary, and her subsequent decision to move back into the chalet. He skulked around all day, taking a packed lunch instead of eating with the girls, and after an early supper, shutting himself away in his room. She knew he was hurting, and ashamed of his outburst, but she didn't know what to do about it. She felt no animosity towards him, only a deep sadness that it had destroyed their friendship, for now she never felt at ease with him. Indeed she was even a little afraid of him.

'Well, I've some good news, at least I think you'll be pleased,' Basil said, when they were alone. She was surprised he'd agreed to go for a walk with her, she'd imagined it might be difficult to prize him away from Maxine. 'As it happens they're looking for an extra teacher at the school in Val de Paix, starting in September. They need someone to teach English to nine-year-olds and assist with the younger pupils in other subjects, can you manage that? I said you were just the person they'd want.'

'Oh, Basil! I hope you haven't overrated me.'

September was two months away. Could she afford to wait that long?

The mid-summer evenings were long and balmy, but since her accident she had a mistrust of the mountain mists.

'I don't want to go any further up the mountain,' she said to her companion. 'We can sit here and admire the view if you like.'

'I heard about your accident,' he said, as if he read her thoughts.

'If it hadn't been for Rudi's dog, Jager I don't suppose I'd be here with you now.'

'And you lost your baby. Maxine told me,' he said. 'I'm so sorry.'

Mary's heart ached. Her baby should have been born any day now had she not been so foolhardy, and mightn't he have lived, had she not been so ill, had he not been premature?

'He was doing so well,' she sighed raggedly, her lips quivering. 'I can't understand why he went so rapidly down hill.' But then, she'd seen with her own eyes the terrifying convulsions. 'Madame thinks he caught a fever from me.'

'Don't upset yourself,' Basil urged. 'I shouldn't have mentioned it.'

'No, no. I want to talk about it. Sometimes I think I'll go mad if I don't talk to someone.' She wanted to tell him about her suspicions—the strange feeling she had that little Tom was not dead, but she couldn't bring herself to say it. It would be a terrible indictment on Madame Steinberger.

'Well,' he said, putting an arm round her shoulder. 'If it helps, I've got broad shoulders. But look, if it's friends you need why move away from here? Why not get a job locally. Isn't there a school in the village?'

'I can't stay here any longer.' She spoke so vehemently he looked at her sharply.

'Why not?'

'Because of Rudi.' She hesitated. She couldn't tell him that either. 'You see, we were sort of engaged. There was an understanding.... But when the baby died....'

'You no longer wanted to marry him,' he finished for her. She nodded. 'And he's taken exception to this?'

It was wonderful how she never had to go into awkward details with him, he was always on track.

'I expect he'll get over it. I know that if I had the chance to be near to Maxine, to worship every day at her shrine of beauty, I should be ecstatic, even if she spurned my love.'

'Would you?' Mary laughed in spite of herself. 'Unrequited love is pretty hard to live with.' It was said with such feeling, he cast a speculative glance in her direction.

'It depends how desperately in love with you he is. But my guess is it won't be long before some other *junges Mädchen* catches his eye and you'll be forgotten.'

'Well, I hope you're right.' She sat with her hands clenched together on her lap. She had told no-one, not even Maxine, about the scene in the bedroom with Rudi. 'But I still think I should leave.'

'I know, you feel you cannot remain indefinitely in someone else's house without contributing in some way, I understand that, but surely....' He broke off as another thought struck him. 'I say,' he said suddenly. 'Why don't you return to England? I mean, you no longer have an...encumbrance, or anything to hide. Couldn't you go home to Yorkshire?'

Mary said nothing. She sat watching a ladybird crawling on the leaf of a plant. The sun, though low in the sky was still warm on her neck. The ladybird took off and landed on another leaf, walked for a bit, then took off again. It was like her, she thought, unsettled.

She was silent for so long, he was prompted to add, 'It seems to me you need to off-load a little, and you needn't feel shy with me,' he laughed. 'I know m' father's a religious man, and all that, but I've been around the world a bit. I wasn't exactly born yesterday. But,' he added hastily. 'You don't have to tell me anything if you don't want to.'

'I know,' she said rather breathlessly. 'But you're right. You've no idea how lonely it can be to have nobody to discuss one's problems with. But I think we should make our way back now. The sun is setting and it'll be dark soon. I'll tell you on the way.'

By the time they reached the chalet Basil knew everything about Colin, from their first meeting, the secret garden and Dickon, to the moment when she discovered she was expecting his child. She told him about her feelings of aversion for Rudi, and how she felt threatened by Madame Steinberger. And when her confession was over it was as if a heavy burden had been lifted from her chest.

Jager came bounding up to greet them. His affection for Mary was obvious, though she was always a little nervous that, huge as he was, he'd knock her over in his enthusiasm.

'He's looking after me,' she said. 'If ever I go walking now he comes looking for me.'

She'd miss him, she thought, fondling the huge head which reached her waist.

It was the end of August. Mary would be leaving soon. Rudi had already begun to prepare for the long winter. She found him in the cowshed, forking over the hay. She wanted to break the news of her departure as gently as possible. They were on friendly terms again but their relationship had been a little strained ever since she'd broken off their betrothal.

'Rudi, I've come to tell you I'll be leaving in two weeks' time.'
His head shot back as if he'd been struck.
'You're leaving!'
He put his hand to her cheek, his eyes scanning her face, her hair, the whole of her.

'Are you leaving me, *liebchen*?' He looked as if he might burst into tears. 'I...cannot...let you,' he said slowly, adding hastily. 'No, no! I won't let you go!' He was on his knees. 'Don't go! Please, don't go. It's because of that row we had, *nicht*? But I've behaved. Since then I've been....'

'You've behaved perfectly. Yes, I know. And it's nothing to do with that...what happened. Can't you see, I can't stay here indefinitely, not if we're not to be married.'

She should not have mentioned that, because he became agitated, a look of despair creeping over his face. 'But I hoped, I thought...if I behaved...you might change your mind.'

'Oh Rudi,' she said, shaking her head.

She was wearing one of Maxine's Swiss blouses, she could not get into her own clothes since the baby's arrival, and its elastic neckline suited her newly matured figure. He came close to her and leaned against the wall, one arm either side of her, effectively trapping her with her back to the wall of the shed. His breath caressed her cheek. There was no escaping him and a feeling of panic rose inside her.

'Why are you so beautiful,' he whispered, gently kissing her cheek, working his way round to her mouth. 'Always tempting me.'

His arms went round her drawing her close, then, feeling her body stiffen in resistance, he became more aggressive, his mouth claimed hers in a fierce, passionate kiss, stifling her protest. At the same time his hand slipped inside the bodice of her blouse and fondled her breast.

'No, Rudi, please!' she gasped as soon as she could speak.

'I want you,' he breathed in a hoarse whisper, 'I've always wanted you. All that time, I never touched you, and I wanted to, so much. And you are not even a woman of virtue,' he added spitefully, his anger rising dangerously. 'You've slept with other men. You must have. You were not married. D'you think I'm a fool, zat I don't know zis?'

A chill entered her heart. Had his mother told him that, or had he really known all along. She couldn't speak. She wanted to die of shame. As far as he knew she was no better than a harlot. What was the use of telling him there was only one man. He probably wouldn't believe her anyway. And it was perfectly true that she'd used him. Why should he respect her? His fingers bit into her chin as he forced her to face him.

'Well? Why should it not be me? Am I not good enough for you? Or is it that you prefer to make love with a man who has no intention to marry you? Well, if that's the way you want it....'

'No, Rudi, don't,' Mary cried, struggling frantically to escape him.

Panic rose in her like a tidal wave. If she screamed who'd hear her? The shed was even further from civilization than the log cabin.

'Oh no, you won't escape me that easily, *mein Liebling*,' he said. Slipping one arm under her knees and lifting her, he carried her kicking and struggling to the pile of hay he'd been forking over. Laughing, he tossed her onto this soft bed and threw himself on top of her, pinning her down with his body. She fought like a tigress, scratching his face, lashing out with her legs, to no avail. With all his towering strength above her, he prized her legs apart with his own, holding her arms above her head.

'No! No!' she screamed, her head thrashing from side to side. 'Don't do this, Rudi!'

But it was no use, he was deaf to her entreaties. Months of pent-up passion and frustration had to be released. He tore off her underwear with his free hand.

'Hush, be still. Don't fight,' he said, holding her arms in an iron grip. 'It'll be alright. I won't hurt you. I'll be gentle if you'll let me....'

But she didn't want to let him!

'Stop! Stop!'

But this was not Colin who had loved her that day at Ravensfell. It was Rudi who's heart was full of bitterness. The encounter was harsh, cruel and degrading, and he hurt her. She wanted to cry from shame. But from somewhere came the notion that if one was raped it was better not to fight it. She tried to disconnect herself from what was happening. It was not happening to her. The meaning of the Victorian adage *Relax and think of England* became clear to her. Suddenly she wanted to laugh hysterically, only it wasn't funny.

But to an extent the exercise worked, for as soon as she let herself go he became less aggressive, even gentle, whispering endearments in her ear, showering her face with kisses.

'Ah, *mein Liebchen*, my love, I love you so, *ich liebe dich*!'

His body writhed and shuddered and became still.

It seemed ages before he moved again, and then, suddenly she realised he was crying.

'I'm so sorry,' he sobbed. 'I didn't mean to hurt you. And now you'll hate me.'

She couldn't speak. It was outrage, revulsion and shame she felt rather than hatred for this inadequate man who continued to weep like a child. He was more to be pitied than hated, but she couldn't say she'd forgive him.

'I'm so sorry,' he kept repeating, over and over again. And, 'I love you so much.'

'All right,' she said, at last. 'Just go now and leave me alone.'

Chapter 22

Colin yawned stretching his long limbs. He hated paperwork. How much longer was this weather going to prevent flying? For the past five weeks storms and high winds had rendered trials on aircraft almost impossible. Instead it had been decreed, in order to maintain fitness among the pilots, that rigorous foot-slogging and P.T. should replace flying practice. At this rate he was more likely to die of boredom than in a flying accident, though there had been rather too many casualties lately, several of them fatal. It seemed that the more sophisticated the machines became the more hazardous the job of flying them.

He'd been a pilot now for a little over a year, having passed his Royal Aero Club certificate in August 1911. He hadn't been home for six months, having had no leave since Easter. Not that he particularly wanted to be at home. With no Mary, no Prince, and a father who'd turned hermit again, it was a depressing place. He was much happier here at Larkhill, or even trudging through the mud at Laffans Plain, among his fellow aviators, who inspired him with their indomitable spirit of adventure. It was a pleasure to work alongside talented men like Geoffrey de Havilland and Ted Busk.

Wandering thoughtfully towards the officers' mess, he was way-laid by his friend John Seymour who had a young lady on his arm.

'Hey, Colin! Come over here. There's someone I'd like you to meet. Let me introduce my sister Louise. This is Colin Craven, Lu. He's quite mad.'

'Aren't you all?' countered his sister.

'Delighted to meet you,' said Colin, finding himself gazing into a pair of laughing eyes. At a guess she stood no more than five foot two, had an impish face framed by honey coloured curls.

'This little minx keeps pestering me to take her up,' said Seymour. 'But I've told her we're not allowed to take females in military aircraft.'

'But I could dress up as a man,' Louise countered with a gurgle of laughter.

'See what I mean?'

'I'll take you up,' Colin offered, wondering what on earth had possessed him to be so rash. 'But not until the weather improves. And not in one of ours,' he added.

'You're even madder than I thought you were!' exclaimed the girl's brother. But Louise cast him a look of appeal. 'Not that I haven't confidence in you as a pilot. I wouldn't entrust my sister to anyone else, I can tell you, but I'm curious to know what machine you intend to use for this purpose?'

'I'm on friendly terms with my old instructor,' Colin explained. 'He lets me borrow his mono' sometimes.'

'I bet he won't if he hears you're proposing to take this little wench for a ride in it. But if it's an instructor's machine, I suppose it must be safe enough. Very well, then,' he agreed, looking indulgently at his young sister. 'Permission granted.'

'Oh, thank you, Mr Craven,' Louise sighed. 'I promise you won't regret it. I'll do exactly as I'm told. I'll be your perfect passenger.'

'I'm sure you will.'

'Don't you believe it,' put in her brother.

'Shall we adjourn to the mess for a drink,' Colin suggested. He was in the best of humour, his spirits having been unaccountably lifted. It was as if the dismal late autumn had suddenly and miraculously turned into spring.

Four months later Louise sat squeezed into the cockpit behind him. He could feel her breath erotically caressing the back of his neck, her knees digging into his sides and her booted feet either side of his seat. His free hand crept down and grasped her ankle.

'Colin!' she piped in mock disapproval, playfully clipping his ear.

'Hey,' he laughed. 'No tampering with the pilot while flying. It could be fatal.'

'I see,' she countered. 'The pilot may tamper with the passenger, but not vice versa.'

He laughed, amused at her humour and quick repartee.

Spring had come at last, the sky was arched and blue, the air clear and invigorating. This is the life, Colin thought irrepressibly. He was never happier than when he was flying, and to be doing it on such a glorious day, with a pretty girl—Louise was not beautiful, at least not like Charlotte, but then he mistrusted that sort of beauty—gave him a feeling of contentment he had not had for more than two years.

A twinge of guilt concerning Mary tugged briefly at his conscience, only to be dismissed. Why should he feel guilty? It was, after all, more than two years since she'd deserted him. There were only two possibilities, either she was dead, or else she had no intentions of ever being found. If she'd really wanted him she would not surely have been so easily put off. Mary didn't give up that easily when she wanted something badly enough. So if this girl, this courageous, vivacious creature, with whom he had such a rich rapport, should fill the void in his heart, would it be so very wrong?

His experience with Charlotte had made him wary, Steady, he told himself sternly. Be ruled by your head this time. But Louise is nothing like Charlotte, his heart urged.

He'd made it his business to find out everything there was to know about her.

'It's a regal name you have, Miss Seymour,' he'd said, the first day he'd taken her flying. 'Are you by any chance a descendent of those Tudor relations?'

She laughed. 'Not directly. Sir Thomas was, I believe, an ancestor, but it's not, I'm afraid, a very salutary connection, probably the wrong side of the blanket.'

'The same applies to most of today's aristocracy, I wouldn't wonder. Speaking of relations, tell me, that's if you don't mind talking about it, what happened to your parents?'

'They were both killed in the Bengal massacre. My sister and I were rescued and brought out by the Indian Army.'

'I didn't know you had a sister.'

'Anna. She's three years older than me, and married. I was only six at the time, Anna, nine. John was sixteen and at school in England. He's cared for us practically ever since.'

'No wonder he's so protective where you're concerned. I didn't know you'd lived in India. My cousin Mary was born there. You must have been there at the same time. Her parents died in a cholera epidemic.'

'There was a lot of it in India.'

'Life is full of coincidences, isn't it? Here's another one. It's just occurred to me that, between us all, we only have one parent alive—my father. What a clutch of orphans we are.'

Things had developed a mite too quickly since then. He'd only met her last November and she'd very soon awoken in him stirrings he'd thought dead. By Christmas he'd invited her and her brother to stay at Misselthwaite. The visit had had the most staggering affect upon his father, who'd come out of his shell for the first time since Mary's disappearance. The other day he'd telephoned him, which was in itself a surprise, demanding to know if there was any chance of him bringing "that delightful little filly" with him at Easter.

However, being at Misselthwaite had a sobering affect on him. Mary's spirit invaded the place, dampening his ardour for Louise. Misselthwaite was synonymous with Mary. Would it always be so? In that case he'd never get married. Or if he did, he might have to sell Misselthwaite, once it was his to sell. It was a dilemma he put to one side for the moment.

'Have you any plans for Easter?' he asked Louise.

'None to speak of. Why?'

'I think my father has taken a fancy to you.'

Louise giggled. 'He's an amusing old thing.'

'That's not exactly how I'd describe my father.'

'Well, I liked him anyway. And yes, I'd love to come and stay at Easter.'

'I haven't asked you yet.'

'But you were going to. Whoops! Colin! Do look where you're going.'

Louise was so taken with flying she begged him to teach her. At first he was a little reluctant, but when she accused him of having a prejudiced opinion that it was exclusively a man's world, and reminded him of women like the Baronne de la Roche, he relented. However he was not prepared to teach her in a monoplane. Because there'd been a number of fatal accidents with them there was a general distrust of monoplanes, and the R.F.C had put a ban on them. But Colin had acquired a biplane of his own, and, with the help and advice of his friend Geoffrey de Havilland, had done it up himself in his spare time.

As it turned out Louise was a delight to teach. She was keen and quick to learn, quicker than many of the young men who were training for the R.F.C.

Louise watched Colin tinkering with his Bleriot BE2.... She was content to hang around for hours with nothing to sit on but a few planks of wood, just to be with him. He was the most exciting man she'd ever met, and she was in love for the first time in her life. All the other young men of her acquaintance, even the more attractive ones, disappeared into the recesses of her memory. Her main aim in life was to please Colin.

'Now,' he said to her once. 'D'you want to know how this machine works. Come here and I'll show you.'

Thus began a new phase of her education. He trained her well and soon she became his helpmate. She was not vain. Without a murmur she'd don an old pair of trousers and shirt of her brother's and get down to it.

'You've got a smudge on the end of your nose,' he teased, kissing the spot where she'd rubbed it with her dirty hands.'

'You've got them all over your face,' she retaliated, laughing.

'You're a most unusual woman, Lu. I can't imagine any other, even Mary, getting herself all mucky doing a job like this.'

She didn't tell him it was a labour of love, especially since he'd mentioned Mary again. Did he think of her all the time? He was always talking about her. She was curious to know why she'd run away.

'Why did Mary leave,' she asked him once.

He was silent, and she knew she'd touched a tender spot, for when he spoke his voice was bitter. 'I don't know.'

'You seem very resentful. Did she run off with a man?'

'I don't want to talk about it,' he said.

'I'm sorry, I didn't mean….'

'I know, it's not your fault,' he said more gently, adding with a sigh, 'I've no idea why she left. Anyway you don't want to know about Mary. She's of no interest to you.'

But Louise did want to know about the woman who appeared to have more influence over Colin than anyone, even his father, and who was clearly far more to him than a cousin, or even a sister. She had an unpleasant suspicion he was in love with her. And she'd left him. She failed to understand why any woman would leave Colin.

There was something mysterious about Misselthwaite and she found it disturbing. There was that garden which Martha had inadvertently mentioned, the one that was locked up. It reminded her of Wuthering Heights. It was years since she had read the book. The big, gloomy house on the edge of the moor, the orphan who came one night and became part of it, all had a familiar ring about it. And wasn't Colin—at least when he was at home—a little like Heathcliff, and Mary, perhaps, his Catherine? In that case what chance had she of winning his heart?

So why was she bothering to try and please him? All the anguish she put herself through, pressing herself to go on when she was dropping with fatigue, forcing her nerve when inside she was quaking with fear. When she stayed at Misselthwaite at Easter she'd trekked for miles with him over the moor, on horseback or on foot, and all the time she had a feeling he was not really with her. He seemed preoccupied, closed off from her.

She was relieved to get back to Larkhill, where Colin was a different person.

And then there were times when he made unreasonable demands upon her.

'How would you like to fly down to Lulworth for the weekend?' he tossed at her one evening after a lesson. 'A group of friends from Cambridge are meeting up there for Whitsun, and they've asked me to join them.'

He may have been invited but she had not. She didn't even know these friends. And she'd always been taught that one did not go away for a weekend with a young man unless one was invited by the hostess, whom one knew. She felt herself blush.

'What's up? D'you think I'm monopolising you? Christmas, Easter and now....'

'No, no! It's not that.' Monopolising her? She could hardly bear to let him out of her sight. But he had not asked her to marry him, and if she did what he was proposing he probably never would.

'Lulworth's a splendid place,' he rambled on. 'There's a lovely beach there, and....'

'Colin, I...I can't go with you.' It was wrenched out of her in an agony of regret.

'You mean you're doing something else?'

She shook her head. 'You see, I've never...been away with a...man before.'

Colin threw back his head and laughed. 'My dear child, I'm not making an improper suggestion. I'm inviting you to a house party given by perfectly respectable friends of mine.'

'But I don't know them, and....' she shifted uneasily.

Colin became impatient. 'Dammit, Louise! Cambridge girls go camping with fellows and think nothing of it. They even, on occasion, share tents. I don't expect you to share a room with me, though I'm perfectly willing to do so if you wish.' His shoulders shook with silent mirth.

She looked at him, her eyes and cheeks ablaze, her breasts heaving with indignation. He was laughing at her! She was not one of his liberated women from Cambridge, and his callous disregard for her honour hurt.

He stopped laughing suddenly, as if he sensed his bantering had gone too far.

'Look, there are bound to be one or two other women in the party.' A house party, consisting mainly of men and one or two unattached females. It all sounded rather risqué.

He took a step towards her, putting his hands on her shoulders.

'What is it, Lu?' he said lifting her chin. His voice was soft, and a smile tugged at the corners of his mouth. 'Don't you trust me?'

His words, the tone of his voice, invoked a thrill of excitement. His head bent towards her, he was going to kiss her...

He knew she was in love with him, that she couldn't resist him, and he was taking liberties. It was so unfair! But she would not let him seduce her. She pushed him away firmly.

'I'll speak to John about it,' she said.

He stepped back from her, letting his hands drop to his sides.

'I'm forgetting,' he said. 'You're little more than a child and still tied to your brother's apron strings.' That stung, and he knew it. 'I shouldn't have suggested it. Goodnight, then.'

He touched her cheek in a brotherly peck, turned abruptly and left.

Tears stung her eyes as she watched him go, and she had to use every ounce of will she possessed not to call him back.

Louise didn't turn up for several days after that, and Colin began to wonder if he had indeed gone a little too far. He made up his mind to write her a letter apologising, begging her to make allowances for a fellow who was quite bewitched by her soft brown eyes. But before he could carry out this noble intention, he was surprised from behind and downed in a rugby tackle, finding himself face down on the ground, his assailant sitting astride his torso.

'What the devil are you playing at with my sister, Craven?' John Seymour bellowed above him.

But with his face pushed into the ground and a dead weight on his back, he could hardly breathe, let alone give an answer.

'Well?' More weight was being applied to his shoulders. 'What have you to say for yourself? She says you want to take her away for a weekend. If that means what I think....'

His arm was wrenched even further behind his back and he couldn't think straight for the pain, but he managed to gasp, 'No.... You're wrong....'

Till All The Seas Run Dry

'Wrong, am I? I wonder. I've met your type before. I've told her to keep away from you, but the devil of it is, the silly chit has fallen in love with you. I'm warning you, Craven, if you hurt her I'll kill you, d'you hear?'

Colin made a desperate effort to speak though he was almost suffocating with the weight on his back. Any moment now his ribs would crack. 'How could I hurt her? I'm madly in love with her.'

To his great relief the iron grip was slackened, and the weight lifted.

'In love with her, are you? Sure you're not confusing lust with love?'

'I'm not. I haven't felt like this about anyone for a long time.' Since Mary he thought.

'Then why are you making her indecent proposals?'

'It's not what you think. You've both misunderstood. I....'

'Well, until you can show me your intentions are honourable,' said John Seymour getting off his back and standing up, 'I'm afraid my sister will remain off limits to you.'

'You can't be serious?'

'I am. Never more so. You obviously didn't take in what I just said. She's very young, sensitive, trusting, and much to my regret, very much in love with you. I won't have her hurt.'

'You can't go on protecting her all her life, you know. But don't worry. I also meant it when I said I love her, and I'd never hurt her, not if I can help it.'

Colin was shaken. The pressure was on from all sides, his father, Louise herself, and now her brother, for him to make a decision about the future. His father seemed very taken with her, last time he was home he'd urged him to marry her.

'What are you waiting for, my boy?' he'd said. 'Mary to come back? It'll never happen. You'll simply waste away your youth like I did.'

He may have been right about that. He'd probably never see Mary again. But why did he have a guilt complex about being disloyal to her. It was she who'd deserted him. Heaven only knew where she was, or if she was even alive. And Louise was here....

There was a remarkable similarity between the two women. They were both strong minded individuals, both rebellious, tenacious, courageous. There were differences. Louise took life less seriously than Mary, she was outspoken and fun loving, yet she pulled her punches, where Mary did not. Mary had the ability to cut him down to size quite painfully. She was silent, controlled, intense, keeping her feelings close to her chest. Louise had a kinder, gentler nature. She was impulsive, more like himself, whether or not that was a good thing he wasn't sure.

During her visit to Misselthwaite at Easter they'd found much in common, she shared his enjoyment of riding and walking on the moor, though there were places he'd never taken her, like Ravensfell. And the secret garden remained locked up, a monument to Mary. She was liked by everyone. Only Dickon and Martha, out of loyalty to Mary, showed any sign of hostility, though not against Louise herself. Their disapproval was aimed in his direction. It saddened him that his friendship with Dickon had suffered so badly from Mary's defection.

Louise was young enough to be malleable, and anxious to please—he would not have found Mary nearly so amenable—and yet she had a substantial will of her own. She'd not be a servile wife, nor did he want her to be. Her refusal to go with him to Lulworth had secretly pleased him. She was a virtuous woman. Not that he lacked respect for Mary or loved her less because she'd slept with him. It had been an unselfish, generous act, and he'd never condemn her for it. But he respected Louise for sticking to her principles.

'I'm due some leave,' he said one day after a flying lesson. 'We could get married, and then fly down to the coast. If the weather's fine we could even swim. What's the matter?'

'Isn't this a little sudden? Us getting married? You're assuming I'll say yes.'

'But you knew it was in my mind. Isn't it what you want, too?' He bent his head and kissed her. She tasted sweet. It was those boiled sweets she sucked when they were flying. 'You do want to marry me, don't you, Louise?'

She hesitated before asking, 'What about Mary?'

'What about her?' She was silent. 'Who's been talking to you about Mary? Dickon?'

'Not just Dickon.'

'Martha, too, no doubt.'

'And your father. He told me how very fond you were of each other, and I'm afraid that if she ever came back....' She broke off, a look of uncertainty on her face.

'She won't come back,' he said, but his voice lacked conviction. 'But even if she did.... Mary is my first cousin. I couldn't marry her anyway.'

'Do you really love me? I couldn't bear it if you were marrying me on the rebound.'

'It's hardly that. Mary's been gone nearly three years.'

Was he still in love with Mary? She was probably the most important person in his life, he'd always love her, but did that mean he could never love anyone else? And was he to live like a monk for the rest of his life? He'd thought once he couldn't live without Mary, yet now he wanted Louise and was perfectly happy to marry her.

'All I can say is I'm happy when I'm with you, Lu. I was desperately lonely before you came along. If that isn't love, then I'm not sure I know what is.' He took her by the shoulders, looking into her eyes. 'So, what's your answer, yes or no?'

'Let me think about it, Colin,' she said at last.

Despite her uncertain answer, he was confident enough of her acceptance to go ahead and ask her brother's permission, and the Colonel's. It was traditional, as in most regiments, for an officer to seek his commanding officer's approval before getting married, though permission was usually granted automatically if the officer was over twenty-five.

'I'm at a loss, Lu,' said John Seymour. 'I understood you were in love with the fellow.'

It was an understatement. She loved everything about Colin. The way he looked at her under that veil of black lashes, his fascinating grey eyes like a whirlpool one could drown in. She loved the way he laughed, the way his mouth curled up at the corners when he smiled, his inimitable humour. She liked it when he teased her. Even little things like the way he raked his hand through his hair and the way he tossed his head. Could she bear never to see him again, walking jauntily, swinging his flying cap and goggles as he came towards her....

Her eyes filled with tears. 'I am, desperately, but....' she said, biting her lip. 'Oh, John! Am I a fool to long for a man to love me to distraction?'

'What d'you want? A spaniel, cowering at your feet?'

'No, but I want to be the most important thing in a man's life. Is that so impossible?'

'It is if you're marrying an aviator. Any woman who marries a flyer must expect to share him with his career, but I'd have thought you and Colin were well matched.'

'Indeed, flying is something I could share with him,' she agreed. But she couldn't bring herself to tell him about her fears, about the nightmare she had that Mary turned up at the wedding and she and Colin went off together leaving her alone. It seemed so foolish.

'Well,' said her brother, after a moment. 'I've known Colin for two years. He seems to be a loyal, reliable sort. Not the type to play fast and loose. No marriage is idyllic, but if you love him I should marry him. If you turn him down, I've a feeling you might regret it.'

What seemed like an astonishingly short time later Louise stood before the mirror, making the final adjustments to her veil. She looked critically at the image she saw in it and wondered if it would please Colin. Her hairdresser had done the best she could with her unruly curls. Doubts raged inside her, and her stomach became a mass of butterflies. How long would it be before he grew bored with her? How long before he left her in that great house in the middle of the Yorkshire moor and went off in pursuit of his own interests?

She was still not certain he really loved her.

But then, how many marriages nowadays were truly based on love?

Her sister Anna burst into the room. Anna never knocked.

'Lu darling,' she cried, holding out her arms. 'You look wonderful!' She kissed her carefully so not to crush her dress. 'John's waiting downstairs. Shall I tell him you're ready?'

'Are you happy, Anna? Really happy, I mean. Not just keeping up a pretence?' Louise asked anxiously.

'My dear child!' Why must Anna always call her "child" when she was only three years older herself. Colin did it too, but somehow she didn't mind it so much coming from him. 'Of course I'm happy. Why on earth shouldn't I be?'

She looked closely at Louise.

'What's the matter, Lu? You look pale as anything. Are you wearing any rouge? Just a touch on your cheek bones wouldn't go amiss.' She began to rummage in Louise's reticule. 'You've got the collywobbles. But don't worry about it. Every bride gets them. Have a small drop of brandy, it's excellent for settling the nerves. You haven't got any!'

'What? Brandy?'

'No, silly, rouge.'

'I never wear it,' said Louise a trifle indignantly. Just then there was a tentative knock on the door. 'Come in, John.'

'Are you ready, Lu? I don't want to hurry you, but...I say, you look as pretty as a picture, as I knew you would....'

Till All The Seas Run Dry

Seeing him standing there, full of affection and admiration— Colin never paid her such compliments—she had to swallow a lump in her throat. He took her in his arms, not caring if he crumpled her dress or crushed the corsage in her hair.

'Are you all right, love?' he asked anxiously.

'She's got a fit of the collywobbles,' Anna explained. 'Give her some brandy, John.'

But he was not listening to her, he was intent upon his youngest sister.

'It's not too late,' he said gently. He could always read her mind, better than anyone else in the world. 'It's not too late, even now, if you want to call it off.'

'What!' exclaimed Anna. 'She can't do that, John. For heaven's sake don't fill her head with such crazy notions.'

'Keep out of this, Anna,' said John, raising a warning forefinger. 'Louise, dearest....'

But Louise had recovered her composure. 'Don't worry, Anna. I'm not going to disgrace you. And you're right, it's only a fit of cold feet. I'll be all right now.'

Chapter 23

'Do you, Colin Craven, take this woman to be your wedded wife ... to keep thee only unto her so long as ye both shall live?'

There was a deathly silence. Louise looked up at him, her heart like lead. He seemed to hesitate for an eternity. At last he said, 'I do.'

'Until death do us part.'

It seemed such a final commitment, and she and Colin had made it together. She looked up to find him smiling at her, his smile so warm, so reassuring she felt aglow with pleasure.

'You look lovely, Lu,' he said. 'More beautiful than I've ever seen you.'

Her eyes pricked with tears and her throat ached. This was a day for compliments, she thought, feeling a little giddy. The strong brandy her brother had administered that morning had made her feel light headed, and she'd sailed through the day as if in a dream. Now there was champagne to add to the affect. She leaned heavily on Colin's arm.

'May I kiss the bride, Colin?' It was Mr Craven. 'Well, my dear, now you are Mistress of Misselthwaite?'

She was Mistress of Misselthwaite!

'There hasn't been a mistress here for twenty-five years,' Mrs Medlock had told her once. 'Most of the staff have never known one.'

But she was conscious of a sinking feeling at the thought of living there.

'When can we expect you home, my boy?' asked Mr Craven, turning to Colin.

'Not for at least two weeks. I'm taking Louise away on honeymoon.'

Relief swept over her. She was not looking forward to the task of running that huge rambling house. Surely Colin would not leave her there alone. She'd much rather rent one of those officer's married quarters at Larkhill. They had not had time to discuss these details.

'Come, darling, we must leave if we're to get to the coast before dark.'

But before they could leave a gentleman wearing a monocle barred their way, taking her hand. 'How d'you do, Mrs Craven. Since that husband of yours seems to have forgotten his manners I suppose

I must introduce myself. I'm Bertie Higginbotham. Colin and I were pals at Cambridge. Get him to bring you to visit us sometime.'

'I will indeed. I've never been to Cambridge'

'You must be hungry,' Colin said when they reached the small hotel. 'You go on up to our room while I secure us a table for dinner. Can you be ready in say half an hour?'

She wasn't hungry. The excitement of the wedding, the apprehension, followed by the long flight had left her feeling exhausted. All she wanted was to lie down and go to sleep.

'Something light, if possible. I couldn't eat a huge meal, Colin.'

Later when they retired to bed she was relieved that Colin, sensitive to her wishes, left her in private to prepare herself for the night. She was sound asleep by the time he slipped in beside her.

But in the morning he turned to her. 'Now, my little dove, what about those vows we made yesterday? You promised to love, honour and obey, and I,' he said, lifting the hem of her nightdress, 'promised to worship you with my body.'

His exploring hands sent little darts of flame rippling from her loins until her whole body was suffused with fire.

'Would you like me to worship you?' he asked, his hand stroking the inside of her thigh. She tried to control it but she couldn't help trembling. She was like an aspen in a breeze. 'Shall I do it now?' She wanted him so much but she couldn't tell him so. 'Louise?'

In answer she wound her arms round his neck and arched her body to his. She gasped at the pain when he first took possession of her, but she would have endured it again and again for the sheer delight of what came after. Never, in her wildest dreams had she imagined such excruciating pleasure.

The honeymoon was everything she'd dreamed of and much more, and it passed far too quickly. They'd laze in the sun, lie on the beach until the sea came up and wet their feet; or they'd walk for miles to find some quiet, secluded spot and make love in the open air, or else they'd rush back to their room in the middle of the day. She tried to behave with modesty but she found it impossible, when he took her in his arms, their naked bodies together, to hide her overwhelming desire.

For nearly a month he was completely absorbed in her and she began to believe he really did love her. If only it could have been like that for ever, their marriage would surely be so happy. But the honeymoon was too soon over, and now she must face reality and Misselthwaite.

****

Basil was beginning to find official cocktail parties around the embassies a dead bore, though he was impressed by Geneva. He was growing tired of Zurich. The weather there had been miserable recently, damp and invariably raining. Summer was almost over and he longed to be in the Alps with Maxine and Mary, specially now that his time in Zurich was drawing to an end. There were important decisions to be made, and there was so little time left.

He was not to remain in Europe as he had hoped. He'd just heard from his superior that his next posting was to be Peking, and he was not sure it was a suitable place to take a young wife. And yet he couldn't bear to leave Zurich without Maxine.

Being in love had certainly complicated his life. On the whole he liked working for the Foreign Office. If he'd been free from attachments he'd be over the moon to be going to an exciting, intriguing country like China. And what would he do if he quit. He was no business man and the thought of a career in the City bored him to tears.

There were other complications, too. Madame Steinberger was a fearsome woman, she'd strongly resist any attempt to take her darling daughter to the other side of the world. And if she was to be his mother-in-law it would be unwise to cross her. Then there were his own, strictly religious parents. What would they think of him marrying the daughter of a notorious courtesan? Yet if he wanted their blessing he'd have to somehow persuade them that, in spite of her mother, Maxine was pure as the driven snow.

And then there was Mary.

It was nearly two years since she had turned up at the Embassy with nowhere to go, in a state as near to hysteria as he had ever seen her. He was thankful that, despite what Rudi had done she and Maxine were still friends. Indeed if Rudi had not been Maxine's brother he'd probably have given him a sound thrashing.

The two girls were now living together in a place called Val de Paix, Mary teaching in the school, while Maxine had a job as receptionist in the little hotel. But Mary would be lonely without her friend. If only she could be persuaded to return to England. Here she was always a little under suspicion, even without the child. People were bound to ask what an English widow was doing living alone in Switzerland.

He could not understand why a sensible person like Mary was still in love with a bounder like Colin Craven. No decent man would treat a woman like that. And yet it crossed his mind suddenly that the whole thing might have been a ghastly misunderstanding.

Well, there was only one way to find out. He was due three months leave in between postings. He was intending to go home to visit his parents in Lincolnshire. While over there he could look up Colin Craven. Perhaps it was interfering, betraying Mary's trust, but if it was to bring about a family reunion, the end would surely justify the means. He would not tell Mary of this scheme. He'd find out as much as possible about Craven without admitting any knowledge of his cousin. If the fellow was the cad he'd always thought he was, he'd leave it at that, and no harm would be done. If he couldn't manage a simple thing like that he had no business calling himself a diplomat.

****

'Where are we going, Colin?' Louise asked, looking at the compass. 'We seem to be going further east. And I don't recognise the landscape at all.'

'You said you wanted to see Cambridge. We've a couple of days to spare. I thought we'd visit Bertie as promised, then you can come back to Larkhill with me. I'm sure we could stop with John for a while, and I can always take you to Misselthwaite later.'

Louise hugged him. 'Oh, darling Colin!' she squeaked, snuggling up against his back, her arms tightly round him. 'You're always so full of delightful surprises.'

'Yes, well…' he said, his hand creeping up her leg towards that most sensitive spot. 'I'm finding it hard to tear myself away from you.'

'Now, Colin!' she scolded, firmly restraining the errant hand. 'Concentrate on flying this aircraft.' Then she kissed the back of his neck and laid her head on his back. 'Oh, I do love you so.'

'That's just as well,' he chuckled. 'Since you're my wife now.'

He might have said, "I love you" back, but he didn't. Indeed he'd never said it, except in the heat of passion. She gave a little sigh of regret.

'Will Bertie mind us dropping in on him unexpectedly?'

'Oh, we can't stop with Bertie,' said Colin, aghast. 'He has rooms within the college and entertaining ladies after dark is strictly forbidden. But there's a little hotel I know.'

They created quite a stir when they landed in a field just outside Cambridge—the same field from which Colin had taken off in that fateful balloon with Charlotte. A large crowd soon gathered, and Louise wanted to laugh out loud when she heard one man say in astonishment, 'One of them's a woman!' Having lived so long in Larkhill where local people were used to it, she'd forgotten that in the rest of the country the sight of an aircraft still drew large crowds.

'Nobody's to touch anything,' Colin issued the warning. 'It might burst into flames.'

'Why did you tell them that?' Louise giggled, when they were out of earshot.

'How else was I to stop them tinkering with it while we're gone? Perhaps Bertie will know somewhere I can keep it under cover. In the mean time....'

By now they had reached the town, and Louise gazed in wonder.

'Oh, Colin, it's unbelievably beautiful. I could become a genius in a place like this. On the other hand, I doubt if I'd get any work done at all.'

'You get used to it,' said her husband, putting a protective arm round her. 'Eventually you take it for granted.'

Someone hailed Colin and came bounding across the road like an overgrown puppy.

'This is Rupert Brooke, Lu. He's a poet and playwright, and he's famous. My wife, Louise, Rupert.'

'I've read some of your poems,' said Louise, admiringly.

The stranger shook her hand affably. 'Your wife! When did you tie the knot, you dark old horse. And where have you been hiding this delightful creature.'

'It's not for lack of trying. I wanted to bring her down to Lulworth at Whitsun. You see, my love, if you hadn't turned down my exceptional offer you'd probably have already met Rupert, among other famous people.'

'Not at Whitsun, you wouldn't,' said Rupert, gloomily. 'I was in Germany.'

'But what about you, Rupert. I thought you'd be married yourself by now. Didn't I hear something about you and the lovely Noële Olivier?'

Rupert winced. 'We're not all as lucky in love as you are, Craven! My life's a mess. Rotten business in Germany. Can't tell you. Truth is, I envy you. To see you with a lovely wife like this.... If you'll excuse me,' he said with a slight bow, turned and walked off.

'I think you've offended him,' said Louise, when he'd gone.

'I don't think so. Rupert doesn't take offence easily. But like many sensitive, artistic people his moods are a bit erratic, according to his personal life at the time. Something is wrong, however, and it must be something serious because he's normally an optimist.'

They later learned from Bertie the probable reason for Rupert's black mood. His long romance with Noële had apparently ended last summer, and in despair he'd turned to Ka Cox, a close friend for many years. She'd gone with him to Germany where they'd become involved in an affair and now she expected him to marry her.

'I see that I've touched a raw spot,' said Colin. 'When I made my frivolous remark about Noële Olivier I had no idea he really cared so much for her.'

'Cared for her! He worships her. Always has done. And you know they were secretly engaged for several years.'

'Poor old Rupert! No wonder he was sore. First he sees me sporting a brand new wife on my arm,' said Colin, placing one round Louise. 'Then I spark the fuse to the black night of his soul by asking about Noële.'

'Are all his poems written about her, I wonder?' said Louise.

'Not all, but a great many, I wouldn't wonder,' said Bertie. 'Well, it's good to see you both, and I don't mind telling you, you look terrific. Marriage seems to suit you. It's good to see you settled at last, Colin. By the way, I think I should warn you...' His voice dropped to little above a whisper. 'Somebody said they'd seen Charlotte last night. She must have heard you were coming. She doesn't give up, does she?'

'If she's thinking of making trouble with Louise....'

Both men glanced in her direction. She wondered who Charlotte was. Then she remembered hearing about the woman Colin had almost married. There'd been a great scandal when he'd broken off the engagement, and then Mary had disappeared. They all hated her at Misselthwaite. She gave a little involuntary shudder.

Colin smiled affably. 'Well, darling, I'd better take you back to the hotel. I'm sure you'd like a nice relaxing bath before dinner. 'I'll see you later, Bertie,' he winked at his friend.

****

When he returned to Misselthwaite Colin realised, quite suddenly, that he had not once thought of Mary since the day he'd married Louise. And then it had only been a spasm, whether of guilt or apprehension, when the vicar asked if he was prepared to make a life-long commitment to the woman standing beside him. A sudden vision of Mary had presented itself, together with the thought "Supposing she comes back?" But he'd dismissed it, telling himself Mary would never come back, not after all these years of dead silence—if she were even still alive.

Yet she had been so much a part of Misselthwaite it was impossible not to think of her whenever he was there, and he could scarcely walk around the grounds without being overwhelmed with poignant memories. It was for this reason he'd spent so little time at home recently. But this was hardly fair to Louise, who, as his wife, would be expected to live here, at least most of the time; nor did he want to be parted from her. If they were to have any sort of life together he must lay Mary's ghost once and for all.

Autumn was in full swing. Soon the trees would be losing all their leaves. He leaned on the little wicket gate which led to the bluebell wood, where the fallen leaves had already begun to form a thick carpet. He remembered how, as children, they used to wade through them, driving before them an ever increasing tidal wave, sometimes knee deep.

He sighed and turned away. It was time to tackle the Secret Garden, in which lay the heart of the matter. He had neglected it for three years, which was a sacrilege, and the last thing Mary would have wanted. The longer he left it preserved as a mausoleum to her the more difficult it would be to extinguish the memories. If he could share it with Louise, it would eventually become their garden. It would come to life again and its healing properties—he was convinced it had them—would overlay any pain he might at first encounter. Yet Mary's spirit would continue to thrive there—a friendly, gentle ghost.

He found himself in the Long Walk which led to the Secret Garden, and it was as if some power, some force he was unable to resist was drawing him relentlessly towards it. He wondered in what condition he'd find it. Dickon would help him put it right.

The door was now quite covered by ivy, difficult to find unless you knew exactly where to look. Colin's fingers felt for the niche in the high wall where he had hidden the key. He might, if his mind had not been occupied, have wondered at the ease with which the key turned....

A feeling of aching nostalgia swept over him, for the place was in a similar state of wilderness as it had been when he'd first seen it....

He could see someone had been here recently... Dickon must have done the same as old Ben Weatherstaff all those years ago, when he climbed over the wall to tend to it. A wave of guilt and sadness swept over him at the memory of the gardener whom he'd been too busy feeling sorry for himself to say farewell to.

Mary's spirit filled the garden. She was everywhere! The honeyed scent from the wisteria was evocative. He could almost see her bending over a rose to inhale its heady perfume, her cheeks flushed from her recent efforts...hear her voice calling his name, and feel the warmth of her body in his arms, her soft lips against his own....

He sat down in the bower....

He had no idea how long he'd been sitting there, but he must have fallen asleep, for now he opened his eyes and, blinking, looked around in astonishment. It seemed as though he'd been transported to another place, for everything was altered. And yet it was the same garden, the same bower. Was he still dreaming?

It was summer, and it was evening, for the sun was low. He felt it warm on his face. The grass was green and neatly mown, and summer flowers were out in profusion, the roses at their most magnificent, their scents bombarding his senses. The whole garden was altered—there were many things, plants, statues, even trees that were strange to him, and many familiar items, such as the pergola he and Dickon had erected some years ago, were missing. But the most noticeable difference was that in place of the old gnarled stump that had been the main stay for the honeysuckle and rambling roses stood a huge tree with spreading branches.

As he stared at it he noticed a rustling noise which at first he mistook for the wind rippling the leaves. He heard also a voice singing—a woman's voice, or it could have been a boy's—a sweet, clear, bell-like sound, coming from its midst. He put his hand up to shield his eyes from the sun, drawing closer to see what it was. There was someone sitting on one of the large over hanging branches, swinging up and down. He drew closer to see who it was. Then he caught his breath....

'Mother!'

'Ah, Colin,' she said in a lilting voice. 'I waited so long for you to come, and now it is too late.'

'Too late for what?' Somehow the sight of her sitting precariously on the branch filled him with foreboding. 'What are you doing up there, Mother? Isn't it rather dangerous?'

'Dangerous, why? I often sit here,' she said, rather petulantly. 'I love this branch, it swings so beautifully. Your father is always scolding me for doing it. Pray don't you begin.'

'What did you want me for?' he asked. Then a dreadful suspicion crept into his head. 'Why is it too late?'

A little tinkle of laughter escaped her. 'Have you really forgotten? This garden, for instance, what does it mean to you?'

'Mary!' he said in a half whisper, a feeling of guilt percolating his whole being. 'Don't tell me she's alive, after all.' Why had he been in such a hurry to marry someone else? But he loved Louise, his soul protested. 'And anyway, why did she leave me?'

'It's too late, Colin, for all these questions. And yet it is never too late exactly. Mary is out of your reach for the time being, but there'll come a time when you will be able to make amends for the wrong you have done her....'

'The wrong I've done her? Mother, you're speaking in riddles,' he said impatiently. 'Please explain.'

'Very soon now you will discover the truth, and all your questions will be answered, but be careful you don't make the same mistake again. It's no use grieving over the irretrievable, Colin. If you go along looking over your shoulder you are liable to fall over the rock right under your nose. In many ways you are very much like my Archie. Don't do what he did.'

'I still don't understand,' said Colin.

'You will,' she smiled at him. 'I cannot show you the future for it is not formed yet and in any case you have the free will to alter it. But I can answer one of your questions. Go over to that sundial.'

Colin obeyed.

'Now,' she said. 'Make sure you are facing due east, and look into the dial.'

He did this, and after a few moments the dial disappeared and a vista opened up, as if he was looking out of a huge window. Mary was in the centre of the picture, surrounded by high Alps. She was holding a baby, cradling it in her arms, cooing at it, kissing it. A moment later the baby was in its cradle and a great shadow hung over it, then Mary was crying, weeping uncontrollably over the cradle, and a tiny coffin was being lowered into the ground. He tried to speak to her, to reach out and comfort her, but he couldn't make her hear. At last everything went blank and he was left staring at the sundial.

'What does it mean?' he cried, turning to his mother. 'I thought Mary was dead. Is she alive? And that child, was it mine?'

But she was no longer listening to him. She seemed unaware of his presence even. She was swinging on her branch and she'd resumed her singing. He feared the branch would break.

'Mother, Mother, take care!'

There was a sound like the cracking of thunder and the branch broke, and with a cry she fell....

Colin found himself still sitting in the bower, the garden in the same state of disarray as when he came in, and Dickon standing before him.

'The mistress sent me t' find thee. She's been looking all over for thee. Thought I might find thee here.'

Still stunned he tried to gather the fragments of his dream together. 'I've just had the weirdest vision, the garden.... Tell, me, Dickon, have you been coming in here during the last three years?'

'Aye,' he said, a defiant note in his voice, adding defensively, 'Do tha mind? Only it were her garden too, tha ken, an' I figured she'd not want it left to die.'

'You're quite right about that. And of course I don't mind. It's a bit like old Ben Weatherstaff, climbing over the wall with a ladder. Do you remember?'

'Aye, only I didn't use ladder,' he grinned. 'I found your hiding place for key.'

'I didn't bury it like Father did. I suppose that shows I didn't really mean to forget it.'

He thought of his dream again. There was one question he could ask Dickon. 'Do you know anything about the tree that was once there?' He pointed to the old stump which was once more covered by rambling roses.

Dickon looked at him strangely. 'Why, there's not been a tree there for twenty-five years, far as I know.'

'But the tree that was there—look, there's still a stump—was it an oak with spreading branches, do you know? And why was it chopped down?'

'How should I know, sir. I were nowt but a wee lad.'

'But have you heard tell? Did my mother like to swing on its branches?'

Dickon looked puzzled. 'Eh, bless me, how d' tha ken that?'

'I've just seen it in a dream. Go on, tell me what you know.'

Dickon's eyes nearly popped out of his head. 'Eh, tha do have some strange dreams, Master Colin. Well, I suppose I may as well tell thee. Tha'rt old enow to bear it now. Tha mother fell from one o' them branches. It were that as brought about her death, an' caused thee to come too soon, an' be born all wrong. Tha father had it cut down after.'

Colin drew in a deep breath. If that part of his dream had really happened, what of the rest? Had he just seen something that had actually happened to Mary?

'Was Mary expecting a baby?' he asked Dickon. 'Was that why she ran away, and why you were so angry with me? Was it my child she was expecting?'

Dickon looked stunned. Nothing Colin said would ever again surprise him. And there seemed little point in hiding it from him when he evidently already knew the truth.

'Aye, she were pregnant, and who else's bairn would it be but yours?' Colin detected a spark of the old hostility in his eyes as he spoke.

He flushed. 'Oh, God! No wonder....' he broke off, wrestling with his emotions. 'Am I forgiven? Can we be friends again?' He spoke so earnestly that Dickon smiled and slowly extended his hand. Colin grabbed it eagerly. 'I can't tell you how much your friendship means to me, Dickon. It was bad enough losing Mary, but....'

A sudden thought struck him. 'Dickon, what if she's alive? In my dream....' Another doubt eased its way to the foreground of his cluttered memory. The vision his mother had shown him might have been symbolic. Why else had she said it was too late—that Mary was out of his reach? If only there was a Joseph around to interpret his dreams. Or did she mean, the spark of hope persisted, that it was too late because he was now married to Louise.

'I'm a bigamist!' he said suddenly. 'Somewhere in the world I have another wife and a child....' No, the child was dead—he'd seen her bury it. Poor Mary! Poor darling Mary—all alone, her child dead, while he....

'I must find her.' he muttered, half to himself. But where would he look?

There were mountains in the background. She was living somewhere where there were mountains. But that could be anywhere.

'If Mary's alive I shall find her, Dickon, if it's the last thing I do.'

Chapter 24

It was three years since Basil had been home for Christmas, and he was shocked to find how much his parents had aged. And they were becoming more and more set in their ways. It was clear they were not very happy about his proposed marriage, though they'd not said so for fear of falling out with him. They would change their minds as soon as they met Maxine. He was confident of that. They would love her immediately.

But what they did voice concern about was the prospect of him going off to Peking for three years. China was a dangerous place for foreigners, they'd heard. Revolutions, massacres, attacks upon embassies. Didn't a whole lot of English people get killed?

'That was the Boxer rebellion in 1900. They're more interested in killing each other these days,' he said in an attempt to reassure them. 'China has recently become a Republic.'

This was small comfort to his father who said, 'It doesn't alter the fact that they don't like foreigners, and the whole thing could blow up again.'

He had to confess he had his own misgivings, but he would not say so to them, in case his alternative plan did not come off. The idea of joining the Royal Flying Corps had emerged since his visit to Cambridge a few weeks ago. After consulting the registrar he'd discovered that Colin Craven had been at Trinity College from 1906 to 1909, he'd become a don in 1910, but he'd given it all up in January 1911 when he'd left Cambridge. That date was significant. It was that Christmas he'd first met Maxine, and, come to think of it, Mary.

His enquiries had led him to Bertie Higginbotham who'd told him that Colin was stationed at Larkhill with the RFC. This piece of information had given Basil a wonderful idea. To be a flyer had been one of his life's ambitions. If he could get himself accepted for the RFC he'd have found himself another career, one that would be far more rewarding than the Foreign Office. Whether his parents would be any more thrilled at the prospect than they were about Peking was another matter. But even if he was not accepted what better excuse could he have to visit Larkhill and Colin Craven?

Till All The Seas Run Dry

****

Christmas this year at Misselthwaite was to be exceptional. Mr Craven had given orders that as many staff as possible were to go home, if not for the whole day, at least for a large part of it. Mrs Medlock, whose family had all flown the nest, and who, in any case, being housekeeper, had responsibility over the others, was herself to wait at table for the Christmas dinner. And afterwards she and the few staff who were left could enjoy as much as they wanted of the remains of the feast.

Jack Frost nipped Martha's nose as she picked her way round the frozen puddles on the way to the stables. She was afraid the ice would not bear her weight, and she didn't want to muddy her Sunday best. The air was so clear she could hear the bells ringing from the next village as well as those of their own little church. She found her brother busily grooming one of the horses.

'Merry Christmas, Dickon.'

'Merry Christmas, Martha. Eh, I'd best not kiss thee, I'm all mucky an' tha'rt clean and neat. Art off already?'

'Aye. Mrs Medlock said I could go soon as I'd finished chores. How long will you be?'

'It's all right for some,' said her brother. 'I've six more horses to groom an' feed yet. Tell Mother I'll not be late for dinner, though.'

'Tha'd best not be. We've got turkey this year, first time ever, thanks to th' mistress, an' Mother'll be mortified if it's marred.' She cast him a defiant look. 'I hope you realise it were her doing, giving us all day off this Christmas. It's unlikely either Mr Craven or Master Colin thought of it for theirselves. Th' mistress is a saint, an' no mistake.'

'Oh, aye,' he said softly. 'I admit I were wrong about her.'

'She's poles apart from that other one.' He realised she was referring to Charlotte. 'She's a real lady. An' she worships th' ground he walks on. I only wish he'd treat her right. He's hardly ever home, and,' she dropped her voice, 'he's gone all queer again these last months. He's got it in his head Miss Mary's not dead, an' he's got all them old photographs up in his room. I thought he'd got over all that.'

'It's since he had that dream int' garden.'

'What dream? Ooh, they are queer folk these Cravens.'

'He thinks Miss Mary's in Switzerland or somewhere like it.'

'Well, I'd love him to find her an' bring her home, but not if it means breaking th' poor mistress's heart. It's not right, him wi' a wife of his own, carrying on like that, leaving her all alone. I hear her weeping sometimes. I bet she were born on a Friday.'

'What's th' day she were born to do wi' anything?'

'You know the rhyme, "Friday's child is loving an' giving." That's the mistress all over. Well, I'll be off now. Don't forget my present when tha come.'

'Tha'll be lucky,' he chuckled.

He watched her trot off down the lane towards the little cottage on the moor. It was true he'd been biased against the new mistress of the house to begin with, as he'd have been against anyone who'd taken Mary's place. But of late she'd won him over. She'd made a habit of coming and talking to him in the stables. She took a keen interest in all the horses and she had a gentle caring way with animals.

He pulled out of his breast pocket the half-hunter they'd given him for Christmas. It was an uncommonly generous present, and though it had been presented by Colin for both of them, he suspected that that too had been her idea.

****

It was cold in the hanger and Colin had to hug and slap himself and jump up and down to keep warm. The aerodrome was very exposed and a biting wind always blew straight into the hanger. It was a difficult task working on machinery with numb fingers, but the job had to be done, and the sooner it was done, the sooner he could get inside beside a roaring fire.

He was missing Louise. The winter was usually a quieter time for the RFC, they didn't do much flying and training was mostly confined to ground work. But they'd all been so busy this year that, with the exception of a few days over Christmas, he had not been home very much at all. And locally there was no suitable accommodation available.

He was about to put the last bits back together and then test run the engine before locking up, when there was a discreet knock on the door of the hanger. He looked up, expecting to see the sergeant or a corporal, but it was a civilian, a man he'd never seen before.

'Captain Craven?' the stranger asked.

'That's me,' said Colin, as he approached. 'You have the advantage over me....'

'My name is Basil Crawford,' said the young man.

'How d'you do. Excuse me for not shaking hands,' he said, holding up his oily ones.

'I say, what are you doing? Working on an aeroplane. May I see?'

'By all means. Are you interested in flying?'

'I'll say I am. It's my second love, after skiing—not that I've ever flown the real thing. But I used to be a dab hand at ballooning.'

'That's how I started. But flying aeroplanes is a little different from ballooning.'

'I bet it is—a lot better, I should think.'

'A lot more difficult, and, I hasten to add, dangerous.'

'Are you going to test run? Can I come up with you?'

'It's too cold to fly today. I was just going to run the engine. But.... You didn't say what you're here for,' he added cautiously. 'Were you hoping to join?'

'As a matter of fact.... Are you looking for recruits?' the other asked eagerly.

'We're always looking for recruits, but I must warn you, we're pretty particular. Getting accepted is not the easiest thing to accomplish.'

'But it's worth a try, and I am looking for a change. At the moment I'm with the Foreign Office and I've just been posted to Peking....'

'The Foreign Office? Where have you been stationed?'

'In Switzerland, Zurich. But, you see, I'm getting married....'

Switzerland! Why did it ring a bell in his mind? For some reason he remembered his dream in the garden.

'Are there many English people in Switzerland, and do you know them all?'

The answer he got was guarded. 'There's a small community of them in Zurich at least, but I don't know them all, by any means.'

Colin looked at him speculatively. He seemed a pretty normal sort of fellow. And why should Switzerland make him think immediately of Mary? She could be almost anywhere.

'Well, if you want to join the RFC as a pilot, you'll have to learn to fly, pass various tests, and get your Aero Club Certificate, or brevet, as we call it. It'll cost you £75, by the way, refundable when you pass.' Basil blanched, and Colin grinned at him. 'Can't afford it? Well, maybe I'll lend it to you. But you'd better damn well pass, or I shall ask for it back.'

Basil didn't know what to make of Colin. Inexplicably he'd taken an instant liking to him. It was as if they'd known each other from time immemorial. He found it hard to equate him with the man who'd treated Mary so badly. Yet married, he certainly was. That became clear the first time he set foot in the Officers' Mess and they ran into Colin's brother-in-law.

'Found a new protégé, Colin?' said the man with dark, wavy hair, a curly moustache and a twinkle in his eye 'I'm John Seymour, and this fellow's married my youngest sister.'

The more he heard about Colin's wife the more confused he became. Even her name, Louise, didn't strike a bell.

'Everyone in the regiment likes her, from the Colonel down,' said a young lieutenant. 'She's always so interested in one, so kind and sympathetic. Captain Craven's a lucky man.'

This description didn't fit the cold, calculating female Mary had described. He almost blundered before he discovered his mistake.

'Did you say you were planning to get married?' Colin asked him during dinner.

'Yes indeed. As soon as possible.'

'Well, it may not be as soon as you would like. It's frowned upon in the army to marry too young. If you're under twenty-five it's called marrying in sin. And you have to have the Colonel's approval, in any case. If you don't mind me asking, how old are you?'

'Twenty-four.'

Colin sucked in a breath through pursed lips. 'You'll have to wait a year at least. And the Colonel will want to meet your intended....'

'But you, yourself were married in sin, as you call it, were you not?'

'Certainly not. I'm twenty-six.'

'But you've been married three years, haven't you?'

Colin pulled an incredulous face, and there was a hoot of laughter all round the table.

'He thinks you're a staid, old married man, Colin,' someone said.

'Where on earth did you get that idea?' demanded his host.

Basil was covered with confusion. 'I'm so sorry. I've made a dreadful mistake.'

'Louise and I have been married just over three months. I've hardly known her a year.'

'Where is your good wife, then. Why isn't she here?'

'Good question,' someone said. 'Why hide her away in Yorkshire, Craven? He's keeping her away from us. That's what it is,' the speaker added with a broad wink.

'As soon as I can get a quarter I shall bring her down here,' said Colin with cool dignity.

'Why didn't you say you'd applied for a quarter. You can have mine,' John Seymour broke in. 'I don't need it now.'

'That's not a bad idea. At least Louise will feel at home. Let's see the Quartermaster in the morning.' He turned to Basil again. 'Tell us about your betrothed.'

'She's not one of those foreigners, is she?' asked one of the others. 'You've come from the Foreign Office, haven't you?'

'As a matter of fact,' said Basil, flushing. 'She is Swiss.'

'German Swiss?' asked Colin, with a frown. 'The Colonel won't like that.'

'Put him down, fellows,' said John Seymour. 'Don't take any notice of any of them, Crawford. It'll be perfectly all right, and I'm sure the Colonel will be charmed.'

'All I can say is I hope you've got more spunk than most of the milksops I've met from the F.O.,' said one rather outspoken man with a handle-bar moustache. He looked a little older than the others. 'It's a pretty tough life in the RFC, I can tell you. None but the most courageous are welcome here.'

'Now that is below the belt, Cricklewood. I won't have that.' It was Colin who came swiftly to Basil's defence this time. 'I don't mind betting Mr Crawford will prove a fine pilot and a distinguished officer.'

Turning in later that evening Basil was in a dilemma. Should he tell Colin about Mary or not? And what should he tell her? That Colin was happily married! Should he exonerate Colin in Mary's eyes at the expense of her happiness, open up the old wound, just as she'd got over it all? It would surely be better that she didn't know. But what if it should come out sometime later, if say, Maxine opened her mouth inadvertently? What would Colin think of him? The trust, the friendship he'd already been shown would be lost, let alone the chance of a career in the RFC. It was a tough decision, but he was prompted to make it when, a few days later, Colin received a letter and challenged him at the breakfast table.

'It's from my friend Bertie Higginbotham in Cambridge. He asks if you have turned up yet,' said Colin, giving him a searching look, and Basil noticed, for the first time, what strange, penetrating eyes he had. 'I'm curious to know why you were looking for me, and why you haven't mentioned it.'

Basil was stunned into silence for a moment. What could he say? Those hypnotic, grey eyes continued to stare at him, seeming to see right through him.

'Oh, very well, I was in two minds to tell you anyway. The fact is I was trying to protect a friend, someone who has been in hiding in Switzerland for the last three years....' He hesitated.

Colin didn't move a muscle except that his eyes opened very wide. 'Go on.'

'It's someone close to you, someone who won't be pleased with me for coming here.'

Colin's face blanched. 'Mary!' he said in a hoarse whisper. 'Where is she?' he demanded, gripping Basil's arm like a vice. 'You'd better tell me, Crawford, or you can go home and forget about learning to fly.'

'I can't tell you,' said Basil, trying to disentangle himself from Colin's iron fingers. 'Don't you see, I've already betrayed her trust by coming here in the first place.'

****

Louise sat sewing by the fire. She hadn't seen Colin since Christmas. He'd promised to apply for a quarter for them to live in, but as far as she knew he'd had no success. This was hardly what she thought of as a marriage, living apart, except for the occasional weekend visit.

Mr Craven sat opposite her, his head lolling forward in sleep. They used the little study on cold winter evenings, it was cosier than the huge drawing room when there were only the two of them. He lifted his head with a jerk.

'I'm so sorry, my dear. How rude of me.'

'It's perfectly all right, Mr Craven. I was happy with my thoughts and my sewing.' She paused thoughtfully, her needle hovering in mid air, before she spoke again. 'Should you mind very much if I went away?'

He looked a little startled. 'Where shall you go?'

'I'm missing Colin.' Those irritating tears pricked her eyes, but she tried to sound cheerful. 'And I'd like to see my brother, too.'

'Of course, my dear. Of course you would. It must be a dead bore for you being stuck in a place like this with a dull old man who falls asleep on you.'

'That's not true, Mr Craven. You're not dull at all,' she said regaining her composure. 'It's just that Colin and I have been married for four months, and I've scarcely seen him.'

'Say no more,' said her father-in-law. 'You shall go as soon as possible, tomorrow, if you wish. I shall put you on the train, and then I'll telegraph that neglectful husband of yours that you're coming. That's more warning than he ever gives me, I can tell you. When he was a young bachelor he'd simply turn up, sometimes bringing a whole flock of his friends with him.'

****

Maxine tore open the long awaited letter, Basil had not written for weeks. No wonder it was a thick envelope, as well as a five page letter to herself there was one addressed to Mary inside.

'He's decided to leave the Foreign Office and join the army!' she told Mary as she handed her her letter. 'He's given notice to the London Office. We shall be living in England instead of Peking.'

'Well, at least you'll be safe there.'

'But will Basil be safe. I fear not. He's joining the Royal Flying Corps. He's going to fly aeroplanes!'

'I'm sure they're no more dangerous than balloons,' said Mary. 'But I wonder what gave him that idea. Did you know he was thinking of leaving the Foreign Office?'

'I knew he was not happy about Peking, in particularly taking me there.'

'Oh, well, at least you'll be able to come home occasionally, and I hope you will.'

'Why don't you come with us, Mary?'

Mary laughed. 'You won't want me living with you. Who ever heard of a third party living with a couple so newly married.'

'But you will come to our wedding, won't you? He wants us to be married in England, and he wants you to come. At least come for that, Mary. Please.'

'Well, we'll see,' said Mary.

Suddenly she longed for home. It would be lonely here without Maxine and Basil. And she'd grown used to the idea of Charlotte at Misselthwaite. Misselthwaite wouldn't suit Charlotte she thought mischievously. Secretly she persuaded herself that Colin had grown tired of Charlotte by now, and her own relationship with him might blossom again. If she could not be his wife at least they could do the things they enjoyed together.

She went to her room to open her letter. Somehow she knew it held some momentous news, or Basil would hardly have written to her at the same time as Maxine. Even so her hand shook when she read that he had met, had actually seen Colin.

'He's desperate to see you,' the letter said. 'And before you go quite hysterical, I have not told him where you are—I believe he thinks you're in Zurich. I've said nothing about the baby either. In fact I told him very little, though he's pumped me with questions. I hope you'll forgive me for seeking him out. I admit I was quite wrong about him. He still loves you, Mary. He's always loved you, and he never married that woman, what was her name? In fact the scandal following the breaking of that engagement was the cause of him having to quit Cambridge.

She'd scarcely had a chance to absorb this news and all its implications when her hopes were dashed by the next paragraph which began:

'Now, here's the rub. He did get married a few months ago, to a girl he met here....'

She had to sit down or her knees would buckle under her. It was as if she'd been kicked in the stomach, or she'd grasped a live electric wire and the surge of current had run through her body, tearing apart her solar plexus. Only a few months ago he'd been free! He hadn't married Charlotte. He had intended to marry her, and she'd run away for nothing. She'd been through all that—lost her baby, lost everything....

She forced herself to continue reading Basil's letter, which spoke of Colin's wife, Louise, '...From what I hear she sounds rather like you, and she's very popular here—the sister of one of the other officers. She likes flying aeroplanes. That's how he met her....' Well, at least he had not been taken in by a beautiful fortune huntress. And they had much in common apparently. It was worse! '...She's from a good family, her maiden name was Seymour....' That would please Colin's father, she thought cynically.

Basil seemed very taken with Colin, who'd been most supportive about him joining the Regiment. She should be pleased that Basil liked Colin, yet she couldn't shake off a feeling of loss. Basil, who, until recently, had been her close friend and confidant, was now friends with Colin. He'd joined the other camp as it were, leaving her out in the cold. And soon Maxine would join him. They'd be a cosy little group of friends at Larkhill on Salisbury Plain, while she....

Till All The Seas Run Dry

The letter ended with the words: 'You can't blame him, Mary. He thought you'd deserted him for good. Until quite recently he didn't even know if you were dead or alive.... I'm so sorry to be the bearer of such bad tidings.'

****

Till All The Seas Run Dry

The young officer looked acutely embarrassed.

'I'm terribly sorry, Mr...'

'Crawford's the name, and I'm a guest of Captain Craven.'

'That's the point, sir. I'm afraid Captain Craven isn't here. He's gone off on leave—some crisis on the domestic front I believe. Obviously he didn't have time to tell you. Anyway, I'm terribly sorry, sir, but as a civilian you can't stay in the mess without a sponsor. Colonel's very particular on that point.'

'It's all right, Merridith,' said a voice behind him. 'I'll sponsor Mr Crawford. Give me the visitor's book and I'll sign it.'

Basil turned to find John Seymour standing behind him. 'Thank you very much.'

'My pleasure. Sorry about that,' said Seymour. 'Colin's gone to Yorkshire, I believe. He and Louise are moving into the house. He should have told you. Anyway, let's partake of some luncheon, shall we? Would you like a drink first? How are the lessons going? Maitland hasn't scared the pants off you yet?'

As they were leaving the mess after lunch a young woman was standing in the doorway looking distraught.

'Louise, my darling!' cried John Seymour, his delight at seeing her as marked as her relief at seeing him.

So this was Colin's wife, a petite, bubbly little person, her fair curls peeping from the scarf she had wrapped round her head and neck.

'Where's Colin, John? Have you seen him,' she asked, anxiously.

'I was just going to ask you that. In fact, I didn't expect you for days. He only left this morning to collect you.'

'Collect me?' She looked blank. 'But I.... Oh, dear, he's going to be so angry when he finds I've taken it upon myself....'

'Is that what you've done? Good for you.'

She looked at Basil curiously, and he, suddenly realising he'd been staring rather rudely, averted his eyes, whereupon she gave him a beaming smile. 'Who is this gentleman, John?'

'Oh, lord! Remind me to remember my manners. This is Basil Crawford, your husband's latest protégé.'

A small hand emerged from the white fur muff she held, and was extended to him.

'How do you do, Mr Crawford,' she said, demurely, revealing a dimple in her left cheek.

What a delightful creature, Basil thought. No wonder Craven fell in love with her.

'It's a pleasure to meet you, Mrs Craven.'

'I don't suppose Colin has told you, you are to have my quarter,' put in John Seymour, catching his sister's attention again. 'I don't need it any more.'

'Our house? You mean we'll be living in our house? Oh, John, that's wonderful!' She almost jumped for joy. 'It'll be like coming home.'

'I thought that would please you,' said her brother. 'Well, I'd better go and get things ready for you. You,' taking both hers and Basil's arm and pushing them together, 'look after each other. Go inside and keep warm. I'll go and see that the fire's lit and so on....' Already he was hurrying off, leaving him with this quiet vulnerable girl.

'Colin will be incensed when he discovers he's made a fruitless journey,' she said, a little crease on her brow. 'Oh, why did he not tell me?'

It was a question Basil would have liked answered. What was Colin up to? He'd been behaving strangely ever since he'd found out about Mary, stalking him at every turn, pumping him with questions, trying to trick him into telling him where she was. Even using blackmail.

'If you don't tell me, Crawford, I'll see that you don't get accepted into the corps. And don't think you can find another sponsor if I reject you. You know what they'll say? It'll look as if you were found lacking in courage.'

'You wouldn't!'

'Oh, wouldn't I? You don't know how desperate I am to find Mary.'

He'd been like one possessed. He seemed to have forgotten he had a wife. Even the RFC and flying appeared to have taken a rear seat. It was Mary, Mary, Mary. And where had he disappeared so suddenly. Had he gone off to Zurich in search of her? It was a chilling thought.

He watched Louise, her quiet dignity, feeling deeply sorry for her. What was she going to think of him when she discovered he was the one who'd thrown a stone at her crystal palace and shattered it? He'd opened Pandora's box and let out a demon that would destroy three people's happiness.

Chapter 25

The ski season was in full swing in Val de Paix. Little fairy lanterns adorned all the houses and many of the fir trees. Maxine came home one day bursting with excitement.

'Oh, Mary, the most handsome Englishman I've ever seen has just arrived at the hotel. And he is so charming. If I had not Basil waiting for me in England, I should fall in love with him myself. I have told him all about you, and he would like to meet you. I insist you come to eat at the hotel this evening.'

'Maxine,' Mary laughed. 'You're an incurable match-maker. Who is this paragon?'

'His name is Charles Cranwell. His friends call him Charlie.'

'You've become very familiar with this Charlie by the sound of it. Christian names, when you've not even been introduced? I wonder what your fiancé will make of this.'

'You will not tell him. Mary, you would not!'

Mary laughed, and then thought sadly how much she was going to miss her vivacious friend.

'And you will come tonight, yes?'

She would, if only to please Maxine, though she didn't feel at all sociable.

She looked at herself in the mirror. This beau Maxine had found for her would not be the least bit interested, he'd probably ignore her and continue to flirt with Maxine. She had dark hollows round her eyes and her suntan, the result of constant exposure to the sun, had faded, making her complexion look sallow. It would take a miracle to disguise these blemishes.

Soon it was time to put on her bonnet and cloak and walk the half-mile to the hotel. She locked the door of the house and turned, feeling her way carefully down the steps. Because the village was situated on a slope, the path which led to the road was both narrow and steep, and there had been a fresh fall of snow in the late afternoon, making it very slippery. The snow clouds had vanished leaving the sky clear and star studded.

She arrived at the hotel in good time and found Maxine in Reception.

'I haven't seen Charlie yet,' her friend told her.

'Mr Cranwell, for Heaven's sake, Maxine.'

'He has not come in from skiing. Oh, I do hope he will come. I didn't make a definite arrangement.'

'I'm rather glad you didn't,' said Mary, with a feeling of relief. She'd been distinctly nervous about meeting this young man. 'If he doesn't turn up we can have dinner together, just the two of us.'

'But I cannot leave the desk. Hanni is not coming in tonight.'

Mary was shocked. 'You mean.... You expect me to eat alone with this young man, a total stranger? Really Maxine! I find that quite outrageous.'

'I didn't plan it that way, really I didn't. Usually Hanni is here to look after the desk while I eat, but they told me just now she does not come in for the duty tonight. She has to visit her mother who is very ill. So I must stay at the desk all evening. You are lucky. Your work is only in the day time.'

'Then, I beg your pardon, but I think I'd better go home....'

'Oh, Mary, here he is!' Maxine burst out excitedly. 'That's him, the one in the blue coat coming in now. Oh, isn't he the most handsome man you have ever seen?' She stopped short, looking at her friend in dismay. 'Mary, *was ist los*, what's the matter?'

Mary was clutching the reception desk as if her life depended on it, her face had gone ashen and she was trembling visibly.

'Colin!' she gasped weakly, as her legs gave way under her.

He was on his knees, gathering her in his arms. 'Mary my dearest, at last I've found you.' He picked her up and carried her to the nearest sofa and laid her down.

'You are Mary's cousin, Colin Craven?' a voice at his elbow asked, and he turned to find Maxine looking at him in stark amazement.

'Yes. I'm sorry I deceived you, but I had to see her, and I knew I'd never get a foot inside the door if I revealed my true identity,' he turned again to Mary who was coming round. 'Oh, May, why must you keep running away from me?'

'Colin?' said Mary, struggling to gather her thoughts. 'How on earth did you find me? I suppose, in your inimitable way, you persuaded Basil to tell you in the end?'

'No, no. Basil is still your staunch ally, I can assure you. I'm afraid I was obliged to resort to the iniquitous practice of spying. I saw a letter addressed to Maxine on his desk and when he wasn't looking I hastily wrote it down.'

'Oh, how wicked of you,' crowed Maxine in delight. 'And how clever.'

'Nobody knows I'm here, or where I've gone. I can't believe I've found you at last.' He was holding Mary's hand as he spoke, then he lifted it to his lips and kissed it. 'Are you all right now? I'm sorry I gave you such a shock. I think I'd better take you home.'

'Will you not have something to eat first,' Maxine suggested.

'I couldn't eat anything,' said Mary.

'Is there no food in your house?' Colin asked, a smile hovering round his mouth. 'I can cook, you know. I used to when I was living in Cambridge. It was a hobby of mine.'

This was a surprise to Mary. 'I never knew that.'

'You don't know everything about me.'

Letting Colin into the house, she wondered why she was doing it. Was she quite mad? Dear God, why did he have this affect upon her—still, after all these years? And she'd thought she could look upon him now with equanimity.

'I like your house,' he said, looking round appreciatively. 'Swiss houses, it seems to me, are warm and cosy, no long draughty passages like at Misselthwaite.'

'They have to be, with temperatures many degrees below freezing outside. And you may've noticed, most of them are built of wood. Surprisingly it seems to withstand the cold better than bricks. Can I get you anything? I shouldn't have stopped you having a meal.'

'I'm not hungry either,' he said, pulling her down beside him on the sofa. Another long silence fell between them, yet the tension was electric. There was so much she longed to say to him, so much to ask, but after all that had happened she felt strange with him, a little shy, even a little frightened. Nor did she trust herself. She was afraid that if she allowed the conversation to become too intimate all the barriers would be broken down in seconds, those barriers she had deliberately built up for her own protection.

It was incredible to think he knew nothing about the most important things in her life. Nothing about the baby, or Rudi, her struggles for survival, sometimes with no money at all, during the last three years. The tears, the pain she'd been through, and here he was beside her living, breathing. It was unbelievable.

But she couldn't prevent him asking questions.

'Why did you run away, my darling? Was it because of the baby?' His words had an electrifying affect upon her. 'You should have told me.'

'You know!' she gasped. 'Basil told you.'

He shook his head. 'Basil told me nothing, except that he knew where you were. But he wouldn't even tell me that.'

'Then how did you know...about the baby?'

There was a long pause before he answered. 'I had a dream.' Then another long pause before he said, 'It was my child, wasn't it?'

She felt the blood rush to her cheeks. 'No, it was a virgin birth,' she retorted. 'What sort of woman do you think I am?'

'Don't take on so,' he said calmly. 'I'm a bit in the dark. I'm never quite sure whether to take my dreams seriously or not.'

'You mean you really did have a dream about...my baby?'

'How else d'you suppose I knew? You didn't tell me. Why didn't you?'

'I thought you were marrying Charlotte. Oh, Colin, must we rake up the past?'

'Rake up the past? For God's sake, Mary! This is my own child we're talking about. Didn't I have a right to know? And I wanted to marry you. What really hurts more than anything is that you didn't trust me. You actually believed I would marry Charlotte.'

She clenched the fist of her free hand, digging her fingernails into its palm.

'What's the use, Colin? Nothing can be done now,' she said, trembling.

'Tell me at least,' he said. 'What happened to our child. Was it a girl or a boy? I know it must be painful for you, but why don't you let me share it with you?'

In truth she wanted to tell him, to unburden, to share her grief. He held her in his arms and they both wept, he no less than she, and he was very tender, very loving. And when she'd recovered she showed him a photograph Maxine had taken so he could see what his baby looked like. For a moment they forgot he was married to someone else. It was as if they were normal parents mourning the loss of their child.

'Why don't you come home, May,' he suggested in a soft caressing voice.

'How can I? You're married to someone else. I don't have to tell you what that means.'

'Does it mean we cannot be friends? I wouldn't expect you to live with us. You wouldn't see much of me anyway, I don't live at home now and I spend little time there, but Father would be delighted to have your company. It would please Lu, too, because then she could stay with me at Larkhill all the time. I don't think she likes it much at Misselthwaite.' She was beginning to feel like a maiden aunt, and wasn't this one of the reasons she'd run away in the first place? 'Louise is quite different from Charlotte if that is what's bothering you,' he added as if he read her thoughts. 'As a matter of fact I believe you two would get along rippingly.'

'I'm sure she's different, but that's not the point.' Or perhaps it was the point.

'Couldn't you come and visit us, at least? Father will want to see you, and....'

'Your father can come and visit me here. In fact I wish he would.'

'I say, that's an idea. I could visit you here, too,' he said, putting his arm round her. 'I could come for the skiing each year. It would be something to look forward to. Now that I've found you,' he added, wistfully. 'How can I let you go again?'

'Don't make it impossible for me, Colin. It's easy for you. You have someone else, someone to love who loves you. I have nobody, now...' She pressed her knuckles against her trembling lips, trying to swallow the constriction in her throat. 'You cannot imagine the grief of losing a child,' she said, in a strangled voice.

'I know,' he said. 'And you shouldn't be alone. You needn't be.'

She shook her head. 'But you can't come here. What if Louise were to find out?'

'What if she does? I should probably tell her anyway. You're my cousin, and as far as she knows that's all there is to it. Why shouldn't I visit you from time to time?'

She shook her head sadly. 'It wouldn't work, Colin. From past experience we both know it's only a matter of time before we.... And then, you'll give yourself away one day. It only needs one slip...'

He stretched out his hand to take hers. 'We're twin souls, May. You've always been the most important person in my life. I was in despair when I thought I'd lost you. And now I've found you, how can I live, knowing you are here, very much alive, and never see you?'

'You have a wife who loves you, Colin,' she said softly. 'Ironically it might have been different if you'd married Charlotte. Believe it or not I had almost decided to come home before I got Basil's letter. In my conceit I imagined you'd be tired of Charlotte by now. She might even have left you, running off with half your money, leaving the way clear for me. But of course that was a pipe dream.'

'You mean you wouldn't have minded about the scandal?'

'Have you ever known me to care two pins what people think? The only thing I'd mind about is getting hurt, or more to the point, hurting someone else.'

'I wouldn't do anything to hurt Louise,' he said. 'She's such a darling, so kind and generous.' She was caught by an unwelcome shaft of jealousy. He did love his wife, in a way that was likely to increase in depth, it was not like the grand passion he'd had for Charlotte. 'But to say 'goodbye' for ever. Must it be so final?'

'Take heart, dear one. I don't believe that even death is a final parting.'

He looked at her sharply. 'You mean, there's life after death?'

But before she could answer there was a knock at the door. Colin looked like a schoolboy caught in the act. Mary laughed.

'Stay where you are. I'll go.'

It was the young footman from the hotel with a message from Maxine. They were so busy, she expected to be working late. She didn't want to walk home late at night, so she would be staying at the hotel tonight.

A warm look came into Colin's eyes when Mary translated the message, a look she knew all too well, and her heart jumped. He still wanted her! But he said nothing. He had himself under control, and she was left suspended between relief and disappointment.

'I suppose I'd better go back to the hotel,' he said reluctantly. 'Are you free tomorrow? There's so little time, if this is the last time we're to meet.'

Her heart did a painful somersault. So little time! 'When must you go home?'

'I've taken a week's leave, but I'm supposed to be in Yorkshire collecting Louise and taking her back to Larkhill. I should go home as soon as possible.'

The thought of parting with him again made her feel sick. 'Can you stay until Monday morning?' she begged. 'I'm free all day tomorrow, and Sunday.'

He nodded. 'And,' he said, kissing her cheek, her ear. 'We've so much to talk about.'

It was true. He knew little about her recent experiences, and she knew even less about his. He was an officer in the Royal Flying Corps, he was what people called a Birdman, enough to make any girl's heart flutter. She wanted to know all about it. She was also curious about Louise, how he'd met her and so on.

'It's so beautiful up here,' said Colin, stopping to admire the view. 'No wonder you don't want to leave it.'
　Mary put a hand on his arm to still him. 'Listen.'
　'What?'
　'That's it. The silence.'
　'But it's not completely silent,' he observed. 'There's a strange, creaking noise.'
　'You can sometimes hear it,' she agreed. 'It's the snow moving.'
　'How eerie. Can we stop a minute? I'm not a very proficient skier and I want to talk to you.'
　'I wouldn't mind a rest, myself,' she said. 'But we mustn't linger long, you can suddenly feel really cold, you know.'
　'This minute I feel quite hot,' he said, wiping his forearm across his brow.
　'I've been meaning to ask you about your dream, the one you had in the garden,' she said. 'Tell me about it.'
　He looked at her speculatively. 'If I tell you something I've never told a living soul, promise not to think I'm crazy.'
　Mary laughed. 'Dearest Colin, I already think you're crazy, but don't let it worry you, I still love you.'
　'Seriously. This is no laughing matter, May. I've always wanted to tell you about it. Do you think dreams are real experiences?'
　'I think some may be. Your dream about me and the baby was quite extraordinary.'
　'And that's not as strange as some dreams I've had. I've seen things that I'm sure were not, as psychologists would have you believe, figments of my imagination, particularly when I was a child. My mother, for instance, would come out of the portrait in my room and stand by my bed. That's why I had the curtain put over it, though it didn't stop her.'
　'You told me you had that curtain put there because she was always smiling, and you didn't like that because you were ill and she'd deserted you by dying.'
　'The truth was she used to haunt me. When I tried to touch her she'd disappear. She'd tell me to get up and walk, and when I tried to do it I'd wake up and then of course I couldn't, though I kept trying. I used to get so frustrated; that's why I had the tantrums. Once I dreamed she picked me up and carried me to the window, then she

threw me out. I thought I was going to be dashed to pieces on the paving stones below, but I simply landed softly back in bed.'

When Mary smiled, he said, 'You think it was all in my mind, but wait... You could argue that I knew what my mother looked like because of the portrait. But I'd never seen a picture of you. How could I conjure up a vision of you from my imagination when I'd never met you?'

Now Mary was shocked. 'You mean...?'

'You see,' he said slowly. 'I recognised you the minute you came into my room that night because I'd already seen you before.'

'But you didn't know who I was,' she protested, feeling a little frightened. 'You thought I was a ghost.'

'Precisely. That was because the only other person I'd seen like that was my mother. I knew she was dead, so I thought you might be too.'

'What did I look like? When you saw me before?'

'A little younger than you were when I actually met you, but otherwise the same.'

'Oh, Colin!' she shuddered. 'You're making me feel creepy.'

'I was about six the first time I saw you. I remember I made a scene about it. I summoned all the servants, insisting there was a girl in the house. "Where's the girl?" I demanded. "Bring her here, I want to speak to her." They all looked at each other and me, in that way, you know, as if to say: "Poor little fellow, he's losing his wits."'

Mary laughed at that. She remembered how imperious he'd been when she first met him, and she could see him behaving in exactly that way.

'I wonder if that was why they tried to keep us apart when you first came,' he continued. 'I suppose they thought I'd go completely round the bend if I saw you. Anyway, after that I kept very quiet about everything I saw that wasn't there. I had no wish to be bundled off to a lunatic asylum. Do you think this is all rather weird?'

'Frankly, I find it a little alarming, but I can't help being fascinated all the same. How often had you seen me, my...ghost?'

'Obviously you weren't a ghost—ghosts are people who are dead. I was dreaming, though I thought I was awake. I had several dreams about you, and we were not always in my room. Sometimes, more often in fact, we were somewhere exotic—there were natives around, elephants and palm trees. I've never been to India, but I imagine that's where we were.'

'No wonder you acted in that strange way when we really did meet.'

'Do you remember our first meeting?'

'As clearly as if it were yesterday.'

'Then you remember trying to convince me you were not one of my dreams?'

'Yes. I seem to recall I offered to pinch you.'

'And you told me to feel your shawl. I remember that too.'

'That was fifteen years ago, Colin. Some moments in our lives are so vivid, they stay in our minds like a tableau or a brilliant painting—captured for all time.'

'Moments like this,' he said, taking her by the shoulders and pulling her against his chest. 'Just look at that, the sun on the mountains. Isn't it magnificent? Hold it,' he whispered in her ear, 'and you and me, a precious memory for the future.'

The scene was breathtaking, the snow-covered mountains, pink in the wintry sun, their smooth, snowy descent to the village nestling in the valley broken only by fir trees coming down in a V shape. Colin's arms held her firmly against him, his breath caressing her ear. She wasn't sure if it was the rarity of the air or the strength of her emotions that made it so difficult to breathe. It was a magic moment.

'I love you, May,' he said. 'I shall always love you. I beg you not to cut me off forever. If I may not see you again, let us at least write to each other.'

'I see no reason why we should not,' she said. 'Though I shall have to be circumspect about the way I write to you. But I shall look for your letters as my only comfort in life. I think we should make our way back now. The sun will be setting soon.'

They were still talking about dreams while they toasted crumpets in front of a roaring fire. Colin, having once begun to reveal some of the strange things that had happened to him, wanted to tell her everything.

'I've never discussed this with anyone before,' he said, 'but have you ever wondered what happens after death?'

'I don't really want to think about death,' she said, thinking of her baby.

'But let's consider my dreams,' Colin insisted. 'Don't you see, you and Mother were on the same plain—she has no body and you have.'

'Meaning that when you are asleep you're on a different level of consciousness and can see and speak to people who are dead?'

'Something like that.'

'If that was so there'd be no need to grieve when you lose someone you love.'

Understanding, he took her hand and squeezed it. 'I believe that's true, May. But not everybody remembers, that's the trouble. Do you remember when I was so ill in London?'

'You mean the time you nearly died?'

'Yes, I had a strange experience then. While I was unconscious I saw my body lying on the bed. I remember thinking what a ghastly sight it looked. And I saw you sitting beside it—my body, I mean—weeping. I wanted to tell you I was all right but I couldn't make you hear, and nothing would have induced me to go back into that pain-racked body in order to do so. Then I flew out of the window and over the rooftops of London. All sorts of weird things happened after that, all a bit muddled, but the bit where I stood and looked at my body and you is still clear as a bell.'

'I've never had an experience like that, but I do remember one of my dreams. It was very vivid, and I've had it more than once. But I don't understand what it means.'

'Go on.'

'It begins a bit like fairy tale, but it ends in a nightmare.' She shuddered. 'I try to wake myself up before the horrid bit, but I can't. I think I'm in ancient Greece, though I've never been there in real life, and I know little of its history. That's why I don't think I've invented it. And... You'll think this is poppycock.'

'Try me.'

'What really convinced me that I had not imagined it was when I saw a picture in an art exhibition of the same temple, the one in my dream.'

'There are umpteen temples in Greece, May, and they all look very similar.'

'Not this one. It's situated on a cliff overlooking the sea. Anyway, my dream.... It begins, as I said, in a very pleasant way. You and I are being married in this temple. I knew it was you, though you looked different. It was very beautiful, dazzling, and there was this priestess who was marrying us.... What's the matter, Colin?' He was frowning.

'It all sounds rather familiar. Go on,' he urged.

'My emotions are so poignant, much sharper than anything I've ever experienced in real life, and the grief.... It's almost unbearable, worse almost than when I lost the baby.'

'But why? I thought we were being married?'

'Later on, I'm afraid you don't love me any more, you've gone off and left me. I'm searching for you, and then...I find you,' she said slowly. 'In the arms of another woman....'

'Good God!' Colin exploded.

'Colin! There's no need to blaspheme like that.'

'But I dreamt exactly the same thing,' he exclaimed. 'It was one of the many confused dreams I had in London. What happened then? Did you commit suicide?'

How on earth did he know that? He must have had the same dream because he knew how it ended. She looked at him in shocked silence for some minutes. 'I threw myself off a cliff,' she said at last. 'Only to wake up in bed, like you did when your mother threw you out of the window.' She paused before adding. 'I've always been terrified of heights, even before I ever had that dream.'

They both sat silently gazing into the fire until an acrid smell tickled their nostrils.

'You're burning the crumpets,' said Mary.

'There's something significant in this,' said Colin, pulling the burnt crumpet out of the fire. 'Both of us having the same dream. And you seeing that painting of the temple.... But hang on a minute. How could anyone have painted that picture? All the temples in Greece are ancient ruins. And the one in my dream at least, was not only whole, but very richly decorated.'

'The painting was a ruin, but it was the same temple, believe me. I recognised its shape and the position on top of the cliffs. Heavens, I know those cliffs well enough.'

You realise what this means, May,' he said, and now he was very excited indeed. 'It means—it can only mean...'

'Reincarnation,' she finished for him. 'You and I have been together before. It makes sense, Colin.'

'Of course we've been together, many times, I should think. That's why...'

'I've always half believed in reincarnation. The Indians believe it, and some of it may have rubbed off on me.'

'But don't you see, May. It explains so much. Why we were attracted to each other, from the beginning. Where did you see that painting? Who was it by? Did you make a note of it? We should try to find out where that temple was, and then we should go back there. Wouldn't you like to go to Greece? I've always wanted to go there...'

'Colin' she said, putting her hand on his arm. 'Calm down. You're not thinking straight. We can't go to Greece, or anywhere, for that matter.' Then she added, gently, 'Haven't you forgotten something?'

He groaned. 'You're right. I'm sorry, I got carried away.'

'But it's a comforting thought,' she smiled. 'To think we may have spent many lives together, and will undoubtedly be together for many more.'

'I don't seem to have learned much,' he sighed. 'I seem to make the same damn stupid mistakes over and over again.'

'I think you are learning. You didn't betray me this time. It was all in my mind. And perhaps I have something to learn too, to face up to jealousy, and live with it.'

'And I must be fair to the wife I've chosen this time, even though I want to be with you. And perhaps,' he said, taking both her hands, 'if we can't be together in this life we can in the next. And let's hope we'll always be friends, forever and ever and ever...

'Until, in the words of that immortal poet, "all the seas gang dry."'

'It's a hope worth hanging on to, my dearest May.'

****

When Colin arrived back at Larkhill the Colonel sent for him.

'What the hell are you playing at, Craven? Where have you been? You asked for leave—of course you're perfectly entitled to take it if you can be spared—to move your wife from Yorkshire. Your wife then turns up of her own accord, and nobody knows where you are.'

'It was a misunderstanding, sir. I've recently discovered my cousin, whom I'd believed to be dead, to be living in Switzerland. I went to see her, then I went to Yorkshire only to find Louise had already left home.'

'Then why the devil didn't you announce your plans in the first place? Oh, I know dear Louise, and we all love her, acted a little spontaneously, but the cat has truly been set among the pigeons this end. You were almost under suspicion of having deserted—though nobody, including myself, could believe it of you. But if you'd been so much as one day late for duty.... Be warned, Colin, this sort of thing will not be tolerated. In future you'll be expected to be more open about your intentions. This is not the Secret Service. You may go.'

'Sir,' Colin saluted his commanding officer and turned to leave.

'Colin,' the Colonel stopped him at the door. 'I'm not the only one entitled to an explanation. I think you'd better go home and see your wife before you do anything else.'

'Yes, sir.'

Chapter 26

Louise would not look at him. She was aloof and dignified.

'It's all right Colin,' she said. 'There's no need to explain. I know where you've been. Did you find Mary?'

'How on earth...?'

'Basil told me. At least he guessed where you'd gone.' She turned a tear-stained face to him.

'You've been crying?'

'I thought you might not come back. I was afraid you'd left me.'

'For God's sake, give me credit for some integrity. So that's why the Colonel thought I might have deserted.'

'Oh, no! I didn't say anything to him. I wouldn't. Nor would Basil.'

'Where is that tell-tale, Crawford? And what else did he tell you?'

'You mustn't blame him. He feels very responsible. He says he should never have opened Pandora's box.'

'Oh, Lu, this is just what I wanted to avoid,' he said, taking her in his arms and feeling her body stiffen. 'I never meant to hurt you.'

'She'll be coming home, I suppose?'

'No,' he said heavily. 'She's determined to stay in Switzerland.'

He tried to make his voice cheerful, but evidently she saw through his bravado.

'You love her, don't you? Why don't you tell me the truth, Colin?'

He couldn't bear to see her hurt, but what could he say to reassure her? She was bound to disbelieve him if he tried to deny his feelings for Mary, and she'd probably misinterpret anything he said. 'Of course I love her. It would be strange if I didn't, she's more to me than a sister. Look, Lu, you have my assurance there's nothing sinister going on between Mary and me, you'll simply have to believe it.'

****

After Colin had gone Mary was in despair. She should be used to it by now, but seeing him, being so close, had opened it all up again. She felt like one of the heroines in grand opera. And yet she was better off. She knew one thing for sure. Colin loved her. She had no doubt about it this time. She'd overcome the despair of parting, she told herself, and if she didn't....

Well, there was an alternative. She could give in to her sometimes violent urge to pack up and follow him and go home to Misselthwaite. Yet she knew what would happen if she did. In a few short days Colin had stirred up all the old emotions and awakened desires she'd thought long dead after Rudi's handling of her. No doubt he loved her now, but for how long? She had a feeling that Louise, with her gentle, loving character would prove a far more formidable rival for Colin's heart than Charlotte ever was. She'd be in a thrall, left high and dry, the eroding pain of jealousy making her more and more bitter as Colin grew closer to Louise and away from her. It was better that she stayed away and tried to forget him again.

Even her letters must not give her away. Nor could she write too often. That, too would arouse suspicion. Yet there were times when she simply had to let herself go.

How she envied Maxine. How lucky she was to be marrying the man she loved, to be with him always, without having to suffer such feelings of loss and deprivation when it was all over and there was nothing left—an enduring, demoralising heartache.

****

'I wish Mary would come back and live in England, at least,' Mr Craven grumbled. 'If she's not careful she'll be stuck in war-torn Europe. If she won't come here, then I must go and see her, and perhaps I can persuade her where you have failed.'

'I wish you would, Father. I know she would like to see you.'

'Then I shall go as soon as the weather improves.'

'What do you think, Colin,' said Louise, hesitantly. 'Could I go with your father. Or would I be intruding?'

'I think it's a splendid idea. I'm sure you and Mary will get along famously. I'll write and ask her if you like.'

Louise wanted to meet Mary. Not only was she curious about her, but she genuinely wanted them to be friends. She hated herself for feeling so jealous. After all, Mary had given Colin up, that was something she wasn't sure she could do. And yet, Colin was different since his return from Switzerland. It was nothing she could put her finger on, he was kind to her, considerate, even loving, but he was more thoughtful, introspective, and there was something missing, a spontaneous easiness between them.

And Mr Craven's obsession with the Turko-Bulgarian war troubled her, too. His head was always buried in a newspaper these days, and he was full of gloomy predictions.

'Is your father a pessimist?' she asked Colin when they were alone. 'Or is there really a threat of war? Do you think the trouble in the Balkans will spread to the rest of Europe?'

'It might. I think we must be prepared for it at least. Some of our chiefs seem to think Europe is heading for a major confrontation. Others doubt if we'll get involved. But don't let it worry you, my love. According to the War Office, even if England does manage to get herself embroiled, our aircraft will only be used for reconnaissance.' Was there a touch of cynicism in his voice? 'Personally I cannot imagine how we could avoid becoming offensive, in which case we're lagging far behind in the race. Other European countries have air forces three or four times our size. We simply can't get the War Office to take us seriously.'

'Colin, you frighten me.'

'Well, my dear, don't be frightened. It may never happen. So far the trouble has been nicely contained, involving only Turkey and the Balkans, and I see no reason for it to spread to western Europe.'

When they got back to Larkhill, Colin found a letter waiting for him from Mary.

'...My new neighbour has a little boy,' she'd written. 'He's two years old, the same age as our little Tom would have been by now. I made her welcome and gave her a cup of tea. And after she'd gone I cried and cried. It was too soon after seeing you. I'm afraid I'm hopeless, I've only to see a mother with a new born baby, and.... But I must not begin again. Oh, my love, if only I could feel your arms around me. I miss you so much....

What am I doing writing to you like this. You'll have to destroy this letter. How simply awful if Louise were to find it. Of course I would like her to come here with your father. I should like very much to meet her. Your father, Basil and Bertie (I recently heard from him, too) all say she is a sweet thing. Indeed I shall look forward to seeing them both. It's lonely here now that Maxine has gone home to Zurich to prepare for her wedding....'

****

Mr Craven almost wept when he saw Mary. Louise felt a little awkward, and she was about to make herself scarce, when they both turned to her.

'Louise,' said her father-in-law. 'Come here, my dear, and meet your cousin.'

Mary smiled at her, such a warm smile, she was immediately drawn to her, and as they grasped hands she felt a surge of sisterly affection towards this woman who she'd always thought of as her sworn enemy.

'Come into the warm,' Mary said. 'I've a good fire burning.'

Mr Craven only stayed a few days. It was his policy never to stay too long anywhere except Misselthwaite. He followed the doctrine of "fish and visitors go off after three days." But Mary begged Louise to stay a little longer, and the latter readily accepted the invitation. Both girls knew that once Mr Craven had gone they'd be able to let their hair down and really get to know each other. They both felt rather inhibited while he was present.

Before he left Mr Craven spoke to Louise.

'If you can't prevail upon Mary to come and live at home, at least persuade her to come back to the U.K. She can go and live in Scotland if she likes, there are plenty of mountains there, but I'd feel a great deal easier knowing she wouldn't suddenly find herself in the middle of a potential trouble spot.'

'If you think it's the mountains, Mr Craven, I'm afraid you've quite mistaken Mary's reason for staying here. Indeed, I believe she prefers her beloved Yorkshire moor. But, seriously, do you really believe this Balkan thing is going to spread to the rest of Europe?'

'I certainly do. There's trouble brewing everywhere, and what with Germany arming to the hilt.... You don't read the papers, my girl. Everyone says war will break out before the end of this year. Mary doesn't believe it, either. She says the Swiss are peace loving people. That may be so, but look at what's around them.'

He gave her a knowing look. 'If you ask her she might come. I've a feeling her determination to stay away may have something to do with not wishing to tread on your toes.'

Louise spent several more weeks with Mary and the two became close friends. She felt that Mary trusted her. She'd even said she might visit Misselthwaite, provided Colin was not there. One day they had a full and frank discussion about Colin. Mary admitted she and Colin had once been in love, but they'd decided not to marry because of their close relationship.

'He's still in love with you, Mary.'

Mary was silent for a moment, then she said quite truthfully. 'He's in love with you.'

Louise played with a bow on her dress, twisting and turning it. She felt agitated. She wanted to tell Mary about her misgivings but she couldn't bring herself to.

'You've nothing to fear from me,' said Mary, as if she'd read her thoughts. 'I shall not attempt to get Colin back. For one thing I intend to stay away from him, and for another.... It was all over a long time ago. There's nothing between us now except fraternal affection.'

Louise continued to fidget. In spite of Mary's reassurances, she still felt unsure of herself.

'You can make him happy,' Mary said quietly. 'You already have. I doubt if he'd have been as happy with me. We were inclined to quarrel. And he does love you. He told me so.'

'Did he?' She tried to imagine how she'd have felt in Mary's position, and her heart warmed to this woman who was prepared to make such a sacrifice. 'I wish you'd come home, Mary, even if it's just for a visit. You could come while Colin's away, which is most of the time. Apart from your uncle and I, Martha, Dickon and Mrs Sowerby would love to see you.'

'Dickon.' Mary's face brightened at mention of him. 'How is he? Colin told me his wife died in childbirth.'

'Yes, she did. And he once confessed to me he still blames himself for her death. He said if he'd got someone to attend to her sooner she might have lived.'

'Dear Dickon. How typical of him,' Mary said. 'He'd be a most caring husband. But remorse is a terrible thing. I wish I could comfort him.'

'Then do come. Let's make a date for Easter.'

Since that conversation they'd grown even closer. It seemed a pity Mary could not come and live in England, Louise reflected. She got on so much better with her than she did with her own sister. She hoped Colin would allow her to come here and visit often. The Swiss air was doing her good.

While Mary was at school she was quite happy pottering around, going for walks, sitting in the sunshine. She must write to Colin. Mary had said she could use her writing paper. It was in the desk, but which drawer? She opened a drawer she'd found locked on a previous occasion when Mary had asked her to fetch something from the desk. Mary must have forgotten to lock it. She was about to shut it again when her eye fell upon a letter in such familiar handwriting it gave her a turn. The drawer was full of his letters. Her hand shook as she took one out. She should not be doing this—it was spying, despicable, but.... To close the drawer and forget she'd ever seen it—a drawer full of letters from her husband to the woman she knew he loved—was more than human nature could endure.

The letter she had in her hand must have been written soon after his own visit to Switzerland. It began: 'My darling....' It was a shock to discover he used that endearment when addressing Mary, though it should have been no surprise. But the words that leapt out and hit her in the eye were further down the page.

'I found your letter rather upsetting. I wish I could comfort you. The loss of our child is bound to be worse for you than it is for me, but I feel it too, you know. If only you'd told me you were expecting a baby. You must have known I'd have married you. I know I've said all this before, *ad nauseam*, and I know it's useless to grieve over the irretrievable, but I cannot help thinking of what might have been....'

So that was why Mary had fled to Switzerland, why she was pretending to be a widow, calling herself Mrs Drummond. She'd had Colin's child. In a way Mary was more of a wife to him than she was. And they were still in love, apparently. Yet Mary had said it was over. For all she knew they were still lovers, they'd resumed their liaison when Colin visited her here.

So much for Mary's avowal that there was only fraternal affection between them. Yet she didn't want to believe her new friend had deceived her. It was as if a beautiful rose had been crushed under a clumsy boot. She felt utterly betrayed, and not only by Colin. As Mary herself had said, Colin was a man. Somehow her betrayal was worse than his.

With shaking hands she put the letter back in the drawer and shut it, hoping the contents had not been disturbed, and Mary would not know she'd been spying. More to the point how was she going to act when she came home from school? Could she behave as though nothing had happened? She was of far too honest a nature to be any good at putting on an act. And yet she was a coward. She cringed at the thought of confronting her with it. One thing she knew for sure. She could not stay here any longer. She'd have to go home at once.

Then she thought of Colin. How would this affect their relationship? How would she behave with him, knowing his guilty secret. If it was going to be difficult to keep her discovery from Mary, how much harder would it be to live with him as if nothing had happened?

****

Till All The Seas Run Dry

The Spring of 1914 was a frantic time for the RFC. The War Office had at last woken up to the fact that Britain lagged far behind France and Germany in air defence, and at the behest of Colonel Sykes, Commander of the Military Wing, a mock mobilization of the Royal Flying Corps was to take place in June. This meant a great deal of work and preparation, including a month's combined training beforehand. Thus Colin was away from home for much of the time, which was as well because he and Louise were not getting on very well.

He lay shivering in a cold, damp sleeping bag. The rain dripped incessantly on the roof of the tent, and everything was wet and soggy. Oh, for a warm, dry house, a hot bath and a loving wife. There was little hope of the latter though, he thought bitterly. He supposed he could not blame her for being cold with him. Not only had he behaved badly, but he'd been rotten bad company recently. But there was no time to dwell upon his deteriorating domestic affairs, when there were more pressing matters at hand. After all, he had the rest of his life to make up to his wife.

Louise stayed in the house by herself. Colin had suggested she'd be better off at Misselthwaite. Was he trying to get rid of her? She knew she was being unreasonable, but she couldn't rid herself of the dreadful suspicion he was involved in a secret liaison with Mary. Yet he'd been perfectly honest with her. He'd admitted having once had an affair with Mary, even about the baby, and he'd begged her forgiveness—on his knees. He'd been as loving as always to her—or he'd tried to be, but she was unable to hide her resentment. At night, when he turned to her she couldn't help thinking of him with Mary; her body would stiffen at his touch and she'd turn her head away.

Then, when he left her alone it was worse. She'd lie awake for hours, fuming with indignation, imagining he was relieved for then he needn't pretend. Once she'd heard him mutter, turning his back on her with an impatient sigh, 'If this is the way it's to be, we may as well sleep in separate rooms.'

This remark had put the fear of God into her. She was desperate to make her marriage work, but she didn't know how to put it right. She was very young and inexperienced. Were all marriages like this? Did all husbands and wives have secrets from each other? Her sister Anna said that love and marriage were not necessarily synonymous, most marriages were a compromise. The married bliss of the romantic novel simply did not exist. She'd had too sheltered a life. She wished she'd never found those dreadful letters. She wanted to try again.

The worst of it was she didn't know what to say to him. He was like a stranger. He no longer teased her, or laughed with her as he used to. He seemed preoccupied. They didn't even argue for he wouldn't be drawn. She supposed there was no fun in quarrelling with someone he felt nothing for.

A car drew up outside the house and Louise's heart jumped. But it was not Colin she found standing on the doorstep. It was her brother John.

'I decided to drive over and see you,' he said. 'Something tells me you need me.'

Louise threw her arms round him and burst into tears.

'Hey, I'm here now,' he said, putting his arms round her and stroking her head. 'Why don't you tell me what's troubling you?'

She told him, as briefly as possible, leaving out the bit about the letter, about her deteriorating relationship with Colin and her suspicions about Mary.

'I'm sorry you've been disillusioned already,' said John, when she'd finished. 'Perhaps I should have warned you what we men are like. I've tried too hard to protect you, I suppose. But I'd be surprised if Colin's deceiving you. He strikes me as a man of principles.'

'I didn't say that he was. He's been quite honest with me, in fact, but I know he still loves her. He writes copious letters to her.'

'Of course he writes to her. She is his cousin, after all. But that doesn't mean she's his mistress.'

She couldn't betray Colin by telling John about the child, even if he was her brother.

'I may as well tell you,' he continued, 'many men do have mistresses, and their wives either don't know about it, or simply have to accept it. But one thing's certain, whether Colin's still in love with Mary or not, if you give him the cold shoulder you'll drive him straight into her arms. When he comes home, I'd give him a warm welcome if I were you.'

The weather was getting warmer at last. She could go for a walk now without getting frozen to a statue, or blown to pieces. Larkhill was almost deserted. Most of the men were involved with the exercises at Netheravon. Even Basil had gone with them, his flying training had been set aside for the time being while he concentrated on the military side. But lonely as she was, Louise would not desert the camp. She'd be there when Colin came home.

Then she had an idea of how to fill the time while he was away. How pleased he'd be and how proud of her if, when he came home, she was displaying a brevet for flying. She was sure she'd been quite close to getting it before they were married, but he'd given up teaching her, indeed he hadn't taken her flying at all, since their return from honeymoon in the summer.

'I expect he's concerned about your safety,' said Basil, when she mentioned it to him. She'd bumped into him while out walking. He'd been on his way to a flying lesson for which he'd returned especially. 'It's a pretty dangerous occupation, flying. I should certainly not encourage Maxine to try it.'

'It didn't seem to bother him before we were married.'

'Ah, but you're his wife now, and more precious to him.'

If only she could believe that. But she didn't say so to Basil.

'Anyway, would you kindly ask Mr Maitland when you see him if he would consider undertaking the training of a frail female, if it is not beneath his dignity. And please don't tell Colin about this. I want to surprise him by getting my brevet.'

'You'll do that, all right. And most of us here, too,' laughed Basil. 'You know, you remind me so much of Mary, no wonder Colin fell in love with you.'

She couldn't help thinking that was a rather back-handed complement.

Maitland agreed to teach her, but he said it would have to be done in his own private plane, which was a mono. And he could not use the military airfield either, so she would have to come some way for her lessons. Well, that was all right. She could drive the car. And Colin didn't need it while he was away on exercise.

All this was agreed secretly with the instructor. She'd pay him a fee to be arranged—he would not charge her the usual £75, since she had already had some instruction from her husband, and anyway he was always willing to do a special favour for a pretty lady.

****

'But, Mama,' said Maxine. 'Basil and I would much prefer a simple, quiet wedding. We don't want all this trouble and expense.'

'I'll hear of no such thing. Your father and I want the very best for our only daughter. There is, however, something you could do while I'm out this afternoon. There's a pile of letters on my desk, and in the top drawer there's a book marked "Wedding." Check the letters against the guest list and mark off those who have replied, those who have accepted and those who cannot come. Would you do that for me?'

It was sometime since Maxine had last been home, and she'd quickly realised she did not like her mother's artificial lifestyle. She was glad she was marrying Basil, though she felt a little apprehensive about living in England, and in particularly Larkhill. She wondered what sort of reception she'd get from the other officers and their wives. Basil had warned her their attitudes and overt jesting might take a little getting used to. One ordeal, at least, was out of the way. She'd already met his parents, and had been most pleasantly surprised. Indeed she felt more at ease with them than she did with her own parents.

As soon as her mother had left the house she dutifully went to the desk to get out the Wedding Book, but she could not immediately find it. It must be somewhere else, she thought. She looked in another drawer. In it were a number of books and files. She looked through them but none were marked "Wedding". Then she came across one and her heart nearly stopped. It had written across the top in bold print, "Adoption Agency—Accounts."

Could her mother be involved in such a business? She was a very secret person, and Maxine realised how little she knew about her. She suddenly remembered Mary's baby, and the mysterious way he'd disappeared. Her heart began to thump wildly as she thumbed through the pages. Entries were in date order so she flicked through the pages until she came to the date Mary's baby was supposed to have died. And there it was. The words almost hit her between the eyes. Received from Horst Franz Engelberg—DM 100,000 for the supply of one boy child, born 30th June, 1911.

Hot and cold shivers ran down her spine. Her mother had sold Mary's baby to the Engelbergs after all. He was not dead. When she thought of all that Mary had suffered, the humiliation, the heartache, the pain....

She heard footsteps in the hall. Her mother was coming back. She slammed the book shut and was about to put it back where she found it when Madame Steinberger entered the room.

'How did you get on?' she asked, amiably. But when her eyes fell upon the book on the desk she went pale. 'What have you been doing?'

'You sold him!' Maxine accused in a voice full of anguish. 'You sold Mary's baby to the Engelbergs. How could you do such a thing?'

'I did what I thought was best, for both Mary and the baby.'

Till All The Seas Run Dry

'You did what was best for you. What about the 100,000 marks you put in your own pocket?'

Madame Steinberger shrugged. 'Well, I could hardly give it to Mary, could I? At least not directly, when she thought the child was dead. But I would have given it to her and much more besides if she had not run away. Anyway, I supported her for almost a year. That must be worth something.'

'You make me sick, Mother. I don't want anything more to do with you. I'm leaving and never coming back.'

'Not so fast, my girl. I thought you wanted to marry Basil Crawford. I could easily persuade your father to revoke his permission.'

'I don't need your permission or my father's. I'm over twenty-one. You cannot stop me, Mama. I don't need any of this either,' she spat, sweeping the letters onto the floor. 'I'll make my own wedding plans.'

'Oh, and what will you use for money?' said her mother sarcastically. 'What if Basil Crawford doesn't want a destitute for a wife?'

Maxine pulled a face. 'You disgust me, Mama. All you can think of is money. I never want to see you again.'

With that she turned and ran from the house in tears. Her mother shouted after her.

'Maxine...wait....'

'Basil?' Maxine's voice echoed down the line.

'Maxine! Darling! Where are you calling from?'

'London. Basil I've left home. For good.'

'Good heavens! What's happened?'

'I'll tell you when I see you. We must change ze plan. We can be married in England, yes?'

'By all means. You know that's what I'd prefer. But...'

'So you can have your regimented wedding after all.'

'Regimental. That's splendid. But tell me, why have you run away from home?'

'I can't tell you on ze telephone. I'll explain when I see you. I'm catching the 2.30 train to Larkhill. Can you meet me?'

'Of course I will. What time does it get here?'

'I don't know, I forgot to ask.'

'Never mind,' he laughed. 'I'll find out. Oh, darling, this is wonderful.'

Till All The Seas Run Dry

Basil was horrified to learn about Madame Steinberger's duplicity. Recalling their conversation on the mountain, he realised Mary must have suspected it at the time.

'Should I tell her,' Maxine asked him. 'What do you think? I don't know what to do.'

'I think it's best if Mary doesn't know about this,' said her betrothed. 'It can only cause her more unnecessary grief. She couldn't get the child back now anyway.'

'Is it really too late? I made a note of the Engelbergs' address.'

'I don't know much about the law in these matters, I'm not a barrister, but I fear Mary would lose the battle. And she doesn't need the money now, though that is something she is entitled to, she's no longer destitute. Her rich uncle knows where she is and is supporting her. And then there's the child to consider. Think about it, Maxine. The little lad is two years old now, he knows no other parents but the Engelbergs, he wouldn't understand a word of English, and the chances are he is much loved—they must have been desperate for a child to pay that sort of money for him. And finally, there is the fact that Mary is not married—your mother had a point there—and Colin, his natural father is married to someone else.'

'Yes, you are right,' she agreed, putting herself not only in Mary's place but also in Louise's. 'It would cause far too much grief.'

'And since there's nothing anyone can do, it's better that Mary knows nothing about it. This is one secret we must keep to ourselves, I'm afraid,' said Basil, remembering the effect his recent revelations had had on the persons concerned.

Chapter 27

Mary alighted from the train and stood gazing at the familiar surroundings. Almost reverently she went and touched the little sign board which sported the words, Thwaite Station. She could hardly believe she was here at last.

Dickon was there, waiting for her. She flew into his arms, not caring that other people were around, some of whom might recognise them. No doubt it would be all over the county by tomorrow. He held her close, stroking her hair, whispering, 'Oh my lass, my little lass.'

She clung to him, her eyes filling with tears. Then she drew away so that she could inspect the dear, familiar face, the round blue eyes, the turned up nose that had been part of her beginnings, recalling to mind the boy who kept rabbits and squirrels in his pockets.

'Oh, Dickon,' she said at last. 'I can't tell you how wonderful it is to see you.'

Mr Craven's motor stood outside the station. Amazing to think Dickon could drive a car now. But why not? There were so many more cars on the road these days. He put her case in the boot, then opened the rear door for her.

'No, I'll sit in the front with you,' she said.

Another memory flashed through her mind, the first time Colin had met her in his car, and how proud of it he had been. She didn't want these memories, yet she knew they'd come thick and fast. By the time she reached Misselthwaite they'd be crowding her out, suffocating her.

'I should not have come,' she muttered, then, seeing the hurt expression on his face, 'I didn't mean that. I wanted so much to see you. You and Martha and your mother, but...'

'I understand,' he said.

He started the engine. It took several goes with the crank handle, but it went in the end. He got in beside her. She was silent as he put the car into gear and eased up the clutch.

'I don't want to meet them...'

'No chance of that. Master Colin is busy with army exercises. He won't be home before th' summer. And as for th' mistress... She never comes here wi'out him, nowdays. She stays at Larkhill.'

'I wish....' she began, glancing sideways at him, 'she hadn't found those letters. We were getting on so well together, but now she hates me.'

He shook his head. 'No, no. I'm sure she doesn't. She's no malice in her, that one.'

'All the same, she cannot forgive me, I'm sure.' She felt the unwelcome tears and pushed them away. 'I don't know how I'm going to cope with this wedding. I'm dreading it, Dickon. They'll both be there—they're bound to be.'

'Tha'll cope all right. I'm confident tha've a sturdy mind on thee.'

'I'd much rather stay here with you. But I can't get out of it. I promised Maxine and she is my best friend. I can't let her down. She wanted me to be a bridesmaid. Thank heaven she gave up that idea.'

'Tha could always just go to church. Tha needn't sit by them or anything. Tha'rt for bride any road—they'd be for groom.'

'Oh, I know. It's just the thought of seeing them,' she said, adding with a wistful sigh, 'I've never seen Colin in uniform. If only I hadn't quarrelled with Louise.' There was a moment's silence then changing the subject she asked airily, 'How's Martha? And your mother? I can't wait to see them.'

'Martha's all of a tizzy to see thee, an' Mother wants me to bring thee to tea. Tha'll come, won't tha?'

'Of course I'll come.' She felt better when she thought of a warm chat with her surrogate mother. 'But I hope she won't go to too much trouble.'

He laughed. 'You know Mother. I expect there'll be cakes an' all sorts, a regular feast, but it's no good me telling her not to.'

By now they'd reached the ridge of the hill and the house came into view for the first time. Mary's heart sank when she saw it, and she caught her breath. Quick to perceive it, he found a suitable spot and pulled in to the side of the road.

'Shall us walk a bit?' He laid his hand over hers. It felt warm and comforting. It was putting off the inevitable, but she welcomed it. She was not ready to face the rest of them yet and anyway she'd appreciate a moment alone with him. It would not be easy to find one once they'd reached the house.

'By all means, Dickon. Yes, let's.'

They walked hand in hand in silence for a while. The gorse was coming out all over the moor. It gave her such an overwhelming, nostalgic feeling of coming home she couldn't speak for a moment. Then she suddenly saw a cloud of blue butterflies.

'Oh, Dickon look. Aren't they beautiful?'

'Aye, they're right lovely.'

'And look, wild orchids,' she exclaimed, dropping on to her knees. 'How pretty they are. I'd forgotten how beautiful the moor is.'

She lay down on a patch of soft grass and stretched out on her back, and he sat down beside her, hugging his knees.

'Aye, it's coming alive, a special welcome for thee. Tha've brought me to life too. I've missed you, lass.'

'Aye, an' I've missed thee, an' all.'

'Tha've not forgot tha Yorkshire, then,' he laughed. Then, leaning over her supporting himself on his elbow, a serious look on his face, he whispered, 'Oh, my lass, my little lass.' He stretched out his hand and gently stroked her face. 'I've sore missed thee. When I thought tha were dead, I wanted my own life to end, then and there.'

'Oh, Dickon!' The ready tears filled her eyes. 'Dearest Dickon.'

'Why don't tha stay home now, lass? What's th' sense going back there? Here's where tha belong. This is where tha were meant to be.'

How could she make him understand that she couldn't because of Colin and Louise?

'I'll stop for a little while, Dickon. But I can't stay here, not for good.'

'Oh, my lass, my lovely lass,' he repeated. 'I've always loved thee, all my life. I know I'd no right but I always have.'

She put her arms round his neck and drew his face down to hers. 'I love you, too, my dear, darling Dickon.' Their lips met in a loving kiss.

****

Colin had not spent one night at home for over a month. Manoeuvres had gone on for most of March and a good deal of April, and even if, for reasons of bad weather, exercises had to be cancelled, there was always something preventing him from getting home. It did nothing to improve his relationship with Louise. But as far as the battalion was concerned, things were looking up. They'd successfully ironed out many of their flying problems, and spirits among the pilots were at a higher level than they'd been for ages, sufficient to justify breaking camp for a few days in order to celebrate the wedding of one of their officers. Colin was dropping with fatigue by the time he got back to base. He hoped Louise had received his message, though he did not expect a very warm welcome.

If only he could make her believe he loved her. Sometimes he felt like taking her by the shoulders and shaking her. Once he'd thought there could never be anyone he loved more than Mary, but he realised now with a heavy heart he desperately loved his wife. He realised that even if she were not his wife, if he could still choose....

But what was the use? He had so mortally offended her she could never forgive him. And now he had neither her nor Mary.

When he got home, however, there was a pleasant surprise waiting for him. A fire was lit, it was still cold in the evenings. The small table had been laid up for two in the sitting room, instead of the cold dining room, and the smell of something delicious cooking in the oven, greeted him at the door. And there was Louise, looking lovelier than he'd seen her for months, in his favourite dress, her cheeks a little flushed and her eyes sparkling. But what caught his eye and sent the blood racing through his veins was the broach she was wearing.

He'd found it in a jeweller's shop and given it to her as a wedding present. It was in the shape of a semaphore signal, very appropriate, he thought, for the wife of an RFC officer, especially when the jeweller told him it meant "I love you." Colin didn't know that particular signal, for it was a Naval one, but he had a pretty shrewd idea that it was not "I love you." But he'd pinned it on Louise's dress and told her that's what it meant. She'd worn it with pride on each occasion she dined at the mess, until one evening she met an officer from the Naval Wing who was visiting Larkhill.

When this gentleman's eyes alighted upon her broach he exclaimed, 'Where the devil did you get that, Craven? It's a famous broach. Once belonged to a certain Admiral's wife. Made specially for her. Can't be two the same. The old girl must have sold it, I suppose.'

Then he'd turned to Louise with a saucy grin. 'Don't suppose you've any idea what it means, have you, my dear?'

Glancing in Colin's direction she'd replied. 'He told me it means "I love you."'

To which the naval officer went into such a convulsion of mirth he almost expired.

As soon as they were home Louise had challenged him.

'Tell me at once, what does it mean? Colin?'

He'd begun to giggle helplessly until she'd flown into a fury.

'Apparently,' he told her, trying hard to keep a straight face, 'it says "Permission to lie alongside".'

Louise had torn the broach off and thrown it into the corner of the room, swearing she'd never wear it again. 'You've made me a laughing stock,' she'd raged.

He'd been apologetic. 'Oh, Lu, I swear I didn't know myself exactly what it stood for until that fellow told me. We have no use for that particular signal in the Military Wing. And it was, after all, made especially for a new wife. Hey,' he'd bantered. 'I thought you had a sense of humour.'

'Not that sort of sense of humour, Colin.'

From that day, until this moment, he'd never seen her wear the broach (he'd promised to get one made for her with the RFC crest on it instead). If ever he'd had an invitation from a woman this was it. The signal was clear as a beacon.

Observing that he'd seen it, she flushed a little. 'Would you like a drink, dearest?'

He took her in his arms and kissed her deeply.

'I'd love one, sweetheart,' he said, huskily. 'But I think I should have a bath first, or I won't be very pleasant company. Why don't you come and scrub my back for me?'

There was no question of her turning away from him that night. Her body was loving and compliant, and it was good between them, better than ever before.

He held her in his arms for the rest of the night, feeling more content than he had for a long time.

As soon as Basil and Maxine's wedding was over, the battalion resumed exercising which kept Colin away for the next few weeks, and Louise continued with her secret flying lessons. She was learning fast; she might have succeeded in her scheme to surprise her husband, but after several weeks she began to feel giddy and sick. She hoped this was not going to be a set back, and went to visit the doctor. It appeared that her sickness was nothing to do with flying. She was pregnant.

This was wonderful, a double surprise for Colin. She would not tell him about the baby either, not until she could display her brevet, so that she could announce, at one and the same time, that she was both a qualified pilot and an expectant mother. There was only one problem. The doctor advised her not to fly again until after the baby was born.

'But I'm ready to take my test,' she cried, in dismay. 'The instructor said I could try for it tomorrow.'

'Have patience, Mrs Craven. Surely you don't want to risk losing the baby?'

But one flight would not hurt, she thought. After all, nothing had gone wrong yet, and presumably she had been pregnant all along.

'I take my test tomorrow,' she whispered to Basil when she saw him. 'Pray for me.'

Colin arrived home unexpectedly, hoping to surprise her, but when he reached the house there was no sign of Louise or his car. He met Basil on the way to the mess.

'Hello, how's the training going? Have you got that brevet yet?'

'No, I'm afraid Louise is going to beat me to it.' He clapped his hand to his mouth. 'Damn! I wasn't supposed to tell you.'

But Colin was not slow. 'You said Louise was going to beat you to it. How come. She's nowhere near ready to take her test yet.'

'That's what you think,' said Basil with a grin. 'She's been having private lessons with Maitland while you've been away. And she's taking her test today.'

'Today!'

'Yes. In fact,' he cocked his ear, 'I think I can hear her now. Shall I get the jeep and we can go over there?'

When they arrived at the airfield, Maitland was about to signal Louise to come down when he saw Colin.

'You'll be delighted to hear, sir, your wife has just become a qualified pilot. I was about to get her down.'

Louise had seen the instructor's signal, but she'd also spotted Colin. Here was her chance to show him what she could do. She did a roll beautifully, bringing the aircraft neatly out of it, straightening up, and preparing for looping the loop. She was elated, she did one beautiful loop, just one more....

She was quite unaware of the men jumping up and down on the ground.

Maitland was tearing at his hair. 'She'll run out of fuel in a moment.'

Colin picked up the megaphone, but it was too late. Halfway through the second loop the engine cut out, and there was that dreadful silence. It had happened before, but that time she'd been the right way up and able to bring the plane down like a glider, landing it rather clumsily, but safely nevertheless. This time she was upside down, and now she was going into a dive....

She struggled to gain control, to bring the plane upright again, but it would not respond to the controls and the ground was coming closer and closer....

On the ground all eyes were glued to the falling aircraft.

'Let's pray she has run out of fuel,' said Maitland. 'Or the plane will burst into flame on landing. If she uses her wits she could jump free, and she may have a chance.'

Colin raised the megaphone to his lips and yelled, 'Jump, Louise, jump!'

She heard him, but it was no use. The falling plane increased in speed as it approached the ground, and she could not release the harness that held her in her seat. It was over in seconds, the plane crashed in a small clump of trees.

Colin was already halfway across the field in the jeep. He had not waited for the others. He reached the mangled aircraft and found Louise's lifeless body among the wreckage. He gathered her in his arms and rocked her two and fro, trying in vain to bring her back to life, sobbing....

'I love you, Lu. I love you so much. Don't leave me! Oh, please don't leave me.'

A sudden breeze whispered to him through the trees. She'll never know, she'll never know. She loved you so, she loved you so. And now it's too late, too late, too late....

Then his mother's words came tumbling into his head. *"Be careful not to make the same mistake again...."*

It was Louise she was referring to, not Mary. *"If you go along looking over your shoulder you'll fall over the rock right under your nose..."*

Chapter 28

Some weeks later Colin stood by her grave. He'd had her body buried in the little churchyard at Misselthwaite, it had to be there. The flowers, the seeds he'd sown after her funeral, were resplendent, a fitting token to her. He laid the bouquet he had in his hand by the headstone. Under her name he'd had the brevet carved. She'd earned it, he thought bitterly. Hot tears stung his eyes. It's so easy to keep saying, 'If only...' Why had he not spent more time with her?

For nearly two months he'd been inconsolable. He could not endure the sympathy of his friends—it required a great effort to avoid breaking down—so he had kept his own council, hiding away to grieve alone. Despite his mother's advice about the uselessness of remorse, he could not help blaming himself for Louise's death.

At the funeral John Seymour had grasped his hand warmly.

'You made her happy, Colin,' he'd said. 'Thank you for that.'

'Did I make her happy, though? I wish I could believe that.'

'Believe it then,' John had said, adding in a lowered voice, 'Did you know she was expecting a baby?'

He hadn't.

That was almost the unkindest cut of all. Twice now he had lost a child before he even knew he was a father.

His own father, with untypical demonstrativeness, had hugged him affectionately.

'My poor son,' he'd said, gripping his shoulders, the tears standing in his eyes. 'I know exactly what you're going through, believe me.'

Of course he did. He was not much older himself when he lost his own wife.

A gentle breeze rustled the trees, bringing with it the scent of mock orange blossom. It was Louise's favourite. June, the month when their romance had blossomed, he'd proposed to her. Was it really only a year ago? And now he'd never fly with her again.

A noise behind startled him, the click of the latch as the gate was opened made him turn, and his heart almost stopped.

It was Mary.

She had come! Incredibly she had appeared like an angel at his hour of need. Now she stood beside him and put an arm round him.

'Your father wrote and told me. I'm so sorry...' she began.
'No,' he interrupted. 'Don't say anything. Don't sympathise.'
'All right. If you don't wish to talk about it.'

He took her arm and automatically they began to walk towards the Secret Garden. And then, perversely, he started to talk about Louise.

'I did love her, May.' It was as if he needed her to believe it. His lips trembled as he spoke. 'If only I could tell her.'

Then he broke down and, screwing up his stinging eyes, buried his face in her neck. 'Oh, May, May, 'I've made such a mess of my life.'

'You and me, both.' Her voice was soft. 'But it's not too late to mend it. We've all the time in the world.'

She held him in her arms until the tension began to ebb from his body, and he knew, in that moment, that this was the beginning of the healing process. Not for the first time, it occurred to him that there was nobody else in the world he'd allow to see him weep. Nobody else to whom he could lay bare his soul. Even Louise, much as he loved her, had not understood him so well. Mary was, in every respect, his very best friend, his soul mate.

'And as for telling Louise you love her,' she reassured him, 'I hardly think you need to. Surely you have not forgotten the discussion we had in Switzerland? It was you who convinced me there was life after death. I'm sure Louise *knows* you love her.'

'Does she? Do you truly believe that?'

'Don't you?'

Colin smiled to himself as relief swept over him. Of course, he knew it was true, for how often had he seen his mother? He felt at peace for the first time since Louise's death.

They walked in silence down the Long Walk, searched under the ivy for the door and found it.

'It's in a sad condition,' she said, with a faint hint of reproach in her voice. 'But we can put that right too with a little loving care.'

Weeds were more prolific than flowers, but it was plain that Dickon had been working at it. Since Colin's last visit nine months ago he'd cleared the roses of bindweed and pruned them all back, cut down most of the ivy that was smothering the trees. And he'd cut the grass.

'Shall you stay, now you're home, May?'

'That depends.' Laughter danced in her eyes, 'Do you want me?'

'What do you think?' he laughed. 'Of course I want you.'

Till All The Seas Run Dry

He resisted the impulse to once more ask her to marry him. It was far too soon after losing Louise, and he needed time to mourn, to adjust to being single. It was enough that Mary would be living at Misselthwaite again, he'd have time to get used to having her around. Besides, he was not sure if he *should* marry her. Twice now he had tried to marry her only to be torn apart by fate.

'There's something else I'd like to show you,' he said.

They left the garden and went to the paddock.

Mary was startled by what she saw there. 'It's....'

At first glance she thought she was seeing Prince's ghost. A beautiful black stallion with an almost identical mark on its forehead gambolled and played around Snowdrop. Occasionally she'd butt him with her head as if to say. 'Enough! Now I want some peace.' Mary stared at him. Then she noticed he was not exactly the same. This horse had four white socks.

Colin giggled, beginning to feel like his old self. 'That's what I thought when I first saw him. He's her foal. Wasn't it clever of Father to find him? He managed to trace him through the people we sold him to, and bought him back. He's three and a half years old now but he's still very skittish, he plagues her to death sometimes. But on the whole she's much happier now she's got him back.'

Watching the young horse dance round his mother, Mary thought suddenly of her own child. The boy would be nearly three by now, if he'd lived. Would the pain of losing him ever leave her? Yet now she had more hope for the future than ever before. She and Colin were together again. In time they would marry, there'd be more children.

'Penny for your thoughts,' he said.

She shook her head. 'My thoughts are worth more than you can afford.'

> Tho' you're ten thousand miles away
> Our hearts will be as one,
> And you will be my dearest love
> Till God puts out the sun.
> So now take heart my own true love,
> In spite of all your tears,
> For we shall meet again my dear
> Tho' 'twere two thousand years!